THE BEST
VICTIM

Also by Colleen Thompson

THE BEST
VICTIM

COLLEEN THOMPSON

Montlake
Romance

Text copyright © 2014 Colleen Thompson

Published by Montlake Romance, Seattle

www.apub.com

Amazon, the Amazon logo, and Montlake Romance are trademarks of Amazon.com, Inc., or its affiliates

ISBN-13: 9781477818466
ISBN-10: 1477818464

Cover design by Inkd Inc

Library of Congress Control Number: 2013920370

Printed in the United States of America

To Mike,

Who believed in my dream before I did…

"Blondes make the best victims. They're like virgin snow that shows up the bloody footprints."

-Alfred Hitchcock

CHAPTER ONE

The news must have severed her mind, shearing it free from her body and its actions. How else could Lauren return, her movements as smoothly automatic as a robot's, to filling the dog's water bowl and loading the dishwasher, the same mundane tasks that had been interrupted by the ringing of her father's old corded phone almost an hour earlier?

The same tasks begun before the police detective had told her . . .

Stomach lurching, she forced herself to swallow. To gulp back the tears, the rage, the raw grief that threatened to consume her.

The knife and fork she'd used last night slipped from her hand, clinking into place in the silverware basket. The spoons came next, spoons she'd used to stir the milk into her coffee, to lift the cereal to her mouth . . .

Had Rachel tested the pistol's weight in her hand while Lauren sat eating breakfast? Had there still been time then, time to make a call that could have distracted her or cheered her up, preventing her from pressing the muzzle to the silky, wheat-blond temple that Lauren had so often stroked when her younger sister was small?

As the kitchen clock's black hands ticked off another minute, a stark image filled her mind: Rachel's beautiful, long hair soaked with blood, her skull blown open, and her face shattered into jigsaw pieces.

The horror of the thought sent the teaspoons clattering to the kitchen floor. Dumpling, the plump, gray-muzzled dachshund Lauren had rescued from a roadside a few days after leaving her California home to pack up the old farmhouse where she and her sister had grown up, bolted from the room, her tail tucked between her stumpy legs.

"It's all right, girl," Lauren called, though it would never be all right again. How could it be if Rachel—? Her throat knotted with the thought.

Maybe, Lauren thought, she should try calling her sister's cell one more time. Her last two calls had rolled straight over to voice mail, but maybe Rachel had decided to start her weekend early and had gone out to a Friday morning movie or the gym or somewhere instead of working at the hospital admissions department where she'd been employed the past three years. With her phone turned off, Rachel would never know about this awful mix up. Would be horrified to learn that someone had mistakenly told her sister she was dead.

When the doorbell rang, Dumpling reappeared, then charged over to bark with all the gusto she usually reserved for eating.

Too overwhelmed to deal with anyone, Lauren turned away, but instead of giving up, the visitor rang the bell again and pounded at the door, feeding her small protector's frenzy.

"Settle down," Lauren managed. Her command ignored, she scooped the struggling little sausage up in her arms and shushed her into silence.

When another knock came, Lauren called, "Not interested," certain it must be someone peddling religion or selling vacuum cleaners. It wasn't as if she'd reconnected with any old classmates who might have stuck around her North Texas hometown, and her few neighbors along the rural road outside of Bright's Prairie never stopped by unannounced.

But then again, neither did solicitors. Then who—?

"FBI, Ms. Miller." The person on the other side answered her unspoken question, the voice deep and masculine and ringing with authority. "I need to speak with you about your sister."

Lauren's hand was trembling so hard, she fumbled with the lock. *Maybe he's here to say the call was a mistake. A wrong number or a cruel prank.* She didn't care which, as long as Rachel was alive.

Heart racing with the surge of hope, Lauren opened the door and peered at a tall, solidly built man wearing a dark suit and sunglasses, despite the swath of clouds. Wind ruffled neatly trimmed, dark-brown hair frosted with silver, and the tips of both his nose and ears had reddened, proof that the forecast blue norther had brought the cold Canadian air mass well into Texas after all.

"Ms. Miller," he said, opening a thin, black leather case he'd pulled from the breast pocket of his suit jacket, "I'm Special Agent Brent Durant, from the Oklahoma City field office. I'm sorry to bother you at such a difficult time, but—"

"It wasn't her," Lauren blurted, shivering in the draft and barely glancing at the badge and ID. Or wondering what a federal agent from Oklahoma City would be doing more than two hundred miles from his home turf. "That's why you're here, right? Because the Austin police messed up?"

Shaking his head, he explained, "I've been part of a joint task force with members of the Austin PD, so they knew I'd be in this area. The officer working your sister's case, Detective Cruz Jimenez, asked me to stop by to talk to you about—"

"No," she argued, desperate to make him see that this was wrong.

Impossible. She had spoken to Rachel only a few days earlier. "My sister's always inviting people to come and stay with her— an out-of-work friend, a neighbor who's having trouble with a boyfriend." *A sister who would rather sit at home with her computers, safe behind her firewall.*

The agent pulled off his sunglasses, the compassion in his brown eyes and his silence speaking volumes. Still, Lauren wasn't having any of it.

"It was someone staying at her place, not her," she said. "Rachel's not dead. Sure, she's been through a lot this past year, with the accident, but she would never—" Her mind spasmed, contracting around the hard knot of what had to be a lie. "She's only twenty-five. She has her whole life. She—"

Agent Durant tried to look past her into the house. "Is there someone here with you? Someone I could call? Your husband?"

"Not anymore. I'm here on my own." Soon after she'd driven halfway across the country to deal with her late father's estate, her husband of four years had informed her that there was no need to come back.

"Have you called anybody yet? Told anyone about your sister?" Concern lined the agent's expressive face. A handsome face, and one she sensed was younger than the early frost of gray suggested. Still, he looked worn, perhaps burdened by the things he had witnessed on the job.

"It really was a mistake, wasn't it?" she pleaded. "Don't worry. I haven't had the chance to let anybody know yet."

She'd been holed up in the old, white clapboard farmhouse for months, with only the throwaway dachshund and the winds that continuously scoured the wide North Texas plains to keep her company. As soon as she'd set up the high-speed Internet connection she needed to keep up with her remote net administrator business, she'd offered to buy her sister's share of the house, saying that the silence suited her.

You can run, but you can't hide—not from life, Rachel had responded. *Believe me, I've spent way too long lately trying. How 'bout you come and see me next week—check out Austin. You might like the techie vibe here, some of the people, too. And I wouldn't mind a roommate for a while if you're up for it.*

"It might be better if we talked inside." Agent Durant rubbed his arms against the crisp chill, and she noticed the small puffs of steam rising off each word. "Mind if I come in?"

Lauren shushed her growling dog just before a gust drew her attention outdoors, where a flurry of dried leaves rattled against the dark-blue sedan he'd pulled into the driveway. The same cold wind bent over the prairie grasses in the front yard and the field across the street. Though it wasn't quite nine a.m., the leaden sky was quickly dimming, whispering a promise of snow flurries. Or perhaps a threat.

She stepped back for him to enter.

Once she'd closed the door behind him, she waved him toward her father's recliner. She hadn't planned to sit, but the graveness in his eyes had her sinking down to a worn, plaid sofa, her soul swamped by the knowledge that he hadn't come to bring the news she'd wanted.

She began to quiver, still clutching the fat dog for dear life. Stalling for time, she stammered, "C-could I get you some coffee? There's a fresh pot, and you look so cold."

Instead of answering, he said bluntly, "I need you to understand, it's true, what the police in Austin told you. After a neighbor reported hearing what sounded like a shot, a blond woman was found dead in the bathroom of your sister's apartment, with what appeared to be a single bullet wound to her head and a gun next to her hand. I understand the police have asked you to come to the medical examiner's office for an official identification—"

"Before five," she interjected. "That's what the detective told me. I was about to get ready, so I can get this straightened out before the weekend."

"But that's just a formality. The responding officers made a preliminary ID from the photo on her driver's license."

Lauren stared into Durant's face, cursing the cold that had come in with him, peppering her like icy pellets. Stinging her skin and intensifying the tremors that racked her body. "My sister would never do this." She shook her head. "She wouldn't. After the accident, she promised me, no matter how down she was feeling, no matter how many idiots trashed her after that stupid cable TV woman—"

"So you were aware your sister was depressed?"

"For a while, of course she was. She felt so guilty, even though it was Megan who begged her to try to make it so she could get home to her kids."

"Rachel was behind the wheel. She felt responsible."

"But she *wasn't*. Even the grand jury didn't think so." Tears blurred Lauren's vision as she rushed to her sister's defense. "It was the storm. The water came up so fast." Seven people had drowned that day. Five of them in different accidents in Austin, yet only Rachel—caught on videotape driving around a barricade into rising waters—had been persecuted.

"No one's here to blame her." He raised his palms to calm her, his voice as patient as it was professional. "I'm just trying to help you understand why she might have been struggling with guilt."

"But she's better now. Much better. Her insurance company had settled on the civil suit, so it was finally all over. She'd just invited me to come visit." *Why didn't I say yes? If only I'd been there, she never would have . . .*

"The medical examiner won't make a determination of the cause of death until the autopsy's completed. But there was a note found that appears consistent with other samples of your sister's handwriting."

"What note? What did it say?"

"She only said, '*Choice is only an illusion. This is what I have to do.*'"

"That's it? Nothing else? You're certain?"

When he nodded, she made him repeat the message, the words burning their way into her memory forever. She tried to imagine her sister, who'd seemed so cheerful and upbeat during their last conversation, saying such a thing, much less writing it before she'd put a gun to her head.

Impossible. "There has to be more."

Special Agent Durant confirmed that this was the information the Austin police detective had relayed to him. "I'm very sorry this has happened. Sorry for your loss. Is there anyone I should call for you?"

"No. There's no one else, no one but me and Rachel. *Why?* Why would she do this now, after everything she's been through?"

"Your sister was troubled," he suggested.

"She wouldn't have bailed now, especially without a word to me." Lauren cried as the old dachshund snuggled against her sweatshirt and licked her hand in an attempt to offer comfort. But there was no easing the pain pulsing at her temples, the nausea threatening to start her heaving. The creeping fear that this was not a bad dream, but a horrible new reality.

"The two of you were close?"

"Very. We didn't see each other a lot, but we text and e-mail all the time. And every week, we talk—I mean, we talked—" Lauren's voice broke as she struggled with the shattering concept of her sister, relegated to the past tense. "We spoke by phone every Sunday. For hours, sometimes. About anything and everything. But never—She was the one trying to cheer me up. Trying to talk me into reconnecting with the world."

"After your divorce?" he coaxed.

Lauren nodded, not bothering to explain that the "getting back out into the world" talk had been a running theme throughout her life. Where Rachel had been generous and gregarious, Lauren had never been able to bond with more than a couple of people at any given time. And now, both of them—her husband and her sister—had been ripped from her life. Taken.

"Rachel hated guns," she blurted, fury surging through her as she leapt onto the detail. "Even after Megan's husband threatened her, she refused to have one in her apartment."

Durant pulled a small, sleek pen and pad of paper from his shirt pocket and jotted a note. "Jon Rutherford, right?"

Lauren looked at him oddly, thinking how odd it was that an out-of-state FBI agent would know so much about Rachel's accident.

As if he'd read her mind, he explained, "Detective Jimenez filled me in this morning on your sister's recent history."

Lauren nodded rapidly. "That night at the hospital, Rutherford said Rachel should've been the one to drown, not Megan. Megan was the one with a husband and two children, another on the way. He said no one"—she choked up—"no one would even miss my sister. As if her friends, our dad, and I didn't matter in the least."

Durant looked up from his writing, his brown eyes as grave as they were thoughtful. "Did he ever threaten her directly?"

Lauren blew out a shaky breath, regretting that she hadn't been there when her sister needed her. *Just like this morning.* "Rachel told me he lunged at her the night of the accident. If hospital security hadn't restrained him, he might've killed her then and there."

"What about afterward? Was there ever any hint of violence?"

She shook her head. "We figured his lawyer warned him off—the one he hired to sue Rachel. But now that the suit's settled, maybe it's just hitting him that money won't bring back his wife. It won't comfort his children when they wake up crying for their mother or help him deal with their boy's special needs."

"Hard to imagine him risking a stint in prison with those two kids to think about," Durant said, "especially almost a year later, when there's been no contact and no threats."

"Rachel did say he moved. He took the kids and went back home to some suburb outside of Houston, where his parents could help him out. But he could have left the kids there and then come back here to hurt Rachel."

"If you tell Detective Jimenez, I'm sure he'll look into it," Durant said, but something in his voice clued Lauren in to the fact that he'd only been pretending to seriously consider Rutherford as a suspect. Humoring the grieving sister of a suicide.

She glared. "He did it. I know it. Or someone else, some psycho or one of those people who kept calling her after that trashy cable 'news' show"—she sketched quotes with her fingers—"first ran on TV about a month after the accident. Did you know she had to change her number?"

"The apartment was locked from the inside, including the deadbolt on the front door. And your sister kept a broomstick in the sliding patio door for security, so it's highly unlikely anyone else could've been with her."

"There must've been an extra key." Lauren knew she was grasping at straws, but she couldn't stop herself. "He locked the door behind him."

Patiently, the agent went on. "You need to understand, the ME's bound to rule your sister's death a suicide, Ms. Miller. I know how hard it is to accept—"

Anger roaring in her ears, Lauren slapped her palms hard against the cushions as she pushed herself to her feet. "You're with the FBI, right? So why are you even here, if all you're going to do is feed me the cops' regurgitated bullshit?"

"I was called in as part of a related investigation. When your sister's suicide was reported, she had my card in her apartment."

"Not a suicide. She didn't. Do it," Lauren insisted, her hand shaking as she raked back her tangled light-brown hair. "That note she left—There's no way she wrote it. It doesn't sound like her at all."

The chair springs creaked, and he rose slowly, moving as though he had all the time on earth. Taking a step toward her, and to Lauren's utter shock, reaching down and enfolding both her hands in his.

His were cool and callused, chapped from winter's cold. The creases fanning from the corners of his eyes crinkled, as if he squinted against bright sunlight often, but beyond the windows, the cold February day had grown as somber as the grim line of his mouth.

"You're right," he said, ignoring the dachshund's low growl. "My Austin PD colleagues and the ME will almost certainly call this suicide, but you and I know better. Your sister might've pulled the trigger, but I swear to you, I swear on my badge, Rachel absolutely *wasn't* responsible for her death."

"I don't understand. What do you—?"

"Whoever this bastard is, your sister isn't his first victim. But I promise you, she's damned well going to be his last."

CHAPTER TWO

"What d-do you mean, last victim?" Lauren stammered.

But Durant knew his words had sunk in. Saw that she understood his confirmation that her sister had been murdered.

He watched her hungrily, wondering what it would feel like having her darkest suspicions confirmed instead of being pacified, ignored, or—worse still—ordered to report for grief counseling and then a psych evaluation. Yet as he suggested she sit down again, she looked more shaken than grateful.

Spotting a box of tissues on the lamp table next to her closed laptop, he grabbed a few and passed them to her. As she wiped her face, its paleness reminded him sharply of her fairer sister. The sister he had failed to save.

On the afternoon he had met Rachel Miller, she'd still been dressed for work in a stylish skirt and blouse, and her beautiful blond hair was neatly swept to one side. But it was her shaking he best remembered, that and the haunted look in her red-rimmed blue eyes.

No, not haunted. *Hunted.* Having failed to recognize the look once, he would never again be able to ignore it. Not that his awareness had done a damned thing to save her life.

"As soon as you're ready to go, I'll explain it in the car," he said, remembering from the background research he'd done before heading off in this direction how Lauren had been more like a mother than a sibling to her younger sister, who had been just ten to Lauren's seventeen the year their mother died. With their father's sales job keeping him away from home for weeks at a time, Lauren had turned down—or been forced to turn down—several scholarships to care for Rachel. Had she resented being stuck way out here in the old farmhouse that had passed down from her grandparents? Or had those years of isolation forged the backbone that would allow her to survive this devastating blow?

Durant hoped so, because she was going to need every bit of strength he could wring from her.

"In *your* car?" Lauren asked. "You mean you're taking me all the way to Austin?"

He nodded. "That's what I'm here for, but we need to get you packed and ready. Then I can answer all your questions. I know you'll have a lot."

Though she brushed aside a tear, her blue-green eyes narrowed. "You'll tell me every detail? Everything you know?"

"You have my word on it," he lied.

"Your word," she echoed, a tic playing at one corner of her mouth. "Could I see that ID again?"

His heart kicked at her question. Was she only being cautious, or had he said or done something to trigger her suspicion? From the little Rachel had told him, as well as the facts he'd been able to uncover through his own sources, the self-taught computer genius behind Siren Sys-Secure was nobody's fool. Not even after receiving what was undoubtedly the biggest shock of her life.

Without missing a beat, he passed her the badge wallet and tried not to hold his breath as she flipped it open and studied his current ID.

When she nodded and handed it back, he relaxed, relieved that the money he'd put into it had been well spent. "Sorry, but if I'm going to leave you down here while I go up and pull myself together, I want to be sure who it is I'm trusting."

"Would you care to confirm with my supervisor?" he asked recklessly. "I have the number in my wallet. Or if you'd rather, you can look it up yourself and call the special agent in charge at the Oklahoma City field office while I wait out in the car."

She hesitated, studying his face. He looked back at her steadily, measured his own breathing. Struggled to ignore the pounding in his chest, the perspiration beading on his back and dampening his palms despite the cold day.

She sighed, shoulders sagging, and her gaze skittered away. "Never mind. I'm just—I'll be back down in a few minutes. Help yourself to the coffee."

Rising, she gestured toward what he took to be the kitchen door before she headed toward the stairway. "Come on, Dumpling. Come up with me."

But the dachshund only made it as far as the landing before she turned and settled herself so she could keep a watchful eye on Brent.

From upstairs, he heard a door close, followed by the groan of pipes and the hiss of running water. Figuring that Lauren would be a while in the shower, he walked into the kitchen, with its faded linoleum and yellowed cabinets, and helped himself as she'd suggested.

The coffee was strong and dark—and best of all, hot enough to burn off the chill still clinging to him. As he drank, he drifted to the refrigerator, where someone had used magnets to hang photos. In several, he recognized Rachel—blond and stunning—as she posed for the camera, modeling stylish outfits, except in one, where she vamped it up in a frilly, hot-pink number so out-landish that it could only be a bridesmaid's dress. Other shots pictured an older man with a smile that made up for his thin-ning gray hair, accepting a plaque in one shot and posing with a fishing rod and a good-sized bass in another. The father, he supposed, who'd died suddenly only a few months after retiring from thirty-six years spent selling farm equipment.

There was only one photo with Lauren, and he couldn't see much of her, other than the hand she was using to try to block the camera. Shy, he remembered Rachel saying. *If she loves you, she really loves you, but she could do without most people.*

It was probably for the best, then, that Lauren ran her busi-ness online. Remote network administrators, who handled mon-itoring and security needs for small- to mid-sized businesses across the country, didn't need great social skills . . .

Nor did part-time hackers.

Remembering the bureau intel he'd gotten on her, he returned to the living room and stared down at the slim lap-top she'd left beside a phone and answering machine so dated that he wondered if she'd kept them as reminders of her father. Reaching toward the computer, he frowned at the colorful Grateful Dead skin that encased it, his stomach twisting at the rock band's skull and roses logo.

I'm so sorry, Rachel. Sorry that it ended this way for you.

When the water upstairs shut off, he froze, glancing toward the stairwell. But she'd still have to dry and dress, then pack for their six-hour drive. So he still had a little time, he reasoned. Time to figure out if Cisco had been right in thinking that Lau-ren Miller was in possession of the exact skill set he needed.

The dog growled at him suspiciously, as if the fat dachshund had the power to read minds. But the momentary distraction had him rethinking what he realized was a terrible idea. Someone in her line of work would surely have advanced security protocols—anything from rotating passwords to fingerprint or facial recognition ID systems. Not only would he get himself locked out of the system, but also his clumsy attempts would be logged and reported.

No, he thought, turning his back to the laptop. There was no way he could risk shattering her trust. Not with everything he'd worked for, everything that meant a damned thing to him, riding on Lauren Miller's willing cooperation.

***

Less than half an hour later, Lauren was packed and dressed in fresh jeans and a scuffed, black leather jacket, which she'd thrown over a purple V-neck sweater. She'd meant to top the outfit with the colorful scarf that Rachel—who was always encouraging her to "brighten up" her look—had sent her for her thirty-second birthday, but the sight of it had her nose running and eyes leaking, so she shoved the length of silk into her pocket instead.

Two quick swipes of the brush were all she needed to untangle her shoulder-length, light-brown hair. Her face was splotchy and her nose red, but she didn't give a damn about that, about anything but getting through what needed to be done.

After shoving her socked feet into a battered pair of motorcycle boots, she clumped downstairs with her purse and a small suitcase.

Agent Durant rose from the sofa, a coffee mug in hand. "All ready?"

She glanced down at the dachshund, who was hopping excitedly at her mistress's reappearance, and shook her head. "Not quite. Dumpling needs her bag packed, too."

He grimaced. "In case you haven't noticed, your dog hates me."

"Maybe you remind her of the asshat who tossed her out along the freeway," she theorized. "I'd bet money it was a man who threw her out like garbage." In her admittedly limited experience, men did that. An image of the man she'd only thought had loved her blasted through her brain, his arm around his pregnant redheaded assistant. The one now living in *her* house.

"I'm not cruel to animals. I like them." The agent gave the dachshund a dubious look, which was rewarded by a curled lip. "Most of them, at any rate."

"Don't worry. She won't do worse than gumming you. She only has a few teeth."

"So where are we dropping it off?" he asked.

"We aren't."

Out of the corner of her eye, she saw his shoulders stiffen. But she couldn't care less about his feelings on the matter.

Several minutes later, she stood by the front door, digging in her purse for her keys. Her laptop bag was slung over one shoulder, and Dumpling's leash was looped over her wrist. Excited to go out, the old dog whined and shuffled her paws, her thin tail whipping.

A few steps away, Agent Durant looked as if he'd eaten curdled yogurt. "You're sure there's not anyone—a friend or neighbor—to look after it?"

Lauren speared him with an annoyed look. "First of all, Dumpling's a *her*, not an it, and, second, even if I knew of someone, I'm not leaving her with strangers, let alone locked up in some awful kennel after what she's already been through. She spent the first two weeks after I picked her up hiding under my bed. I had to stretch out on the rug and coax her to eat bits of boiled chicken."

Durant eyed the little dog, whose belly nearly touched the floor. "You sure you weren't slipping her brownies and ice cream for dessert?"

She snorted. "Everybody knows you can't feed dogs chocolate. And she was terrified. You have no idea what it's like, being—being abandoned like you're *nothing* . . ."

Her words choked down to silence as an aching void opened just beneath her breastbone. The dark emptiness spread through her, whispering that it was her own abandonment that had left her clinging to whatever comfort a fat, old dog had to offer.

So what if it was? Why the hell not? She straightened with the thought, lifting her chin and staring at him boldly. "She comes with us, or I'll drive my Jeep down. I'm perfectly capable, you know."

"*No.*" That single word was hard enough to break a tooth on. "We have to talk, for one thing. And you're obviously in no condition."

"I'm tougher than I look," she assured him, though she felt translucent as a moth's wing. And every bit as fragile.

She started when the phone rang.

Before she could answer it, he shrugged, "Fine. We'll do it your way," and picked up both her suitcase and the duffel she had loaded with dog food, treats, and Dumpling's favorite chew toys. "Let's go."

"I should get this," she said, despite the sick feeling crawling up her throat at the memory of the last call she had taken.

"You don't need to—"

The answering machine came to life, her father's once-reassuring voice making her wish she'd forced herself to rerecord his message.

"Ms. Miller? Lauren Miller?" The caller was male, with an accent that left no doubt that he had spent at least part of his childhood south of the US border. "Please pick up if you're home. This is Detective Jimenez again, from the Austin PD Homicide Division."

Did he imagine she had already forgotten? That she would ever forget the voice, the man who'd told her of Rachel's death? Something in his tone warned that he had more bad news to deliver.

Dread poured thick as concrete. It dripped down through Lauren's body, filling up her hollowed legs and cementing her in place. A few steps away, Durant slowly lowered both the duffel and the suitcase, his face tense and expectant, his color gray as winter's chill.

Dumpling strained against the leash and whined, clearly impatient to begin the walk she'd been expecting. Lauren shushed her, as if she feared that Jimenez might hear.

On the answering machine, the detective sighed. "Your cell phone keeps rolling straight to voice mail, but if you're hearing this message, you need to turn the lights off, all of them, right now, and wait inside an interior room for your local sheriff to send out a deputy. Until you hear from me, don't open your door for anybody. If a stranger comes, you hide. Hide and call me right away—especially if you see a tall, white male, late thirties, most likely in a suit."

Her gaze snapped to the face of the tall stranger inside her house, but his eyes had gone as flat and unreadable as a shark's. His face hardening, he turned away, moving quickly for the phone as Jimenez went on warning her, "This man may be representing himself as a federal agent. He could be going by the alias—"

In one swift and shocking moment, Durant jerked both the phone and answering machine from the wall.

Sucking in a painful breath, Lauren wheeled around to race up the only avenue of escape—the empty stairwell. But in pivoting, she wound the dog's leash around her ankles, sending herself crashing to the wooden stairs.

She cried out, more from terror than the bolt of pain exploding in her elbow where she'd struck it. As she struggled to untangle herself, Dumpling snarled and snapped at Durant. Brushing the animal aside, he leaned over, then lifted Lauren to her feet by her uninjured arm.

"Wait," he pleaded. "Don't fight. I swear, I didn't come to hurt you."

He turned her to face him, his dark eyes boring into hers and his face flushed with emotion. "Just let me explain, please."

"Get. Out." Though a tremor ran through her voice, she didn't look away from him, she couldn't, with her brain parsing the meaning of the flash of metal she'd glimpsed in the split second his jacket had swung open.

He has a gun. A gun. The image of her sister's blood-soaked hair flashed lightning-swift through her brain, followed by the resolve that no matter what, she would survive this. Survive to make this bastard pay for what he'd done to the last person on this earth she'd ever love.

CHAPTER THREE

To say this was Brent's worst nightmare was nowhere close to accurate. He had already survived the worst life had to offer, though for a long time and maybe even still, he would have rather died.

But Lauren's panicked reaction to Jimenez's phone message was easily a bottom-five moment. How the hell would he gain her cooperation now?

"I'm not going anywhere," he said, struggling to keep his voice low and soothing. As if there were any words that could undo the damage. "Not without you."

As they stared at each other, the fluid play of her emotions—from fear to hatred to determination—submerged into the depths of her gaze. But she could no more hide the tension in her arm where he gripped it than she could disguise the wild thumping of her pulse beneath his fingertips.

As vital as his goal was, he hated himself for scaring her. And hated himself more for what he intended to make her do.

"What is it you want?" she asked. "To kill me, like my sister?"

Ignoring the dachshund's ominous rumbling, he said, "I know what you're thinking, Lauren. May I call you Lauren?"

She shrugged. "You're the one with the gun, *Special Agent.*"

He considered the sarcasm a good sign. Better than dealing with hysteria, anyway. "I have no interest in hurting you, no interest in anything but catching your sister's killer."

Her shaking stopped, and she straightened her spine, though she couldn't be more than a slim five-five or five-six, even in her boots. *And beautiful, in her quiet way*, he couldn't help but notice. The first noticing he'd done in so long, it surprised the hell out of him and, almost as quickly, filled him with remorse.

"Why do you care?" she demanded. "And who the hell are you?"

"Exactly who I told you: Special Agent Brent Durant. Or at least I was up 'til six months ago." He relaxed his grip. "Did you hurt yourself when you fell? I saw you hit that elbow." He nodded toward her left arm.

Pulling free, she rubbed it and made a scoffing sound. "I'm supposed to buy concern? From you? A man who hasn't given me a single straight or honest answer?"

"I haven't lied," he said, though at least in part, this, too, was a falsehood. "Everything I've told you about your sister's death is true."

Pain arced over her expression, and she looked away a moment. When she regained control and blinked at him, her eyes had filled again. "How would you know anything about her?"

"I have sources, sources who haven't heard—and a couple who don't give a damn—that I'm on leave from the bureau. And I knew Rachel. Or at least, I've met her."

Lauren scowled at him. "She would've told me if she'd spoken to someone claiming to be from the FBI. Or did you tell her a different lie? Pretend to be someone else so you could—What did you do to her, you bastard? Why is Rachel dead?"

As Lauren's anguish echoed in the entryway, the dachshund bared her few teeth, the reddish hair along her spine raised.

He shook his head. "I tried to tell you earlier, she had my card on her when she died. That's why Detective Jimenez called me. We worked together in the past. But apparently, word about my recent issues hadn't reached him down in Austin."

She gestured toward the dead phone. "Well, clearly, that's changed, and he sounded pretty upset about it. So what'd you do? Go crazy? Start beating suspects or harassing witnesses or what?"

Ignoring her questions, he asked, "Where's your cell phone?"

She hesitated a moment before answering, "After the detective called this morning and told me about Rachel, I was so upset I dropped it—drowned the thing in my dishwater."

"Let me see that," he said, pulling the purse off of her shoulder. Heedless of her protests, he plucked out a cell phone. Along with an item that surprised him even more.

It was a little .38 revolver, of the hammerless, snub-nosed variety some women liked to carry. But slim as it was, it was plenty big enough to kill, and he'd bet what was left of his savings that she knew how to use it.

"Hey! That's mine," she cried. "You have no right."

"How about the right of self-defense?"

"I'm calling bullshit on that. You don't get to claim self-defense in a kidnapping. Especially when *you're* armed."

"It's not a kidnapping," he argued, though from her point of view, he was sure it must seem that way.

"I doubt the detective would agree," she said, "and that gun's my legal property. I have a concealed carry permit," she explained. "Rachel hated that I have it, but out here in the country, it makes me feel safer. Because you never know when somebody's going to stop by for a *kidnapping.*"

He slipped both the gun and phone into a pocket of his jacket. "I'll return them later."

"When?"

"When I'm sure you're not going to call the cops or drill a few holes in me."

She glared at him, her gaze assuring him that if she managed to get the weapon, it might be more than a few holes.

On second thought, he added, "Come to think of it, I might hold off until we catch the son of a bitch who killed your sister—and I make damned sure he never gets the chance to drive another blonde to suicide."

***

As he marched her into the yard, Lauren's every instinct screamed that she shouldn't get into his sedan, with its darkened windows and the driver whose grim determination chilled her to the marrow.

But whatever lies he'd told her, she recognized one sure truth. He wasn't out to just arrest the man responsible for Rachel's death. Durant meant to kill the bastard.

The idea burned like straw thrown on the hot coals of her anger, and bloodlust leapt like flame inside her: the desire to see the monster who had taken Rachel from her dead. Need burned even brighter, the need to know for certain that her sister had not willingly chosen to leave her, to leave life behind, without so much as a goodbye.

Though the first few flakes swirled on a bitter breeze, Lauren didn't feel the cold as their feet crunched over frozen gravel. She picked up Dumpling and climbed into the passenger seat while Durant put her bags in the trunk.

What are you doing? Rachel's voice was in the car, so clear and so urgent, Lauren swung her head to stare at the seat behind her. And nearly wept when she found it empty.

Get out, Lauren, now. Run, while you still can!

Deeply shaken, Lauren fought back her terror, telling herself it was her own subconscious speaking, not her sister. And knowing she could never hope to outrun Durant, let alone a bullet. Besides, as dangerous as the man seemed, he offered the answers she craved—and maybe even the chance to avenge Rachel's death.

Still, Lauren's muscles remained coiled, begging her to listen to the voice of reason.

The driver's side door opened, and he climbed in and started up the engine. When he put the car into gear, a loud click echoed in the silence: the sound of the door locks automatically engaging.

She forced herself to swallow, though her throat felt hard and tight. As he backed onto the empty road, she managed, "You promised me you'd answer all my questions."

He didn't say a word but instead flipped on the headlights against the bruised-sky gloom. Flurries spun away, parted by their passing, and her nerves stretched taut, as if one end remained anchored back at home.

His gaze remained fastened to a country road pockmarked by potholes. They passed another farmhouse, but the lights were off, and the neighbor's truck was gone.

Angered and frightened by his silence, she tried again, her mind assembling truth from disparate pieces. "You said 'we' before. 'Until *we* catch' the person who killed Rachel. So that means you need my help, right? It's why you came here, isn't it?"

Remembering his recent access to FBI records, she ventured yet another guess. "You know about me, what I do, and you think I can help you somehow."

"Something like that," he admitted.

"*Exactly* like that, and if you want my help, you're going to have to answer my questions like you promised, Durant. Or whoever the hell you are."

"They might've drummed me out of the bureau, but they didn't take my name. It's Brent Durant, just like I told you."

She wouldn't bet on it, but right now something else he'd said pricked her attention. "Drummed you out? I thought you said you were suspended."

"It started out that way. But when they figured out I'd never stop, they made it permanent."

She digested this new information, wondering if this man ever opened his mouth without spewing lies or half-truths. "Never stop *what*?"

He slowed to turn onto the same state road she would have taken if she'd gone to visit Rachel, as she should have. As Lauren stroked the dog on her lap, she struggled to keep her head above the sense of unreality rising like an icy tide, threatening to drown her. She had nearly forgotten what she'd asked him when he finally deigned to answer.

"I never stopped ignoring my assigned cases and looking into suicides across the country. Looking for connections where nobody else sees them."

"What sort of connections?"

"Younger women—all blond and attractive—with no history of depression or suicide attempts."

"What else?" she asked. "What else did you find that linked them?"

"Not enough to convince the SAC—that's the special agent in charge—to pull me off drug trafficking and let me run with this full time. But then again, he wasn't really listening, only watching me like I was a damned time bomb ready to go off any minute."

Smart guy, Lauren thought, remembering how swiftly, how violently Durant had ripped out her phone and answering machine. Putting the memory aside, she said, "Well, I'm not him. I want to hear it. What else connected these women?"

"Every one of them had been involved in some recent tragedy, one receiving widespread negative publicity."

Lauren frowned, thinking of Rachel's accident, of the news stories surrounding both the drowning and the lawsuit, along with the heartbreaking photos of the pregnant victim and her children splashed across the evening news. There had been interviews with loved ones, too, friends talking about Megan's devotion to her church and family, her many acts of kindness, how she'd sold her own car to help pay for therapy for their little boy, an adorable, blond four-year-old born with Down syndrome.

In the eyes of the media, Megan—a pretty blonde herself—became the perfect mother, a sainted victim who inspired candlelit services and roadside memorials heaped with flowers, teddy bears, and crosses. Rachel, on the other hand, was just as quickly vilified after former judge and current cable TV darling Jaycee Joiner had unearthed a tagged Facebook photo showing Rachel, clearly buzzed, at a friend's bachelorette party months before. It had been enough for the host to brand her a party girl, a reckless threat to respectable married women, and lambaste the grand jury for failing to punish the perpetrator of this "blonde on blonde crime."

After a couple of hellacious weeks—weeks in which Rachel was publicly crucified as the "Blonde on Blonde Killer"—the furor was drowned out by an even more sensational news story involving a drug-addled young starlet accused of murdering her own baby. Still, Lauren had regularly searched the web for anything and everything to do with Rachel's case. Unlike her sister, she was net-savvy enough to stop short of reading various forum comment sections, knowing that the conversations on these websites often were both personal and painful.

They're just stupid trolls, she'd warned Rachel the day her sister called in hysterics over a rash of particularly cruel comments. *Pathetic losers who'll say anything to get a reaction. They'd come out against fresh air, sunshine, even the damned Easter Bunny if they thought it would get them five minutes' attention.*

Recalling what Durant had just said about the other victims' tragedies, Lauren asked him, "What kinds of tragedies? Were there similarities?"

"Sad stuff, all of them." His mouth tightened before he added, "You're sure you want to hear the details?"

No, she wanted to shout, but she had to understand. Had to know if Durant could be right—or if he was completely insane. "Yeah." She nodded. "I have to know."

"One was a young mother whose baby died after she absentmindedly left him to roast in her hot car. There was a teenaged girl, too, who'd been blogging about her struggles with anorexia for about six months when another set of parents accused her of 'encouraging' their daughter to starve herself to death. And then there was the woman whose—"

"Enough, please." Lauren raised a hand, bile burning in her throat. Sickened, she turned her head and stared out the window at the bleak, brown farmland sliding past, stark behind the rippling veil of snow.

"I'm sorry," he said somberly. "It's just—I know you're already in shock, overwhelmed."

"Don't tell me what I'm feeling," she interrupted, too upset to care that he was right on both counts. Not when he'd added raw fear to the mix. Fear that she was blinded by grief—and as crazy as her captor for believing anything that came out of his mouth.

"I think I do know," he had the balls to answer, "I know because I've—"

"You've *what*? Delivered bad news to a lot of people? *Abducted* them from their homes, too?"

He glanced over, his jaw clenched and his brow furrowed. "I am not abducting you."

"You scared me half to death at the house. You still do."

"I'm only trying to make sure you'll listen long enough for me to explain the truth to you. The truth you'll never get from the police, the FBI—not from anyone but me. I'm giving you the information I've spent the last year gathering, and I'm letting you decide for yourself if you want to help me catch your sister's killer."

"And if I don't believe you?"

"Then when we get to Austin, you're free to go and grieve your sister's suicide."

As the flurries in the headlights dwindled, sunset peered beneath the cloud cover to stain the flat horizon as red as fresh-spilled blood. She wasn't ready to let her fury die, too, to leave herself in the grip of an endless winter mourning and questioning her sister's choices. Questioning, too, whether her own first instinct—that Rachel never could have done this—had been right, or she was merely being sucked into Durant's delusion.

"I'll listen," she agreed. "I'll listen and then decide. But first I want to know, when did you meet Rachel? What did you talk to her about?" *Why didn't you protect her, even from herself?*

"She agreed to meet about a week ago, at a coffee shop."

Her gaze narrowed. "Which coffee shop?"

"Ah, I don't recall the name. Some trendy little place on Chicon Street—great espresso."

Lauren nodded, remembering her sister taking her there on one of her rare visits. Rachel had started mooching the shop's free Wi-Fi back in college, but the hazelnut lattes were what kept her coming back long after leaving school to work in hospital billing.

Still, Lauren reminded herself that anyone could figure out as much about Rachel's habits by checking out her Facebook page or Twitter account, or reading a review of the café she'd posted online somewhere. As often as Lauren had warned her about blabbing her whereabouts to the world so casually, Rachel had only laughed off her concern, accusing her of letting her cyber-security work make her paranoid.

Frigid waves of nausea broke Lauren out in gooseflesh. If she only had the chance to annoy her little sister with another lecture . . .

Durant took her silence for permission to continue. "I wanted to see if she'd received any direct communication from a troll who was leaving comments in the discussion sections under online news stories related to her accident. I'd been scanning social media and forums, checking out the conversations, looking for similarities in the wording, threatening statements—"

"I'm surprised all that ugliness didn't melt your eyes in their sockets," she said bitterly. "I'll never understand the kind of person who gets off on leaving sick, judgmental comments about people involved in tragedies."

"Actually, you just nailed it right there."

"What?"

"They get off on it, at least that's what the bureau experts and the forensic psychologists have to say about the subject."

She made a sound of pure disgust. "Sexually, you mean?"

"A lot of times. But sometimes, it's just a matter of relieving their own stress or boredom by inflicting pain on others. And just like with face-to-face bullying, it can get competitive. Like a sport."

"A *blood* sport," she corrected, her short nails digging crimson crescents in her palms.

"I'd been following discussion threads related to women I believed might fit the suspect's profile," Durant continued, "when I noticed a similarity in the wording of some of the most vicious comments. And there were personal details in them, details I suspected could have only come from Rachel. How she blamed herself. How she was seeing a counselor to help her with the bad dreams she'd been having—nightmares about Megan Rutherford's unborn child coming to accuse her of murdering her mother."

Lauren's heart raced, hearing Rachel's anguish in the words. Or had she sent them in an e-mail? "He could have hacked her phone or maybe her computer. If her password wasn't secure enough, or she logged in on a public access wireless hotspot somewhere—"

Somewhere like the coffee shop.

"Or if he somehow got her number and spoke to her by phone," Durant said. "She denied speaking to him, but she wouldn't look at me when I asked. She became defensive and asked me to leave soon afterward."

Lauren shook her head. "Maybe she wasn't lying. Maybe she was just sick of talking about it. That's why she left counseling. She said it was bad enough she'd had to survive the accident once, let alone rehash it again and again."

"She was lying, Lauren. And it fits this suspect's pattern, digging up his targets' numbers somehow and phoning to torment them."

"If some creep had called her, she would have freaked out," Lauren insisted, "and I would've been there in a heartbeat. Would've made her report it to the police and even slept on her damned doorstep if I had to, with my gun in hand."

"Before I, um, before I left the bureau, I was able to subpoena a couple of the other victims' phone records. Right around the time of their deaths, both had dozens of calls from private numbers, numbers that turned out to be from burner phones, disposables paid for in cash from various locations. Little mom-and-pop stores with no security cameras—or old, low-tech systems where nothing could be made out but a blurred figure in a hoodie sweatshirt."

"So how can you be sure it's always the same person?" *And how can I be sure you're not making all of this up?*

"I can't. Not for certain. And I can't prove he's connected to the troll on the forums. But I damn well know it's him. I swear, I can practically feel the evil welling up in the final message he posted in relation to each victim."

Durant's reasoning might not completely hold together, but the utter conviction in his voice drew a shudder from her. And a question, too. "What was it he wrote? What did he say about my sister?"

Durant braked hard as a coyote dashed across the road a few feet from their bumper. Her grip on the dog tightened as the tires squealed. There was a moment the car lost its grip, the rear end sliding sideways. But the ex-agent kept them on the road, and the coyote vanished into the tall grasses.

"You okay?" he asked her.

"Sure. Fine. Never better," she said, though her heart was pounding with the near miss. Clearly upset with the jostling, the dog whimpered and struggled in her arms until Lauren helped her climb down to the floor of the backseat. "There you go, sweetie. Curl up down there. Good girl."

Turning around, Lauren strapped herself back in and focused on the agent. "Now tell me, what was this troll saying on the forum?"

His gaze locked on the road, Durant said, "You don't need to hear it. Trust me, you don't want it in your head."

"I want to know. I *have* to. I owe that much to Rachel."

The car grew so quiet that Lauren could make out the chatter of each pebble that passed beneath the tires, every breath the driver took.

When he spoke again, his words were scarcely louder. "That's what I thought once. But I was wrong, Lauren. I never should have—"

"But it's your job," she argued.

"No, it *wasn't*," he ground out, "as the special agent in charge, all my colleagues, and the damned psychologist they made me see, were all too quick to remind me. But because I had to know what he said, this investigation—this *hunt* for the twisted animal who killed her—is fucking all that I have left."

By the dim light of the glowing dashboard, she studied the tension in his handsome features. The tautness of his square jaw, the way he gripped the wheel so hard, it looked as if he might rip it from the column. Though she wasn't particularly bothered by the language, she took the harshness in his voice as another warning. A warning that this man was skating dangerously close to the edge.

"All? I don't understand." Hardly daring to breathe, she asked, "You're not talking about Rachel, are you?"

He shook his head before confirming, "Hell, no, I'm not talking about Rachel. This all goes back to the very first victim that I know of. Her name was Carrie—Carrie Wilkinson . . ."

There was a weighted quality to his pause, like a heavy stone dropped onto the frozen surface of a pond. With the cracks in the ice spreading toward her, Lauren knew instinctively that he had something more to say, something that would change everything she thought or guessed about him.

"Carrie Wilkinson Durant," he said, his words as cold and empty as the emerging starlight outside. "We'd been married for ten years when she took one of my razorblades out of the package. Took it with her to the bathtub. I found her floating hours later. Just the way he'd planned."

CHAPTER FOUR

The mention of his wife's name reopened old scar tissue, and Brent was there again, seeing the streamers of pale golden hair floating on the surface, hearing the splash of blood-tinged waves as he'd dragged Carrie from her bath.

But the water had long since grown cool, just as she had, her flesh pale and wrinkled from the water, her hazel eyes wide and fully dilated. Worst of all had been the absence in them, the yawning emptiness that told him his frantic efforts at resuscitation had come far too late.

Yet he couldn't make himself stop, not even when the paramedics—responding to a call he would never remember making—had tried to pull him away. Maybe it was because he knew, knew it to his marrow, that this cold kiss would be their last, this damp embrace final.

"Your wife," Lauren was saying, her words ringing in his ears like the distant tolling of church bells. "Of course. It all makes sense now. How long ago?"

Caught in a memory of the funeral, he didn't answer until she repeated the two words, "How long?"

The death knell in his head fell silent long enough for her question to sink in. A question, as simple as it was impatient, without a trace of the pitying condolences he was so damned sick of hearing.

"Two years," he answered. "Two years ago today."

"The other killings," she continued, sounding as detached and clinical as a federal agent investigating strangers' deaths. "Did at least one of them happen on the first anniversary?"

Recognizing the coping mechanism for what it was, he shook his head and clamped down on his emotions, too. "No. And there's no correlation among any of the other dates, except that the suicides I'm tracking have all been in Louisiana, Texas, Arkansas, and Oklahoma. One possible outlier in Albuquerque, but that's the farthest I've found."

"So you're thinking that this troll—this killer—is located in Texas and choosing victims within driving range?"

He would almost swear he heard her plotting points and drawing lines between them on a mental map, the way one of the bureau's data geeks would. If he hadn't seen the other Lauren, the one who'd pleaded for him to tell her the news of Rachel's death was a mistake, the one who doted on a throwaway dog, he might have believed she was some sort of robot.

"It's a pretty broad range, considering the size of Texas, but yeah," he said, gratified by how quickly she had grasped an argument that no one in the bureau had been willing to consider. Or maybe they had looked into his theory, just as Special Agent in Charge Fremont Daniels had sworn, leaving Brent out of the loop because of his relationship with an alleged victim. In the end, though, they'd refused to see it, figuring the connections he saw so clearly as figments of a guilt-stricken mind. A mind broken on the rocks of his wife's suicide.

"Why'd she kill herself?" Lauren asked him bluntly.

"She didn't. Kill herself. She was fucking *driven* to it, same as Rachel," he barked, the frustration of not being heard for two long years beating at his temples, "the same as if he'd slashed her wrists himself. So don't ask that again."

She flinched, grabbing the door handle beside her as if she might bail out at any moment. As if she thought he would try to hit or even shoot her.

Her reaction stopped the red wash of his anger cold, filling him with shame. Was he really so far gone he'd take out all his fury on a frightened woman? A woman grappling with what was undoubtedly the worst shock, the deepest grief she'd ever known?

Yet *she* was the one who burst out, "I'm sorry. I'm not always so good at—Rachel always says I cut straight through the niceties, get to the point without all the useless verbal foreplay."

He'd be willing to bet her bluntness didn't get her a lot of second dates, or maybe even first ones, in spite of her trim body and unusual blue-green eyes. But he wasn't here to make friends with her, much less teach her social skills. In the past two years, he'd been having trouble enough managing his own. Or so the exodus of his friends had informed him. Not even his own sister called him anymore.

Still, what was left of his conscience nudged him, and common sense said that acting like a crazy man was no way to gain her cooperation.

"I'm the one who should be sorry. I didn't mean to scare you." He casually hit the child safety lock button on his own door to be sure she didn't hurt herself with an unscheduled exit. "But Carrie *didn't* kill herself. She was forced into it, coerced."

"Rachel always *said* I cut straight through, not *says*." Lauren corrected herself with a frown, as if she hadn't heard his half-assed apology. "I keep forgetting that she's gone now, so she can't tell me—All I want is to hear her yell at me about my lousy manners one more time."

He glanced over and saw her wipe her face. But if he'd expected a full meltdown, she surprised him, instead murmuring, "This isn't real. It can't be."

He grimaced, wondering how many times he'd thought the same thing, had prayed for it to be true, since Carrie's death. Two years out, he'd come far enough to recognize her denial. And far enough to understand why others believed his theories about the bastard he thought of as "the Troll King" were denial, too.

Lauren shook her head. "When I asked why your wife had done it, I only meant to ask, what was it he used? Which tragedy did this guy blame her for? You said that was his pattern, to guilt blondes into—you know."

He tried to answer, but the words knotted low in his throat.

"Jesus, Durant," she blurted. "Please don't tell me she was the one who left the baby in the car. *Your* baby."

"It's none of your damned business," his voice rumbled through clenched jaws.

"You said you'd tell me everything if I came with you."

"Everything about your sister."

"Whose death, you're claiming, is related to your wife's. So convince me."

She was persistent; he would give her that much. "It wasn't the kid in the car. The rest—I can't talk about it right now." Or ever, if he had a damned thing to say about it.

As they approached a speed reduction for the town ahead, she heaved a sigh. "Okay, I guess, for right now, anyway. But at least tell me the last thing he posted about Rachel, this troll on the net. Otherwise, whatever you want from me, forget it."

"All right," he said, grateful to get her off the unbearable topic of his late wife. "Just last night, this guy put up a photo of Megan Rutherford from her last Mother's Day. Gorgeous picture, taken in the sunshine. She was hugging two cute kids, the younger one with Down syndrome—"

"That would be Luke, four years old, and his sister, Molly."

"—and this big, fluffy puppy."

Lauren nodded. "Yeah, I've seen that picture, with the Newfie mix named Badger, paws like dinner plates. Huge by now, I imagine."

"They were all laughing at something," Brent continued, wondering if she used such details to keep emotion at bay. "Underneath the shot, the sick bastard posted, '*Anybody with a single scrap of decency would blow their head off. Rot in Hell, Whore!*'"

Lauren pinched the bridge of her nose and turned her face to the glass. After collecting herself, she asked, "Did she—do you think Rachel read it? Surely, she wouldn't have—I begged her not to look at that trash, not to pay attention to those monsters. And never, no matter what, to feed the trolls with any response."

"I don't have access to her laptop, so I can't say whether or not she ever read it. But if he'd been calling her on the phone like the others, spewing that same bullshit—"

"Like I said, she would've told me."

"She didn't tell you about me."

She waved a hand at him, as if she could somehow push him farther from her. "I need to think. It's too much."

They rode in silence, the tiny towns they passed through like islands dotting the vast stretches of rangeland, much of it nearly emptied of cattle thanks to last summer's drought and sell-off. He fiddled with the radio for a minute, searching for a decent station, but seeing Lauren's pained look, he quickly cut it off.

He understood her need for quiet, her inability to take in any more at this point, so he waited until they'd passed through Dallas before he spoke again. "We're going to have to fill the car up, so we might as well grab something for ourselves while we're at it. How 'bout you? You ready for a stop yet?"

She shook her head. "I just want to get to Austin as fast as possible, so we can get this all straight."

From behind the seat, the fat dog scratched the floor mat and groaned, resettling her old bones.

"Sounds like our passenger could use a break, too," Brent told Lauren. "Don't want her springing a leak on my upholstery."

"Dumpling's perfectly housebroken," she said before qualifying, "unless she gets upset."

"Do long car rides generally upset her? We've been on the road more than three hours already."

After a measured silence, Lauren said, "Maybe we should stop, then."

With little to choose from this far out of town, he pulled into the lot of a restaurant called Burger Palace, which boasted a grassy margin that looked decently dog friendly. Still, he would need to leave her to go inside for a few minutes. The question was, could he trust her to still be here when he returned?

"The way I see it," he told her, "I've got a couple choices here. I could cuff you to the steering wheel and leave you 'til I get back. But I figure that would make Detective Jimenez in Austin right about me, and I don't want him to be right, don't want to be the kind of man who'd—"

"Go to prison for decades, maybe, on a charge of armed abduction?" One corner of her mouth rose slightly.

He nodded. "There is that. And if I end up rotting in a cell, that'd leave the Troll King free to go after other women, to destroy their lives and the lives of their families."

She looked at him for a moment, a frown tugging at one corner of her mouth. "Where would I go, even if I did run? One way or another, I have to get to Austin to fix this, and you're my fastest way there."

The words told him she was still bouncing between shock and denial, still hoping she could bargain her way out of Rachel being dead. Grief would do that to a person. He'd gone through it himself with Carrie. Was still going through it on an unconscious level, waking up with a sense of crushing loss after dreams of finding her, alive and well—really well and not the shattered shell she'd become throughout the last months of their marriage, nor the obsessed and anxious woman she'd been before Adam.

"Just hurry up and go inside already," she said. "I'll need you to hold Dumpling's leash so I can visit the facilities, too."

He did as she asked and was relieved to see that she was still there, walking the dog among the frost-crisped weeds when he came out of the restroom. Watching her through the glass, he took a chance and ordered a couple of burger baskets and drinks for the road, which he paid for and told the clerk his friend would pick up in a few minutes.

As he came out, he said, "You mind grabbing our order on your way out if it's ready?"

"Our order?" She waved off the idea. "I told you, I don't want anything."

"If you don't want it, you don't have to eat, but we still have a long drive. You might change your mind."

She shrugged in answer and returned about five minutes later, just as he was wondering if she'd slipped out the employee exit or talked the manager into calling 9-1-1.

He unwrapped his burger, and they were underway again. Maybe it was the smell of the food, or maybe she'd paid attention to what he'd said before, but about twenty minutes later, she picked at the fries and nibbled one end of her sandwich. Every so often, she leaned back and shared a bite of grilled beef with the dachshund, who was making obnoxious little grunts, snuffles, and whimpers as she begged from the backseat.

He increased their speed as they rolled beyond the edge of town, the road slicing an arrow-straight swath across more empty land. Or nearly empty, save for a single dun-colored horse that jerked its head from grazing to watch them pass.

It should have a pasture mate, he thought, remembering the horses he'd grown up with on his grandparents' ranch in far West Texas. Like cattle, equines were herd animals, always jittery and uncomfortable, sometimes flat-out crazy, if they were kept too long on their own.

Just as he was growing crazy, cut from his familiar herd of spouse and friends and fellow agents. *This has to stop, Brent,* Carrie whispered, his dead wife's voice inside his head.

Beside him, Lauren balled up what was left of her meal and stuffed it in the bottom of the bag.

"I think the dog got more of that than you did," he ventured.

"Tasted like old grease," she complained. "I hope it doesn't make her sick."

"Trust me on this. The food wasn't the problem. For a long time, everything will taste off, or it won't have any taste at all." He recalled how little appetite he'd had in the months after Carrie's death, how his old clothes seemed to swamp him. "Remember that and make yourself eat anyway. Go through the motions, or you won't have the energy to handle all the things that have to be dealt with."

"I don't want to handle anything. I don't want to 'get through it.' I just—I just want Rachel, that's all."

"I know," he said, not trusting himself to say more, to tell her how two years later, he still wanted Carrie, the way she'd once been. How he would doubtless want her until they someday buried him by her side.

Lauren said nothing, but her misery spoke for her, the wounded silence radiating off of her in waves. And vulnerability, as well, as cruel a fate as the one the Troll King had inflicted on her sister.

"There's something else we need to talk about," he managed, hating the emotion running roughshod over his voice.

"I don't want to talk anymore."

"Then listen, just listen. Because this bastard isn't through yet."

"You have to understand," she said, turning on him viciously, "I don't give a rat's ass about other people. I don't have room left in my head for that now."

"In the last few months, he's escalated, coming after his victims' family members, too," Brent explained, "harassing them about their loved one's suffering and their failure to see it. To stop them from taking their own lives. The calls and messages have been beyond cruel and extremely graphic. He's been torturing these women with excruciating details of their relatives' deaths."

"These women?" She shook her head. "You mean, he hasn't called you?"

"I wish to hell he would," he said, "but he has a type, and I'm not a pretty little blonde."

"Neither am I. So if you're thinking of using me for bait—"

"You've got the young and attractive part in spades, and you'll be plenty blond once we lighten up your hair and get you saying the right things in front of the news cameras—"

"What the hell? No," she shouted, her voice so sharp it made the dog behind the seat yip. "I thought you wanted me to help you track him electronically—because of my experience with—with networking."

You mean hacking, he wanted to correct her, thinking about what Cisco had called her, "an old-school white hat freak." Meaning that she liked breaking in for the thrill of breaking in, not doing any harm. For her clients, her work had another purpose: finding and closing security rifts before malicious hackers could exploit them.

"I do need your experience," he told her, "but the surest way to draw him out is for him to see you as a potential target. And the easiest way to do that is to disguise you as a potential vic—"

"Screw that. I'm not some dancing pony for you to trot out for a performance. And I'm nobody's damned *victim*. Including yours. You got that straight, Durant?"

***

They were closing in on Austin when Durant grimaced and turned an accusing look toward Lauren. "Tell me that's not you."

"Ugh. *Dumpling*." Her nose wrinkling, she turned to look back over the seat at the dachshund, who had a pained expression on her graying face. Or maybe she was just embarrassed. "Sorry about that."

Lauren was apologizing to the dog and not Durant, since the way she figured it, he deserved worse than a little stink. She put her window down a couple inches.

Durant was quick to follow suit, creating a cold cross-breeze that did a lot for the air quality. "Do we need to pull over? Because I am not going to be a happy man if she loses it in my car."

"I think she's okay." Lauren waited a beat before laying her hand over her own stomach. "But I'm not so sure about me. I knew that greasy junk you picked out was a bad idea."

"It's not like there were a lot of better choices. Besides, *you're* the one who decided to feed most of your lunch to that over-stuffed sausage."

"Poor Dumpling," she said, feeling guilty for intentionally upsetting her dog's digestive system. Though her own stomach felt fine, Lauren squirmed uncomfortably and tensed, groaning as she cupped her hands over her waist.

Durant glanced at her, concern in his brown eyes. "We're about ten minutes out from Char-Lee's on 35—the one that advertises such great restrooms—and I'm sure they'll have all kinds of stomach medication, too. Think you can hold out that long?"

Having made this trip to visit Rachel, she would have put it at more like twenty minutes. Feigning a distressed look, she asked, "Do I have another choice?"

He shrugged. "Maybe we'll come up on another fast-food place or a gas station. Or if it's a dire emergency, there's always the side of the—"

At her look of horror, he shut up.

"I'll hold out," she said. "But please don't dawdle."

They were quiet as he kept on driving, Lauren bending her knees and bracing them against her door. She thought about adding another groan or two, as well, but decided to go for pained stoicism instead.

Since she hadn't tried to duck out of the Burger Palace, she was counting on having earned his trust well enough that he'd never suspect her plan to ditch him at the always-crowded travel plaza. As frightening as she found the thought of going to a stranger, perhaps one of the employees, and asking to use a phone to call Detective Jimenez, she was more worried about allowing Brent Durant to continue to control her—feeding her only the information that would allow him to manipulate her to his end . . .

Including his shocking plan to transform her into the Troll King's wet dream. She hugged herself and shivered, sickened at the thought of attempting to remake herself in Rachel's image. And even more terrified to imagine herself in front of a battery of cameras.

Yet as disturbing as the thought was, Durant had by now, at least, become something of a known quantity, a man grappling with a grief too huge for him to contain. She sneaked a look his way, seeing the creases in his forehead, the tight grip on the wheel, the hard set of his square jaw. Seeing absolute obsession, clothed in well-toned flesh. As noble as it might be, chasing down some mysterious tormentor he blamed for his wife's death, she reminded herself his dark fixation was no less dangerous to both of them.

And not one iota less insane.

Still, somehow, the fear of walking into the crowded travel plaza and spilling her story before total strangers darted beneath her skin like tiny electric minnows. She told herself the fear was baseless, that she'd be far safer among so many witnesses, but the nearly pathological social anxiety she'd always grappled with only tightened its grip.

Not for the first time, she wished she'd inherited a fraction of Rachel's trust in her fellow humans. But the thought of where such trust had gotten her far sweeter sister made Lauren's breath hitch and her eyes burn anew.

"You're looking pretty pale." Brent sounded genuinely worried. "If this is something serious, maybe I should try to find a clinic."

"It's fine," she said. "Or it'll be fine, anyway. As soon as I take something for my stomach."

"Getting there as fast as I can," he assured her, though she noticed that he was driving only a few miles over the posted speed limit. Which made sense, considering how much trouble he could be in if they happened to be pulled over and she asked the officer for help.

Fortunately, Dumpling's stomach issues settled enough that they were able to make it to Char-Lee's without another stop. After a brief wait in traffic to pull in, Brent had to make a full circuit of the packed lot before finding a distant parking spot. "You want me to walk your mutt while you go inside?"

She froze, realizing she hadn't thought about poor Dumpling, who wouldn't be allowed inside; she wouldn't be able to take Dumpling out through the huge plaza's other entrance, either. It was a weak point in her plan—she, who was so adept at carrying out the most sophisticated online incursions.

It was one more sign of how this morning's phone call had knocked her world off its axis. Of how she couldn't trust herself to make good decisions. But the one thing Lauren knew for certain was there was no way on God's green earth she was going to leave behind her best friend. No way she would risk Durant dropping off Dumpling at the nearest animal shelter—or worse yet, another roadside—where a fat, gray-muzzled dog like her wouldn't stand a chance.

"Do you think you could go inside, and I'll stay with her?" she asked. "I think I want the fresh air, some of those Pepto-Bismol tablets, and a clear soda first. One with real cane sugar, if they have it."

He hesitated for a moment, his face an unreadable mixture of emotions.

Sensing that he was trying to figure out whether to believe her, she opted for as much of the truth as she could risk. "It's really crowded in there."

She looked anxiously in the direction of the travel plaza, shuddering at the swirling chaos of so many people going in and out. After spending the last few months alone at the farm, except for brief forays into a town where she wouldn't see this much traffic if she stood on a corner for a solid month, it made her feel like an overloaded circuit.

"I don't—I don't do crowds," she confessed, darting a look his way. Because it was easier, she'd found, focusing on one person at a time. "Not well, anyway."

Durant nodded. "All right, Lauren. Just deal with the mutt, and I'll go get your medicine and your 'real cane sugar.'"

He did so, taking the keys with him. Too bad, she thought, he had both her phone and her gun on him as well.

But it couldn't be helped, any more than she could help her nervousness as she scanned the people going to and from their vehicles. Most of them were paired or in groups, so she settled on taking Dumpling to the marked dog-walking area. There, she saw a tubby, middle-aged man picking up after a couple of tiny, white hairballs and a big, blond bodybuilder type who was jerking around an equally muscle-bound tan dog with a choke chain.

The first man looked like the type to ask his wife, who might tell him to call the cops and keep his nose out of a stranger's business. The second looked as if he might chop her into pieces and feed her to his sidekick.

She looked around for a third choice, praying there would be a single woman . . .

And knowing that the time for choosiness had passed.

***

Brent trotted outside, carrying a small bag containing the medicine, the soda, and some saltines, which Carrie used to nibble when she had an upset stomach, and realized when he saw the car, its back door standing open, that he had utterly been had.

After looking around for any sign of her and realizing that her bags were gone, too, he blurted, "Son of a bitch!" furious at himself for being so gullible, so stupid that he'd fallen for a story a first-year rookie cop would have suspected . . .

A story she'd trumped up using a freaking farting dog.

Struck by the sheer ridiculousness of the situation, he snorted, thinking this was the kind of self-deprecating and ironic tale that would have his fellow agents springing for round after round at their off-duty get-togethers for as long he would tell it.

An instant later, his amusement crashed and burned— because if he didn't get out of here this minute, this was a story he wouldn't get to tell *at* bars but *behind* them. And he wasn't about to let the cops be the ones doing all the laughing.

Grimacing at the thought, he kicked shut the back door, piled in the front seat, and started the sedan. Or tried to.

A few minutes later, he laughed, louder and longer than he had laughed in years. People turned to look at him. One young mother snatched up her children's hands and veered in the opposite direction—as if his insanity were some dangerous disease they might catch.

Maybe it was, and surely he needed to put some distance between him and this car before the authorities showed up to arrest him. But for some reason, he couldn't help but give it up for Lauren Miller, a woman who, with every reason to be a quivering mass of tears by now, had had not only the presence of mind and the know-how, but also the pure brass balls to do something to his car's ignition before she'd left.

As he glanced up, he spotted a big, red pickup leaving the lot, the kind of pickup with a lift kit, giant tires, and a monster dog chained in the back. Inside the cab, there was a flash of movement, the top of what looked like a woman's head ducking out of sight.

And pressing its nose against the side window, a flatulent little sausage wagged its tail as if to say goodbye.

"See you again soon," Brent rumbled, his voice a throaty growl. Because the better he got to know the woman that Cisco had informed him was known among white-hat hackers as *Litef00t*, the more certain he was that she had what it took to finally bring the murderous Troll King to his knees.

And the more determined Brent was to convince her that her sister had been willfully, methodically killed.

CHAPTER FIVE

When a woman needed a quick getaway, she could do worse than a truck-driving guy with a dog that probably left backyard land mines bigger than her dachshund, Lauren decided. Just as she'd hoped, the blond bodybuilder who called himself Big Mel had turned out to be the type to act first and consider the consequences later rather than sit dithering over whether the authorities should be called or the woman with the awful story of the abusive boyfriend could be trusted.

Instead, Big Mel had asked her just one question. "You want this bastard flattened, or you just want to take off?"

"Distance—that's all I need. As soon as I make sure he doesn't follow."

Clearly fascinated, the huge man had kept watch while Lauren raised the hood and found the ignition fuse. Crossing it over the car's battery, she'd shorted it in record time before lowering the hood and grabbing her things.

"You look like you know your way around an engine." Sparing her an admiring glance, Big Mel pulled onto the feeder road. "So, your boyfriend a mechanic?"

Lauren tried and failed to picture Durant with his white sleeves rolled up and his tie spotted with grease. "Not him." And her ex-husband had been absolutely helpless, insisting on hiring someone for every repair or maintenance chore, even those she had repeatedly offered to take care of. It had taken her a long time to clap onto the fact that Phillip was embarrassed at the thought that neighbors in their upscale community might see her draining the transmission fluid or rewiring a broken outdoor light.

She still didn't get why it would matter to him what anybody else thought. When she'd asked, he had put on his most pompous real estate attorney face and told her, *That question, in a nutshell, Lauren, encapsulates everything that's wrong with you. And our relationship.*

"Your daddy, then, or a brother?" asked Big Mel, who looked older than she'd first thought, or maybe the leathery tan, blurred tattoos, and an assortment of scars weren't so much about years as hard-won miles.

She shook her head, more amused than surprised that he assumed a man must have been the source of her unexpected knowledge. "Self-taught, or mostly, anyway. When there's no money to get things fixed, somebody's got to learn."

He grunted his agreement. "Sounds like we grew up on the same side of the tracks, girl. So where to now? Maybe you could use a place to lay low for a few days? My little house ain't much, but I'd gladly share what I have."

She gestured toward the dashboard clock, which read 3:38.

"I have to get to the medical examiner's office on Sabine Street before five." Her nerves jittered a warning that she'd somehow given him the wrong idea. Possibly by dint of having breasts. "The police called me this morning. They need me to— to sort out a mistake there."

"The *medical examiner*? Who's dead?" He bypassed the freeway's entrance ramp, keeping to the access road.

"They're saying it's my sister." She rocked in her seat as Dumpling snuggled closer. "But I-I told him—I told him that can't be right."

"You mean that jackass of a boyfriend would pick a fight with you the same day you found out that your sister . . . ?" The huge man grunted in disgust. "You sure you don't want me to head back there and mess this dude up? Seriously, it would be my pleasure."

"Thanks." Was it possible that, beneath his rough exterior, Big Mel's heart had lain in wait his whole life for an opportunity to play the hero for some damsel in distress? But Lauren didn't want Durant, who was a victim of his own tragedy, hurt so much as she wanted clear of the insanity that gripped him. At least until she could establish whether anything he'd told her had been truthful. "But I just need to get over to Sabine Street. Is there a rental car place around here where you can drop me?"

She'd need wheels, anyway, to get around as long as she had to stay in Austin. And more important, to keep herself from having to beg rides from the Big Mels of this city.

He thought about it for a minute, slowing for traffic as they passed a number of businesses, from self-storage units to an auto supply store to an urgent-care center. "You know, between this, um, mix-up about your sister and your fight with your jackass boyfriend, I'd feel a whole lot better about it if you'd let me drop my dog off back at home and drive you over there myself, Miss— you never did tell me what your name was, did you, sweetie?"

"Celia Blanchard," Lauren said quickly, using one of the false identities she often employed on the Internet. One she could afford to burn. She was beginning to understand: she'd already given the bodybuilder more personal information than she should have. And her instincts warned her that the more pieces he had of her, the more he'd want to claim. It could be he was simply lonely, or maybe he was hoping for a sexual payoff for his good deed of the decade. A payoff he might be willing to use coercion, or maybe even force, to gain.

A warning coiled just beneath her belly, shaking its rattles as it tasted the air inside the truck cab. She wished she were back inside the car with Durant, whose guns and grief and delusions suddenly seemed less threatening. Or why hadn't she simply sucked up her fear of crowds and gone inside the travel plaza, where scores of witnesses would have served as her shield while someone called the police for her?

A line of brake lights brought them to a stop. Though she couldn't make out the reason, she spotted flashing emergency lights at the intersection up ahead. Had to be a wreck, she figured, her right hand inching closer to the door handle.

"Well, Celia Blanchard," Big Mel said, grasping hold of the false name in the casual way a man picked up a knife he'd owned for years. A knife that could be used for a variety of innocent reasons—or could serve as a reminder that he was the one with all the power. "It seems to me that the Good Lord might've put you in my path for a reason. Maybe it's a sign I need to see that you get through all this safely."

She felt the sting of perspiration dampening her back beneath the jacket as her instincts told her the shift into the territory of God's will was a bad sign. "That's very kind of you, Mel. I can tell you're a good man, and I want you to know I appreciate what you've done for me so far. But any more's too much of an imposition on a stranger."

"Don't think of me as a stranger, Celia. I'm a new friend, that's all. A friend who wants to help." There was something brittle in his voice, so brittle that she half expected his clenched, yellow smile to shatter.

"Right now, I need to be alone, Mel," she insisted, the few words hammered thin and flat as foil. Ice cold, Phillip would've called them, another example of a "deficiency" he'd used to excuse his own.

She might be wrong about the man next to her, as she so often was when it came to people, but having just escaped one stranger who'd wanted to manipulate her, she wasn't about to fall prey to someone even worse.

"But Celia, honey—" Big Mel started, creeping her out more with every second.

"You might want to take my word for it on this one," she said, grabbing the dachshund as she opened the door, "unless you want to see a brand of batshit crazy you'd never come up with in a hundred years."

***

One thing about wrecker drivers: they could sniff out a disabled car from miles away, like vultures on the scent of a fresh kill. Within minutes from the time Durant popped the big sedan's hood, he had several noisily vying for his business.

Brent gave it to a driver standing behind the others, a dark-skinned man with a shot of silver through his springy hair and his thumbs hooked in the pockets of his stained coveralls as if he had neither the time nor the inclination to fight the young pups for a tow.

Once the others had hurried off, responding to an emergency call on somebody's scanner for an additional ambulance, he used his smartphone's flashlight app to show the driver the fried filaments in the ignition fuse. "Instead of a tow," he asked, "how 'bout I pay you for a lift to pick up another one of these?"

"S'posed to tow you to the boss's shop with no 'ceptions," the driver said before adding a shrug. "But on a day as cold as this one, cash don't leave no footprints."

They negotiated a price somewhere between high and extortionist, but Brent was in no mood to argue. So it was that he was riding in the cab of a truck that smelled of old coffee, stale sweat, and about a million cigarettes when he spotted a bright red pickup with a familiar dog chained in its bed. The truck had pulled over on the feeder about fifty yards ahead, near where scores of vehicles had backed up, waiting for a wreck to clear.

"Up there! Up ahead," he shouted, as the driver prepared to pull into the lot of an auto parts store.

"We'll miss our turn and have to go clear 'round, through all that traffic," the man warned.

"Fifty extra for your time," Brent said, as ahead, the passenger side door opened and a slim figure stepped out, lost her balance, and spilled to the ground. As if she had been given a shove as she got out. "That woman—she's my—she's a friend."

Like the dachshund in her arms, who immediately popped up and started barking, Lauren Miller didn't stay down. Scrambling, she ran after the red truck before the driver could nose his way back into traffic. Horns blared as the occupants of nearby vehicles honked warnings, but Lauren didn't give up. Before Brent wondered if he could make it to her faster on foot, she reached in and snatched her bags, which she tossed onto the roadside, shouting a few choice words if her body language was any indication.

As the pickup pulled away from her, the wrecker driver shot Brent a skeptical look. "She looks madder'n a skin't cat. You sure you want any parta that?"

A reasonable question, he thought as she turned his way while checking her dog for injuries. Even from this distance, he made out the stiffness of her posture and the torn knees of her jeans, neither of which gave him much hope that she'd be grateful to see him.

"Yeah, I do," Brent told him, swearing he would find a way to harness every bit of the raw anger and determination he saw in Lauren Miller and mold them to his purpose. Because it would take that kind of guts and grit to help him hunt down the animal who had tortured his Carrie until she'd broken.

It would take a woman tough as nails to look away while he permanently ended the Troll King's chances of legally maneuvering his way out of the situation. While Brent left the bastard awash in the same blood that nightly haunted his own dreams.

An hour later, he and Lauren were back on the road in Durant's sedan, with Dumpling comfortably settled on the back seat floorboard.

"For what it's worth," Brent said, hoping it was safe to risk another stab at conversation, "it was a pretty good escape plan. I still have no idea how you managed to fry my fuse so quickly."

"Obviously, some *man* must've shown me how to do it."

He snorted at her irritation but managed to hold back a smile. "So exactly what was it that happened between you and your knight in shining pickup before he threw you out?"

"He didn't *throw* me out." Her indignant glare bounced off him. "I was *getting* out. Leaving on my own."

"Apparently, not fast enough to suit him. So what happened? He try something?" Anger cracked through Brent's composure at the thought of some Neanderthal who couldn't wait two miles before trying to cop a feel.

It made him feel like a creep himself for noticing the swell of her breasts, though they were mostly hidden by her jacket. For noticing the way her soft hair framed her face and how pretty she looked, her cheeks pink with a mix of embarrassment and exasperation.

"If you don't mind, I'd rather not discuss it," she said, holding the cold pack they had purchased against one of her knees.

Though she'd seemed intent on ignoring her injury, he'd found a first aid section in the travel plaza and insisted that one of them put on the antibiotics and bandage her abraded flesh. After skewering him with an annoyed look, she had done the honors, and then swallowed the two headache tablets he'd given her to help with pain and swelling—after insisting that he show her the bottle.

"So we'll just go with, you missed me," Brent suggested.

She rolled her eyes. "Yeah, sure. That was it. Big Mel got jealous when I told him how you make psychosis look so sexy. Or maybe it's paranoia. I don't know. You ever get an official diagnosis?"

Brent tried to chuckle, but the sting went too deep. Too close to what his superiors, coworkers, even trusted friends had told him. "You, with all your hang-ups, you really want to give me grief about that?"

"Probably not, considering that you're the one who has the guns."

He frowned at the reminder. "You know, you didn't have to come with me. Didn't have to climb into that tow truck on the feeder. There were cops up at that wreck at the intersection. Cops who would have helped you if you'd gone and told them you were being kidnapped."

"I know." She shook her head, a flush suffusing her face. "But all those people. They were watching me from their cars. Staring at me, honking."

"Well, yeah. That's my point, why I couldn't have done anything, even if I'd been of a mind to."

"You might have your issues," she said, "but I realized that it's getting late, and you're my last shot to get there before five o'clock at this point. And I realized, too, that you won't hurt me. Because you really do need me for whatever it is you're scheming."

"That's right, Lauren. I would never hurt you. Even if you decide to walk away from this after I drop you off at the morgue."

He felt the weight of her stare, the gears clicking in her sharp mind as she appraised and analyzed his claim.

"You mean it." She stated it as a fact, not a question.

"I mean it absolutely. If it's what you want to do, listen to whatever the cops and the ME's office are going to tell you. Accept Jimenez's version at face value. Then grieve for Rachel's suicide and move on with your life."

She crossed her arms in front of her chest, hiding those breasts that kept stealing into his thoughts with a relentlessness that made him wonder if his libido was making up for two lost years.

"Maybe I don't have a life to move on with," she told him, "not without my sister."

"Could be you'll find the path to a new life begins with doing all you can to make sure this never happens again."

"Revenge, you mean," she corrected. "That's what you're really after."

"Revenge won't bring her back. Won't bring back any of them." He parroted what the bureau psychologist had told him, knowing it was the right thing even as he dreamed of smearing the Troll King's brains across the pavement, of painting Carrie's name in blood across the sides of buildings.

Was he sick to think those things, unworthy to live past what had happened? And was he wrong to wish the same, obsessive rage on the shell-shocked woman he had with him?

He didn't know; he'd never know, but he was grateful when she let silence spool out in the space between them. It gave him time to breathe a little, to reacquaint himself with the beautiful city, nestled among rolling hills and flanked in part by the sparkling Town Lake. Though many of the trees were bare, he drank in the greenery of the live oaks and magnolias, which kept their leaves all through the winter, allowing himself to shake off the bleak expanses of North Texas. To shake off his own grim mood as he considered how to let Lauren go without losing her forever.

Soon, they made it to a narrow street, where Brent parked near a nondescript, three-story building. Beside him, Lauren stiffened, glancing at the dashboard clock, which read 4:36.

"I told you I'd have you here in time," he reassured her.

"I only hope they aren't so eager to go home and start their weekends, they'll want to rush through this instead of listening."

He could have pointed out that they'd have been here a whole lot earlier had she not felt the need to try to escape him. Instead, he assured her, "They won't rush you on something this important. The reception area might be closed, but they'll have people on duty all through the night, people who will help you through this."

Her body stiffened, the tension rolling off of her in frigid waves. "But will they believe me when I tell them it's not my sister?"

"If that's what you think, once you see the photos."

"You mean they won't take me—that I won't go in to see her?"

He shook his head. "Each municipality is different, but I'd say most likely not. They'll show you a picture of her face, or maybe of some distinguishing mark if she has any—"

"Rachel has a little tattoo." Lauren rubbed at her eyes. "A hummingbird on her right shoulder. She begged me to come down for a visit, to come with her to get its match, but I was too—the thought of all those needles piercing my skin . . ."

He nodded, adding sharp objects to her list of phobias. Or maybe it was the thought of the germs they might carry. "When you go inside," he said gently, "I want you to focus on your breathing. On counting how many breaths you take until it's over."

He wasn't sure exactly why he offered her the lifeline, unless it was because he needed her, her skills and spirit, intact.

She looked into his face, her own as frightened as a lost child's. "I wish you'd come in with me."

"I'd figured you'd be glad I'm not. Didn't you just try to dump me?"

"I've found out there are a lot scarier things out there." Her blue-green eyes glittered. "And I'm pretty sure this is one of them."

He thought about it for a minute, weighing the possibility that she'd still file a complaint, have him arrested for aggravated kidnapping. She had already proven she was more than capable of subterfuge. Still, the fear on her face was so familiar and so piercing, he doubted she would be his biggest issue.

"I wish I could go in with you," he said, "but the Austin authorities might very well be waiting to take me in for interfering with their investigation. Besides, you need to hear what they say and make up your mind for yourself."

She nodded. "Then I'd better go. Before I do, though, can I have my cell phone?"

He fished it out of an inner coat pocket but pointedly didn't offer to return her gun. "Would you like me to check you into a hotel room, take your things there? There's a Sheraton right down the street, and I'm almost positive they're pet friendly."

Ignoring him, she stared down, her face paling as she looked at the phone.

"What's wrong?" His stomach falling, he kicked himself for not sparing the screen a glance in hours. Earlier, he'd deleted some missed calls from Jimenez, but since then, he hadn't felt her silenced cell phone vibrate.

She shook her head. "I-I'd better go, before it gets too late."

"What's on the phone?" He reached for it, fearing that the Troll King had already found her, but she snatched it out of range and dropped it in her pocket.

"Tell me right now, Lauren," he pressed, fear slashing through him at the thought that this was how it began—how he would end up losing her, too. Because once the Troll King truly got his claws into a vulnerable woman's psyche, she rarely, if ever, managed to break free. Not even a woman as resourceful and intelligent as Lauren had proven herself to be.

Ignoring him, she grabbed her purse and opened the door a split second before he could hit the locking mechanism.

"Hold on just a minute!" he said, upset he had forgotten about the child locks on this leg of their journey. But she had bailed out of the car already. A moment later, she was reaching for the back door to claim her dog and luggage.

His foot flashed to the gas pedal, his instincts telling him that this would be the only way to ensure that she would talk to him later. She cried out, her horrified plea for him to stop spiking through his white-hot conscience. As he sped off, she ran after him a few steps, giving him a last glimpse of her red face as he took the corner fast enough that the sedan's tires squealed a protest.

"It's for your own good," he said, telling himself he only meant to help her as he left Sabine Street behind.

But as he drove, an image vibrated through his brain, a vision of a small and tasteful tattoo. Though he had never had the occasion to see Rachel's, he knew damned well that Lauren was about to.

About to see it for the last time, in colors so vivid they would sear themselves into her brain forever, the wings and feathers blazing against the snowfield of her sister's death-pale flesh.

Because of his cruelty, Lauren Miller would have to walk into that cold and faceless building all alone and face the worst hell of her life without even the comfort of the fat, old dog in her arms.

***

Lauren's knees were shaking as she walked up the concrete ramp leading to the building's entrance. With her throat aching and her nose running, she wanted to find a ladies' room and indulge in a good, old-fashioned cry—or maybe scream and smash the mirrors since Brent Durant wasn't around for her to strangle.

But with time running out, she couldn't spare a minute for histrionics, nor could she risk pulling the phone out of her back pocket to reread the message that made the world spin around her each time her thoughts glanced off it. So after breathing a quick prayer that the rogue agent would take Dumpling and her bags to the hotel he'd suggested, she swallowed back the threatening nausea and went inside.

After taking an elevator to the third floor as signs directed, she found an empty waiting area painted in shades of institutional oatmeal and tapped at the frosted window with a knuckle. When no one answered, she knocked harder, praying that the office hadn't closed early for some reason.

Moments later, the glass slid to one side, revealing a jowly, middle-aged woman whose dark unibrow made her look permanently annoyed. "May I help you?"

Her heart stumbling, Lauren could barely force the words

out. "I, uh, I was asked to come here, to identify a—they think it's my sister? Rachel Miller? But I can't imagine she would . . ."

The receptionist's expression softened. "Ah, yes. Rachel Miller. I was asked to keep an eye out for you, Miss . . . ?"

"It's Miller, too. Lauren Miller."

"You're here alone?" The woman rose slightly from her seat and craned her thick neck to look out into the waiting area.

The wariness in her expression made Lauren suspect that she'd been asked to watch for Brent Durant as well. Would he have been arrested, as he had feared, if he had come inside? Would they send someone to lock him up if she told them to check the Sheraton?

Yet Lauren simply nodded, too nervous to answer all the questions such a demand would entail. Not until she got through this part, anyway.

The receptionist pushed a clipboard toward her. "If you'll fill out this information and let me see a photo ID, someone will call for you in a few minutes."

Lauren took the form back to a chair and completed the required blanks before fishing her driver's license from her wallet. After returning to the counter, she peeked into the open window. But the receptionist had left her desk, so Lauren, unable to resist the impulse, pulled the cell phone from her pocket and opened the messages.

Her pulse pounding like a war drum, she stared at the name on top of the screen. Her sister's name, which meant that the text had been sent from Rachel's phone.

The text containing six words that sent fresh fault lines snaking through Lauren's frozen heart. *"NEED TO TALK TO YOU. SOON."*

CHAPTER SIX

Lauren wondered, could it be true? Could her sister have been crying out for her one last time? The thought made Lauren want to weep, too, want to make these cold, beige halls echo with her screaming. But the timestamp on the message stopped her, telling her it had been delivered at 10:23 a.m.—more than two hours after Detective Jimenez had broken the news of Rachel's death to Lauren.

Was it possible that the delivery of her sister's final message had somehow gotten hung up in the system? Though SMS—short message service—was becoming more and more reliable, Lauren knew that delays of hours or, on rare occasions, days still happened.

But as she stared at the unchanging screen, other possibilities whispered in her psyche. Could someone have maliciously sent the text—perhaps someone who had stolen the phone from Rachel's apartment? Jon Rutherford sprang to mind, her suspicions about the widower returning to the forefront. But she couldn't rule out Durant's mysterious Troll King, either. Maybe this alleged tormenter was more than a dark figment of a grieving man's imagination.

Or Rachel could be alive still. Alive and in hiding. Reaching out to let me know my instincts have been right all along.

Like a bird clipped by a passing car, hope fluttered desperately inside her. Struggling for altitude, it flapped its ruined wings, rising on Lauren's promise that—if it were only true—she'd go to church again, she'd put in time at the local food bank. She'd give a fat donation to save orphans, rescue lost puppies—start a sanctuary so the orphans could run and play with the damned lost puppies. She'd sacrifice all she had if she might somehow buy her sister one more chance.

But just as gravity would sink the wounded bird, it came calling for Lauren, too, in the form of a balding man wearing khakis and a navy polo emblazoned with the logo of the Travis County Medical Examiner's office. Pushing a pair of steel-framed glasses onto a beaky nose, he offered his hand and introduced himself, giving Lauren a name that she forgot the instant she heard it.

With polite efficiency, he gestured toward an unmarked doorway. "Shall we go back to my office, where we can talk in private?"

Lauren looked around, half expecting to discover that others had filled the empty lobby while she'd been distracted. Other individuals, maybe even families, experiencing the worst day of their lives. But no one else had come in, and the only one watching was the sad-eyed receptionist with the unibrow.

"Sure," Lauren finally answered, her knees threatening to give out as she meekly followed. Followed knowing that, whatever happened, she would not be the same woman as when she'd arrived.

***

Whatever the nameless man had told her after showing her the photos, Lauren hadn't heard. She couldn't, not with the buzzing noise that filled her head, a sound that vibrated in her brain and filled her mouth with the bitterness of bile.

After pushing a box of tissues toward her, he said something—or at least his jaws were working—and gestured to indicate she should wait for him to come back. As if she could get up to leave, with her legs, her hopes, her throbbing heart cut out from underneath her. As if there were anywhere she could go to hide from the sight of her sister's lifeless face, bloodless in the photo and somewhat distorted from the hidden wound to her head, and the tattoo Durant had warned her to expect.

Before he left, the man opened his top desk drawer and dropped the folder containing the photographs inside it. If she wanted to, she realized, she could pull out the file and take another look.

She plucked a tissue from the box, but didn't move a muscle. There was no need when she could see those images as clearly as if they sat in front of her.

She had no idea how long she sat there, too numb to weep, too lost to move, before someone tapped at the door. Unable to find her voice, she didn't answer, but the door cracked open anyway, and a Latino man in his later thirties leaned in, his thick, telenovela-worthy black hair contrasting with a conservative charcoal suit and subtly-patterned tie.

"Ms. Miller? I spoke to you on the phone. Detective Cruz Jimenez." Entering the cramped office, he offered her his hand, his deep brown eyes as sympathetic as his smooth, accented voice. "I'm very sorry for your family's loss."

Looking up at the too-handsome face, at the flash of whitened teeth, she kept her own palms on her thighs. "There is no family. Only me now."

"In that case, I'm doubly sorry. Mind if I sit down so we can talk?" He pulled back the chair beside hers rather than taking the one behind the desk.

When it became apparent he meant to pull close to her in the already-cramped space, cutting her off from the door, she blurted, "Yes. I do mind. I mind very much."

He hesitated, surprise and something else—maybe annoyance—sparking in his eyes, before he straightened, schooling his expression to polite concern. "Where would you like, then? Behind the desk? Or would you prefer I do this standing?"

She tipped her chin toward the desk chair. "Over there is fine. I just—my stomach's pretty iffy, and I wouldn't want to stain your nice suit."

Though it was the thought of him trapping her without an exit that made her sick, he nodded. "It's only natural, after what you've been through. The loss of a loved one, especially under such tragic circumstances—"

"Rachel *didn't* kill herself, no matter what it looks like."

Mr. Made-for-Spanish-Soaps took his seat and pulled out a silver pen and a small, blue notebook. "I want you to know that I'm here to listen to you. To listen and explain. But before we go any further, I need to ask you, did you get the message I left earlier?"

She hesitated for a moment, remembering how Durant had ripped the phone from the wall, how he'd sped off with Dumpling and her luggage. How she'd been scared enough about what he'd suggested—about the state of his mind—that she'd risked trying to escape him.

He lost someone he loved, too. And he believed you when you said that Rachel wouldn't take her own life. Not like this Jimenez; she could tell already. He'd tipped his hand the moment he had told her he was here to listen and *explain.*

"What message is that?" she asked, shaking her head slowly. "Did you leave something on my home phone?"

"I started to. Your machine cut me off. And my calls to your cell number weren't returned, either."

She shrugged. "Heaven knows how long my dad had that old answering machine, but you probably would've missed me anyway. It's a long drive here from Bright's Prairie. A long way from anywhere."

"So you drove here? On your own?"

Again, she hesitated, a lie on the tip of her tongue. But her knee-jerk instinct to protect Durant didn't pass the logic test. Telling herself she wasn't going to become the latest textbook example of the bonding of hostages to their kidnappers, she forced herself to tell a version of the truth. "No. Why would I, after you sent Special Agent Durant to come and get me?"

Jimenez stiffened, nostrils flaring. "So Brent Durant did come there? He didn't—where is he right now?"

She shook her head. "I have no idea. He promised to drop my things off at a hotel not far from here." Or at least she hoped that's what he'd done. "But he didn't say where he was going afterward."

"I'm afraid there was a mix-up at the scene. Agent Durant's card was found in your sister's apartment, and as a professional courtesy, another detective called and shared relevant information without knowing that Durant had—"

"He mentioned that he'd met with Rachel. Something to do with a case he's working on." Lauren pinned the detective with her stare, the one Rachel had always complained made people squirm. *You could at least blink now and then, try to look a little human.*

But as miserable as she was now, Lauren was more inclined to lash out than worry whether she made Detective Jimenez uncomfortable. "A case involving the stalker who's been driving women to their deaths."

Jimenez sighed and dragged the ringless fingers of his left hand through his hair. "That's what I was afraid of, that he'd tell you all about that crazy theory of his."

Lauren turned in her chair to face him directly. "Why crazy? Considering the kind of attention Rachel received after her accident, the harassment she suffered after that TV show, it's easier to believe she could have been goaded into doing something like this without a word to me."

She scooped out shallow breaths, numbness needling her extremities. A sense of unreality shrouded her awareness, a growing conviction that none of this was real.

"When loved ones take their own lives," Jimenez told her, "it's difficult to accept. I spoke with the special agent in charge who was Durant's superior at length today, and according to him, Durant was dismissed for his inability to move past his wife's suicide two years past. Did he mention that to you?"

Wanting him to elaborate, she tried to look surprised. "Dismissed? Over his wife's death? He didn't tell me that, no."

Jimenez nodded. "The bureau did its best, I'm told. Offered counseling, extended leave, a change to a more closely supervised assignment. But the erratic behavior, the unauthorized investigation, the continued abuses of authority to advance his baseless theory didn't stop."

Lauren came to her feet, unshed tears making her vision shimmer. "How *could* he quit with other women still in danger? Women like my sister? She might still be alive today if anyone had listened to him."

"I'm very sorry you were caught up in this wild theory of his." Jimenez's voice was sympathetic. "But you need to understand,

Miss Miller—Lauren. If the human mind focuses long enough on any array of data, however random it might be, it will perceive linkages. Connections that aren't there. Our brains are hardwired that way, and with grief stripping away every bit of objectivity Agent Durant's training and experience should have afforded him, it was only natural that his brain would invent some mysterious, malicious phantom pulling the strings."

Hating the dismissive tone in the detective's voice, she argued, "But he has evidence. He told me."

"What he's suggesting has been thoroughly investigated, but it simply isn't there."

"Then why would he wreck his career, risk his freedom?"

Sadness tempered the detective's handsome features. "Look at all the crazy conspiracy theories out there, fantasies spun of TV snow, white noise, and paranoia. Even when these notions are disproven time and again, they still persist."

"So you're saying that Agent Durant's no longer an agent. That he's some kind of nutcase instead. Insane."

Jimenez shook his head again. "I've worked with him before, considered him a good friend at one time, and I'd never go so far as to call Brent Durant insane. But for the last two years, he's been a little . . . The best word might be *lost*. Overwhelmed by his own personal tragedy."

"*Overwhelmed* . . ." Lauren sank down to her seat again, thinking how pathetically inadequate the word was to describe the landslide of raw emotion—the horror, grief, guilt, even the irrational anger—that came with knowing that a loved one had deliberately chosen to check out.

"I can see why you might sympathize with his situation right now," the detective said, "why you might even be tempted to think of him as someone who can help guide you through this—this situation with your sister. But my best advice is to stay as far from him as possible. The delusional are dangerous—to themselves as well as others."

As sincere and concerned as he sounded, Lauren couldn't argue.

"Once we've finished here," Jimenez offered, "I'll help you get your things, and we'll move you to another hotel. The Omni's quite secure—or do you need somewhere more budget friendly?"

"You think I give a damn about money right now?" If she had to, she'd spend every dime of what her ex had been forced to pay her to gain clear title to the house in California. Spend everything she had to get to the bottom of what had happened. Hostility draining from her voice, she heard only defeat as she added, "As long as it's safe, clean, and they'll take my dog, that's all that matters to me."

"None of that should be an issue there." The detective passed her a card imprinted with his name and contact information. An additional phone number was written in ink on the bottom. "But if Durant somehow tracks you down and shows up there, day or night, you need to call me. That last number's my personal cell phone."

"You aren't planning to arrest him, are you?" she asked, her pulse bumping faster at the thought.

Jimenez shook his head. "I hope to hell not. Brent's a fine man and a top-notch agent—one of the best I've ever worked with, but this obsession's going to get him locked up or even killed if somebody doesn't shake some sense into him. So whatever you do, don't let him into your room. And especially don't let him in your head."

"You really think he'd hurt me?"

"The guy's lost his job, his wife, most of his friends—this theory of his is all he has left. Except he's completely off base about the connections, and I'd bet my badge that he's dead wrong about your sister."

Her heart twisted, not wanting to believe it. "You're sure about that? Because Rachel—I can't wrap my head around that idea that she'd even have allowed a gun in her apartment, much less touch one. She would never—"

The detective touched her arm gently, his gaze earnest and voice steady. "Before you go any further, Lauren, before you let Durant's grief poison your life the way he's let it ruin his, let me tell you what we found inside your sister's apartment."

The memory of the text message she'd received leapt to mind. "Her cell phone—did you find that?"

Jimenez blinked at her abruptness. "It was taken into evidence at the scene, yes."

"This morning?"

"Officers spotted it when they first went inside. It was on your sister's coffee table. But don't worry. We'll return it after a check of the contents."

"I'm not worried about the phone. I'm wondering how it was I received a text message from it, hours after Rachel—" Lauren forced herself to take a deep breath, to keep her thoughts trained on her question. "After she died."

"What sort of message?"

"One saying that we had to talk."

Regret filled his brown eyes. "So she *did* reach out to you, or tried to. I know it will be hard, but try not to blame yourself for not reading it in time."

"That's just it. I should have." Lauren pulled out the phone and opened the message from her sister. "You see the time delivered? It was late in coming to me. Hours late, it looks like."

Jimenez took the phone from her to study the message. "Were you in an area with limited reception? That could've held it up."

"Not before she—before she died," said Lauren. "I have a microcell—it's a signal booster—at my house, for my business. And Rachel's reception at the apartment was always fine. We've never had an issue. Never."

"I'm very sorry the service picked today to malfunction."

"Maybe it didn't. Maybe someone else sent that text."

Jimenez sighed. "Listen, I know Durant might have suggested that, and I can see why you'd want to believe it, but we both know the most likely explanation is that—"

"Check it for me, please. Check her cell phone when you get back to the station. See if the text is listed in her sent messages mailbox. If it's there, I'll accept that Rachel tried to reach me." If it wasn't, the only explanation, however unlikely, that Lauren could come up with was that some other individual, someone who had both her sister's and her cell numbers, had spoofed the message's point of origin specifically to screw with her. It was simple enough to do using any number of shady websites online. Lauren had used at least one herself to fake a text message. With it, she had tricked an employee who ought to have known better and gained entrance to a supposedly secure site, a breach that she immediately reported to her client.

"It'll be there," the detective assured her, "but I promise you, I'll check it out, whatever I can do to put your mind at ease."

"Speaking of minds, it sounds as if yours is already made up. Or maybe I should say closed."

Jimenez shook his head. "It can't be and it won't be until the autopsy's completed and the ME makes his ruling. But considering the other items arranged around your sister, I'd be remiss if I failed to warn you this truly looks like suicide."

"What items? What did you find?" asked Lauren, a buzz building inside her head. A buzz that warned her that more bad news was bearing down . . . bad news that she was powerless to evade or outrun.

***

Brent knew that time was running out, that the longer Lauren had to think about it, the greater the chance she would be talked into accepting the official version of her sister's death. Once that happened, he would lose the help he'd risked so much to gain— and the expertise he needed to stop the Troll King for good.

But that evening, his calls to Lauren's cell phone went unanswered, and when he stopped by the Sheraton, the hotel desk clerk informed him she'd taken her dog and checked out instead of staying.

He tried to imagine where she might have gone. Certainly not Rachel's apartment on the east side, even if the police had cleared the crime scene. He couldn't believe she would have the stomach for tackling the mess on her own. Having the dog with her, however, limited her lodging choices—along with the places he would have to look.

Still, since no reputable hotel would give out a guest's name, it took him until dusk the following day to track her down. He only managed that by a stroke of fortune, when he spotted her coaxing the dachshund to walk near a small downtown park.

By the time he parked the car and caught up, she was sitting on a park bench in the deep shadows beneath the trees, the leash held slack in her hand. Chilly as the evening was, her jacket was unzipped, and her gaze was distant. Dangerously distant, as he stole up on her and called her name twice before her protector's barking finally made her jerk her gaze in his direction.

"Durant," she said, her voice as flat as her expression.

Though he'd meant to try his hand at charm, anger ignited in an instant from her careless disregard for her own safety. "Lauren Miller, you mind telling me what the hell you're doing out here in the darkest spot you can find?"

"Sitting. Thinking. Thinking about my little sister."

"And getting yourself mugged or raped or murdered's going to help?" he demanded. "Is that what Rachel would want?"

Lauren shushed the dog and surged to her feet. "Why should I give a damn what Rachel wanted? She was clearly only thinking of herself. Too selfish to think of anybody's pain except her own."

At the sound of her anger, his own faded, overwhelmed by bitter memory. "For a long time, I was pissed at Carrie, too. Sometimes, I still get mad. But when a person's pushed beyond her limits, she's pushed out of her right mind, too, beyond sight of anything but her own torment."

She crossed her arms over her chest. "The Troll King's torment, I expect you're going to tell me."

"Judging from the sarcasm, I take it Jimenez had a nice long talk with you."

"He did. He told me about you, for one thing, how you've lost perspective."

"The cops and the agents from the bureau, they're the ones with no perspective. The ones so busy looking for horses, they wouldn't know a herd of zebras if it stampeded over them." He set his jaw, thinking of how lazy investigators could get, how prone to thinking that every incident fell into one of a few familiar patterns. Like cataracts, routine blinded a person over time—as if any family's tragedy could ever be rightly called commonplace.

"My sister, it turns out, had an apartment full of pharmaceuticals," Lauren said. "Drugs prescribed for people suffering from severe anxiety and depression."

"Of course she was anxious and depressed. She was being stalked relentlessly, sharpened bamboo shoots jammed up underneath her every weakness."

"She told me she was better because that's what I wanted to hear. But she wasn't better, Durant. Secretly, she never got past the guilt she felt for the accident. For killing her own friend—that was how she put it."

"That's wrong, Lauren. Utter bullshit. Your Rachel might have struggled for a while. Anybody would have. But she would've gotten past it, would've leaned on her friends and her boyfriend, her sister and her—"

"They broke up a while back. She and her boyfriend, I mean. He got into some graduate program overseas, and they decided the whole long-distance thing was going to be too complicated. The way she talked about it, she seemed more relieved than upset, but I don't know now . . ."

"You know your own instincts," he argued, "the ones that told you Rachel had been murdered."

She looked at him, her expression lost in the deepening gloom. "My instincts might've been wrong. Especially the ones that kept me from filing a criminal complaint against you."

"Because you know I'm right about your sister."

She huffed out a sigh. "You know what, Durant? I was going for a simple 'thank you.' Not an argument, and definitely not any more of your Bigfoot theories."

"You can help me stop this, Lauren, make sure this doesn't happen to anybody else. And the Troll King isn't Bigfoot, or the Loch Ness Monster, either. He's out there. He's real. And he's going to strike again."

"People—people fall into despair and end things."

"Sometimes, they do. But other times, they're pushed. Like *this* time, no matter what Jimenez told you."

She shook her head. "Listen, I need to get back to the hotel. It's getting really dark, and tomorrow's going to be a long day. I have to—They'll be releasing the r-remains, and I'll need to find a funeral home. Order the flowers and pick out a nice c-casket for her."

"Let me walk you."

The look she turned on him was hammered flat by disapproval. "Don't take this the wrong way, but I'd rather you didn't know where I was staying."

"And I'd rather you didn't end up murdered between here and the hotel."

***

The Internet was his home, a home he counted on for everything from communication to entertainment to sex, but the library, too, had its guilty pleasures. Back among the dustiest of stacks, he found the most harrowing of reading. True facts from times that made so much more sense to him than this one.

Times when the wise, the superior, had been free to judge the weak and foolish, where injury was repaid with injury, theft with the loss of the offending hand. Times when the guilty were shamed publicly, in stocks or on ducking stools, when women were stripped and shorn of their hair, then driven through the streets for consorting with the enemy.

In those days, those who caused the death of others weren't treated to counseling, probation, or even a fine and an insurance payout but the ax, the noose, or the firing squad instead.

Yellowed and brittle though they were, the pages excited him in a way no porn site had in months. The dry, Victorian prose described the most salacious details, and what photos there were depicted women suffering for their sins, women weeping, bleeding, or lying pale and stiff as marble, their hands clasped over their still chests.

Footsteps closed in from behind him, swiftly padding on the carpeted floor. "Didn't you hear the announcement? The building's closing in ten minutes, and we'll need to get these put away." As she gestured toward the open volumes spread around him, the Stealth Librarian, a gray-haired grandma whose thick-framed half-glasses hung around her neck, sounded irritated. Probably because she'd already warned him earlier about the noises he was making.

"I heard," he said, picturing Her Bitchship dressed all in black as she lay in one of the stiff, post-mortem poses. Then, at least, she'd keep her mouth shut instead of wasting his time. "I'll be out of here by closing."

As she pulled on the old-lady glasses, her small eyes narrowed. "Just so long as you are before the security guard does his final walkthrough. Otherwise . . ."

He glared at her, holding a gaze that increasingly reminded him of a teacher he had always hated. "Just let me finish here, all right?"

She opened her mouth as if to protest, but there must have been something in his eyes that warned her that if she didn't hold her peace now, she'd be looking over her shoulder all the way to her car. Looking for a brand of retribution she still might not see coming.

Instead, she nodded, though she couldn't resist one last, pointed look at her watch, one pained arch of her drawn-on eyebrow, before turning crisply on her sensible shoes and retreating.

Ignoring her, he returned his attention to the oldest book he'd pulled today, one describing the implements of medieval torture. As he carefully tore out several of the illustrated pages, he told himself he should have lived then, back in the days of the breast ripper and the iron maiden, the cat's paw and the witch's chair. He should have been the one coolly watching the proceedings while the torturer awaited his nod, his permission, to put an end to the entertainment—and the prisoner's suffering.

Though born to the wrong century, he knew enough to understand that the use of such devices would be unthinkable in this coddled age. Still, he had instruments at his disposal, instruments as cruel and diabolical as anything centuries of dungeon torturers—or even the Church—had ever produced. He had the phone, the net, and best of all, he had his target's conscience.

Prodded by the right words, by the skill and experience he'd honed over the last two years, these were all he needed to bring any sinner to her knees. Sometimes, as with Rachel, even sooner than he'd wanted.

The thought left him restless, the bitterness of disappointment, the ache of newfound emptiness, cold and leaden in his gut. After ripping free one last page—this one featuring an adulteress being burned at the stake—and stuffing it in the inner pocket of his jacket, he headed for the door.

For now that Rachel had escaped him, someone had to suffer. If he could only find someone worthy of his interest . . .

Someone to keep the anger and the boredom and the aching loneliness at bay.

***

"Seriously? In Austin, you think that something's going to happen to me?" Lauren asked, gesturing at the clean, well-lit sidewalk, where a young couple was walking hand in hand in the direction of the Sixth Street clubs that made up the heart of the city's vibrant music scene.

"Austin's not immune to violence," Brent warned her, "and for all I know, direct contact might be the Troll King's next escalation."

Shaking her head at him, she said, "Get some help, Durant."

He gave her a slow once-over, taking in the dark circles beneath her eyes and the fact that she was wearing the same torn jeans and purple V-neck under a battered leather jacket she'd had on the day before. "I could say the same for you. Seriously, Lauren, when's the last time you slept or ate?"

Turning on her heel, she hurried away. Or tried to anyway, before, within a few steps, Dumpling sank down to the concrete to form a panting puddle.

"She's not down with this whole exercise regime I've put her on," Lauren confessed as she bent to scoop up the fat dachshund. With a grunt of effort, she added, "*Or* the diet dog food I bought either."

"Let me guess. She's more inclined to whatever's coming to you on your room service tray."

"Something like that," Lauren grumbled, turning from him to resume walking, her strides quick and purposeful.

He hurried to catch up with her, her avoidance cluing him in. "Wait, don't tell me there haven't *been* any room service trays."

"All right. I won't tell you."

"Then you've gone out and picked up meals, right?"

"I picked up some chips and stuff when I bought Dumpling's dog food."

"Some chips. That's all, right, in the whole time since I've seen you? And I'd be willing to bet the dog ate more than you did."

Planting her feet, she swung an annoyed look his way. "What're you, my mother now? You want me to report my bowel movements to you, too?"

He grinned and shook his head. "Definitely a *no* on that one. But let me take your friend there, at least. It—I mean she—looks kind of heavy. No offense, dog."

But the dachshund growled when he reached for her, and Lauren turned away. When her cell phone started ringing, she stopped short. "On second thought, I'd better get this. Behave, Dumpling."

When she shoved the dog at him, he took her, despite the display of the animal's few teeth.

"Has to be Rachel's friend, Nikki," said Lauren as she pulled the phone from her back pocket, "calling about the services."

Shaking her head, she quickly stopped the ringing and said to Brent, "Oh, never mind. It's just a private number. I reject those junk calls."

She put the phone away and continued walking. But she didn't get three steps before the ringing resumed.

Clearly annoyed, she muttered, "Let me just mute this, if this telemarketer's going to be a pest." But as she glanced at the phone, her face reddened. Fumbling to accept the call, she raised it to her ear.

"Hello?" she asked, her voice shaking. "Hello? Who is this? And what the hell are you doing calling me from Rachel's phone?"

CHAPTER SEVEN

"Your sister died because of you."

The voice Lauren heard was not the speaker's. Of that much, she was certain as she recognized the electronically slowed tones that deepened the words . . . the words that made the fine hairs behind her neck stand on end and her stomach shrivel to a hard knot. That made her realize, for certain, that Brent must have been right all along.

"Died sobbing," the caller went on, *"as she slipped the muzzle past her teeth, tasted the hopelessness, the bitterness—knowing that you didn't even care enough to pick up the phone and answer her text."*

He went on speaking several minutes longer, the relentless cruelty of his words inserting more unwanted images into Lauren's mind: her sister kneeling on the hard tile, her beautiful face streaked with tears, her hand shaking as gunmetal rattled against her teeth. Heart fluttering like a panicked hummingbird inside her own chest, Lauren felt her sister's hopelessness, her desperation, the crushing pain she couldn't bear another instant.

But this bastard—this subhuman piece of garbage—wasn't going to get his rocks off hearing Lauren's reaction. Fighting to recover her voice, she ignored Durant, who was gesturing as he tried to get across some message, and let her sneer bleed though.

"So I'm supposed to be impressed that you know how to spoof your message and phone calls and use an app to make yourself sound like Freddy Krueger?"

"*You want to know how brains look,*" the distorted voice went on as if she hadn't spoken, "*when they spray out the back of someone's head and hit the bathroom cabinets? The globs are silvery, with swirls of blood and clumps of blond hair sticking in them. When they slide down, they look kind of like oatmeal, with clots of flesh and splinters of her skull poking through—*"

"Get fucked, freak," Lauren told him, barely noticing the sharp looks of disapproval from two passing older women as she cut off the caller.

"You hung up on him?" Durant asked, his face flushed and stubbled with a day's growth of beard, though he wore a clean shirt and a fresh jacket over his western boots and jeans.

"Are you serious? Of c-course, I hung up," she said, breathing so hard she could barely stammer out the words. Hands shaking, she moved to shut off the ringer in case the jerk called back, but the phone slipped from her shaking hand and clattered to the sidewalk.

Brent picked it up and checked it, relief written on his face. "Not broken, anyway. But if he calls again, I'll need you to—"

"Forget it." She snatched the phone from his hand and made sure Durant was watching as she powered down the device. "I'm not listening to one more minute of that psycho's garbage. Not playing anybody's game."

"But, Lauren. We can stop him, stop him before he ever gets the chance to kill again."

"Stop him how? It's not like spoofed calls can be traced— unless you still have the resources to—"

He shut her down with a shake of his head. "But there are other ways, ways of messing with his psyche."

The hard shell of her demeanor cracked with her voice. "I-I just can't, Brent. Can't stay on the line while he . . ." The grisly details slid through her mind, the bloody bits of brain and bone oozing their way down a bathroom cabinet.

"He—he *knew* she'd done it in her bathroom," she added. "Knew about the text, too, if it was really from her."

"It's what he does, and what he'll keep right on doing until we find a way to stop him."

With the streetlight shining down on him, she caught the predatory gleam that had replaced his troubled look. A gleam that confirmed that he wanted more than the revenge of seeing the Troll King locked up in a cage, where he could never hurt another woman.

He wanted the man dead. Wanted to be the one to kill him.

At the moment, Lauren could think of nothing on this earth she would like more. Still, she looked over the disgraced agent carefully, wondering if he was half as unhinged and even a quarter as dangerous as Detective Cruz Jimenez had suggested.

Or if he was exactly the brand of crazy that she needed to bring her sister's killer down.

***

What the hell had that son of a bitch said to make a woman as strong and smart as Lauren Miller go all tight-lipped and ashen faced? What words could the troll have used to have her choking out, "My room—I have to get back," and striding away without even glancing back to make sure he followed with her dog?

As he hurried after her, Brent wanted to ask Lauren for specifics, to tease out of her exactly what the Troll King had said. With her eyes fixed on her goal and her pace quickening with every moment they drew nearer, Brent feared she'd race away if he tried to bring it up now. Might even run out into traffic in her haste to get away.

So instead, he bit back his questions, knowing that if she shoved him away now, she might end up as dead as Rachel. All he could do was be here to support Lauren as the cruel words chewed through her defenses like carrion beetles gnawing on a corpse.

On a couple of occasions during their walk to Lauren's hotel, Brent tried putting down the dachshund on the sidewalk. But Dumpling only whined when he whistled and tugged on its leash, looking up to plead for help with plaintive brown eyes.

Lifting the animal and tucking her under one arm like a football, he called to Lauren, "So tell me, exactly how long has it been since this little sack of goo has acknowledged it has legs?"

Distracted for the moment, she glanced back and shook her head at him. "Dumpling's a *she*, remember? And please don't hold her like that. You'll need to support her with both hands. Otherwise, you'll hurt her back."

He grumbled, but shifted his burden and was gratified when Dumpling wagged her scrawny tail at him instead of biting. "Guess I'd forget about my legs, too, if I got too fat to see 'em."

"Don't worry. I'll have her slimmed down before too long," Lauren assured him.

"I think you might have a bit of a fight on your hands," Brent said, stroking the animal's sleek side. "She reminds me of my mother-in-law, a real master when it came to weaseling out of anything good for her."

He frowned at a memory of his wife cajoling Imogene, telling the woman she wouldn't live to see her grandchildren if she didn't stop sampling the sweets she loved to bake and do something about her sedentary lifestyle. But it was Imogene, for all her diabetic issues, who had lived to attend her only child's funeral. As far as Brent knew, she and Carrie's father had never recovered from the shock.

I should make the trip, check on them. Guilt pierced Brent's obsession, the knowledge that he'd deliberately kept himself too busy to visit them in Iowa because their pain only magnified his own grief. His own sense of responsibility for failing to protect their daughter.

I'll go later, he told himself, anticipation sharpening inside him. He felt a surge of optimism that since Lauren must surely believe him now, she would cooperate as he'd hoped. With her help, he would someday soon be able to report to his former in-laws that the person responsible for their daughter's death had been made to pay for what he'd done. That the very last word the son of bitch heard had been Carrie's name.

As Brent caught up to Lauren, they turned a corner and hurried toward the massive, glass-fronted Omni hotel, which was abuzz with activity this particular Saturday evening. At the front drive, several well-dressed couples were leaving in a sleek, black town car and several expensive European imports. A half-dozen laughing women emerged from the building, all dressed to the nines and sparkling with jewelry. Brent overheard the doorman tell them to enjoy the play they were attending.

Lauren, on the other hand, spared none of them a glance, nor did she make eye contact with another doorman, who welcomed them into the beautifully appointed lobby. As they passed the front desk area, Brent scanned other groups preparing to head out for dinner, gathering near the bar, or waiting to add their names to a list to dine at the hotel's restaurant. A couple of diehard laptop warriors were at different lobby seating areas, soaking up some free Wi-Fi or trying to be seen as hardcore by their bosses, but for most, the workweek was no more than an unpleasant memory, leaving guests eager to enjoy whatever the city's downtown had to offer.

But Brent could not ignore the possibility that any one of the guests or visitors, even someone masquerading as an employee, might have a darker purpose. Might at this very moment be taking stock of Lauren's reaction to the phone call he had made.

Or she.

After studying the Internet posts and talking to those few relatives of victims who had been willing to tell him anything, Brent was nearly convinced the perpetrator was a single, socially maladjusted male between the ages of twenty and thirty-five, probably someone with a history of restraining orders or stalking charges filed on behalf of other women he'd encountered.

But long ago, Durant had learned the hard way that it never paid to cling too tightly to a theory, or to rule out half the population from a possible list of suspects. So he scanned the crowd, paying careful attention to the loners but noticing no one who sent up red flags.

Glancing in Lauren's direction, he wondered if she felt self-conscious about being underdressed for this crowd, the way his Carrie would have. But Lauren appeared to be beyond that, her face chalky in the lobby lights, her gaze glassy as she cut through a clot of people, bisecting their conversation. Without giving a single indication that she saw anything except the elevator doors that were her goal.

"Excuse us. Sorry," he said for her, hurrying his pace to catch her by the elbow. "Slow down a second, Lauren. No need to mow anybody down—or attract any more attention than we have to."

She jerked to a stop. "What? Am I embarrassing you? Is that what you're trying to tell me? Because if that's going to be an issue for you, you may as well hand over the dog and take off now."

"This isn't about me. It's you I'm worried over—and whoever might be watching."

Lauren blinked in surprise before darting nervous looks around the lobby. "I-I didn't think about that. All I can think of was getting away from all these people. And what that bastard said about my Rachel. How she put the gun in her mouth, how her blood and brains—"

Shifting the dog, he laid his free hand on her shoulder as he leaned close to her ear, "Not here, Lauren. Not now. Don't give him the satisfaction."

She sucked in an audible breath, stiffening before she drew away. Her gaze locking into his, she nodded. "You're right, Durant. I'm okay."

"You should call me Brent," he said, "if we're going to be partners."

She studied him intently before saying, "Oh, we're going to be partners, all right, or at least we will on one condition."

"What's that?"

She gestured toward the elevators, stepping inside when an empty car appeared and pushing a button for the sixteenth floor. As they glided upward, she held another button, stopping the car in place.

"If your condition's elevator sex," he said dryly, "you should've picked one of the glass ones."

She snorted and shook her head. "If your next career ambition's comedy, *you* should maybe think again."

"You're probably right on that count." He bent to put down the dachshund. "So what's the condition, Lauren? Or are you planning to hold this elevator up all evening?"

"When we do hunt down this bastard," she said, her gaze shifting from amused to deadly serious in the blink of an eye, "I want you to promise that I'll be there when you kill him. That I'll get to watch him die."

His heart jerked in his chest. How the hell had she guessed? "I can't—"

She shook her head, raw determination burning in her gaze. "Don't lie to me. And don't try to manipulate me, either. Because if I'm in, it's as an equal partner. All the way, or not at all."

Still holding the elevator button with her left hand, she offered him her right.

Blood rushing in his ears, he stared at her hand as if it were a live bomb, one that might blow up on both of them at any second.

"Earlier today," she said, "I was checking out what you said, looking into some of those forums where no-life losers feel entitled to pass judgment on anybody in the news. And I think I've found something. Something you might not have."

"What's that?"

"Moderated comments over at *The Vigil*'s website—you know, Jaycee Joiner's TV show?"

He nodded, remembering how the judge-turned-jackal had been the one to catapult Rachel from storm victim to "Blonde on Blonde Killer" with one broadcast. How Joiner's fans, who, both male and female, called themselves the "Vigil Aunties," had jumped on the turn of phrase like starving dogs on bloody scraps. "If they were moderated," he asked, "that would mean the site administrator took them down from the web, so how would you get—"

"Deletions leave behind 'ghost copies,'" she said, "that can be viewed if a person knows how to locate and restore them. The stuff I found was . . ." Revulsion pulled her mouth into a grimace. "It was seriously messed up. Suggestions that Rachel should be—that somebody ought to beat her, choke her, rape her with—you get the picture."

"God, Lauren, I'm so sorry you had to see that garbage." He had waded through enough of it himself on various websites, where sick individuals mistook the right to free speech for the right to incite violence. At least *The Vigil* tried to police the worst of the ugliness; many other sites had devolved into a total free-for-all.

"I'd like you to look at the phrasing on the messages," she said, "to see if any of this garbage might be *his.*"

Brent's mind raced with the possibility that, whipped into a murderous frenzy, the Troll King may have let down his guard. *If* any of these were from the Troll King. "You'll show them to me?"

"I'll show them to my *partner.*"

His hand engulfed hers, and as the two shook, he nodded at her. "Partners."

"Brent," she said, making it official.

He liked hearing her call him by his first name. He found he liked her, too, with her odd mix of tough-girl cunning and the vulnerability she fought so hard to hide. Or maybe he recognized a woman skating on the same edge he was, a woman who would either prove his salvation or send him plummeting to ruin along with her. But since he was already sliding toward a wreck, he was perversely glad to have someone else along for the ride.

On the sixteenth floor, she let him into a room done in restful browns and blues. He went first to the window, where he took in the tall buildings and snaking line of freeway traffic that made up Downtown Austin. When he turned around, Lauren was sitting cross-legged on the bed, with her laptop on her knees while the dachshund snuggled close beside her.

"I'd like to see those posts," Brent said, "but first I need to know, exactly what else did he say to you?"

She winced, keeping her gaze latched to the screen. "Only the ugliest things he could think of."

"I know it will be hard, but I need you to tell me everything, while it's still fresh in your mind. How he sounded, what he emphasized, every detail you remember."

Lauren closed the laptop lid, pain clouding her expression. "All right. Sure. He . . ." She took a deep breath. "The voice was digitally altered, slow and deep, like in one of those scary movies teenagers like to watch."

"Male?" Brent asked, trusting that she wouldn't be as easily fooled by the machine-generated tone as others.

She nodded. "Male, yeah. The syntax, the word choices. I'm almost certain of it."

"What did he say, Lauren?

She shuddered, the way an animal will when a fly walks over its back. "Terrible things."

"What things, Lauren?"

Her hands curled into tight fists, and she glanced at him. "You're sure you need to hear this?"

"To stop him, I'll need everything. Everything you've got."

She nodded, her gaze emptying as she stared straight ahead. Slowly, haltingly, she recounted all that she remembered, with a couple of detours to double back to fill in some detail she'd forgotten. She never looked at him as she spoke, never shed a tear or shifted her stiff posture, but Brent could see how each word cost her, how the Troll King's cruelty was carving bloody slivers off her even now.

His own soul bled as well at the cruel reminder that the same sadist who had called her had tormented so many others in the same way. Had tortured the woman he should have protected until she could no longer bear it.

Maybe it was his thoughts of how he'd failed to recognize the depth of Carrie's pain that had Brent crossing the room to Lauren. Or maybe it was the emptiness of her expression that had him taking her hand gently and pulling her onto her feet and into his arms.

She gasped, her body stiffening. "What are you—I-I don't want . . ."

She let the protest die, slowly thawing to lay her head against his shoulder. Though she went still and quiet, he felt the bumping of her heart beneath his hand. Felt her struggle between her natural independence and a very human need for contact in the wake of tragedy.

"I promise you," he murmured, "we'll make him stop. We'll make him pay." He rubbed her back as he might rub a child's to offer comfort. But the feeling of her soft curves pressed against his body, the warmth of her flesh in his arms evoked a far more complex reaction—one that had him aching to lower his head and claim her mouth, to push her back down to this huge expanse of bed and make her forget the vicious phone call. Make both of them forget everything for a while . . .

Breathing hard, he stepped back, gritting his teeth and reminding himself that, employed or not, he was still a professional and she was still a grieving woman. A woman who was shaking so hard, she felt as if she might collapse as any moment.

Praying she hadn't felt the hard ridge of his arousal, he said, "I'll help you through this, Lauren."

"How?" she challenged. "How are you going to do that, when two years after your wife's death, you're still not . . ."

She didn't finish. Didn't have to, but they both knew she was right, both knew that he hadn't moved on. That he wouldn't until he fully understood his loss and until he settled his accounts with the murderer they hunted.

Mercifully, she changed the subject, reaching for the laptop. "Let me pull up those deleted comments."

He pulled out an old business card with a secure e-mail address printed on the back of it. "Send me copies, will you? I'll want to compare those to the posts I have saved on my computer."

But as badly as he wanted to go over what she'd found and get her input on the case, the dark circles that underscored her eyes served as a reminder that she was too exhausted to think clearly. Hungry, too, he was sure. "How long has it really been since you've slept or eaten? Or cleaned up and put more antibiotics on those torn-up knees?"

She shrugged. "I'll be okay. I'll order up more coffee."

"You'll order up some food," he said, "and eat it."

"Are you kidding? Do you honestly think I could keep anything down after what that monster said?" She frowned. "I have to track him down. Have to find him tonight."

"I know you're wired right now, but when the adrenaline wears off, you're going to crash hard. Trust me."

She opened her mouth as if to argue, but cut herself short with a shake of her head. "How did he even get my number?"

"It's probably safe to assume he hacked your sister's cell phone at some point, or maybe her online contacts list from her computer. Pretty sure it's how he operates, taking potshots here and there to see who he can get a rise from."

"Hope I didn't disappoint him."

Brent smiled at her sarcasm, which he considered a good sign. Sobering quickly, he reminded her, "The thing is, Lauren, we need to pique his interest. To get him really focused on you before he moves on to the next blonde in the news."

"To pique his interest," she repeated. "You're talking about TV again. I told you, I could never go on—"

"The Internet could work as well, maybe even better. We could set up some kind of website, a blog in memory of your sister, with lots of photos of her, a personal note from you and her friends on how much she'll be missed."

Lauren let out a shuddering sigh. "Troll bait, that's what you're talking about. Right? A place to let those slimy pieces of garbage rip her to pieces even now."

He nodded, knowing as well as she would how often memorial sites and social networks brought out cruel bottom-feeders. And considering Rachel's recent notoriety, which had already drawn so much negative commentary, the outcome was even more certain. "I'm sorry, Lauren. Sorry to cause you pain. I'm even sorrier to have to ask you to post photos of yourself, too. Your blond self, that is."

Putting down the laptop, she began to pace the room. "I-I walked to a drugstore earlier today and picked up the hair coloring. I thought about what you said, thought I might as well . . . but I couldn't—I can't—go through with it." She shook her head, covering her face with her hands. "There has to be another way. Some way to track him from what we've got."

"Maybe you're right." He took a step nearer to her. "But before we get started, you'll have to have some food and rest."

"But we have to—"

"*You* need to take care of yourself. How're you supposed to think straight when you're so exhausted, you can hardly keep your eyes open?"

Anger flooded her face, making her look anything but sleepy. "I thought we were equal partners, so who are you to tell me when to—"

"This is how he does it, Lauren, how he starts breaking down his victims. When Carrie—when my wife died, the autopsy showed she was twenty-one pounds lighter than she'd been at her last doctor's visit—twenty-one pounds in just a couple of months, and she was never a big person. She was barely sleeping, too. Up padding around the house night after night, staring out into the backyard, refusing to talk to me about what happened, no matter how I begged her." His mind drifted back to the nightmare they'd been living in the months after Adam's death. He remembered wondering if it was possible that their marriage would survive it, or if she'd grow so sick of the way he'd buried himself in his own work, she would one day leave him.

Regret surged up, bitter bile, at the memory of those times he'd imagined that it might come as a relief if she did go. But he'd never for a moment dreamed of the way she would depart or the gaping hole her death would leave in his life.

"You never told me," Lauren said, "what was it he used against her? What was it your wife blamed herself for?"

He went to the desk, picked up the room service menu and started flipping through it. "So tell me, what do you want? Or would you like me to go get us something while you're in the shower? Steak? A salad? Sandwiches? I'm up for anything."

When he glanced back her way, her brows were raised, her gaze assuring him she hadn't missed his change in subject.

"How about answers?" she asked pointedly. "Because *partners* share things."

"*Relevant* things. My personal history's not one of them."

"Are you kidding? Your personal history's at the very heart of this, if your wife really was the Troll King's first victim."

"First things first," he said, looking down at the room service menu. "What do you want?"

"For you to quit ordering me around and start playing fair."

"No one's ordering you. I'm just trying to help you get out of this alive."

Her gaze cut through all his pretenses.

"Here's the deal," she told him, passing him her card key. "Go find us some pizza. Really *good* pizza, not the chain stuff, with extra cheese, no other toppings. You do that while I get cleaned up, and then we'll get to work."

"Pepperoni on my half okay?"

She shrugged. "Whatever floats your boat. Unless it's anchovies." She made a face at the thought.

He nodded and started for the door before hesitating, troubled by how agreeable she'd grown. Or eager to get him out of the room.

"There's just one more thing I'm going to need," he told her.

"What's that?"

In two steps, he reached down and scooped up the sleepy dachshund from her spot on the bed. "To be absolutely certain you'll still be here when I get back."

***

Lauren paced the hotel room's narrow confines, almost as furious at herself as she was at Brent Durant. Clearly, she'd allowed her lack of sleep and the troll's disturbing phone call to throw her off her game, enough that she'd somehow given away her change of heart about allowing the former agent to come up to her room.

Despite Jimenez's warnings, she was no longer worried about Durant being a physical danger to her. Instead, it was her own response to him that scared her, her dizzying impulse, that moment he'd pulled her into his arms, to raise herself on her toes and devour the sensuous-looking mouth of his. To shed her grief, her guilt, the tight confines of her isolation, losing herself in him—and the bed that dominated this room. Shame burning her face, she tried to push the thought away, but there was no stopping the insane need that their brief contact had ignited. The reminder of how very long it had been since her body had responded to a man's touch . . .

You mean how long it's been since you were dumb enough to make that mistake, she told herself, her skin crawling at the reminder of how she'd mistaken a handsome real estate attorney's single-minded focus as a balm for the loneliness that had whispered there was something else out there for her, something more than the comfortable rut she'd allowed herself to fall into.

Naïve as she was, she'd never guessed that Phillip's attention had been snagged by her repeated refusals to go out with him after they'd met at a party her biggest client had strong-armed her into attending. Apparently, rejection had proven a novelty he couldn't resist, one that had appealed to him just long enough to charm her down the aisle after a whirlwind courtship. Long enough for Lauren to imagine that she had what it took to be a wife, even a mother. And long enough for him to grow disgusted that she was no Eliza Doolittle awaiting his "improvements"— including the attentions of the prominent plastic surgeon he'd suggested could bring her up to what he'd referred to as "Southern California standards."

I've learned my lesson, learned what I am, she told herself, but still, the ache continued, the grief and loneliness that demanded comfort. Which meant she had to limit her contact with Brent at all costs.

She stopped her pacing for a moment, her attention drawn to the square of paper on the desk, where he'd written down his e-mail. Like her, he was using a disposable address made up of a seemingly random series of letters, numbers, and symbols. A secret, frequently changed mailbox meant to keep him a step or three ahead of any authorities who might care to track his movements online.

As she used a throwaway account of her own to forward him the files she had promised, she told herself that it meant nothing that the two of them thought alike in that regard, just as it meant nothing that they both shared the same goal of destroying their loved ones' stalker. They were two loners, temporarily sharing a single orbit, and the sooner they could complete their mission and move on with their lives, the better off they both would be.

But as long as the Troll King still lived, she could never return to the solitude she needed. And she knew of only one way sure to draw the bloodsucker like a fly to a fresh corpse.

Sucking in a deep breath, she headed for the bathroom and tore into the package she'd left on the bathroom counter with shaking hands. On the box, a model smiled at her, a sunny smile that matched Rachel's personality as much as it contrasted with Lauren's.

The hair color's shade, called Moonlight Magic, seemed right, too, so perfectly reminiscent of her sister that Lauren's stomach did a slow roll. The thought of lightening her hair this way, of baiting the Troll King publicly, left her nauseated. But didn't she owe it to her sister, to herself, to make the effort? To do whatever she must to put this whole nightmare, along with the temptation of Durant's big hands and his dark eyes, his moments of kindness and his maddening high-handedness, far behind her.

Some forty minutes later, Durant hadn't yet returned. But Lauren stood before the mirror drying her newly pale-blond hair, her body wrapped in a thick, white towel as tears rolled down her face. Tears for the sister she could almost see, imploring her from the steam-fogged mirror. Begging Lauren to run as far and fast as she could rather than doing all she could to make herself another target.

Instead, she moved like a sleepwalker to the closet to complete her transformation. As she dressed, she choked up, thinking of how her choices would have pleased the man who'd wanted nothing but a different wife.

But the fact was, she no longer gave a damn what Phillip wanted. Instead, she dressed to fuel a monster's fantasies.

CHAPTER EIGHT

As Brent returned with the pizza, he nearly drove past the hotel. Not that a building of its size was easy to miss, lighting up the night sky like a beacon as it was, but the thought of Lauren, of that body that called to his, broke him out in a cold sweat.

Behind him in the back seat, Dumpling snuffled and licked at her chops. "Pretty sure handtossed's not part of your diet, so quit your begging," he said as he turned into the hotel drive, thinking that maybe he should try to bribe a bellman to carry both the pizza and the dachshund upstairs to Lauren's room.

He'd send a message, too, saying he was tired and would meet her in the morning. And in doing so, he'd avoid the temptation of those sweet curves of hers, still damp and fragrant from the shower.

At the thought he sucked in a deep breath, filled with wonder that the libido he'd imagined gone forever had come roaring back. Grateful, even, though the guilt that followed hit him even harder. How could he imagine that he'd felt a powerful connection with a woman who was still reeling from her own tragedy?

What you felt, he warned himself, *was two-and-a-half years of pent-up lust.*

But what he really needed was her willing cooperation if he was to finally put an end to his hunt. Which meant the last thing he could do was to risk offending her. Or being such a selfish ass that he'd consider, even for a moment, using her heartbreak to slake his physical needs.

Swearing to himself that he was not going to be that guy, he turned into the parking garage at the last moment, taking the ramp that ended below ground and claiming one of the spots. But he didn't get out right away, not until telling himself, in no uncertain terms, that he wasn't *touching* Lauren again for any reason.

"Now get your shit together and get up there," he ordered himself.

After bribing the greedy little dog with pinches of crust, he convinced her that it was worth her while to use those stubby little legs of hers to follow him—or the handiest human food source. The scent of yeasty dough, oregano, and cheesy tomato sauce wafted up and made his stomach growl.

"Just don't tell the boss I spoiled your appetite," he told her, wondering if Jimenez had a point about the state of Durant's own sanity, since he'd been reduced to talking to the world's most obnoxious dog.

Eyes brightening, the fat little wiener sat up on her hind legs and waved her paws in an entreaty. And made him laugh when she sweetened the deal by tilting her head and giving him a growly sort of whine.

"All right," he relented, lifting the edge of the box once more and swearing, "but if you gas us out of the hotel room, I'm pleading ignorance."

By the time they reached the sixteenth floor, Brent was pretty sure he would never again have to worry about the toothless wonder gumming him to death. But his amusement faded when he knocked and Lauren didn't answer.

Knocking harder, he wondered if she might still be in the shower. Or if, as exhausted as she'd been, she might have passed out on the bed. But considering what she was dealing with, he was worried enough about her to use the key card to unlock the door, to slip inside the room and see . . .

The woman leaning toward the dresser mirror, tying a brightly colored scarf around her neck, looked so much like the young woman he had met that he had to remind himself that Rachel Miller was lying in the morgue now rather than standing right in front of him.

Clearly, Lauren had done more than lighten her shade to match the sister she'd lost. She'd curled the ends, letting them tumble in sideswept splendor—exactly like Rachel had been wearing hers when he had seen her.

The black, scoop-necked tee and body-skimming jeans she wore were subdued enough, and the dark colors made the brightness of her hair and the colorful punch of her scarf stand out even more. Brent knew he should say something, at least to ask if she was all right, but for the moment he was speechless. He was still at a loss for words when she finally turned to face him.

The cosmetics she'd applied made the resemblance even more uncanny—the subtle reshaping of her brows and shading of her eyelids, the light dusting of blush, and the red lipstick applied with an expertise that surprised him, as he'd never seen Lauren wear a lick of makeup. But what made him set down the pizza, made him forget his hunger altogether, was the glazed desperation in her blue-green eyes . . .

It was a brand of hopelessness that reminded him painfully of Rachel, when she'd refused to admit that the harassment he'd found signs of had been happening to her, too. A brand of hopelessness he'd failed to act on when he'd seen it in his own wife's eyes.

He dropped the dachshund's leash, forgetting all about the animal.

"Here you go," she said, her voice husky. "This what you were after?"

"It's more than—it's amazing, Lauren."

Grimacing, she handed him her phone. "I'll need you to—to t-take some photos. Pictures we can put up on the tribute site I'll design."

Taking the cell, he swallowed past the painful lump in his throat. "Are you—are you okay, Lauren?"

She grimaced, firing back, "What the hell do *you* think?"

"Honestly?" he asked. "I think you're as brave a woman as I've ever met in my life." *And as beautiful*, though somehow he'd liked the real Lauren, natural and unpolished, even better.

"Brave," she scoffed. "I don't feel brave, Durant. I feel sick. I feel like—this is a mockery of Rachel. A mockery I'm using to draw ugliness from hateful clowns who've never met her, never known her, yet will still feel entitled to judge every aspect of her life."

"We're not out to draw those losers," he said. "We're out to catch that one troll. The one who went from judge to executioner."

He took several shots of her, haunted and unsmiling, with a glint of pure rebellion in her eyes. Raw hatred of the animal who'd deliberately destroyed the person she loved best in the world. But to Brent, Lauren's anger only made her look more vulnerable. When the Troll King got a look at these images, he'd be salivating in his eagerness to take her apart, piece by piece. But could the hope of stopping him, of seeing the sadistic son of a bitch dead, if she and Brent got lucky, possibly be enough to save her? Or was she already far too close to shattering to survive any more harassment?

Brent hesitated, and Lauren scooped up Dumpling and unhooked her leash before carrying her to the window overlooking the city lights.

"Hey, wait. I'm not finished," he said.

She pressed her forehead to the cool glass, a single tear glistening along the curve of her cheek. "That's too bad, because I am."

In that unguarded moment, he snapped one last photo of her, an image that etched itself into his brain. And made him swear he wasn't losing her, too, wasn't letting her out of his sight until this was over.

"Rachel was always after me to do the girly-girl routine," Lauren said as she set down the dog again. "Go to a spa with her, get our hair done, shop for clothes we didn't need. She would've loved a sister like that."

Remembering his conversation with Rachel, he shook his head. "She *loved* the sister she had. I could see it when she talked about you. You raised her, sacrificed your own chance to go to college, and then paid for her to—"

"Let's get one thing straight, Brent. It was never, not for a single second, any kind of sacrifice. Rachel is—she was—my *family*. I'd walk through fire for that girl. And I'll walk through hell for her, too, even through this travesty." She gestured to her altered hair, her made-up face, the red, yellow, and white scarf that made either an elegant accessory . . . or a hangman's noose.

Their gazes locked, and within the shining prism of that moment, Brent saw a reflection of the pain, the guilt, the need for atonement that had ruled his life for two long years, driving away the friends and coworkers who had tried to help him. Isolating him, just as she'd become an island unto herself.

But as much as he liked to pretend otherwise, every human had his limits, times when every cell of him ached with the need to hear another human voice, another mind that could be a sounding board for his ideas, another body to hold, to pleasure, to keep back the tide of darkness. In spite of all the promises he'd made to himself that he would never again touch her, of the dozens of good reasons to keep that vow, of their dinner cooling in its box on the table, his hunger for food vanished.

A sharper, deeper hunger than he'd ever known awakened in its place.

***

One thing about Rachel Miller's girlfriends, they sure liked to talk. Though they'd been tight-lipped and defensive back when Rachel had been drawing so much fire after the accident, tonight, grief had loosened their lips—or maybe it was the tequila the eight of them were going through in the hole-in-the-wall neighborhood cantina where they had gotten together to drink in their friend's memory.

The occasion started out quiet and respectful, but after a few rounds, tongues loosened and the women laughed or cried— sometimes both at once—as they shared their favorite memories of their friend. Soon, those few other patrons around them faded from notice, especially the loner in the baseball cap and sunglasses, a man who'd turned up the collar of his black jacket while he paged through last week's newspaper and pretended to sip at a single mug of beer.

They forgot about him, but his attention was riveted on the women who had gathered. Especially the blonde wearing a crimson wrap dress that hugged her curves, whose bell-like voice carried better than the others. It was Nikki Watson, thought the watcher. He recognized her from the Facebook file he had set up under the name of one of Rachel's former classmates. Though he'd never posted a single message, he'd gotten to know Rachel well, poring through her photos and posts from her party-girl friend. And despising the bitches more every time that he logged on.

"Yeah, I asked her if she'd like to come tonight," Nikki was telling the others, "but she said she wasn't up to it."

"Poor thing," said an exotic-looking dark-haired woman whose identity the watcher wasn't sure of. "Rachel said her sister's really shy."

"One of those computer freaks," said Nikki, a snotty edge to her voice. "I swear, the woman has no idea how to hold a simple conversation. And as for manners—"

"She's probably pretty freaked out. She's not staying in Rachel's *apartment*, is she?"

This question created a buzz of sympathetic protests about how it would be too horrible, too disturbing, with all the blood and mess. But the man behind the newspaper already knew that Lauren wasn't at her sister's. He'd checked out that possibility earlier today, eyeing the crime-scene tape with a rush of shame and horror, though he knew he should feel nothing but joy.

Blond Nikki waved her manicured hands dramatically, tamping down their outrage. "No, of course I wouldn't allow that. I invited her to stay at my place. Thought maybe I could help her with all the arrangements and the other stuff. After all, *I'm* the best friend, and somebody who knows Rachel's style ought to be the one to pick the clothes out for her."

The watcher stared over the top of his newspaper, his heart pumping. Was that where Rachel's sister had gone? If so, maybe he could get there while beautiful Nikki and the others drowned their sorrows. Maybe he could—

A tiny young woman with short, auburn hair and huge hoop earrings interjected, "Um, Nikki, I don't think it matters. I mean, after what—what happened to Rachel, I can't imagine she'll have an open casket."

"Oh. Oh, God," Nikki clapped a hand over her mouth and dabbed at her eyes with wadded tissues. "I didn't think of that. Still—Rachel would want to look nice. And after everything she went through, she deserves that much at least. Doesn't she?"

The long table went quiet before the auburn-haired woman asked in a small voice, "Should you have left her at your condo, Nikki? All alone, tonight?"

Say yes, the watcher silently pleaded as he dug in a pocket for his keys. *Say, Lauren likes it that way, say that she prefers to be alone. Alone, where I can find her while you idiots drown your sorrows until you're so damned hammered the waiter takes your keys. That should give me time enough. Time enough to—*

But Nikki was shaking her head. "Oh, no. She said no. Didn't want to stay with me, didn't want me helping her tomorrow."

"Well, that was kind of rude," slurred one of the others, who seemed drunker than the rest. "Rachel only said that she was shy, not a Grade A bitch."

Nikki shrugged. "I'll try again, for Rachel's sake. But Lauren said she was already checked in at the Omni. She *said* she wouldn't want to crowd me, but it was obvious she wanted no part of my help. If you ask me, she's just plain antisocial. Rachel could hardly ever talk her into . . ."

But the rest of their gossip was lost in a rattle of newspapers. The noise of a man in a hurry to track down the woman he had come to find.

CHAPTER NINE

Lauren's skin rippled, a delicate shiver that made Brent wonder, was she frightened of what she saw in his eyes? Terrified of getting too close to a man she'd surely been told was having an emotional breakdown—a man who'd given her plenty of reason to distrust him?

But in her trembling exhalation, in the dark dilation of her pupils, he saw not fear but the lit fuse of something far more dangerous. He fought to stamp it out, to remind himself he needed her help, not her body. Still, he would swear he smelled the smoke, heard the crackling of that tiny flame in his ears, a flame burning inexorably through his self-control.

"Brent," she said, speaking only a split second before she took the first step toward him. When he went to her, pulling her against him, a cry rose from her throat like the resurrected dead.

They came together like two storms, spawning something even fiercer the moment his mouth slanted over hers. The heat, the moisture, the rough plunder of their contact sent shock waves through his body, leaving him painfully hard.

As the stubble of his whiskers scraped her skin, he felt her teeth sink into his lip, returning pain for pain. But the sensation spiking through him felt so damned good, after years of numbness, that he lost himself in the thrust of tongues, the sensations of her hands reaching up beneath his shirt, the pressure of her lithe body against his erection—followed by a grinding that ripped through the tattered ghosts of his doubts.

In those frenzied moments, there was no finesse, no gentleness between them. Nothing but raw sensation as he pulled up her top and cupped her breasts with rough hands, as he thumbed the buttons he needed so badly to devour through the layers of her clothing. Too damned many layers . . .

Her arched back and soft moans gave him all the encouragement he needed. Pulling the tee off over her head, he removed her bra, too, within seconds.

"God, Lauren, how I want you," he groaned as he filled his hands and leaned in to claim another blistering kiss. A kiss that ended with her taking a few steps backward and pulling him onto the bed with her. There he drove both of them to madness as he suckled and stroked her before fumbling with the closure of her jeans, his own growing impossibly tight.

When the button below her navel proved stubborn, he kissed his way down her belly—and smiled when she whimpered and wriggled beneath him.

As the button succumbed to his efforts, he moved to unzip her, but some instinct—or perhaps it was only a fragment of conscience—broke through his lust, making him hesitate a moment.

"You're sure?" he asked her, the scraping of his own breath, the pounding of his heartbeat loud in his ears. "Because it's been a hell of a long two years for me, and you're so damned—I swear to you, once I get a taste of you, there won't be any turning back. Make no mistake, I mean to be inside you, Lauren. I mean to take you, long and hard."

She shook her head and whispered to him, "No turning back. I swear it."

But the streamers of mascara running down her pale face told another story. The story of grief so deep, it formed a stark, black line he couldn't bring himself to cross.

***

Lauren reached for him, her stomach dropping, but he was gone from her already, rising from the bed and stalking toward the bathroom, his face a stony mask.

"I'm sorry. I'm so sorry," she called, the harshness of her ex's judgment ringing in her head. *Don't be such a little prick tease.* It hurt a man, he'd told her, to get so worked up, and let him down, especially with useless tears and drama.

But she'd been left aching, too, when Brent had pushed himself off the bed. When he'd raked his hand through his silver-tipped hair with the deepest sigh she'd ever heard.

"We can't—I won't do this," he had told her, his voice gruff as he turned from her, an erection straining at the front of his pants.

An impressive erection, from the look of it, but she would never know for sure. Would never get the chance to use it—to use him—to drive every last thought from her mind.

"Please, it's okay," she called after him. "I swear I'll pull myself together. I can—we can still—just tell me what you want."

He walked back out, and in his face, she saw not anger but contrition, a sadness so deep it must have been etched into his soul. In the face of it, she felt her skin flush, felt shame that this man remembered his dead wife where she had forgotten Rachel. Or wanted, needed desperately, to forget for a short while.

Snatching up her shirt, she used it to cover her breasts.

"You're nowhere near ready for this." His voice was a low rumble as he reached to smooth her hair with his fingertips, that bright blond hair that her sister had sometimes complained attracted the wrong sort of men. But then his hand dropped to gently move a strand of Lauren's hair aside, and he looked longingly at her bare breasts before shaking his head. "Damn it all, I have to go before I—I'll see you in the morning. All right?"

She turned from him, her face molten, but somehow managed to spit out, "Yeah, sure. *Whatever*, Agent Durant." She wasn't about to make the mistake of thinking of him on a personal level again, or as anything but a means to the end she sought.

"Lauren . . ."

She sat there frozen, refusing to look at him until, finally, she heard the door to the hallway snick shut.

As Dumpling looked up at her mournfully, Lauren sat there for a long while before she dressed again and forced down two slices of lukewarm pizza—with the consummate beggar scoring a few tidbits. Afterward, she brushed her teeth and repaired the mess of her face before beginning to work on Rachel's memorial website.

But Lauren couldn't do it, couldn't face the photos of the beautiful, young sister who was lost to her forever. Couldn't bear the sight of the pictures Durant had taken of Lauren herself with her phone, either. Even worse were the images running in an endless loop through her brain—images of her pathetic, humiliating entreaties to the man who'd walked out on her.

How would she ever face him again?

Pacing the room, she fought to convince herself that the man's opinion didn't matter. That she didn't really even know him, with all the secrets he was keeping from her. Secrets that put him in the driver's seat, where he called all the shots.

Caught up in a whirlwind of frustration, anger, and distress, she stalked back to her laptop and plugged a name into her browser's search box: *Carrie Wilkinson Durant*. Because if nothing else, she should at least verify those few details he had shared and look for other similarities to her sister's story.

The horror of what she read writhed like live eels in her stomach. Liquid heat streaked down her face as she imagined what this poor woman must have gone through, how she must have blamed herself—even before the purveyors of human-misery-as-entertainment started speculating about the "shocking motives" behind the "so-called accident" that had cost the life of an adorable three-year-old named Adam. Though Lauren hadn't heard about the case, which had taken place in a suburb of Oklahoma City, Internet trolls had eagerly leapt into the fray, every one of them feeling qualified to judge the "blond bitch of an ice queen" who'd robbed another family of their precious child. As the trolls called her far worse, Lauren found her heart breaking and her eyes filling at the display of the ugliest side of human nature.

Painfully reminded of the attacks that had cost her sister her life, Lauren closed the laptop and picked up Dumpling, hugging the fat dog tight to her chest.

Feeling more restless than ever—and vaguely ashamed of prying into Durant's private tragedy—Lauren got up and again began pacing the room, whose walls seemed to close in on her. She'd been cooped up here far too long, she realized, boxed up in this tiny cell. If she didn't get away, get out of her own head soon, she was afraid she would burst out of her own skin. So after making a nest of towels for Dumpling, Lauren grabbed her purse and headed downstairs to the lobby.

It had been on her mind to take a long walk, to lose herself in swift strides. But seeing the darkness just beyond the glass gave her pause, along with Durant's earlier warning about putting herself in danger.

A part of her wanted to rebel, to recklessly head out in the hope that she might draw the killer she had dyed her hair to lure. If he was really lurking nearby, it would certainly be swifter. But chances were the monster was hunkered down in a stained and ripped-out recliner somewhere halfway across the state or country. For all she knew, the sadist could be halfway around the world.

He's not that far, her instincts whispered as she remembered how Durant had plotted suspected victims and found that they were centered here, in Texas. The Troll King's use of the phone, as well, spoke of a stalker who preferred to get closer to the victim than the net alone could afford. Maybe close enough that he would eventually work up the nerve to personally go after the next one.

If she'd only had her gun, Lauren would have welcomed the opportunity of a personal confrontation, the chance to shoot down her sister's killer and call it self-defense. But at the thought, her stomach spasmed and a thrill of fear chased up her backbone.

She was a network security administrator—at best a part-time hacker—a woman whose risk taking was confined to the virtual world. *Unless you count the bedroom,* she thought, a wry smile pulling at one corner of her mouth. But the thought oozed greasily around her stomach, and she made an abrupt turn toward the lobby bar.

Despite her ex's efforts to "refine her," she'd never taken to his fancy wines, nor did she like champagne. Beer tasted bitter to her, but the last time she'd gotten together with her sister, Rachel had introduced Lauren to the sweetness of minty-lime mojitos. Lauren had, she thought, found her on-ramp to inebriation. Lightweight that she was, she hadn't gotten through the second drink that night before she'd found herself completely wasted.

Tonight, she told herself as she found a seat at the bar, she was going to break her record. Three ought to be enough, she thought, to drown the memory of her behavior with Durant.

But no amount would ever wash away the ghost of her vivacious sister, who appeared in the empty seat beside her, the words she'd uttered so often hanging in the air like cigarette smoke.

Come on, Lauren. Drink up. It's time to live a little.

"Not for you. Not anymore," Lauren murmured to herself as the bartender showed up with her first mojito.

She paid him for the drink, ignoring his attempts at small talk. And paying absolutely no attention to the man reading his newspaper in the corner of the room.

CHAPTER TEN

As he sat in the parking garage inside his car, Brent cursed himself in frustration. He'd been an idiot, letting his conscience stand between him and the woman who had only wanted whatever solace meaningless sex would offer.

He reminded himself that Lauren was struggling through the same hell he was still trying to survive. With her, he wouldn't have the stupid platitudes or pity, wouldn't have anything but a chance to forget himself for a while, to put someone else's fresh suffering ahead of his own.

He chuckled at himself, acting as if making love to her would make him some kind of damned hero. As if her soft curves, her breathy moans, her red-hot kisses hadn't sent raw need streaking straight to his cock. The trouble was, what they'd been leading up to wasn't making love at all but the kind of sex that left marks. As it was, his lower lip was swollen, even a little bruised, where she'd nipped him, and he had seen the reddened flesh around her mouth and breasts where his beard had scraped raw the sensitive skin.

She deserved better, he told himself. Deserved gentleness and understanding, a man who didn't take off at a damned run over a few tears. And what if, in his absence, she received another phone call? Was he leaving her wide open, in her vulnerable state, to the Troll King's monstrous manipulations?

Pulling the keys from the ignition, he dropped them into his pocket and got out of the car again. All the way back upstairs, he warned himself—or more accurately, his body—that he wasn't returning to get laid. He was instead going to apologize and talk her through what would surely be one of the roughest nights of her life.

Though he no longer had her key for access, he managed to slip onto the elevator with a couple of hotel guests without eliciting suspicion. Once they'd gotten off at their floor, he went on up to the sixteenth and back to Lauren's room.

She didn't answer her door, and he couldn't say he blamed her. But the dachshund barked at his knocks, and he didn't hear Lauren shushing the dog, either.

"You okay in there?" he called, wondering whether she had jumped back in the shower. Washing away the memory of his caresses.

He tensed and told himself that she hadn't decided on a bath instead. That she hadn't gone there like his Carrie, taking her razor with her. Yet the thought lodged in his mind, raising the short hairs behind his neck.

As his pounding grew louder, the door next to Lauren's popped open, and a balding head appeared. "Jeez, Einstein," a jowly older man said, "She's not in there. Don't you get it? I passed her as she was heading for the elevator about twenty minutes back."

"Sorry, man, and thanks." Brent turned toward the elevator, imagining Lauren walking through the darkest shadows of the park where he'd first found her, without even her toothless old dog to sound the alarm in case of trouble.

In his hurry to head out, he nearly missed her. But in the glass-and-marble lobby, certain sounds carried, especially the unexpected notes of a woman's laughter.

Turning, toward the dimly lit bar, he caught the bright tumble of blond curls, now spilling loose around her shoulders. Caught the flash of white teeth and red lipstick as she smiled at a sandy-haired man whose back was to Brent, her glass rising before she brought it to her mouth and tipped it back.

Heat rose to the surface, his skin heading toward its melting point. Had hers been the laughter that had snagged his attention? Laughter from the same woman whose tears had driven him away?

And more to the point, would the golden boy talking to her be taking Brent's place in her bed tonight? The thought made him want to march over to the bar, punch out the guy she was talking to, and haul her back up to her room upstairs.

Sure you don't want to beat your chest and throw in a Tarzan yell while you're at it? Brent shook his head, disgusted with what he realized was a raging case of jealousy. Jealousy over a woman he had no claim to, regardless of whatever connection he'd imagined.

A connection based on each of them having lost a loved one to the Troll King, on the desire to see the sadist dead and buried? *Yeah, that sounds like the start of a real healthy relationship*, Brent thought, gritting his teeth and taking one last look. And telling himself that if she was that determined to use sex to take her mind off her problems, it was none of his damned business.

Or could it be? He moved nearer to the bar entrance, watching the pair for a few more minutes. His stomach clenched as he saw what looked like a normal conversation between Lauren and a guy in his mid-thirties, a business type with neatly trimmed hair wearing a sport jacket and tie. A mid-level corporate sales rep stuck away from home and family for the weekend. Brent would bet money that if he moved a little closer, he'd be able to spot an indentation from the wedding ring the jackass had left up in his room.

The thought made Brent grind his teeth, but a philandering salesman hitting on a hot blonde on a Saturday night was business as usual in hotel bars around the world. And since Mr. Clean Cut didn't come anywhere close to matching the profile Brent had developed of a maladjusted, socially immature hacker with no idea of how to carry on a reasonable conversation with a woman, *he* was being the creep standing here and watching, praying he'd see Lauren revert to her usual antisocial self and send the joker packing.

So you could sweep back in and coax her upstairs?

Scowling, Brent tried to tell himself that it was time to head back to the nearby motel where he was staying. He'd had his chance tonight and blown it. Sitting here and watching any longer was only going to make it tougher for him to get to sleep tonight. And impossible for him to work with Lauren in the morning, especially if she looked up to catch him skulking.

Still, some lingering instinct—most likely paranoia—made him linger until a tall, dark-suited man with the vigilant look of hotel security came over to ask if he could help him find something.

Brent cursed his luck, realizing there'd be no way he could continue hanging around now that his surveillance had been noted by a pro. "No, thanks. A friend and I were thinking about meeting for a drink here, but he hasn't shown yet, and I can't reach his cell phone."

"So you're not a guest here?" the man asked, his clear gray eyes sizing up the potential threat.

"Nah. It was just a convenient central meeting place."

"Sixth Street should be getting cranked up by now. You might want to head on down and check out the music there. Who knows? You may just spot your friend if you're lucky."

Brent nodded and thanked him for the tip, though he understood the subtext just fine. *I don't believe there is a friend, and you've loitered in our lobby long enough.*

To insure the message sank in, the security officer took up a position between the bar and front desk, his hands folded before him as he waited Brent out. Unwilling to call more attention to himself, Brent spared Lauren a last, regretful glance before he finally withdrew.

He might have lingered in the hotel garage for a while, but an attendant wandering with a radio in hand was walking the aisles, craning his neck as he looked for signs of trouble. Or signs of Brent, if he'd been tipped off from Mr. Security upstairs.

With no other choice except to leave the property, Brent tried to tell himself that Lauren was more than capable of handling herself. Then he headed to his motel, to a decent room with a good bed that might as well have been built of rocks and cactus for all the rest it offered him that night.

***

"You ready for another?" Lauren's new friend asked eagerly. If "friend" was the right word for the handsome, sandy-haired salesman who had put down his newspaper before striding over to buy another round and strike up a conversation.

Lauren raised her glass to show she was only halfway through her second. Already regretting the new hair, the makeup, and the splashes of color that had drawn him to her like a shark on wounded prey, she tried to think of how to get rid of this guy so she could sit and drink in peace. But earlier she'd spotted a tall silhouette near the lobby entrance of the bar, and she wasn't about to give Durant the satisfaction of seeing her blow off her company so quickly.

Instead, she answered, "Still working on this one. You wouldn't be trying to rush me, would you?" *Or get me drunk so you could offer to walk me to my room . . .*

He smiled smoothly, his gaze swallowing her up. "Absolutely not. I could enjoy this view all night."

But as he clinked his glass against hers, there was a tremor in his hand, and he glanced at his cell phone for the third time. Probably waiting for a phone call from the wife at home, she decided, noticing how he kept his left hand out of sight.

As tempted as she was to glance back toward the doorway, she didn't want Durant imagining she was looking to him for a rescue. Still, she would almost swear she felt his disapproval, his wish for her get the hell out of this bar and head back to the safety of her room.

Anger burned away the pleasant buzz she had felt starting. What did he care whom she had a drink with? What right did he have, after the way he'd left her?

Maybe it was the unfamiliar effects of the alcohol, or maybe it was her wounded pride, but Lauren continued her conversation with the salesman, laughing a little harder at his jokes than she should have, even flirting a little—as lousy as she was at it— as she finished her drink.

Mostly for Durant's benefit, she pretended she was some other woman, some carefree business traveler looking to kill a lonely evening. But it wasn't her false name and cover story that intrigued the salesman, no more than it had been the real her who'd been responsible for the lapse in the ex-agent's self-control. All they really wanted was the pretty mannequin she'd made of herself.

"So you work in insurance, Celia," said the salesman, interested enough to probe beyond the surface of Lauren's lie. "What exactly is it that you do?"

She shrugged and embellished her story, the first time she could remember ever having been called upon to do so. "Nothing too exciting. I'm in the actuarial department. We run forecast models predicting the likelihood that things will fall apart—business ventures, buildings in hurricane-prone coastal regions, the human heart."

"The heart?" The man who'd called himself Jack Steelman leaned forward, seemingly entranced.

Lauren nodded, thinking the advertisers of Moonlight Magic ought to print something on the box about how this shade made even insurance irresistibly fascinating, at least to horny salesmen. "When a person's applying for a policy, we calculate the chance of death and use it to establish a premium that affords the company a reasonable profit margin."

After risking a peek toward the doorway, she wondered how long ago Durant had left. And cursed herself for impersonating the personable for no damned reason. "See, Jack? I told you it was boring."

"Not at all. I promise." Blue eyes twinkling, he shook his head and held up his right hand, Boy Scout style. "So how would you compute the chance of us sharing another round? Maybe an appetizer or even dinner if you're hungry?"

"You're sweet to offer," she said, pushing back her glass, "but I think I'd better head on up. I have an early meeting in the morning."

"*Sunday* morning?" he asked, an edge coming into his voice. "Seriously, Celia, if you're trying to blow me off, just say so. It's not like you'd be the first."

She sighed, hating that she never knew how to get out of these things gracefully. Which, come to think of it, had started her down a path that had led her to the altar the last time she'd found herself in a similar situation. So she pushed aside her worries about being nice and told him bluntly, "I'm trying to blow you off, John, because I'm not interested in married men. Or any man, right at the moment, but thank you for the drink."

In spite of the dim light, she saw his face darken. "It's *Jack*, honey. And there's no need to be a bitch about it."

She cocked her head and frowned, "I thought you said I should just tell you."

"But I didn't mean—and anyway, what makes you think I'm married?"

Rising from the barstool, she said, "Interesting tactic, asking how you were detected instead of denying the transgression. But I'd rather not help you fool the next woman, assuming she's the type to care."

Disgust twisted his handsome face. "You're a real piece of work, you know that?"

"Better than an easy mark." As she put down money to pay for her own drinks and a generous tip, she felt a moment's gratitude to her ex for teaching her to cut her losses early.

The thought made her realize, as she headed for the elevator, that she'd dodged a major bullet when Brent Durant had left her bed. And she would be damned smart never to offer him another invitation.

Once she returned to her room, she worked as long as she

could, clamping down on her emotions, to put the memorial page together. Pretending she was ghostwriting web content for a client, or working on one of the complicated schemes she sometimes used to lure a cyber-creep into revealing himself to the authorities, she wrote a glowing tribute to her sister, deliberately making her sound like the saint she'd never been.

But Lauren could only lie to herself for so long, so by the time she added photos from her phone of her beautiful young sister smiling, laughing, clowning for the camera, her own head was aching from the struggle to hold back her tears.

"Why?" Lauren begged the images, so full of life, so vibrant that they made the memory of the stark morgue photos seem obscene. "Why couldn't you come to me? I would have tracked that son of a bitch down and killed him, if that's what it took."

With a shaky sigh, she moved on, going through the pictures Durant had taken earlier that evening. She ended up choosing the one of herself holding Dumpling by the window, though she hated the way the shot left her grief as exposed as a raw wound, exposing her to the judgmental comments she knew would soon appear.

Her vision swimming with exhaustion, she clicked the Publish button, posted the link on Rachel's favorite social network—after easily guessing the security question and resetting the password—and switched off the lights. For a long time, she lay curled on her side, staring into inky darkness before she finally tumbled to its depths.

***

From the shadowy recesses of the budget hotel room he'd checked in to, sleep mocked Durant through the long night. Twisted by his tossing and turning, rough sheets tied him in knots, yet the rest he needed proved as elusive as the quarry he had hunted for the past two years.

Hours later Brent dropped into a light doze, only to jerk awake what seemed like a few minutes later, disturbing images of Lauren and the man he'd spotted her with earlier still spinning through his brain. Only in his dream, Lauren was straddling the businessman, both of them naked on the bar. Slowly, she lowered herself onto him, her head tipping back as she cried out Brent's name.

She was silenced when her lover's monstrous hands shot upward to clamp around her pale throat, to choke the life out of her as a hideous barbed crown burst like antlers through the surface of the Troll King's bloody scalp.

Gasping for breath, Brent sat up and clicked on the light. "Shit," he said, heart stampeding as he fought to shake off the nightmare, to remind himself it was nothing but a tangled dream. *She's safe, safe in her bed, sound asleep. Alone now.*

But anxiety clung to him like greasy smoke, so he reached for his laptop computer. If he wasn't going to sleep, he might as well get back to work.

Bringing up a search engine, he typed in Rachel Miller's name, along with the word "suicide." A number of hits came up, most of them links to local reports on the discovery of her body with what a preliminary investigation led authorities to believe was a self-inflicted gunshot wound. Most of the stories went on to identify Rachel as the driver once accused of recklessly causing the drowning death of coworker Megan Rutherford in last fall's flood. But as Brent moved from the hard news websites to those belonging to what he thought of as the "tragitainment" outlets, he found several luring the curious with clickbait headlines such as *"DID GUILT OVER FRIEND'S*

DEATH DRIVE BUSTY BLONDE TO SUICIDE?" and *"WAS BLONDE ON BLONDE KILLER'S SUICIDE TRAGEDY OR JUSTICE?"*

Predictably, the comments sections contained a few sympathetic postings lamenting the loss of another young woman's life, along with one hoping she found peace and mercy in the great beyond. Soon, however, the more reasonable statements were buried beneath a landslide of harsh judgment—words Brent would have thought he'd become inured to by now. Nausea swirled as he imagined Lauren reading them, her grief as fresh and raw as his had been two years before.

Bitch got what she deserved.

Finally. Took the bimbo long enough.

Wish I was there to help steady her aim.

In a response to that last comment, he found another response that stopped him cold. **I* was, and it was totally worth the price of admission, watching those silvery globs sliding down the bathroom cabinet, chunks of skull and tufts of hair stuck in them.*

"There you are, bastard," he said aloud, his skin crawling at the similarity in the wording to the phone conversation Lauren had described. Could the Troll King have really been there, with Rachel, in the flesh? Brent sincerely doubted it, figuring the asshole for a coward who would never risk a physical altercation. But as Lauren had mentioned, the man had known that Rachel took her own life in her apartment's bathroom, a detail that Brent hadn't spotted in any of the news stories.

He was probably on the phone with her, urging her to do it, just before her death. Just as Brent had found a record of a conversation between some untraceable caller and his own wife, the Troll King would have wanted to be directing the action this time, planting his cruelly detailed fantasies into the latest mind that his malice had broken.

Grinding his teeth, Brent clicked the profile link the Troll King had used for his posting—an eye-roller of a new name, Un$toppable69, another fake account clearly set up to cover his tracks. Just as in the previous profiles, he'd given no location, and if Brent went through the time and trouble to have Cisco, who was one of his last remaining friends inside the bureau, run it down, he knew he was going to find that Un$toppable69 was posting using a proxy server, which would transmit his messages from one server to another, a string of them that would likely span much of the globe.

The FBI, and some of the government's other intelligence agencies, had methods that were capable, with time and the right team on it, of piercing the veil. Unfortunately, access to those coveted resources was strictly regulated—and normally required a subpoena from a federal judge.

Which was about as likely, given Brent's current status, as the current FBI director showing up to pump his hand and pin a medal to his chest.

Frustrated as ever, Brent opened up another tab to check out his e-mail accounts. Finding a message with attachments filed under the address he had given Lauren, he opened it and was surprised to see that she'd attached the files he had asked to see.

Looking at the timestamp on the message, he smiled, gratified—and more relieved than he would admit—to think that she was spending a restless night as well. A night alone, he figured, banking that her natural reticence would keep her from sending the screen shots while another man was in the room.

Moments later, Brent's smile fell at the idea that she might have just as easily gotten the sex she craved and then sent her lover on his way. Cursing himself for being a jealous fool, Brent wished like hell he could un-flip whatever switch had flooded him with testosterone.

For with desire came the risk of hoping for a different out-come than the imprisonment or death he knew awaited him at the end of this long nightmare. The risk of hoping for a different future than the one that he deserved.

CHAPTER ELEVEN

It was still dark hours later when Lauren opened her eyes to find Rachel standing over her, shaking her and sobbing, "If only you'd told me you were coming to Austin, I swear I would've waited!"

Lauren tried to answer, tried to explain that she'd had no idea Rachel was so depressed, but the words caught in her throat and her limbs refused to move. *Paralyzed*, she thought at first, before she understood that the stillness extended through her entire body, right down to her stone-cold heart. Because *she*, and not Rachel, had been the one who'd stuck the muzzle of her .38 in her mouth and ended the pathetic whimpers of an empty life with one explosive bang.

A loud ringing jerked Lauren from the nightmare, and her heart thumped a wild reminder that she was painfully alive. Realizing it was the landline she'd heard, she reached for the phone on the nightstand. She propped herself on her elbows, her shell-shocked brain warning her that calls that startled a person awake often brought the worst of news.

As she reached for the handset, a glance at the clock told her she'd slept later than she'd thought. With the heavy curtains closed, she never would have guessed it was already 7:40.

"Hello?" she asked, bracing herself to deal with Detective Jimenez. Or maybe it was Durant, wanting to get back to work in the same room where the two of them had almost—

"*It's no fucking wonder your husband wouldn't put a baby in you, Freak-bitch*," the distorted voice said. The voice of a stalker who had somehow tracked her here, to this hotel.

Panic jolting up her spinal column, she opened her mouth to ask how he had found her. But only a choked sound emerged as she thought of the salesman she had angered last night, a man who'd sat so close to her she could have touched him. Could have used her nails to gouge the blue eyes of what might have been her sister's killer. Had it really been him?

"*But your Phillip wasn't nearly as careful to keep from knocking up his pretty little assistant, was he? I can hardly blame your ex, though, for not wanting to mix his DNA with a pathetic creature like you. Considering what I've seen, I'm surprised he could even bring himself to fuck you in the first place. Maybe he felt sorry for you. Too bad for you I never will.*"

"M-morning, Jack," she ventured, her heart stuttering as she tried out the name the businessman had given. "It was nice to meet you last night."

"*Dreaming of me, darling?*" the Troll King gave an ugly chuckle. "*Guess that's as close as a sad-sack little bitch like you'll ever get to meeting—*"

"So did you crawl out of whatever nasty hole you're living in to meet my sister, too? Wasn't it enough, stalking her long-distance from whatever pathetic basement hideaway you're—?"

"*Speaking of holes,*" he told her, a depraved sneer bleeding through the digitized cruelty, "*you'll find that I paid sweet, sweet Rachel a visit before she died. A very personal visit, you might say . . .*"

In hideous detail, he went on to describe the sickening things he'd done to sexually degrade her sister, things Lauren would have never thought of, let alone imagined possible. *Lies*, she told herself, or more likely wishful thinking, the sadistic fantasies of a sick mind. Still, she felt her gorge rising as she struggled to push back the horrific images, to think of how to lure this nightmare into range.

He feeds on weakness, she reminded herself, *so if you want to keep him engaged, you'll have to play the victim*. Her lungs emptied at the thought, every atom of her being rebelling at the thought of playing to his twisted daydreams. But what other choice did she have if she wanted him to pay?

"Everyone who really knew my sister knows she was a good girl." Outrage shook through Lauren's voice like a cold wind trembling through the prairie grasses. "She would've never done those things you said, would never let a monster like you touch her!"

"*When the pain's bad enough, a person will do anything—or anyone—to make it stop.*" He was gloating now, clearly wringing joy from deliberately inflicting pain. "*What would* you *do to stop me from calling? To get me out of your life forever, Lauren?*"

She desperately wanted to suggest, *How about an electric carving knife castration?* Instead, she said what she supposed a normal woman would have, the perfect victim of his dreams. "I'm calling the police! They'll make you stop this. They'll lock you up where you belong."

He only laughed at what they both knew was a meaningless threat. "*Don't worry. Now that I've had the pretty sister, I can't imagine being satisfied with the family freak. So we'll just keep in touch this way for a while, shall we?*"

"Don't call m-me again, or I'll—" she demanded.

His mocking laughter silenced her. "*You'll do whatever I tell you to do*"—the monstrous voice grew somehow more horrifying as it dropped to a near whisper—"*because only you and I know how much you deserve this. How many times you blew your sister off, how often you embarrassed and disappointed her before she finally gave up.*"

Her attempt at meekness forgotten, Lauren's temper exploded. "I will hunt. You. Down." But it was already too late. The Troll King had disconnected.

Shaking with fury, she called down to the front desk and was quickly connected. "The client who just phoned me was somehow accidentally cut off," she said, unable to disguise the tension in her voice. "Could you reconnect me with that party? Please."

"I'll be delighted to assist you, Ms. Miller," a male voice replied, sounding as if he really meant it. "If you'll hold for just a moment . . . Oh dear, I see the call came from a private number, so unfortunately, I won't be able to—"

At the sound of a firm knock at the hotel room door, Lauren nearly jumped out of her skin. Over the riot of the dachshund's barking, she told the hotel operator, "Thanks, anyway. I have to go now."

When another knock came, she put down the phone and shushed Dumpling before creeping closer to the locked door. When no one called, "Maid service," she peeked through the peephole and blew out a sigh. She'd almost forgotten she had let the police know where to find her.

Grateful that she'd fallen asleep in her clothing last night, she raked still-shaking fingers through her hair and opened the door. "Detective Jimenez, I'm so glad to see you." After the phone call she'd received, she would have welcomed even Brent Durant, with all his attitude, as long as it came with strong arms and a gun.

"Would it be all right if I come inside for a moment, Miss Miller?" he asked. "I have a couple of things to tell you, and with the hotel so close to the station, I thought I might as well stop by on my way in."

"I'm kind of a mess right this moment," she said, referring to her mental state as much as her appearance, "but, sure. Come on in. I was just about to call you anyway."

He stepped into the room, smelling of soap and after-shave and looking as crisp as she was rumpled. His dark eyes appraised her, taking in the new hair color, the smudged remnants of makeup she'd been too exhausted to wash off last night. "Everything okay here? Are you doing all right, Lauren? You—your hair—"

"Of course I'm not all right. My sister's dead, and I've been getting—" she began before cutting herself short. "Wait. You said you came to tell me something? Is there news on my sister's case?"

He looked both concerned and curious, but after a beat, he let his questions go. "First of all, I thought I'd let you know your sister's apartment has been cleared. There's a key waiting for you in the manager's office on the ground level."

"It's been cleared?" she asked. "Does that mean—is it . . . you know, where she was—where Rachel was found the other morning . . . ?"

"Apartment management called in a crime-scene remediation company to see that everything's made clean and safe for you. Once they're finished, you're fine to go inside and start packing up the contents."

At the thought of going inside Rachel's apartment, of packing up the remnants of a wasted life, Lauren shuddered, though she knew there would be no way to avoid it.

"Also," Jimenez told her, "I thought you'd want to know that your sister's remains were released to the funeral home you designated earlier this morning."

Lauren nodded stiffly, grateful that Nikki had stopped her drama queen theatrics long enough to recommend someplace local, since Rachel would have surely wanted her service to be held here, where all her friends were. "So the autopsy's been completed, then?"

"With the exception of the toxicology report, yes. There's a backlog on that testing, so we're probably looking at a few weeks before you receive the official report. But the preliminary results, from the bullet trajectory to the gunshot residue on her hand, all point to your sister's death being self-inflicted."

Lauren had thought she was prepared for this news, but the words still hit her like a doubled fist, especially after hearing the Troll King's gloating. "She might have pulled the trigger, Detective. I'll concede that, but I have solid reasons to believe that she was forced to do it. Which makes this a murder, as far as I'm concerned."

"Why don't you sit down?" the detective said in the patient, measured tones he undoubtedly reserved to calm hysterical relatives, "and I'll be happy to discuss your feelings."

She didn't move an inch, but remained standing as she looked up into the too-handsome face. "I was about to call when you showed up, about a disturbing phone call I had a few minutes ago on the room phone."

"Who called you?"

"I wish I knew, because whoever it was, I'm almost certain he's the one who was calling Rachel. The one who made her feel she had no choice, just like she said in her note."

What looked like real interest sparked in his dark eyes. Before he could frame a question, Lauren explained, "It's the second call I've gotten. Last night he reached my cell phone, even though I rarely give the number to anyone but clients. And now he's found me here, too, at the hotel. Trying to rattle me."

"So this anonymous caller, what did he say?" Jimenez's accent deepened, like the worry lining his forehead.

"The sickest stuff imaginable, in this digitized voice to make him sound like some kind of horror movie psycho."

"Please, sit down." Jimenez gestured toward the armchair. "You're looking very pale right now."

She perched on the seat's edge, mostly because it was easier than arguing with him. She must really look like hell, though, because the detective stepped into the bathroom and came back with a glass of water.

Accepting it with a nod of thanks, she choked down a swallow.

Jimenez turned around the desk chair and sat facing her. "Miss Miller—Lauren, if I may . . ." He waited for her nod before he continued. "I know this will be difficult, but I need the specifics if I'm to catch and stop this person."

She shook her head. "We both know you aren't going to catch this guy, let alone keep him from calling. He knows enough to block his number—or to spoof Rachel's like he did yesterday to freak me out."

"He spoofed her number, the same as with the text you received?"

Lauren's vision blurred with sudden moisture. "So Rachel really didn't send that message?"

"She definitely didn't, according to both her phone's logs and the cell phone company's records. That's one of the things I needed to tell you."

Lauren blinked away the tears, her emotions a jumble. As relieved as she was that she hadn't missed Rachel's attempt to reach out, her rage redoubled at the maniac who would torment her with such a message.

She felt hurt, too, that after everything the two of them had been through together, Rachel had never thought to call her, not even to say goodbye.

Lauren sniffled, and Jimenez left the room, only to return a moment later with some tissues for her.

"Thanks," she managed, wiping at her dripping nose.

Nodding, Jimenez returned to his seat. "What did this man say?"

Lauren's mouth went dry again, but she forced herself to go on. "He told me how Rachel suffered, how she gave up because I didn't visit. Because I didn't return the message she sent."

"Sick piece of *garbage*," the detective burst out, the last word sounding strange and harsh in his accented English. "I hate it when this happens, when tragedies bring out unbalanced bottom-feeders who get their kicks preying on the families of victims. I hate to say this, but it happens more often than you think. These people, they're like a cancer. They can't help but chew through whatever's good and decent in society."

"This isn't just some random psycho trolling for reactions. This guy knows things about me and how my sister . . ." She swallowed hard and forced herself to continue. "He described the scene where she—He gave specifics, horrific details. Things that only someone who'd been there would know."

"What specifics? Tell me."

She heard a thumping sound and looked down to see Dumpling wagging her tail against the chair leg, distress in her big brown eyes in reaction to her mistress's emotion. Lifting the dog into her lap, Lauren drew a deep breath. "He talked about her p-putting the gun in her mouth, about the—the pieces spraying onto the bathroom cabinets behind her."

"It could've been a guess. The presence of a handgun got out to the media. And in my experience, a lot of suicides tend to choose the bathroom, especially when the—um—when the manner of death chosen involves blood loss. Still," Jimenez said, his tone thoughtful, "I see your point about this caller. We have to consider the possibility he may have information not released to the public—or may have enough experience in law enforcement or emergency services to make that assumption."

"He has my name, my cell phone number," she said, convinced this was more than a random stalker, "and he knows where I'm staying. He knows details about my life, too, private information he seemed to get a lot of sick joy out of rubbing in my face. What if—what if this man was calling Rachel? If *he* was the one who gave her the gun?"

Jimenez shook his head. "I know you said your sister hated guns, but there's no question she purchased that one. When I went back to the scene yesterday, I was able to find a recent bill of sale from a local pawnshop. I followed up, spoke to the clerk at the shop she visited the afternoon before her death. He told me she didn't say much, but she did ask him to show her how to load it."

A wave of grief threatening to submerge her, Lauren wondered if things would have turned out differently if Texas had a waiting period for gun purchases. Or would Rachel have simply found another way to end a torment that she couldn't bear?

"What about you?" Jimenez frowned, his gaze laden with suggestion. "Do you have any enemies who might try to take advantage of this situation? Someone who knows you well. Say, for instance, an ex-husband?"

"You're thinking *Phillip* might've heard about my sister and made these calls to upset me?" Incredulous, she made a dismissive sound. "Believe me, no. He's selfish, not a psycho. Besides, he got exactly what he wanted months ago—rid of me, at no cost to his cheating self, except my share of the equity in our house, most of which I'd pulled out of my personal savings in the first place."

"Sorry to pry, but was that a substantial sum? Did he contest it at all?"

Lauren waved off the questions. "You're barking up the wrong tree. Considering the circumstances, I could've nailed him to the wall, gone after him for everything he's worth instead of only reclaiming some of what was mine."

"So why didn't you?"

She sighed, remembering how lost she'd felt, how empty, grieving both her father and the life she'd made in California. An elaborate illusion built of thin air and an even less substantial hope. "I just wanted the humiliation to be over, that's all, with no more fighting. And I didn't need his money to survive." *Or his love, apparently*, though she'd long ago realized she had never really had it in the first place.

"Anyone else you can think of, Lauren? A business rival, a client with a beef?"

She shook her head, knowing that there were those who would love to harm her—or *Litef00t*, anyway. But the kind of people she'd pissed off online didn't bother with harassing hackers; they would simply have her arrested or outright killed instead, providing they could ever catch her.

"It's not about me," she insisted. "Durant told me my sister was harassed, too."

"Durant, huh? But your sister never said anything about that to you?"

"Not a word," Lauren admitted.

Eyes narrowing, Jimenez asked, "Has he tried to reestablish contact since you've been over here? Or have you spotted him anywhere, even in passing?"

"You don't—you can't possibly think he was the one who's been calling me."

"As we discussed before, Durant was inadvertently given details about the case after he failed to disclose he was no longer with the bureau. And he was given that information only because his business card was found on the coffee table, beside your sister's cell phone."

"Are you trying to tell me Rachel talked to him that morning?" Lauren's pulse jumped at the thought of Brent failing to mention a conversation with her sister on the morning of her death.

But the detective shook his head. "The phone records show they had a couple of brief conversations about a week ago, but nothing since then. Nothing we can prove yet, anyway."

"What do you mean, 'nothing we can prove *yet*'? Are you trying to tell me you suspect he might have done something to my sister?"

"Not at all," Jimenez assured her, "but if I find out Durant was stirring her up about his crazy theories or stalking you with insane phone calls in order to trick us into investigating what's clearly a suicide as something else . . ."

"Listen, it couldn't have been Durant," she admitted, "not when he was standing right next to me last night, when I heard from this mystery caller."

"He was standing—so you *have* had contact with him."

"Never said I hadn't. And I'm telling you, this creep on the phone was someone else, someone seriously unbalanced. He was saying things about my sister, claiming he did sick things to her before she died. Sexual things." Lauren heard her own voice rising, squeezed tight by a rising tide of panic. *Tell me it was all a lie. Tell me that he never touched her.*

"Then he was lying to upset you," Jimenez assured her. "The preliminary report I saw noted no signs of sexual battery—or any intimate activity at all."

Eyes closing, Lauren bowed her head and blew out a breath she hadn't realized she'd been holding. "Thank God for that, at least."

Tail wagging, Dumpling tipped back her head and licked a single tear from Lauren's chin.

Detective Jimenez crossed the room and squeezed her shoulder. "I'll check with your cellular provider, see if I can track down your mystery caller. Meanwhile, you should block all private callers—"

"I've already done that. And I'm blocking every number he's spoofed, too."

Jimenez smiled. "Good move. Probably pissing him off, though."

"You really think I care if I make this guy mad?"

"No, but you should be aware that sometimes these guys take it personally when they're thwarted. Then they escalate."

He's already killed my sister, Lauren wanted desperately to say. *How do you escalate from there?* But she didn't say it out loud, didn't want to hear Jimenez return to his pat answer about some garden-variety sicko who got off on calling the families of the dead.

Jimenez nodded his approval. "Good. Then you'll need to get clear of this hotel as soon as possible."

Nodding, she said, "It makes sense for me to stay at her apartment while I work on packing things up."

His dark eyes captured her gaze. "Are you sure you want to do that, Lauren?"

"I don't want to do any of this. Who would?"

He frowned, that pondering look drifted through the inky depths of his eyes. "I have some time coming, personal time, I mean. I could take the day off, help you with any arrangements, take you over to get boxes, even help you sort through things if you'd like."

"Why, Detective? Why would you want to do something like this on your day off? Don't you spend enough time on the job surrounded by death?"

He pressed his lips together, considering for a moment before answering. "It's Cruz, please, Lauren. And maybe I still feel lousy about exposing you to Durant and his nonsense. Or maybe I just think you could use a friend."

So he felt sorry for her, did he? The poor, deluded family member getting phone calls from a random nut job. But something beyond sympathy swam in the depths of his handsome gaze, something that nudged a suspicion that he wanted to do more than simply protect and serve.

Her guess was that, more than anything, he was out to catch his old friend Durant "happening by" again to see her. Out to conduct an intervention—or lock Brent in a cage.

The question was, would she be better off hunting the Troll King without the renegade agent—better off freed of an attraction that could shatter what was left of her heart? Or in accepting Cruz Jimenez's help, was she simply trading one danger for another, for a man who might arrest not only Durant, but also throw her in jail while he was at it . . .

Because whatever laws stood between her and the bastard known as the Troll King, she damned well meant to shatter every one.

***

The moment the memorial website appeared in his search alerts, a slow, cruel smile pulled at the hacker's face. As he clicked the link, he laughed, thinking how little Rachel, the "sweet angel" her sister had described, resembled the tramp whose carelessness and impatience had killed a decent woman, thinking how the bitch had damned well earned the death that he had plotted.

But the photos made him miss Rachel, too, for she had been his favorite in a long time, more spirited than any of the others he had . . . *massaged* into the deaths he'd dreamed. A fighter to the last, she'd instead done the last thing he'd expected: gone into a pawnshop and picked up a handgun for her protection. As if she'd sensed how close he really was to her, how tempted he had been to break into her apartment late one night and act out his less-than-lethal fantasies in person before he finished with her.

Defiant as she'd proven, he'd been nearly certain she was the one worthy of taking his game to the next level, so sure that he'd been stunned when she had instead broken, turning on herself with a sudden violence he hadn't quite seen coming—or planned so meticulously, either. Furious that she'd deprived him not only of the real-time sexual adventure he'd envisioned but of the exquisitely choreographed ending he'd devised especially for her, he'd lashed out at her sister instead.

Describing to Lauren Miller the things he'd meant to do to Rachel before her death, though, had only left him more frustrated. He'd felt a slight rush to discover that the sister had a streak of Rachel's spirit—a toughness he would enjoy breaking, but the fact was she wasn't his type.

Or so he'd thought at first, when he'd had only a few photos from Rachel's hacked cloud storage photo vault to go on. But now that he'd seen what Lauren *really* looked like, how stunning she was with that flaxen hair and those heartbreaking blue-green eyes, he reached for himself reflexively, his jaded eyes closing as he dreamed of her playing her sister's part in the most gruesomely creative death he'd ever devised . . .

A death that would bring the medieval torturers he so admired rising from their dark and distant graves to applaud his work of genius, clapping as the bones of their long-dead hands slowly crumbled into dust.

CHAPTER TWELVE

Sitting in his car in the crowded parking lot of the apartment complex where Rachel Miller had once lived, Brent swore in frustration. Four-forty in the afternoon, and he remained cut off, unable to get near Lauren as Detective Cruz Jimenez stuck to her like glue throughout the day. And not only in his official capacity, Brent noticed as he took in the jeans and running shoes, the casual, rolled-sleeve shirt that Jimenez had at some point changed into—maybe after Brent had tailed them to the funeral home, where the detective had driven her so she could tend to the funeral arrangements.

Brent had left them for a while then, figuring that surely Lauren would soon send Jimenez packing. But after checking the lot and finding Jimenez's Explorer missing, Brent's knock at the apartment door had gone unanswered, as had the one text message he'd dared to send to Lauren's phone.

With no better choice, he'd settled in to wait a while, hoping that eventually Lauren would come back here rather than checking in to yet another hotel. But if she'd wanted to remain in a room, why not just lengthen her stay at the Omni, that is unless Jimenez was trying to help her ditch him again?

Unfortunately, when Lauren did return, she was walking beside the detective, her face pale, her eyes tired, and the pale sweep of her hair pulled back in a simple ponytail. Yet she still managed to smile at something the detective said as he carried a stack of flattened moving boxes. Beside her, the leashed dachshund wagged her whip-thin tail as if she quite approved of the proceedings.

"See if you get any more pizza crust from me, you little traitor," Brent grumbled, frustrated at the complication of his old friend's presence. A complication that could end up getting him detained for questioning or worse if he were caught here.

Still, Brent lingered, hoping that Jimenez finally would go home to his wife—and take his male-model good looks with him. But the detective didn't come back down, not in five or fifteen or even fifty minutes.

As time crept forward, Durant's knuckles ached from his death grip on the wheel. He tried to tell himself Jimenez was only being a decent guy, giving Lauren rides around an unfamiliar city. Surely, a standout police detective—a married man—wasn't spending his off time hitting on the sister of a suicide he was investigating. Wouldn't be attempting to take advantage of her.

Still, Brent thought of last night's salesman and how vulnerable a grieving woman could be to seduction, especially by a man who looked as if he'd talked his share of females into abandoning their better judgment. Eyes narrowing, Brent felt the burn of resentment low in his gut, and his mouth filled with an emotion as thick and coppery as blood.

It wasn't jealousy, he told himself as he climbed out of the car and stalked in the direction of the staircase. He had sacrificed his home, his career, maybe even his *grip* in the hunt for the Troll King, and he wasn't about to lose Lauren's cooperation to some local cop who wouldn't see the full picture if Brent framed it and nailed it to his freaking forehead.

Far worse, though, than the thought of losing Lauren to the detective was the idea of leaving her vulnerable to any more of the Troll King's torments. Of losing her the same horrific way he'd lost her sister.

I shouldn't have wasted time trying to confirm what was happening to Rachel and gain her willing cooperation. Should've taken her from here instead, kidnapped her if I'd had to, tossed that frigging cell phone, and gotten her miles away from here.

As insane as the thought was, the Troll King had made Brent a desperate man. Unstable enough that before he knew what he was doing, he headed straight for the apartment.

He had nearly reached the staircase when his better judgment caught up with him. For all he knew, Jimenez was here not to seduce Lauren but here in the hopes of finding and locking up the man who had impersonated a federal agent and abducted her from Bright's Prairie. Even if he weren't out to arrest Brent, charging upstairs like a maniac wouldn't do a whole lot to convince the detective that his old friend was not a danger to the public.

As he debated his next move, one of the two doors sharing the landing above him opened. Brent stepped off the sidewalk and behind the shelter of a bushy evergreen with the goal of avoiding the detective as, with any luck, he left alone.

"Are you sure, Lauren?" Jimenez asked, his voice echoing off the landing's concrete and carrying well enough for Brent to make out every word. "I'd be more than happy to stay a while. We could get started with that packing or at least get things organized for when you're ready to—"

"Thanks," she cut in quickly, "but the people from the car rental place should be here to deliver my ride any minute. And after that I'm—um—Nikki Watson wants to come meet with me about the services. She's known Rachel since their freshman year at UT, so I can't exactly leave her out of things."

Brent smiled to himself, recognizing a blow-off when he heard one. But Jimenez didn't seem to take the hint.

"When I spoke with her," he said, "she seemed really broken up about your sister. Sounded like the two of them were pretty close."

"Rachel had a lot of friends. Everybody loved her—the people who knew her, anyway," said Lauren. "They all supported her after the accident and when that ridiculous 'Blonde on Blonde' crap started."

"Except, the thing is—" Jimenez began before deliberately cutting himself off. "Oh, never mind. It's not important."

"Except what?" Lauren was quick to ask, and Brent grimaced to hear her take the bait. "Please don't leave me hanging."

"*Except*, I was going to say," Jimenez told her, "Nikki and the others, the ones who knew her well and worked closely with her at her job, didn't seem nearly as shocked as you were about the idea that Rachel might have ended things."

"What are you saying?"

"Rachel's friends knew she'd been struggling lately, morbidly focused on the way Megan Rutherford drowned, tangled in her seatbelt while Rachel had fought to get her out of the car. They claimed they did what they could to distract her, but nothing seemed to work. Lately, they'd been talking among themselves, trying to figure out what to do before she—"

"You mean to tell me that they *knew* my sister was suicidal? Knew it and said *nothing*? Why wouldn't they reach out to me? Or someone, anyway."

"Before she got any worse, I was going to say. At the time, none of them thought she'd actually harm herself, but looking back, they've realized there were warnings, comments she made to one or another of them that didn't seem so bad until they put them all together after her death. Nikki was worried, but Rachel told her she'd been to a doctor and gotten medication. Nikki thought that was a good sign, that Rachel was dealing with her issues with the help of a professional."

"I—I never knew. I never—I was so wrapped up in putting my own life back together. In getting past the divorce. I thought it was the worst thing that could ever happen. How stupid could a person get? How blind and self-centered?"

Hearing Lauren's grief, the regret and the self-loathing that swamped her, made Brent ache to step out from his half-assed hiding place, take the stairs two at a time, and hold her tight while he told her what a fool her ex had been.

"Lauren . . ." The detective's subtle accent made her name sound almost musical. "I've been through a divorce myself, just last year, and it's like—it feels like someone's blown a hole in you with a shotgun. It's impossible to pay attention to anybody else's issue when every glass of water you drink comes gushing out your side."

Lauren said something in response, speaking too quietly for Brent to make out, but he heard Jimenez loud and clear when he told her, "You don't have to do this all alone . . ."

You son of a bitch, Brent thought, wondering if Jimenez was gaming her with all this crap about his marital status and his offers to help in order to get her to cough up what she knew about Brent. Or was Jimenez really so hard up that he would jeopardize his reputation in the cop shop, maybe even his job, moving in on the bereaved sister of a woman whose death he was investigating.

But Lauren, apparently, had heard enough. "That's what people always say when they don't know me," she said, "like being alone's some kind of hardship instead of what I need right now. Time to process, time to grieve, time to make all the decisions that I need to."

Though her voice was cool and smooth as window glass, Brent heard the fragility beneath the surface. Sensed the small cracks threatening to shatter her hard-won composure.

"Do you really think it's the best thing for you to stay here? In the same place where your sister—"

"If I change my mind, you'll be the first to know."

"All right," Jimenez said gently, in spite of her abruptness, "but call me—especially if you hear from that lunatic again. Because if there's anything that I can do to put human scum like that in prison, it'll be my pleasure. Trust me."

Brent bit back a curse, now certain that his former friend was working to turn Lauren against him. And maybe even get laid in the process.

"Oh, believe me, I'll let you know if I hear from him again," she assured him. "And thanks for everything, Cruz."

Cruz . . . Brent's gut churned to hear her call Jimenez by his first name. Moments later, Brent stepped back behind the shrub as footsteps warned that his old friend was heading back downstairs. Tempted as he was to confront the detective, Brent remained hidden, considering his next move, until Jimenez started up his dark-gray Explorer and pulled out of the lot. Before Brent had taken two steps, Lauren called down from the balcony, "Okay, Durant. You can come on up now."

Brent froze, wondering how the hell she could've possibly known that he was here.

She leaned over the railing. "Don't think you're going to fake me out. Dumpling keeps whining and wagging her tail in your direction. And the detective's back might have been to it, but I can see you plain as day in the reflection from that window across the sidewalk."

Brent moved to the bottom of the stairs, where he scowled up at her. "You sure you don't want me to take off? Or are you trying to keep me long enough to call back your new friend, *Cruz*, and let him know 'that lunatic' is back?"

With an exasperated sigh, she waved him up. "Come on up here, you big idiot. I've got stuff you need to hear if we're still going to work together."

Shaking off his hesitation, he headed up the stairs, where the dog greeted him with a happy little woof when she set eyes on him. Even though she'd ratted him out, Brent reached down and scratched the little sausage, who lost interest the moment she determined that he had no food in hand. What a mercenary.

"So that stuff you and Jimenez were plotting, about putting me in prison—"

"This might come as a surprise," she told him, "but not everything revolves around you. And I don't rat out my partners. Ever."

He let that sink in for a moment before changing the subject. "So we're really still partners? After last night, I wasn't so sure."

Looking into his eyes, she narrowed her eyes as if she were seriously considering telling him to take a hike. Instead, she sighed and told him, "You might be infuriating, but you've still spent the past two years eating, sleeping, and dreaming about how to hunt down the Troll King. And you know more about his habits than I'll ever be able to uncover working on my own. So, yeah. We're good. Except for one thing, Durant."

"What's that?"

"This 'relationship' we've got going." She made air quotes with her fingers. "It's strictly business, that's all. And it ends the day the Troll King does."

"That's probably a good idea," Brent said, as if her words weren't boring a hole straight through his chest wall. Even though he knew she was right, though he'd told himself the same thing. Told himself that, for him, he had no future beyond stopping the man he meant to kill.

"It's more than a good idea." Lauren's beautiful gaze drilled straight through what was left of his defenses. "It's non-negotiable. So are we on the same page?"

He hesitated for a moment before jerking a nod. A nod that filled him with oily, black regret as he agreed, "Same page."

"You want to come in?" she asked. "Or are we going to stand out on the porch all day?"

"I'm coming." He figured if Lauren could stand going into the apartment where her own sister had been driven to take her life, there was no reason for him to be balking. Yet despite the fact he'd entered many crime scenes in his career in law enforcement, he hesitated in the doorway, halted by the memory of the evening he'd pounded on this very door, the evening Rachel had called through it, *Leave. I don't want to talk to you*, until her neighbor, a bearded, middle-aged guy, came out and threatened to call the police.

Lauren watched Brent carefully, an unreadable emotion crossing her pale features. "You've been here before, haven't you?"

He shook his head. "Not inside it, no. The day after I met her at the coffee shop, I decided to take another crack at getting her to talk. I knocked, but she insisted I leave. So I just left another of my cards here; I stuck it in the door to replace the one she ripped to pieces at the café."

"She must have taken the new card inside, at least," said Lauren. "Jimenez said they found it on the coffee table by her phone. If only she had called the number, reached out for help instead of . . ."

Frustrated, Brent bumped the back of his fisted hand against the doorframe. "I should have come back, fought harder to save her."

Sadness dimmed the light in Lauren's eyes as she turned away to walk inside.

As Brent followed her into a freshly vacuumed space that smelled of cleaning products, he noticed that an oscillating fan had been set up in the living room, and he heard exhaust vents blowing in both the kitchen and the bathroom. Otherwise, the apartment looked clean and comfortable, with a living area dominated by potted trees, a flat screen TV, and a big, ivory microfiber sofa with a flock of colorful pillows of different shapes, sizes, and textures. The coffee table held a few magazines and a tattered paperback romance, which someone—presumably Rachel—had left facedown and open, as if she'd meant to come right back and continue reading its yellowed pages.

He'd be willing to bet it was one she'd read many times before, like the "comfort reads" Brent's wife went back to whenever she was stressed. Before Adam's death and the Troll King's secret harassment had pushed her beyond the point where she could focus on the written word.

Looking away, he swallowed back the lump forming in his throat.

"I'm not sure anybody would've been able to get through to her," Lauren told him, "not even me, while the devil had her in his grip."

"The Troll King, you mean?"

She nodded and sank down to the sofa, grabbing a sunflower-yellow pillow and squashing it in her arms. "He took another ugly swipe at me bright and early this morning. Over the hotel phone."

Brent swore under his breath and sat on the other end of the couch to keep her at eye level. "He found you at the hotel? How?"

"I'm not sure. It could be something as simple as him staking out the medical examiner's office, following me from there after I left." Shuddering, she hugged the pillow tighter. "For all I know, I could've met him last night . . . down in the hotel bar."

Brent's heart spasmed. "You don't mean to tell me that guy I saw, that asshole hitting on you—was—"

"Aha!" She slung the pillow at him. "I *knew* that was you, spying on me last night."

Feeling the heat of her accusation creeping up from his collar, he caught the pillow and laid it between them. "It's called protective surveillance, not *spying*. I was watching out for you. But I figured you might take it wrong, act like I was some kind of jealous stalker."

She sliced him with a look that should have drawn blood. "Jealous? Why should you be jealous? It's not like you couldn't have had what he was after. Like you didn't walk away from it. From me."

"C'mon, Lauren. Let's not argue over this. Not now. So was it him in the bar, do you think?" Stricken by a new fear, he felt his blood freeze. "You didn't—tell me you didn't take him upstairs."

She huffed out a dismissive sound. "Are you seriously asking me that?"

He met her gaze and held it. "I've never been more fucking serious in my life. If this was really the Troll King . . ."

She shook her head, insisting, "This wasn't our guy, just some sales rep far from home and looking for a little action."

"The Troll King's smart enough to have escaped detection for at least two years that we know of. And more than twisted enough to use it against you if you took him upstairs with you."

Her already-pale face blanched, her eyes avoiding his. And Brent was hit with a wave of pure physical revulsion imagining that the abomination he'd be hunting, the monster who had coldly and methodically dismantled the psyche of woman after woman, had put his filthy hands on Lauren. Had touched the places Brent had caressed, and those he still wanted so badly, that the memory sliced straight through him.

"Trust's never been easy for me, Brent, hasn't since the other kids made my life hell back in school—the ones who'd have anything to do with me at all, that is." Lauren confessed, an admission that seemed to come out of left field. "My husband turned out to be a cheater, a player who wouldn't let a little thing like a wedding ring get in his way. Whatever capacity I had to ever take a man's words at face value, Phillip Bell Worth the Third gouged it out of me and stomped it to death."

"Everybody knows you can't trust a man with that many names. But that's no reason to—"

"This guy last night," she said, "Jack Steelman, or whatever his name really was, was just another cheater, looking to break his vows. You think I'd do that to another woman? You really think I'd do it to myself?"

Brent felt himself unclench inside, felt himself breathe again. When he could once more think straight, he asked, "So how did he react?"

She shrugged. "Called me a bitch and let me go. Which makes him a jerk but not a homicidal stalker. Doesn't it?"

Brent nodded grimly, realizing she was more than likely right. He still figured the Troll King for a socially maladjusted misfit, a description that probably fit Lauren herself better than a run-of-the-mill salesman. "So let's assume it wasn't him. Is there any other way the Troll King could've tracked you? Electronically, I mean, since that seems to be his MO."

She shrugged. "I suppose it's possible he's found some way to deliver a virus to my smartphone and track my GPS. Something like a—oh, my—I'm an *idiot*."

"What?"

She bowed her head, groaning as she kneaded at her forehead. "That stupid app. A few days before she—before Rachel died, she e-mailed me the link to download it so we could privately message each other without paying an added fee for texting. Only it never really worked, so I deleted it from my phone. And I never got the chance to ask her about it."

Shaking her head, Lauren looked up, her face flushed with chagrin. "Of all the people in the world, I should have known better. I'm always so careful with my laptop and the servers, but like a lot of people, I take my phone for granted, forget that it's as vulnerable as any other computer."

"So you figure the original e-mail was really from him, and the app you downloaded was a Trojan with a viral payload?"

She nodded and pulled the phone out of her pocket. "These kinds of things have made their way into the various app stores in the past. Some have even slipped past the big boys, which is like the achieving the holy grail for malicious code creators."

When she started messing with her phone, Brent said, "Don't send that virus into oblivion quite yet, Lauren."

Hand freezing, she looked up at him. "Why on earth not? Otherwise, he could track me down here, too."

"You and I both know he probably has already. He's probably got his program automatically logging and recording all the coordinates you visit."

"You're right," she admitted, "which means that I'm not safe here, especially not since I launched the memorial site with my new photo."

"You have it up already?"

"Uploaded it late last night," she said, "and posted links on Rachel's Facebook profile, though I hate exposing her friends to what's coming."

"Have you checked it yet for comments?"

She shook her head. "Not since hiding in the bathroom with my phone first thing this morning. I didn't want Jimenez to know about it. Didn't trust him not to try to make me take it down, because of the calls I've been getting."

"So you did tell him about those?"

"Of course, I did. He stopped by to check on me right after the troll called and woke me up this morning, spewing these horrible, perverted things he'd done to Rachel. Jimenez confirmed that they were lies, thank God, or fantasies, most likely. But I can tell you, I was really shaken up."

"No wonder. So does the detective buy my story now?"

She shook her head. "He's still clinging to the idea this guy's some random ghoul, one of those sickos who harasses families of the dead. Although Cruz *did* suggest it could've been you, out to prove your whack job theory."

"*Whack job*?" Brent gritted his teeth.

"I don't think he used that term exactly," she admitted, "but that was definitely the gist."

She cocked her head, looking at him oddly. "I didn't hurt your feelings, did I, calling you a whack job?"

Taken by surprise at her concern, he laughed. "Believe me, I've been called worse, especially lately."

Her serious expression remained firmly in place. "But that doesn't make you crazy, even if you have been acting that way lately."

He snorted. "Thanks. I think." But he was gratified to hear that she'd seen past behavior that even he had to admit must seem bizarre or frightening. That she understood his reasons, and didn't judge him for it.

"It's understandable," she said, "considering what you're facing. Who *we're* facing, together."

He grasped her hand, which had been resting on the pillow he had placed between them. "I'm not going to let you down, Lauren. Not going to let him get you."

Tensing, she looked down at their linked hands and shook her head at the sight. "This doesn't feel like 'professional,'" she warned as his callused fingers bumped across her knuckles. "Doesn't feel like 'non-negotiable,' either."

"Then how about we renegotiate?" he asked as he pulled her closer, studying her widened eyes as her pulse thrummed in his grasp. "Because I'm pretty sure I'm about to make another of my trademark whack job moves."

***

Lauren tensed, ready to order Brent out of the apartment. Didn't he understand how it was hard enough to be here, to feel Rachel's presence pushing in on her from all sides and bear the weight of what her sister had done and what had been done to her? Couldn't Durant see how she struggled each time she passed some trinket she had given Rachel as a gift or glimpsed the framed photo on the countertop that separated the living room and kitchen, a shot of her with her younger sister from last spring?

Lauren's throat tightened, her eyes burning as the vision swam before her, the image of them wading through a swath of spring bluebonnets with their arms linked. Rachel had been smiling, her face turned toward the camera, toward her boyfriend of the moment, who'd taken the shot. Lauren, on the other hand, had been gazing off into the distance, unsmiling but at peace as a sun-warmed breeze made streamers of her light-brown hair.

At peace as she would never be again, she knew. For even if she and Brent should be successful, if they should find the Troll King and stop him, what would that do to restore what had been shattered? What would it accomplish in terms of bringing Rachel, Carrie, and the others back?

She studied Brent's brown eyes, her heart brimming with a pain so deep, she couldn't get the words out. But when he reached for her, encircling her with his strong arms, she felt her breathing deepen. Felt the tension drain away as she laid her head against his shoulder, as she allowed herself, maybe for the first time ever, to lean into, to accept, the solid strength of a man. And not just any man but one crossing the same dark chasm she was facing. He might not have made it yet, might still be swallowed by its depths before he found a way to bridge it, but somehow, maybe they could help each other.

Holding her, he rubbed her back, a soothing, age-old rhythm that had her drifting back to that sunlit field, to the music of her sister's laughter as it competed with spring birdsong. And a tear slipped free as Lauren acknowledged a slice of joy that would never come again. A joy she hadn't even recognized back inside that golden hour.

They sat like that for several minutes, the only sound that of Dumpling's toenails scratching at Brent's pant leg in a bid for attention. Long after the dog gave up and waddled off to lie down, Brent gently pressed his lips to Lauren's temple and whispered, "So far, how are the negotiations going?"

Lauren turned her head in answer, and their mouths met softly, tentatively, a gentle, questing dialogue far more subdued than last night's violent storm.

Pulling back a few inches, he whispered, "I was afraid Jimenez had talked you out of coming near me. Or that I'd lost you myself, when I walked out last night."

"Jimenez thinks you're dangerous," she said, "to yourself as well as others."

As Brent cupped her jaw with his hand, it came to her, with an electric thrill of fear zinging through her nervous system, how close his splayed fingers were to her throat. And how quickly, how irreversibly, a man pushed beyond his endurance might snap. Even a man as decent and honorable as this one.

Even a man whose serious gaze and gentle touch, whose devotion to finding justice for his wife and others like her, tempted Lauren to give trust another shot.

"You'd be wise to listen to Cruz," Brent admitted, his deep voice as troubled as his eyes. "He's probably right about me."

"I have to admit, I'm still on the fence about you," she admitted, reaching up to stroke his hair, to feel the slightly coarser scattering of white, a silvering that lent him a gravity and maturity that made men like her ex-husband and Jack Steelman look like selfish, shallow children.

"So what can I do," he rumbled, his gaze hot enough to burn away her willpower, "to push you over the edge?"

Afterward, Lauren would never remember the moment when she tipped, when a combination of her need and his voice, of their mutual goal and their mutual attraction, pushed her into his arms. All that mattered was the press of his lips against her own, the smooth dance of their tongues, and the glide of her hands over the hard planes of his body. His touch thrust her into a world of pure sensation, a world where it no longer mattered where she was and what the two of them were facing. In the back of her mind, she remembered his warning from last night, about how it could never last, how they would only have until Brent captured and destroyed the man whom they sought. But instead of scaring her off, the impermanence of their actions made her explorations even bolder, made her arch her back and help him pull her shirt off, allowing him to reach behind her and unhook her bra with one deft motion.

Where his hands went, his mouth soon followed, driving every other thought from her mind.

As she tipped back her head, pleasure winding tight inside her, she was dimly aware of a rapping sound, followed by Dumpling's barking.

When the knocking continued, Brent swore quietly, and Lauren wanted to sob with frustration.

Instead, she sighed and glanced over at the closed blinds before whispering, "That's probably the rental agent here with my car."

"Nikki?"

Lauren shook her head. "I only told Jimenez she was coming to get him out of here. She's offered to help me several times, but I can't deal with the way she tries to take over."

"We'll go pick the car up later," he promised, in a voice drugged with need. "Until then, I'll take you wherever you want to go. Take you as far as you can stand."

When he kissed her, Lauren forgot about the car, forgot all the reasons she should want her independence. The knocking faded from her consciousness, then vanished altogether as Brent removed his own shirt to reveal a chest that might've been chiseled out of fantasy.

She peeled off the rest of her things, watching him do the same. And marveling at the strength and masculinity of his body, a body that took her breath away . . . especially when her gaze strayed lower. When the length and thickness of his hard shaft made her ache to touch it.

When she did touch him, he groaned like a man in pain, reminding her of how long he'd told her it had been for him, how long since he had made love with the wife he'd lost.

So she caressed him carefully, settling on him a flurry of touches gentle as the wings of butterflies. But when she slid down to her knees, meaning to please him with her mouth, he grasped her wrist. "Not that. Not now. I've been dreaming of this since I met you and . . . I want to make it last. I want to make it perfect for you."

After insisting they switch places, Brent kissed his way down to her navel, teasing with hot licks before driving her into a frenzy of need when he zeroed in on her very center. After that, coherent thought deserted Lauren as he took her over the edge again and again with his clever mouth and fingers. She cried out her pleasure, the world around her splintering into a kaleidoscope of color.

Finally, he pulled a condom from his wallet and then sheathed himself. Then he kissed her again, teased and touched her until every atom of her wound deliciously tight with anticipation. His breathing fast and hard, he darted his tongue into the shell of her ear, eliciting her whimpers. "Please, I need you inside me. Need you, Brent, right now."

Parting her legs with a knee, he filled her emptiness in one swift motion, and they rocked together, finding a rhythm that knit light from both their strands of darkness. A rhythm that pushed them beyond their grief, their worry, spiraling them ever higher . . .

And lifting them to heights so dangerous, so lofty, that neither noticed the soft "whoosh" tone as Lauren's cell phone, still lying on the coffee table, e-mailed a recording to a waiting listener.

CHAPTER THIRTEEN

They slept spooned on the sofa, neither suggesting a move to what had been Rachel's bedroom. Brent woke disoriented hours later, his neck aching as he turned toward the chiming trill of an electronic alert. But the unfamiliar sound ceased, so he ignored it, allowing his blurred awareness of the woman in his arms to convince him he'd slipped into another dream of Carrie.

The curves he felt were fuller than he remembered, the feminine sound of her breathing so relaxed that he imagined he'd gone farther back this time, to the memory of the days before grief had left his wife emaciated, and far too wired to rest easily. Far too broken to accept his touch, let alone to make love.

To make love . . .

He jerked awake, heart racing, and his nostrils filled with a clean, light scent different from the woman he had loved and pitied and sometimes, on the worst days, even hated. The scent of Lauren and not Carrie.

What the hell have you done?

But as much as making love to Lauren would complicate things between them, Brent couldn't bring himself to regret it. Not with the slow pulse of her heart quieting the gnawing sense of doom, the certainty of having failed so badly that had been dogging him for two years. More than that, he realized, for it had been two and a half since he'd frowned down at his ringing phone, annoyed that Carrie would interrupt an important meeting with a potential informant, a cartel middleman who'd been paranoid as hell—and for good reason considering the grisly example his organization had made of the last man who'd broken faith by talking to a Fed.

Brent's first impulse had been to let his wife's call go to voice mail, where she could, depending on today's mood, either babble excitedly about the latest breakthrough in fertility treatments—no matter how expensive or unproven—or weep with envy, raw and ugly, because a friend had "callously" announced she was pregnant or didn't "properly appreciate" the children she'd been blessed with. The truth was, after eight years, Carrie's need for a child of her own had mushroomed into an envy-soaked obsession. A fixation that made every day emotional roulette and sex a joyless chore.

Though he would have loved a biological kid of his own, Brent had repeatedly assured his wife that she would always be enough for him and that any time she wanted to talk about adoption, he would throw everything he had into supporting her decision. But his attempts to ease her mind had only made her tearfully accuse him of "giving up on her." And when he'd suggested she consider going back to teaching—she'd quit, believing that the stress of her job might be what was keeping her from conceiving—in order to take her mind off the issue, she'd come completely unglued over the "pure torture" of facing another classroom of beautiful kindergarteners when she might never have one of her own.

By the afternoon of that fateful phone call, he'd begun to fantasize about a different life, one on his own, without the constant strain, the ovulation calendars, the emotional and financial fallout every time she begged to try "just one more round" of in vitro. With Carrie flatly refusing to go with him for counseling, he'd gone so far as to discreetly ask one of his fellow agents, who'd recently divorced, for the name of his attorney. Though Brent hadn't yet gotten up the nerve to call the guy, he'd felt so damned guilty over the phone number in his pocket that he'd impulsively told his potential informant, "Sorry, man. I have to take this," and then got up to accept the call.

And listened to the soul-wrenching sounds of his wife screaming Adam's name, cries whose echoes would haunt him as long as he lived. Cries that marked the beginning of the end of everything.

"Hey," Lauren murmured, shifting beneath the light throw she'd used to cover both of them. "Something wrong? You're all tense."

"Cramp in my back. That's all," he told her, pushing himself to the sofa's edge and swinging his bare feet to the floor.

Using the throw to cover her breasts, she sat up as well. "You aren't regretting—?"

"Hell, no." He wrapped an arm around her. "Not for a second, Lauren. What about you?"

She snorted. "Did I *sound* like a regretful woman? Back when you were—when we were—"

"You most certainly did not," he said, smiling at the shyness choking down her words.

"And it was okay for you, too? I was, I mean?"

His lips found her cheekbone, kissed it. "*Okay* isn't the word I'd go with." He realized it wasn't simply shyness, but insecurity he'd heard. Which made him want to hunt down and punch her dick of an ex-husband. "Being with you was amazing. *You're* amazing, Lauren. Generous and sweet and smart, not to mention sexy as hell."

"Gotta be the hair," she murmured, trying to make it sound like a joke.

Knowing better, he pulled her close to him. "I won't lie to you. You make one knockout of a blonde, but as far as I'm concerned, the natural look is even hotter. Besides, with what you've got—looks are only the icing. Don't ever let what your idiot of an ex-husband did convince you otherwise."

Leaning against his chest, she let a sigh slip free. "It's not just him, Brent. It's—I keep hearing the Troll King's voice on the phone. The things he said to me, the way he zeroed in on every weakness."

"What weakness? Because, I swear to you, you're one of the strongest women I have ever known, one of the bravest and the smartest."

"But he knows things about me." Anxiety pinched at her voice and tightened the skin around her eyes. "Details about my marriage. Private things I never shared with anyone but Rachel. And even though I totally know better, know he's just using details he jacked from my sister's phone or laptop, he knows exactly how to burrow into my brain."

Brent took her by the shoulders, turning her to face him and staring into her face in the dim light sifting through closed blinds. "I'm not letting this happen, Lauren, not to anybody else again—and especially not to you."

She shook her head. "Don't worry, Brent. This isn't my first time around the block with trolls. And I can promise you, on my sister's memory, this monster's day is coming. I'm going to find him for you. And for everyone he's hurt."

He pushed her hair behind her ear, loving the cool sleekness of the strands beneath his palm. "What's he saying to you, Lauren? Because I can tell it's eating at you—"

She shook her head. "It's not important."

"It's critically important. Because once you let his words get inside, once you wall yourself off like Rachel and Carrie and the others, you'll be lost. And I swear to you, I'll die before I let that happen."

A frozen silence stretched between them, the thinnest layer of ice over deeper waters. In their murky depths, he read the conflict, her natural reticence warring with the sense of what he'd said.

"I'm not like Rachel," she swore, heat flaring to life as she pulled away from him, "not like any of them. I understand exactly what this jerk is doing, how he's just taken trolling to another level. For sick kicks, I imagine. The tragedies he's attacking don't matter in the least. They're nothing to him but a lever, a way to pry his victims from their sanity. "

"If the details don't matter, then you can tell me, Lauren, tell me everything. Bringing secrets out into the light will rob them of their power and help me keep you safe."

"I can keep myself safe," she insisted, "at least I can if you give me back my gun." She reached forward, grabbing for her clothing.

He shook his head. "I don't want you armed right now, not with the grief so fresh. And definitely not with the Troll King playing with your head."

She slipped into her bra and hooked it before poking her head through the neck of her top. "Coming from you, that's rich," she scoffed. "If it hadn't been for Google, I still wouldn't know what really happened with your wife."

He froze, heart thundering, not only at her words, but the flat bluntness of the way they'd come out. Maybe it was just her way of regaining distance, the kind of defense mechanism she used to push everyone away. But whatever her reasoning might be, it pissed him off. "What the hell? You looked it up? Read all those lies, the accusations those bottom feeders posted on the forums?"

"What did you expect me to do?" She threw a hand up to underscore the question. "Take everything you said at face value? Some stranger who abducted me at gunpoint?"

"I thought we'd gotten past that," he said, grinding his teeth as she turned from him to slip back into a pair of bikini panties. "Way past it."

"Look, I was upset, upset with you for leaving me there at the hotel. It made me question myself, wonder if I was thinking halfway straight about you. And along with everything else, I had Jimenez's warnings running around in my head. So, yeah, I checked out your story, checked out what would motivate you to throw away your career, maybe even your freedom."

On one level, Brent understood, but after what they'd just shared, her snooping still smacked of betrayal. As did the thought of a tragedy that made him want to put his fist through a wall whenever he allowed himself to think about it. "So now you know about—about Adam. Or at least you think you do."

His guts churned as he spoke the name for the first time in more than two years. The name of a little boy he couldn't have loved more if he had been Brent's own. It hadn't started that way, hadn't started out as anything but Carrie's doing a favor for a neighbor, a harried young mother whose husband's job involved a great deal of travel. With finances tight, Annabel had needed to return to nursing, but her long evening shifts and irregular hours had made finding decent childcare a nightmare.

Soon, Brent had found himself spending a lot of time with the rambunctious three-year-old. At first, he'd been none too thrilled by the disruption of his after-work routine, but it didn't take long for him to fall into the habit of burning off some steam by wrestling with the little guy in the backyard, tossing a squishy ball for him to catch, or watching him splash around in a kiddie pool Brent had picked up, their "guy time," giving Carrie a chance to put together dinner uninterrupted. But story time quickly became the high point of Brent's day; it was when he would use a bunch of goofy voices to act out each book's parts, often with the aid of the stuffed animal "friends" Adam brought over in his little backpack.

During those few months, Brent had gone from indulging, or maybe tolerating was the right word, Carrie's desire to be a parent to really getting it—and seriously looking forward to the day he could claim the role for real.

But apparently, some people weren't cut out to be parents. Didn't deserve to be entrusted with a helpless child's life.

Not him, that was for damned sure, and after Adam's death, Carrie must have felt the same, for she'd quit going to the fertility clinic. Quit mentioning the idea of a baby, which had for so long been her favorite topic of conversation. Quit speaking of any future at all as she struggled to survive an unendurable present.

Lauren touched his hand. "I'm sorry for what your poor wife must have gone through. What it must've cost you."

"You have no fucking idea." He could still hear his wife's sobs as he'd tried to protect her from Annabel's grief-spawned breakdown and her husband's towering rage. As he tried to explain that it had all been his fault, really.

Splotches of color came to Lauren's cheeks, as if she had been slapped. "You know what? I'm burying my sister tomorrow afternoon, so let's not act like you've got the market cornered on suffering."

Realizing how he must have sounded, Brent quickly back-pedaled. "I didn't mean it like that. I only—"

He was interrupted by the chiming sound, the same one that had awakened him earlier. Still barelegged, Lauren stood and padded to the countertop.

"I heard that noise before. That your e-mail?" he asked gruffly.

"Not e-mail, an alarm." She woke the dark screen with the touch of a key. Light flooded the dim room, illuminating the look of concentration as she typed in commands.

She dropped down some mental rabbit hole, focusing so intently that it was as if he'd vanished from her notice. Or more likely she was angry after the way he'd chewed her head off. He was pissed at himself, too, for the way he had reacted, not to her digging into his past as much as to the guilt he'd been carrying so long but had never been called to account for.

Instead, Carrie had been the one to pay the price for a tragic series of mistakes, an accident that had left her broken and vulnerable to a monster intent on exploiting her grief, for no better reason than what Lauren had rightly called "sick kicks."

So explain the rest to Lauren. Just tell her—if she really matters to you. But as much as Brent wanted to make her understand, he was held back by the knowledge that a future with her, with anyone, was far out of his reach. Better she should think him a temperamental jackass than get any more attached to a man who, at best, could expect a life on the run, if not in prison or the grave.

Still, it ate at him, that nagging voice that told him he'd only hurt her more by shutting her out. Not to mention the desire, which had taken root despite his best intentions, to claim something he had damned well proven that he did not deserve.

The chiming sound repeated, again and again. The tone, and Lauren's attention to her laptop's screen, dragged his mind from the past.

"What's it mean?" he asked.

"Bastard's persistent. I'll give him that," she murmured, seeming not to hear him as her hands flew over the keys. She shifted through several screens, giving him a glimpse of graphs and strings of HTML coding that went far beyond his own mostly self-taught knowledge.

His heart knocked, jolted with excitement. "Who's persistent? The Troll King, you mean? You've found him already?"

She smiled at the screen, her eyes bright with excitement. And not only excitement, but a brand of beauty that lit her from the inside. "Not yet," she answered, her voice leaving little doubt that she expected that to change soon. "But he's out there right now, trying to post his hateful garbage on the memorial page I set up for my sister."

"How can you be certain it's him?"

"It's him. I'm sure of it."

Vulnerable as she'd seemed before when she was wondering if he'd actually *enjoyed* making love to her, her voice now brimmed with a calm certainty, a confidence that sent a jolt of raw lust streaking through him.

"I couldn't prove it in a court of law," she said, "but I doubt any other troll's going to sit there trying to get in using one VPN after another, not for this long."

"So you're somehow denying access to anyone using virtual private networks?" He hadn't even known it was possible to block anonymous visitors from websites. But then, until he'd been unceremoniously stripped of his clearance, Brent had relied on the bureau's tech specialists to know that sort of thing for him, while he focused his own efforts on investigations in the field.

"Not exactly," she explained, "but I have blocked a list of known VPNs—a list that's updated hourly—from accessing the web form that will allow him to post comments. It's always possible he'll find a way to work around it; and even though I've been dutifully playing the broken-winged bird like you want, I've also been blocking his calls to my cell from every number he's spoofed to harass me. And now this, of course, in the hopes that he'll get frustrated enough to crack before I do and give himself away."

"Why do I get the distinct impression that this isn't your first troll hunt?" Brent put in, feeling his admiration for her surge, along with the suspicion that she'd been doing more than the recreational hacking the FBI knew about.

She returned a sphinxlike smile but didn't miss a beat. "Mad as he's likely to be getting, it's going to be a whole lot easier for him to drop his guard, maybe use a public access point, like a library or a café, even a fast-food place with free Wi-Fi, to get through."

"And that'll lead us to a physical address."

She nodded. "If we're lucky and he skips the VPN stage or gets careless enough to use one with a DNS leak. If I push him hard enough—and not with any more of this perfect-victim garbage, either."

"Push him how, then?"

Anticipation gleamed in her eyes. "You'll see."

"You're enjoying this, aren't you?"

"Who *doesn't* love taking down the bastards? Especially this one. My sister—Rachel was only twenty-five years old, Brent. *Twenty-five*, with her whole life ahead of her."

As her voice choked down, he went to her. Arms wrapping around her, he kissed the top of her head. "I know," he said, stroking the silky hair that tumbled down over her shoulders. Unable to stop himself, he added, "And I'm sorry for being such a jackass before about your running an online check on what I'd told you. Especially since, if it were me, I would've done it a lot sooner."

"Well, I'm sorry it upset you. And I'm sorry I've been holding back what the Troll King's dredged up from my marriage. You're probably right that that's a bad idea, so let me slip my jeans on. I feel ridiculous enough without adding pantslessness to the mix."

He pulled away, pretending to consider, and ran his gaze down her legs. "I don't know, Lauren. I could go with 'sexy,' 'tempting,' maybe 'distracting.' But *ridiculous*, with those gams? You've got to be kidding."

"*Gams*. Really?" She laughed to hear a word straight out of a noir flick. "What are you now, channeling Sam Spade?"

"If that's what it would take to make you smile like that again." He knew he sounded corny, but they had enough issues without adding cynicism to the mix.

But her smile faded quickly as she found her jeans and finished dressing. He dressed, as well, abruptly conscious of his own nakedness.

When they had finished, Lauren flipped on a light and offered to make coffee. "Or there's some soda in the fridge, too."

He opted for the latter, while she got herself a glass of water. After she muted the computer so they wouldn't be disturbed by the occasional chiming of another alarm, they returned to the sofa.

Her body tense and her expression anxious, she said nothing for a long while.

Finally, he prompted her, "Come on, Lauren. Tell me what the Troll King's digging in with. Whatever it is, we'll rip that lever out of his hands and shove it up his—"

"You'll think this is stupid, knowing the kind of person I am." She wrapped her arms around her waist. "But I wanted—really wanted to be a mom for real. I mean, I practically raised my little sister, but I love the idea of having someone all my own, a little person entirely dependent on me to love and guide and teach things. I wanted someone who would always be mine, no matter how messed up life got. Someone who would think of me as just Mom, not the school freak no one would look at, unless they wanted a handy target to humiliate."

His heart contracted, hearing the pain in her voice and a yearning he knew too intimately. A need for acceptance, love, and family that he had once upon a time shared. But it scared him, too, reminding him how slowly, insidiously, frustrated desire could morph into envy, resentment, and obsession, as it had with Carrie.

"So did you—did you have problems," he managed, "with fertility?"

Lauren shrugged. "I have no freaking way of knowing. Not with Phillip putting me off with one excuse after another. He was too busy with this real estate development he was fronting, or he thought he should take more time to make the adjustment to being a husband before he thought about 'the dad thing.' Then, there was the deal where I should work on convincing his family not to hate me before we brought another human being into the equation."

"In-law problems, huh?" he asked, realizing how lucky he had been with his own, who had been like the parents he had lost in a car wreck as a kid.

"The thing is, his mom and his sisters were really nice, even after I threw up when they pushed me into going to this crowded restaurant opening with them. It was Phillip who was ashamed of the way I ducked parties or always said the wrong thing when he did drag me anywhere near the superficial, cynical snobs he called friends. I embarrassed him too much for him to want to have a child with me."

Wincing, Brent fantasized about booking a flight to California to break the jerk's face. "Sounds like the kind of guy who's just too selfish to want to share time and attention with a kid, so he blamed it all on you."

"Except it wasn't the kid part he objected to." She spoke quietly, not meeting Brent's gaze. "Or at least, it wouldn't appear so, considering how soon after I left for my dad's funeral Phillip knocked up his office assistant. His gorgeous, fun-loving, *socially appropriate* assistant. As we speak, the lovebirds are decorating a damned nursery in *my* house, all because I'm too—"

"Whoa," Brent slid close to her, taking her by the arms so she'd be forced to look into his face. "Lauren, slow down. Can't you see it? This says *nothing* about you. And everything about the kind of man this Phillip proved himself to be."

"I know. That's exactly what my sister told me." With a groan, Lauren pressed her knuckles to her forehead. "And in my head, I get it. But that didn't keep the Troll King's words from stabbing straight through my heart when he started with his garbage."

"Because some part of you believes that you deserve it, right?" From his own experience, he knew exactly how that worked. "Well, I'm here to tell you it's a part of you that couldn't be more wrong."

She nodded, but in her eyes he saw the horror of having her sister's killer twist his knife in the still-fresh wound. But there was a core of strength there as well, a flicker of defiance that blazed brighter until it banished her shadows and the monsters crouching in them.

"You just wait," she told him, "because I'm about to start speaking his language on my website. See how he likes it when I reflect back all that ugliness at his psycho ass."

He grinned, loving her fierceness. Loving this woman more than he would ever let on. But the more he came to care about her, the more worried he was to think of the target they were both making of her.

Sobering, he said, "You know what? It's not the Troll King's head games that I'm most worried about now. You're too strong for that, too tough and savvy. I'm more worried about what he might do as you continue pissing him off, how he might escalate straight past making a careless mistake that could get him caught and come after you physically. Especially now that he knows exactly where you are."

"So you'll give me back my gun?" she asked, sounding so eager that it made him smile.

"Sorry, no. But before you argue—"

When her cell phone started ringing, she flinched involuntarily before glancing at the screen and saying, "It's Jimenez. Or at least that's what the caller means for it to look like."

"You can do this," Brent assured her, anticipation coiling in his gut at the thought that, if it was really the Troll King spoofing the call, he might have the chance to hear the bastard at work.

She came to her feet to answer the call, listening a moment before her tension eased. "Glad to hear it's you, Detective."

Moments later, she blinked hard, shaking her head and saying. "No, Cruz, no. I haven't heard from—Oh, God. Please don't tell me that she's—"

Brent stared a question at her, but Lauren was pacing the apartment, paying him no attention whatsoever. After listening to Jimenez for several minutes more, she said, "I understand. I'll call you if I hear anything. Please let me know when you find out more."

"What is it, Lauren?" Brent demanded as she ended the call.

She looked around wildly, her face pale and her mouth gaping. "It's Nikki—Nikki Watson. Her landlord f-found her apartment's front door standing open, and there was blood, lots of it, but no Nikki."

"Shit!" Brent swore, immediately leaping to the same conclusion that Lauren clearly had.

Just as they'd both hoped, the Troll King had been goaded into escalating his behavior. But instead of giving himself away or coming straight for Lauren, he had lashed out at Rachel's best friend . . .

Another drop-dead gorgeous blonde.

CHAPTER FOURTEEN

Blondes broke so easily in real life. Unlike their minds, which often took him weeks or months to shatter, their flesh and bones had proven far more fragile. Still reeling with the discovery, he tasted bitter rage, his expectations of hours or even days of carefully planned torture obliterated in a desperate scramble, a struggle where kicks and fists and brute strength conquered restraint.

All too quickly, it had been over. Even more upsetting, *he'd* been over, too, so excited by the fight she'd put up, by the torn clothing, the warm flesh and the red-hot panic, that he'd come the instant he had thrust his way inside her, his hands clamped around her throat to keep her still.

He didn't think he'd squeezed all that hard, but there had been a crunching sound and a slackening, followed by an awful stench as the bitch's bowels and bladder gave way. And everything was ruined, reeking with filth and tainted with failure. *His* failure to live up to those medieval torturers, the *artists*, he had somehow imagined he would be equally skilled as, equally worthy of being written up in history books.

Were these long-dead masters laughing at his arrogance? Doubling over at the idea of some soft, pathetic American who'd been gouged by his victim's nails and fouled by her disgusting waste? Though he'd scrubbed and scrubbed after removing her rug-wrapped body, he imagined people could still smell him as he sat trying to pull himself together. The sound of laughter lingered, too, not only that of those he sought to emulate, but that of the woman who'd called him a basement-dwelling freak, who had blocked his spoofed calls and kept him from posting on that lame-ass memorial site like he was nothing but some punk kid. The woman who felt safe in the company of the man the troll kept hearing in the garbled audio recordings her smartphone periodically sent each hour to his account.

"Let her have her little laugh now," he mumbled, thinking of the surprise he had in store for her, a shock that would teach her once and for all that she wasn't dealing with some ordinary lame-ass troll who was too scared to come out of the shadows. Not only that, but it would serve to separate her from the man who'd brought her here from that pissant North Texas town where she and Rachel had grown up.

At first, he'd figured the guy for some kind of law enforcement officer, what with that overconfident cop strut, the neat haircut, and the big blue sedan he drove. The cut-rate motel where he was staying was another tip-off, the type of old-school, two-story firetrap the troll imagined that a traveling cop's expense account might cover.

But though the troll had never been able to discern the words of conversation he'd recorded, he'd recognized the wordless moans and cries he'd heard fast enough. Whoever this guy was, the little slut was screwing him, only days after her sister had blown her brains out in the same apartment.

"Enjoy it while you can, bitch," he said, knowing that Lauren's lover wouldn't be a factor for much longer; for as soon as the tracking device stuck to the blue Taurus's undercarriage alerted him that the sedan with the Oklahoma plates was on the move, he could knock the bastard out of play with a single phone call.

Eventually, he figured, the guy might escape the vat of grease he was about to be thrown into. But by then, the troll would have grabbed Lauren, this time learning from his errors—and remembering the lessons he'd torn from the pages of the flaking, yellowed books. This time, he swore to himself, he would keep his victim alive and conscious while he did as he pleased.

He would do all the things he'd dreamed of until he finally tired of her . . . and gave into her pleas for the chance to end things exactly the way he planned. While he sat and watched and filmed her last hours, to play them and replay them the next time he was bored.

***

With Dumpling whining at her mistress's distress, Lauren paced the confines of the sanitized apartment, anxiety gathering around her like the early evening gloom. "It's my fault Nikki's dead, my fault for antagonizing him the way I have been."

Brent moved to intercept her. "We don't know for certain she's dead."

When he reached for her wrist, Lauren snatched away her arm, unable to bear the thought of being touched. "I'm almost afraid she isn't."

Brent's grave nod told her that he understood what she was thinking, that he feared the kind of torment someone as unbalanced as the Troll King would inflict now that he'd gotten his hands on a living, breathing woman.

"We have to find her," Lauren said. "Have to stop him before he—before any chance slips through our fingers."

"But we still don't know where he is. Have you checked the memorial site lately to see if he's gotten through?"

She rushed to her computer on the pass-through counter between the kitchen and the living room, and flipped open the skull-and-roses lid. A couple of clicks, and the site popped up—looking nothing like the loving tribute she'd designed.

"Oh my God. My—" She bolted from the room, slamming the bathroom door behind her. But there was no escaping the horrific images that had exploded on the screen. Crudely doctored versions had replaced the photos she had posted. In one, her sister's laughing face had been made to look as if she were performing a pornographic act on a sweaty, naked man. In another, a hand meant to resemble Rachel's own pressed a gun to her head, and comic-book style "BLAM!" and "KAPOW!" were emblazoned over top.

But as horrific as those photos were, the one that had Lauren retching showed her own head grafted onto the blurred image of a nude and battered female body, sprawled on an Oriental rug. From the awkward arrangement of the limbs, the woman had to be either dead or deeply unconscious.

Sick with shock, Lauren barely heard the soft knock or the sound of her own name. As she finished washing up, Brent cracked open the door.

"I'm so sorry," he said. "I should've checked it before you opened—"

"Th-that's Nikki in the picture. It's her." Lauren had been braced for the troll's cruel words, but the vision of her own head grafted onto that battered body had panic clawing at her throat.

"You're sure?"

"D-did you notice the tattoo? You can see the edge of a wing on the back of her right shoulder. It's the match to Rachel's hummingbird. Nikki got one with her . . . because, of course, *I* wouldn't do it."

Self-loathing stole up on her, stealing the breath from her lungs. If she'd only been there for the sister she had claimed to love, none of this would have ever happened.

"I want you to drag that idea out of your head and set fire to it. And then I'm stamping out the ashes." Brent dragged her into his arms, hugging her so fiercely there was no escape. "This has nothing to do with anything you did or didn't do with Rachel. Whatever's happening, the blame's on him, every bit of it. You hear me?"

"It's hard not to with you smothering me." She might have sounded surly, but her arms snaked around his waist and she learned her ear to his chest until she could breathe again.

"Too bad for you," he assured her, "because I'm not going anywhere."

She pulled away to look up at him. "Maybe you'd better rethink that. Jimenez is sending over uniformed officers, right away, he told me. They want to get me out of here, to a different hotel."

Brent nodded and guided her out of the cramped confines of the tiny bathroom. "Glad to hear he's finally taking the threat seriously. But it won't do you any good to move unless you do something about that virus on your cell phone."

"You're right." Lauren picked up the cell phone and played with the settings for a few moments. "I've turned off the GPS location services."

"Are you sure that'll do it?"

"Not entirely, depending on how sophisticated this guy is. So I'm powering down the phone for now, and later, I'll do a full system restore, which should work because the—"

"This is probably one of those situations where I don't need to know the details."

"Right." Her face heated, and she wondered what he must think of her talking like a damned computer when Rachel and her best friend were both . . .

No. Maybe there was still time. Nikki could still be alive. Which meant there might be a way, at least if they got lucky.

As she made a beeline back to her computer, Brent said, "Don't, Lauren. You've seen more than enough already."

She shook her head, both annoyed and oddly touched by his desire to protect her. "I have to check the log to see how he got past my block on private networks. But shouldn't you head out now? If the police find you here, they might arrest you."

"And if the Troll King finds *you* here between the time I leave and the time the cops arrive . . . ?"

She held out her hand and looked at him expectantly. When he didn't immediately catch her meaning, she struck out her index finger and raised her thumb to form an invisible gun. "How 'bout handing it over?"

He grimaced and unzipped an inner pocket in his jacket. Reluctance etched in his face, he hesitated until her patience ran out.

"C'mon, Brent. You can't still be thinking that I'm going to shoot you? I mean, I hardly ever blow away the men I've slept with. Not literally, I mean."

He didn't smile at her jest, nor did he give her any sign that he considered their time together more than a lapse in judgment.

The thought twisted uncomfortably inside of Lauren, but what else had she expected? A declaration of undying love from a man consumed with revenge? A declaration that would have sent her running anyway?

He returned her revolver, its snub-nosed muzzle pointed downward. "Just don't do anything idiotic with this, all right?"

"Still loaded?"

He nodded. "With the same hollow-point bullets you left in it."

She shrugged off what she took as disapproval. "Hey, if I ever have to shoot somebody, I *really* want him dead. And that goes double for this bastard."

"I'm still not leaving you alone."

She thought of arguing that she'd be fine until the police arrived, but when she looked up into his handsome face, there was no give in his expression, not the slightest hint he would abandon her before he knew for certain she'd be safe.

Maybe this was as close as a man like Brent would ever again get to admitting he cared for any woman. God only knew, it was as close as she could bring herself to accept. Even that was difficult with the knowledge that he might be risking his freedom to stay with her. And more than that, the chance of revenge, which would slip away if he were locked up.

"Just watch the window. All right?" she said. "Then maybe you can slip out when you see the black and white pull up."

She claimed one of the pair of stools next to the counter and laid down the revolver a few inches from her laptop. Dragging in a deep breath, she forced herself to wake the screen and then deliberately focused only on the website tracker icon she was clicking.

But as the new page came up, Brent walked up behind her, apparently less worried about the police than he was about the Troll King. "Wait a second. Go back."

She slanted an annoyed look his way. "Weren't you the one who didn't want me looking at those pictures?"

"Move over and let me look, then. I thought I caught the edge of another photo we missed. Or maybe he just posted it."

Lauren shivered, her flesh crawling with a fresh outbreak of gooseflesh. But not knowing would be torture, so she told herself that if Brent could stand the sight, so could she.

Another click, and the memorial website refreshed. Seeing the corner of an unfamiliar photo near the right edge of the screen, Lauren dragged the image to the center. And stared, not at the bloody or obscene image she'd expected, but at a photo of the entire Rutherford family with the words "FINALLY, JUSTICE" centered on the dark frame about them.

But it was neither the message nor the face of Megan Rutherford, beams of light creating a digitally rendered halo over her head, that struck Lauren speechless.

"I saw this the other day, over at *The Vigil*'s website." Regret sifted through Brent's grim words. "I imagine it was someone from the torches-and-pitchforks crowd who put it up there."

Lauren shook her head, beyond caring about the "Vigil Aunties" and so many others who imagined that they knew her sister. "I-I don't give a damn who made the stupid picture. I only care who's in it. Do you recognize this man?"

Chills racing along her scalp, she pointed out the smiling man beside Megan Rutherford in the photo. The same man Lauren had been all too close to, though the neatly trimmed facial hair evident in the picture was now missing, and last night's attire had been far more businesslike.

Brent shook his head, but a moment later he burst out, "Fuck me. That was *him*, in the hotel lobby bar last night. Jon Rutherford was there, using some fake name to try to worm his way up into your room."

Lauren shook her head in disbelief, trying not to imagine what he might have done if things had gotten that far. "How could I not have known the man? It's not like I haven't seen this picture before. Without Megan's halo, anyway."

"Clean shaven, he looks different, and he's lost quite a bit of weight, too."

"You're right about that," said Lauren. "And *I* was right, too, about him killing Rachel. Only now, he's clearly focused on her loved ones."

"But why would he be? That makes no sense. And why go after Nikki?"

Throwing up her hands, she guessed, "Psychotic break? Transference? Maybe blaming our influence for Rachel's irresponsibility that stormy day last spring?"

At his look of disbelief, she added, "Come on, Brent? Don't tell me that you, of all people, can't see how his wife's death could drive a basically normal computer salesman to insane extremes."

His jaw clenched as he slanted a hard look down at her. "Me, of all people?"

"Sorry," she said, cursing her genius for always popping out with the wrong thing. "I didn't mean—But anyway, isn't that more likely than some troll-turned-serial-killer dating all the way back to your wife?"

Brent shook his head. "But the messages he posted online and these phone calls you've been getting—it's the same troll, the same language as the animal who went after my Carrie and the others. Unless I've been driven to such 'insane extremes,' you figure I'm imagining the whole thing?"

His gaze latched onto hers, tension crackling between them, and it occurred to Lauren that any man willing to risk everything to stalk a monster could practically be the poster child for Insane Extremes.

But for once, she kept the thought to herself, instead shaking her head and saying quietly, "You're not nuts, Brent Durant, or at least no crazier than I am."

Unexpectedly, light splintered his darkness, the hint of a smile creasing the corners of his eyes. "Is that supposed to be comforting? You forget, I've seen you in action."

"If you're going to be like that, forget it. It's obvious *you're* crazier."

"It could be argued that *you're* the one who slept with me," he teased.

"You caught me in a weak moment."

The two of them shared a fleeting smile, but a queasy flutter reminded Lauren that no matter who was responsible for taking Nikki, she and Brent couldn't afford to waste another moment. Returning to study the listings of visitors to her sites, she scanned the domain names and IP addresses and prayed she would find something, anything to explain how someone had hacked her site.

Brent gestured toward a cluster of visitors listed in red. "So what're these ones?"

"Trolls, most likely, trying to post comments through the virtual private networks I've been blocking." She pointed out several tight groupings where someone had made dozens of attempts in rapid succession. "See how close together these are? That's the Troll King, from earlier, before I turned off the alarm. And see this long gap? That'll most likely be the period when he was—when he was busy grabbing Nikki earlier."

"But here he is again, right?" Brent said, gesturing to another clump near the end of the list, indicating a cluster of attempts about three hours beyond the first.

Lauren's hopes for Nikki faded as it occurred to her the renewed effort might indicate the troll no longer had his hands full.

"Right," she managed, "but see this, where the most recent listings shifted from red to black? This has to be where he found his way in, maybe through a VPN too new to be blacklisted." Staring at the timestamp column, she said, "Looks like he did his last uploads only about—that's just ten minutes ago, Brent. Wherever he is, he could still be there."

Brent asked another question, but Lauren's entire awareness had funneled into data usage, uploads, and IP addresses. She flipped from screen to screen in rapid-fire succession, the same hands that had earned her no better than a D+ in the one high school typing class she'd taken now flying quick as thought across the keyboard.

As was often the case, the stats, the analytics program, and even the IP geolocation website offered no absolutes in terms of answers. But taken together, the facets merged with her intuition about a possible public hotspot with a DNS leak—a gut feeling that had Lauren's heartbeat revving.

She looked up to find Brent lifting a slat and staring out into the parking lot. "Are they here yet?"

"I don't see them."

Maybe she should wait, she thought, should tell the police what she was thinking rather than letting Brent race off to confront a killer on his own. But if she chose that course, how much time would be wasted trying to convince a couple of street cops to act on a hunch they wouldn't comprehend instead of following the orders they'd been given?

Was she willing to take the chance of letting the Troll King escape into the night and missing whatever hope they might have of finding Nikki?

At the thought, Lauren snapped shut the laptop. "Forget about waiting for the cops. We're leaving. Together."

Brent's sharp eyes studied her face. "What is it? What did you find?"

"I can't be sure I'm right, can't guarantee a damned thing. But if we hurry, we *might* catch the Troll King or Jon Rutherford, or whoever the hell this is, over at the—"

Brent ripped the car keys from his pocket while she grabbed her purse. Dumpling raced for the door and yipped, hopping and whining in her eagerness to come along.

"Sorry, mutt," Brent told her, "this is strictly a no-canines operation."

Realizing he was right, Lauren shut the dachshund into Rachel's bedroom with a bowl of water and a couple of dog biscuits.

When Lauren returned, Brent didn't move from the door.

"Aren't you forgetting something?" he asked.

Confused, she shook her head before following his nod in the direction of the counter, where her loaded revolver still lay, all gleaming menace next to her computer. Exasperated with herself, she grabbed the gun and tucked it into her purse's outer pocket . . .

All the while praying to whatever god looked after girl geeks and wannabe warriors that she was not about to have to use it.

CHAPTER FIFTEEN

The bitch's lover's car was on the move now, heading back in the direction of the motel where he was staying. The same motel where a very special package awaited its discovery.

Inside the small restroom, the troll had taken off his earbuds, yet his foot tapped out a breakneck rhythm as he spoofed a phone call to the motel's front office. Once connected to a gruff-voiced older desk clerk, he reported water gushing from a broken toilet. "You better get here fast," he added, "before my downstairs neighbors get the freaking ceiling dropped down on their heads."

"What the hell does a person have to do to break a *toilet*?" the manager ground out. "Did you at least cut off the water valve and throw down towels?"

"Hey, man. That's on you. I didn't pay to stay in this dump just to do your job for you."

"I'll be right up, goddamn it. Just what I need with the rain coming."

After disconnecting, the troll laughed, imagining the grumpy old bastard's reaction when he uncovered the stinking lump beneath the blankets. Grinning broadly, he grabbed the computer he'd left balanced on the restroom sink before returning to his table.

Once there, he tipped back the espresso he'd been nursing for the past hour and grimaced at the cold grittiness of the dregs. As he banged the cup hard into its saucer, the noise drew jittery glances from the couple sitting at the nearest table along with a frown from the broad-assed brunette behind the counter.

But they were nothing to the troll, not even worth the trouble it would take to put them in their places. Ignoring them, he popped his earbuds back into place and returned his attention to Rachel's memorial website.

Hopped up on adrenaline and caffeine as he was, the words fell from his fingers like razor-wire streamers. Cutting words for Rachel's sister, who dared imagine she was smart and bold and enough of a bitch to stop him.

As he crafted each incision, his mind filled with those images he held most holy: a woodcut print of a woman forced into huge-eyed silence as she was paraded through the streets, a scold's bridle caging her head and holding her tongue flat. Another scene sprang to life, this one of a goodwife, tarred and feathered, the skin peeling from her burned body in agonizing sheets. And then there was the black-mouthed scream of some blond harlot as her bare breasts were torn away before a jeering crowd, an image so compelling he amended his plans for his target . . .

A target the police would soon ensure he had all to himself.

***

"Stay down, Lauren," Brent warned as they slid past a police cruiser. To his relief, neither of the two officers inside seemed to notice as he turned onto a street washed in the lurid tones of twilight. Beneath a thick bank of cloud cover, the purplish-crimson glow struck him as eerie. The harbinger of a storm that might break any moment.

"You need to go the other way," Lauren called from where she knelt on the floorboard, hunched awkwardly over her laptop on the seat, its lid only partly open. "I can't narrow down the exact coordinates, but the geolocation's coming up with a cross street over near the intersection of Rosewood and Chicon—"

"It's the coffee shop where I met Rachel," he guessed. "You mentioned they offer free Wi-Fi, right?"

"Yeah. That's what I'm thinking, too, but are they still open in the evenings?"

"I'm sure of it." It made perfect sense to Brent that Rachel's stalker might hang out at one of her favorite places. Clearly, the bastard was holding fast to Rachel's memory, using her sister, her friend, even her neighborhood to wring out every poisonous drop of the power and control he'd felt in driving her to her death. "I'll turn and head back that way at the next corner."

"I'm pretty sure our guy's still there, probably posting more horrible pictures, or his usual charming comments."

"The drive's about ten minutes. Is there any way you can engage him, keep him there instead of letting him get back to wherever he's stashed Nikki?" Brent seriously doubted the Troll King would have intentionally left his victim alive, but at the very least, they might be able to recover the poor young woman's body for her family's sake.

"I'm on it," she said, peering at her satellite connection.

With his jaws clamped and his hands steady on the wheel, Brent made a right at the next cross street, heading toward another route that would parallel his original choice. "Okay. Coast is clear now."

When he glanced over, she was still kneeling, her face lit by the screen as she jabbed madly at her keyboard.

"Come on, Lauren. Get back up in your seat and buckle up."

"Hang on just a second . . ." A moment later, her seatbelt clicked into place. "Pretty sure I just out-trolled the Troll King."

The smug certainty in her voice made him ask, "What exactly did you say to him?"

When she told him, Brent blew out a long breath. "Yeah. That certainly oughta do it, except . . ." If the profile he'd worked up proved to be close to correct, the Troll King would be too incensed by her blatant disrespect to do anything but respond by attacking the website.

"Except what?"

"Except when we get to the coffee shop," he told her, "I'll need you to stay inside the car."

"You have to be kidding if you think I'm hanging back while the son of a bitch who killed my sister—"

"You just posted calling him, and I quote, 'a pathetic, pencil-dicked loser who gets off upsetting decent people with his childish faked pictures.' Accurate as all that may be, you know he's in there reading it right this minute. Which means he's likely to completely lose it if he sets eyes on you now."

"I can—You don't have to worry. I can take care of myself."

Behind the boldness of her words, there was a moment's hesitation. Willing to use it if it kept her safe, he drove home his point. "Yeah, but can you take care of everyone else inside that coffee shop if this guy pulls a gun out and starts shooting? Are you trained for that, Lauren? Or what about a hostage situation? People could be hurt, more innocent people, if this isn't handled right."

A gust of wind shoved at the big sedan, sending leaves and litter skittering across the road ahead.

"You're figuring he's armed?" asked Lauren.

"He's already crossed the line from verbal manipulation to a physical attack. But his previous known behavior indicates he's more comfortable lurking in the shadows, which means that he's most likely employing some sort of equalizer."

She considered his assessment. "Jon Rutherford's plenty big enough to thrash me physically. Or try to."

"Doesn't mean he isn't carrying insurance—or that Rutherford's necessarily working alone, if we're even right about him being involved in the first place. So stay in the car, Lauren. Stay and keep your head down, for everybody's safety."

As the first few fat raindrops exploded against the windshield, Brent cursed himself for a fool for rearming her. It meant there would be no restraining her by force at this point. And no protecting her from the fallout of his actions, either.

"I want to be there when he goes down." The threat of tears bled through her plea. "You promised that I could, for Rachel."

As the small pale-yellow and blue café came into view, Brent was shocked by his own impulse—after two and a half years of hunting—to drive past it, to drop her off someplace safe, to shove her out and leave her at a nearby park or school, or maybe on the porch of one of the small bungalows that lined this older residential street if need be. When he'd first dragged her into this investigation, he'd been thinking only of *his* goals, *his* revenge, but that was before he'd come to know Lauren Miller as a woman. Now, the thought of letting her get hurt or implicating her in his illegal actions broke him out in a cold sweat.

"You either agree to stay inside the car, or we're not doing this at all," he said, raising his voice to be heard over the rattling of the rain against the hood and roof. "There's no compromise with this thing. Too many lives could be depending on it. Including Nikki's, if there's any chance at all she might be alive."

"So you're not planning on shooting whoever this is on sight?"

"In a public place, with a woman missing?" He shook his head and switched on the windshield wipers. "If everything goes the way I hope, I'll have that bastard cuffed and on his belly ten seconds after I walk in."

There was a flickering above them, followed by the thunder's low complaint. Sounding equally unhappy, Lauren asked, "And then you'll call Jimenez, let him help sort out the rest?"

Brent knew that might be a good idea, but resentment boiled over at the memory of the detective's attempt to steer Lauren clear of his "delusions." And then there were the vows that he himself had spoken at his wife's grave . . . the wife he'd helped to put there. "Let's cross that bridge when we get to it, okay?"

Lauren finally relented. "All right, Durant. I'll wait. But I'm rolling down the windows, and if I hear or see any sign of trouble—"

"You'll pull around the corner there and call 9-1-1 if I don't come out and signal you within two minutes. And then you'll take off, and we'll catch up later."

"Are you serious? I can't just—"

He pulled into a curbside spot not far down the street from the café's front door, the car's headlights gleaming off the wet street and the wipers squeaking until he shut them off. His eyes locked onto Lauren's. "You damned well can and you will. This isn't just some online game."

The rebellion written in her gaze reminded him that she was used to calling her own shots. "You seriously think I don't know that, Durant? With my sister lying in a refrigerated drawer?"

"Maybe you need a reminder that you could end up in one just as easy. And I won't have it, Lauren. Not even if that means driving away now."

Within seconds, the wall crumbled, leaving worry in its wake. "All right, all right. Just be careful in there, will you?"

The rain sounded like corn popping around them; he nodded. "Just wait behind the wheel, in case this thing goes to hell and we have to get out in a hurry."

***

Inside the café, the troll wanted to shout out loud, to rage and bellow at the new words that came up on the screen before him. Her words—that little bitch's—daring to mock and disrespect *him*. All too aware he was in public, his fingers pounding out his fury instead, all steeped in the vilest, most vulgar language he could think of. But the torrent of hatred drained him; her insults still mocked him even after he hacked into the site and tore them down.

That was when it came to him that things had changed for him forever, that *he'd* changed. And he knew the hands powerful enough to choke the life from one blonde would never again be content with hurling stupid words at any other.

A tone intruded on his thoughts, as repetitive as it was insistent. The GPS alert, he realized, only it was growing louder, as if the Taurus he'd attached it to was no longer drawing nearer the motel but instead . . .

No, that couldn't be, he thought, barely noticing the rhythm of the rain on the roof above. But people kept darting annoyed looks in his direction, so he shut off the alarm and switched to the tracker screen.

An instant later, he rocketed to his feet, his chair crashing to the floor behind him. They were all staring at him now, but it didn't matter. Nothing mattered but the silhouetted figure he saw approaching the front door.

As it hit him that he'd screwed up, underestimating those he'd preyed on, panic sent him hurtling toward the shop's rear exit—and his one chance of escape.

***

When she was focused on her work, Lauren could sit for hours, until her spine stiffened, her stomach rumbled, and her bladder howled in protest. But as wound up as she now was, she didn't last a minute before she bailed out of the car, telling herself Brent should've known a loner like her sucked at taking orders . . .

Especially when she was scared out of her mind at the thought of what he might do when he finally faced the man he had been hunting for so long. Or with the man he *thought* he had been hunting, if Rutherford would really prove to be Rachel's, and now her own, stalker and Nikki's abductor.

As soon as Brent disappeared inside, Lauren popped out of the car and slogged through a small drift of damp leaves as she hurried after him. She didn't mean to go inside; she intended to slip around the corner of the building and peer into the window she had spotted during their approach.

She was a few steps from the corner when the front door abruptly burst open, and a young couple boiled out past her into the rain, their faces flushed as they made a beeline for a scooter. Next came a bearded guy with dreadlocks that stuck out from underneath his beanie, his dark eyes wide as he jerked a cell phone from his pocket. He started to punch in a number but noticed Lauren near the door. "Don't go in! He's got a gun!"

"Who does?" Lauren asked desperately, but he was already hurrying away, giving their location to what had to be a 9-1-1 operator.

As the couple's scooter buzzed to life, another woman raced out into the rain, her face as pale as her white apron.

"They're gone now," she shouted to the guy with the dreads. "The guy with the badge chased that weird dude who's been hanging around out the back door."

"Hey, Miss! Don't go back there!" the barista called to Lauren. "Didn't you hear him say there was a gun?"

But Lauren was already racing along the side of the building, adrenaline propelling every step. A distant streetlight and the occasional security light formed misty haloes in the rain, but there were spilled-ink pools of shadow, too, where anyone or anything might be lurking.

Where are you, Brent?

On the street beyond the café, an old beater of a car slowed, its driver peering at her before flooring the gas to squeal away. That was when it registered that she held the revolver, though she could not remember pulling it from her bag. She felt like a fool, a fraud, as she trotted along the rain-slick street, pointing the gun at everything, at nothing, and starting at each branch that rattled in the breeze.

Like the sky above, her frantic heartbeat thundered. She had no idea what she was doing out here or what she'd do if she ran headlong into the Troll King. She was in so far over her head, she'd need an elevator to reach rock bottom.

If she had any sense, she told herself, she would wait back in the car the way Brent had told her to, wait for someone in uniform to show up, or phone Detective Jimenez and beg him to hurry over. Yet when she heard an eruption of barking from a yard not far ahead, she hurried in that direction, her focus less on the man responsible for Rachel's death than on the man who chased a monster all alone.

As the rain soaked her hair and clothing, her attention narrowed to a yard ahead, where two barking dark shapes rattled a chain link fence as they repeatedly hurled themselves against it. Big dogs, mean dogs, from the sound of them, but Lauren plunged past anyway, praying that the fence would hold and she'd be spared a mauling.

Once beyond the noise, she made out a clattering up ahead—a trash can falling, she thought—and an elderly male voice shouting from a porch, "Get outta here, you bums! Or maybe you wanta spend the night in jail?"

Lauren hesitated, gasping for breath, and registered the sound of sirens. More than one patrol car, she thought, and they sounded as if they were closing in fast.

Worried that Brent might be arrested, or maybe even shot in the confusion, she pushed on, flinging herself across a narrow intersecting street—to the sound of screeching brakes and a blaring horn. She spared the gray pickup's driver the barest glance before she took off toward what looked like movement about forty yards ahead.

She realized it was Brent, turning into an alleyway between two sets of back yards. But he clearly didn't see her, his attention riveted on something ahead.

Panic wound tight in her chest, a bone-deep foreboding warning her to call to him before it was too late. But her lungs were on fire by now, her legs so heavy she could barely lift them, and every powerful stride he took widened the gap between them.

A moment later, he vanished behind a house as he proceeded down the alley. *Call him back before it's too late*, her instincts screamed, but she didn't have the breath.

From somewhere down the alley, a woman's cry rose, and Brent's deep voice echoed in response.

"FBI, ma'am! Get back inside! I'm not here to hurt you!"

Lauren heard the sharp slam of what she thought must be a back door.

Gunshots followed, two of them, as sharp and shocking as twin thunderclaps. The blasts echoed through the alley, rattling Lauren to her core.

And leaving her with no idea if Brent had been the shooter or the target—or if she would be shot down the moment she stepped into the alley to find out.

***

Brent staggered as the pain exploded in his lower right arm, pain that sent his pistol flying, along with a shower of debris from a nearby gatepost. Ducking down, he scrambled to grab it, but he couldn't make his hand close, so he used his left one to pick it up and lost his footing.

Getting up was harder than it should have been: dizziness was breaking over his head like a huge, black wave. He turned to look for the shooter, and felt a burning in his neck, like the sting of the scorpions he'd once encountered on his grandparents' ranch. Confused, he tried to swat at it, which caused him to drop the pistol again.

Just as well, he quickly realized. He was going to need his left hand to apply pressure to the wound on his neck—the wound pumping out more hot blood with every heartbeat.

His vision tilted wildly, convincing him that his hunt, for now, was over. But the sound of fast-approaching sirens had him staggering off into the shadows—and praying that he wouldn't bleed out before he got to Lauren and the car.

CHAPTER SIXTEEN

As she stood motionless near the entrance to the alley, the roaring in Lauren's ears rose to a crescendo, the soundtrack of her adrenaline rushing through her system. *Get away*, her body urged her, but the thought of leaving Brent, possibly injured or even dying, threatened to cut her legs from under her.

Equally terrifying was the suspicion that if she stepped into that alley she would find him bent over the unarmed body of Jon Rutherford. As much as she hated the thought of what the bastard had done to her sister, her mind snapped back to those two little children in the family photos. Would they be orphaned, and Brent incarcerated, for something as stupid, as ultimately useless, as revenge?

In the crucible of that stunned moment, the realization came with a clarity as clear and sharp as broken glass. Only it sliced straight to her pounding heart, because her sweet sister was still lying in that cold drawer, still going into the ground tomorrow afternoon, never to return. And Carrie Durant's body wouldn't magically reanimate, no more than the killer's death would heal her husband's broken soul.

But if she acted now, Lauren could do something. She could get Brent out of this rain-soaked hell before the approaching sirens closed in on them, before either an ambulance or a police car carried him away.

Her extremities tingling with nervous energy, she lurched forward, the gun still shaking in her sweaty hand. Before she made it three steps, a gangly male figure with a backpack slung over one shoulder exploded from the alley, moving so fast she nearly tripped over her own feet trying to avoid a collision.

"Stop!" she cried, reaching reflexively for what she realized, from the floppy, dark hair and the gawky features, was a kid—a witness maybe?

But she snatched at empty air, watching him sprint away, the Converse sneakers flying at full speed. Within a few strides, a book—no, it was a laptop computer—tumbled out of the unzipped backpack and smashed down on the street's edge with the sound of shattering hardware.

He clearly heard it, too, for he staggered to a stop to look back over one bony shoulder. And something in his face swept away her foolish notion that this coltish, black-clad teen was only a panicking bystander and not the very monster whose torments had destroyed her Rachel.

He must have recognized Lauren, too, for his face contorted with a shout of pure rage. His left hand swung in her direction, grasping the gun he clearly meant to fire.

With her own weapon in her hand, she froze, unable to pull the trigger or run for cover or drop to the ground. As she waited uselessly for the bullet's impact, the wail of sirens, the hiss of rain, and the rush of her blood were swallowed by the throaty roar of a huge engine as a dark blur came out of nowhere.

The pickup slammed into the boy, sending him tumbling over the hood with a sickening *th-chunk* as his body slammed into the windshield. The driver jammed his brakes and then reversed to send the teen rolling off the front end.

Stricken mute by an unholy combination of relief and horror, Lauren backpedaled a few steps, as if she might escape the nightmare. As she watched, the pickup came to a rest, and a huge, broad-shouldered man unfolded himself from the cab.

He looked around wildly: compared to the bright wash of his headlights, the spot where Lauren stood must have looked blacker than a crow's wing. She tried to say something, to at least tell him she would call for help, but she couldn't force the words free and couldn't make her shaking hands pull out the cell phone, either.

She could only stare, her pulse still throbbing madly, as the bull of a man knelt beside the boy. Checking on him, she thought, but the driver's back was to her, and she saw little beyond his dark ball cap and jacket.

Seconds later, he stood, cursing quietly as he slipped his hand inside an inner pocket of his jacket. Had he put something in there, something he'd taken from the kid? Lauren couldn't be certain, but as the man looked around once more before returning to his cab, she realized that he had no intention of calling the police.

He's going to take off. But instead of reversing to get around the body, he put the truck back into drive . . .

And deliberately ran over the crumpled form, which made a sound like a tree trunk snapping to pieces in a windstorm. Hot gorge rising, Lauren raised her hand to her mouth, but not fast enough to silence her own instinctive cry of protest.

For one terrifying instant, she looked into the truck's cab and saw the driver looking back at her, his deep scowl and stubbled jaw shockingly familiar. Before she could react, he sped off, leaving her certain that this was the same man who'd nearly struck her in the intersection only minutes earlier. But he was gone now, gone before she'd gotten more than a tear-blurred glimpse of the truck's rear plates.

Less than ten feet from where she stood, the boy who'd meant to kill her lay broken and unmoving, his blood washed toward the gutters by the falling rain.

Fat, white blobs erupted in Lauren's vision before she realized that she wasn't breathing. She forced herself to drag in the damp air as several neighbors ran toward the teen, apparently having witnessed the hit and run from their homes.

Had they seen the driver, too, watched him stealing something from the victim? And had anyone else heard the gunshots from the alley, or had she only imagined that part? Realizing that Brent might well still be back there, bleeding, Lauren finally recovered her wits enough to move in that direction.

But first, she stooped to grab the dead boy's laptop, tucking it under one arm before darting back into the deepest shadows. Someone yelled at her to stop, saying the police would want to talk to witnesses.

"I'll be right back," she answered, not certain that she meant it.

Not certain of anything but the need to find Brent alive.

***

It was something from a nightmare, the rain and the thunder and the pain that shot through him with every step. Still, Brent fought his way to the mouth of the alley, battling dizziness and nausea to get back to Lauren.

Then he saw her moving toward him, a sight so welcome he might have taken it for a hallucination if she weren't soaked and shivering and white-faced in the weak light. He rasped out her name, his voice no match for the cold rain and nearby sirens, yet somehow, her gaze found him anyway.

"He was—he was going to shoot me, but the truck rammed him. It hit him and then backed up. The guy got out to check and then ran right over him. There was this awful sound and so much blood . . ." She blinked at him, her lips parting as she saw his hand holding on to what he prayed was just a graze wound. "You're hit! He shot you, didn't he? It was the troll—the Troll King. Just a kid, but he's dead—There's no way he could've made it, the way he—"

"Listen to me, Lauren. You need to tell Jimenez. Tell him all of it, but say you came here alone, that you were so upset about your sister and those phone calls, you tried to track him down yourself."

"What are you talking about? You need help. You're bleeding."

"Just give me the keys, Lauren. Give me the car keys, and I'll deal with this on my own. Then I'll come and find you, and we can figure out—"

"Don't you understand? It's over. The troll's dead. I'm sure of it."

"We don't know it was really him. No scrawny little punk could've driven my wife to—"

"We can prove it"—she showed him a laptop, with one hinge broken and askew—"once I pull the hard drive out of his computer."

"Work with Jimenez," Brent repeated, "and I'll find you when I can."

"You're not thinking straight! You're in shock."

"It's not so bad." He prayed that he was right about it, that he hadn't lost too much blood already. "Not so bad I want to end up jailed on whatever charges they dream up."

"You could *die* if you don't let me help you. Besides, Jimenez won't believe me. Those people in the café are all going to say they saw you!"

"Give me the damned keys, right now."

"Forget it, Brent. I'm not letting you bleed out—or kill somebody on the road when you pass out driving."

He let go of his neck for a moment to clamp down on her arm.

"Ow! You're hurting me. Let go!"

"Please, Lauren, I'm begging you. Don't make me take those keys by force. This is wrong. It's all wrong. I-I saw him, too, saw his face, and it can't be just some kid, some freaking high school boy destroying all these lives for—for nothing. There's more. There has to be more."

She stared at him, real fear blooming in her eyes. "Jimenez was right about you. You've totally lost it. You know that?" Though the rain made it hard to be sure, she seemed to be crying as she dug the keys out of her pocket, weeping as she slapped them into his bloody palm.

"We'll catch up later," he swore, the throbbing agony of his wounds intensified by her loss of faith. "I'll make you understand, and I'll make it up to you. I swear it."

"You want to go on with this craziness, let it run you into the ground?" she shouted. "Do it without me, then, Durant, because I'm getting off the roller coaster ride from hell right now!"

***

Lauren watched Brent disappear into the deepest shadows, his departure from her life somehow coming as more of a shock than his arrival. Stricken by a vision of him dying alone in some hotel room, she took a step after him and called his name, but he was already out of earshot.

Shivering with cold, she thought of telling the police about him, giving them the location of his car to head him off. But when she returned to the scene of the hit-and-run, she saw that no officers had arrived yet. As an ambulance pulled up, its head-lights illuminated several neighbors getting soaked in the rain as they held umbrellas over the teenager's limp body. An older man kneeling on the ground beside him looked up and shook his head, the grimness of his expression confirming what Lauren had known from the start.

She wondered if she should try to head back to the café, to see if the police were there yet. But there was a good chance she would miss them as they hastened over here, and she was half-afraid of overtaking Brent before he reached his car.

Her skin broke out in gooseflesh as she imagined what might happen if she ended up between him and his goal. Over the past few days, the two of them had pieced together slivers of trust like a castle built of twigs, but tonight's events had splintered the illusion.

He'd never hurt me. Never . . .

Strong as the instinct was, she dismissed it as wishful thinking, knowing that a man half out of his mind with pain, blood loss, and emotion might do anything. She felt shot herself, her heart and soul pierced as she realized that the same man who had so tenderly, so fervently made love to her only hours before might now prove a danger to her.

So instead of going after him, she waited as the slackening rain washed away all traces of her tears' warmth. Only later, when one of the arriving officers came to question her about what she had witnessed, did she finally turn over the laptop she'd been holding on to for dear life as she broke down weeping with suppressed emotion.

It was after eleven-thirty that night when Detective Cruz Jimenez finally walked into the interview room where Lauren had been taken. In contrast to his normal camera-ready appearance, he looked tired and rumpled, his dark hair clumped as if he, too, had spent a portion of this stormy night out in the rain.

She adjusted the blanket wrapped around her and set down the cup of coffee she'd been given on the table. "Some day off, huh?"

He offered her a warm smile and pulled out the chair beside her. "At least it started out well. But it's been all downhill from there."

"No kidding."

"Are you all right? You need more coffee? One of the guys just brewed up a fresh pot."

She waved it off. "I'm good, thanks. The officers have been nice."

He lowered himself into the chair and eyed her skeptically. "So why, then, do you keep lying to them about your FBI friend?"

"I'm not."

"I'm insulted you would try to con me. I thought we were better friends than that."

When she said nothing, he pushed harder. "Come on, Lauren. I already know the two of you hooked up sometime after I left the apartment and arrived at that coffee shop together. We have witnesses who saw you in Durant's blue Taurus."

Too worried to keep up the pretense, she asked, "Have you—have you found him? Is he all right?"

The detective peered at her intently. "What is it with you and him? Why're you so worried?"

"Because the last time I saw Brent, he was bleeding badly. That kid—the boy killed in the hit-and-run—shot Brent back in the alley just around the corner."

"He was *shot*? And you didn't say a word about it?"

"He insisted I keep it quiet, right before he took off. He wouldn't listen when I begged him to get help." She prayed she hadn't made a costly mistake in honoring his wishes. "Wouldn't listen, either, when I said it was all over."

"And you're still sticking to the story that the driver of the vehicle who struck him was a stranger to you?"

"It's not a story. It's a fact. Like I told the officers, the man was driving a newer pickup, dark gray, I'm pretty sure. I think it might've been a Chevy or a GMC. First digits of the license plate were D17."

"Texas plates?"

"I think—" She shook her head and sighed, remembering her blinding tears, her shock and revulsion and relief that she'd been spared a bullet. "I'm not really sure. It all happened so fast. But it definitely wasn't Brent behind the wheel, if that's what you're getting at. The man was huge, a white guy, and he had dark whiskers—or at least I think he did."

"Age?"

"I don't know. Maybe thirties? Forties? I was scared out of my wits, and he was gone in a split second."

"Did this driver see you standing there?"

She shook her head. "At first, he didn't. Then he got out and checked the kid to see if he was alive. Or at least, that's what I thought he did. When he turned around, I could've sworn I saw him jamming something in his pocket."

"A wallet maybe? Or a cell phone? We found neither on the victim."

"Maybe both. I'm not sure."

Jimenez looked disgusted. "So he wasn't just a hit-and-run driver. He was some low-life opportunist."

"He climbed back in the truck and didn't hesitate a second before he ran right over the kid—deliberately this time. That's when I finally unfroze and came unglued."

His hand moved closer toward hers, but he didn't try to touch her. Instead, he gave her a look steeped in sympathy. "I'm not surprised. That must've been horrible to witness."

Her skin crawled at the memory, her stomach threatening upheaval. "The thing is, I'm pretty sure he saw me just before he sped away."

"I doubt it even registered. He was probably panicking by then, wanting to get out of there before someone caught him with that poor kid's valuables."

As horrible as the troll's fate had been, Lauren couldn't stand to speak of him as though he'd been nothing but an innocent victim. "That 'poor kid' had already shot Brent and was about to shoot me, too. They did find the gun, I understand."

"About ten feet from the body, yeah. It must have been sent flying by the impact. So why were you two chasing this kid in the first place?"

"I know you must've been briefed. I explained all this to the other officers when I turned over his laptop."

Jimenez's dark gaze bored into hers. "Tell me anyway. Why chase him?"

"Because this kid was the same freak who called me and stalked my sister. And maybe others, too, if Brent's right. That hard drive'll tell the story."

"It's pretty badly damaged, but we're sending it to a computer forensics specialist to see what we can get."

"So did you find out who this kid was? And why he'd be so fixated on—"

"No ID, but the detectives assigned to the case are working on it."

"Not you?"

He shook his head and speared her with a look that sent fresh chills cascading through her. "I've been busy on another case. It's why I'm here to see you."

"Which case is that—Don't tell me it's Nikki?" Forgetting herself, Lauren grabbed his wrist and squeezed it. "Is she—please, Cruz, tell me she's been found!"

"First, I need to tell you we've found the car Durant's been driving, outside the Slumbertime Motel, just off the freeway."

She stared at the detective, and her heart began to pound. Because in his dark eyes, she saw worse news was coming. Saw it as clearly as a pair of headlights bearing down on her with lethal speed.

CHAPTER SEVENTEEN

As the driver tapped an inch-long cylinder of glowing ash against the lowered window, a few cinders spilled inside. He didn't give a damn, though, about the ragged out van he'd taken using the kid's keys. Soon enough, he'd ditch this piece of shit, just as he had the pickup he'd stolen hours before.

Though the truck was gone, the driver could still see its apparition in his mind's eye. In crystalline detail, he saw—and savored—the dent that marred the hood and the web of cracks where the kid's skull had bounced off the windshield. His memory lingered, almost lovingly, on those few dark strands of flesh-gobbed hair sticking to the glass. Or maybe that had just been dirt, washed there by the rain. Either way, it didn't matter. He found the recollection as satisfying as the Havana cigar he'd allowed himself for a job well done.

Or almost done, at any rate.

"The little psycho's finished," he told the contact over the burner cell phone he'd picked up.

"You're sure?" Smooth as it was sexy, her voice was a liquid fire that traveled straight to his groin.

Deceptively deadly, too, from what little he had figured out about her in the three years they had worked together. A man might be her top operator one week and the target of a cleanup the next.

He ought to know. With no remorse and no emotion, she'd ordered him to take out a guy he believed to be one of his peers a few months earlier. The incident had served as a powerful reminder that however often he dreamed of tracking her down to find out if she was half as hot as she sounded, acting on his fantasies was likely to prove fatal.

"As you've reminded me on more than one occasion, I'm paid to be sure." The caller sucked in another lungful and reminded himself to take the cigar's butt with him. The gloves wouldn't do him much good if he was idiot enough to leave his DNA for the cops.

Bad enough there had already been one screwup, one his instincts warned him would be best kept to himself. But a fraction of a second later, he reminded himself that holding back, omitting it, would be more dangerous. So despite his reluctance, as coarse and heavy as wet sand in his gut, he forced himself to confess, "Unfortunately, there could be one . . . difficulty."

"What's the issue?" she asked, the sultriness he loved giving way to a mechanical detachment.

He mouthed the smoke, tasting its acrid richness before admitting, "He didn't have the laptop on him. And I didn't find it in his van, either."

"Wait. I thought our bad boy still had his mama's car?"

"Nah. It was recovered back in Houston, not ten miles from the house. Can you believe the dumbass swapped his mama's fifty-thousand-dollar Beamer for some rattletrap molester van? And here I thought he was s'posed to be some kinda freakin' genius."

"He was psycho, maybe, but not stupid, especially if he was living out of that van on the road."

"From the looks of it, he was," the caller allowed. "I did get his cell phone, but that damned laptop's nowhere to be found. I'm not sure where else to look. Unless . . ."

"There's no 'unless' about it. Find it. There's a hell of a bonus riding on keeping that phone and laptop out of the wrong hands. But only if we can deliver the whole package in the next few days."

"That could be . . . complicated." He liked money as much as anybody, but it'd be hard to spend from the inside of a prison. And impossible if he ended up a corpse. "I was seen tonight, right after, by some woman standing maybe a dozen feet outta the action."

"A witness." Judgment hardened the two words, judgment against him for allowing such a thing to happen.

The driver swallowed back a pellet of fear. "Standing in the shadows, yeah. And she might've seen me goin' through boy genius's pockets. But maybe not. My back was to her."

"You think she was a bystander or maybe involved with him in some way?"

"She was a blonde," he said suggestively, "and a damned scared one at that moment."

"So she was good looking?"

He hesitated, listening for some sort of trap hidden in the question. But the contact, who dealt directly with the clients, always knew more about the target than she told her operators, so it was possible she'd have something that would help. "Pretty sure she would've been, if somebody'd handed her a towel and a blow dryer."

"Was she holding anything? Anything that could've been our missing laptop?"

He sucked in a mouthful of cigar smoke and frowned over the memory. But there was nothing more than the quick glimpse of pale hair and a white face, an impression of a woman too petrified to move.

"I don't know. She might've been. Just like she could've been with him, close as they were."

"Make it your business to find out who this woman is, why she was there, and what, if anything, she's saying to the cops."

"Hell, for all I know, she's already turned the laptop over to 'em. Or they've gone ahead and found it on their own. But even if they have it, between the rain and the beating it would've taken when I clipped him, I can't figure that computer's giving up anybody's secrets."

"You'd better hope you're right about that. And anyway, if this woman was really somehow involved with the kid, she could be more of an issue, you know? And considering she's a blonde, I'm thinking, just to be safe . . ."

"I've gotcha," he agreed and stubbed out his cigar. As the contact ended the call, he was already looking forward to lighting up his next Havana—once he'd extinguished this job's final complication.

***

As somber as it was sympathetic, Jimenez's expression had Lauren's vision swarming and a buzz building in her ears.

"Blood was found in Durant's car," he said, "mostly in the driver's seat."

"I told you he was injured."

"We found bags as well, torn wrappers. It looks as if he found an all-night drugstore—maybe a drive-through—somewhere and did his best to stop the bleeding."

"Thank God." She prayed it meant he wasn't too seriously injured. Or maybe he'd opted for self-help out of desperation, since she'd heard that emergency rooms were required to report all gunshot wounds. *But why abandon his only means of transportation?*

"About twenty minutes after we found the car," Jimenez told her in that gentle tone she'd come to know he used when delivering the worst of news, "the bodies were discovered in one of the motel rooms."

"The bodies . . ." she repeated, struggling to peel away the layers of a reality too huge, too horrendous to absorb all at once. "I don't under—Why would there be . . ." He'd said *bodies*, hadn't he? The plural.

But she couldn't form the question. Couldn't hold on to a coherent thought. Numbing cold and blazing heat twisted through her like strands of lightning. Braided among them were her last memories of Brent, injured but insistent, before running from her at a pace she couldn't hope to match.

"Impossible," she murmured, dizziness fraying her vision. But Jimenez was still talking.

"One was identified as the hotel manager. He told his son on the phone he had to go deal with a water leak up on the second floor. When he never called back like he promised, the kid swung by and started looking. Found the door to Room 226 ajar and then the woman, dead there. He didn't see his father lying behind the bed until he stepped inside. The old man had a bad heart, and we suspect the shock of discovering the victim—"

She sucked in a breath that cleared her vision. "Then Brent wasn't there? Y-you didn't find him dead, too?"

"We don't know where he's gone without his car, but we do know the bodies were found in his room. He'd checked in under

216

the name Stephen Teller, but the manager's son, who works there part-time as a desk clerk, identified Durant from a photo."

"And the woman? Was it—" Fear clamped its icy hands around her throat. "Was it Nikki?"

With a grave nod, Jimenez told Lauren he was sorry. Though she could see how much he hated slamming her with another piece of bad news, she crossed her arms at her waist to keep from flying at him and attempting to claw the useless regret from his face.

Rising from her seat, she asked, "How did Nikki die? You aren't going to try to tell me it's another suicide?"

The detective came to his feet to face her. "Unofficially, it does appear to be a homicide. I can't say more until the autopsy's been completed. And the family hasn't been notified yet, so please don't share any of this information."

"Don't worry. I wouldn't dream of being the one to—" She shook her head. "How is it you do it, Detective? Collect a paycheck every week for breaking people's hearts."

"I remind myself I'm not the one who engineered their heartbreak." His subtle accent underscored an inner strength. "I'm simply helping them navigate the strange hell where they've just landed, leading them to whatever answers there are to be found."

"So lead me to some answers, shepherd. Help me understand this. Why would the Troll King have left Nikki Watson's body in the motel room Brent rented?"

Jimenez said nothing, but his troubled silence spoke volumes.

"Wait. You can't mean that after everything I've told the other officers and all the evidence I've handed over, you still don't buy there was ever a Troll King in the first place?"

"I'm not trying to minimize what you've been through, but all the evidence will need to be reviewed, all the theories carefully considered."

"Including the idea that *Brent* did this, right? That's ridiculous. He was with me, at Rachel's apartment, starting about half a minute after you left this afternoon."

"You misunderstand if you think I mean to rush to judgment. I know Durant, respect him. If he's done something drastic to reinforce his 'theory,' the waste alone . . ." He shook his head.

"But you told me you know him. Then you must know he would never hurt a woman." Despite the boldness of the claim, she thought about the last time she and Brent had been together. She'd doubted, even feared him, so how could she blame Jimenez for refusing to ignore the presence of Brent's car and a murdered woman in a room he'd rented?

"I *knew* him," the detective told her, "before guilt changed him to a different person."

"Why would he feel guilty?"

"Maybe you can answer that one. Why does any survivor of suicide feel guilt? For not seeing the invisible? For not stopping what his wife shared with no one? But I've heard that in Durant's case, it goes back even further, to the death she blamed herself for."

"The little boy's drowning, you mean." It struck Lauren again, how similar the case was to the drowning believed to be the catalyst for her own sister's suicide.

The detective nodded grimly.

"You know something more about it, don't you?" she asked. "Why he blamed himself for that death?"

"It's very late, and you've been through a lot." His tone matched his gaze, both full of compassion. "Why don't I have an officer take you to pick up a few things and then get you settled into a hotel room?"

"Don't patronize me. I want answers. I deserve them."

"We all do. The *right* answers. So it's high time you went home so I can get back to finding them."

She tried staring him down, but her eyes kept sliding to half-mast no matter how hard she resisted.

"I'll go," she conceded, knowing there was no way she'd be able to face tomorrow's funeral if she didn't get some rest, "but not to any motel. There's no need now that that damned troll's in the morgue where he belongs."

"Forget it. You're not staying alone in that apartment. Not as long as Brent Durant's at large and knows to look for you there," he insisted. "Go now, without giving me any more grief about it, and I'll authorize the release of one other item we found in his vehicle: a laptop with your name on it. Someone locked it in the trunk."

With both fatigue and sadness weighing on her, she drew in a deep breath and nodded. Because there was a part of her—maybe the traitorous, disloyal part or possibly the wiser portion—that shared the detective's fear.

***

Weak with pain and blood loss, Brent watched the tow truck hook up his sedan and drag it from the motel's lot. He knew the police would be locking it up in a secured impound lot, where there'd be no chance of recovering the damned thing legally—or by any other method.

Just one more setback in a night of setbacks, a night that should have been the happiest he'd experienced in years. Again and again, Lauren's voice trailed through his throbbing skull: *Don't you understand? It's over. The troll's dead. I'm sure of it.*

Could it really be true? Could something as random as a hit-and-run have ended the manhunt that had driven him to such extremes?

After doing his best to tend to his wounds with the supplies he'd bribed a homeless man to purchase from the drugstore, Brent had tried to make himself believe it, to imagine some kind of life on the other side. He struggled, too, to accept Lauren's take on the story at face value, to absorb the mind-bending idea of some bored teenager wreaking all this havoc.

Then he'd stepped into his motel room . . . into an unimaginable hell. The battered body he'd recognized as Nikki's had been cold, but not that of the older man whose feet he'd spotted sticking out from behind the bed. Despite the pain of his injuries, Brent had dragged the man out to a position where CPR would be possible and had torn open his shirt. That was when he'd discovered the man, too, lacked a heartbeat. Judging from the lingering warmth and color of the body, he must have died only minutes before Brent came up the steps.

His stomach plunged at the realization that if the Troll King had meant to set him up, he'd done one hell of a job. With Brent's fresh prints all over the room and the room booked under a false name, he'd face countless hours of questioning—and most likely an indictment.

So what the hell did he do now? And who on God's green earth did he have left to turn to, especially now that Lauren had turned her back on him?

CHAPTER EIGHTEEN

After an officer helped Lauren move her things to yet another downtown hotel, she was quick to double lock the door and turn on every light, to check behind curtains and the shower door as if she expected to find Norman Bates hiding somewhere.

Dumpling's big brown eyes seemed to sense her worry. The dachshund waddled into Lauren's path, pawed her ankle, and rolled over, wagging her tail and snuffling for attention. Stressed as she was, Lauren squatted down, hoisted the dog's bulk to the bed, and rubbed her plump belly.

The stroking did them both good, enough that Lauren felt her breathing ease a little, her mind relax its death grip on the horrors she had witnessed. "Thank God for you at least," she told the dog and wondered, not for the first time, who had rescued whom that day along the roadside.

She thought she wouldn't sleep, couldn't imagine how she'd close her eyes after everything she'd witnessed tonight. But after a long, hot shower, fatigue quickly pulled her under—the backwash of the adrenaline that had flooded through her system.

Or maybe it was the need to escape, the desire to vanish into oblivion, away from guilt and worry. But Lauren didn't get her wish, for the nightmares were relentless: her mind replayed the hit-and-run, her argument with Brent, and the scene of his hotel room as Jimenez had described it. As if that weren't enough, the dreams soon devolved into gruesome mix-and-match scenarios—disjointed images like frames from an old-fashioned horror movie film reel: Rachel sprawling broken on the pickup's hood, Brent gaping and glassy-eyed in the motel room. Lauren even saw herself, running from the huge truck driver in the alley. Running until she stumbled, her hand pressed to her spurting neck.

So it almost came as a relief when reality at last intruded, in the form of her cell phone ringing beside her. Half-surprised the phone still worked considering how soaked she'd gotten the previous night, she fumbled to pluck it off of the nightstand.

As she registered the time on the clock radio—8:39 a.m.— her gaze flicked to the phone's lit screen, hope crowding into her chest but just as quickly falling. It wasn't Brent calling to tell her that last night had been another nightmare, or that Nikki wasn't dead, and he had never been shot.

Instead, the number was unfamiliar, except for the area code, which she recognized as one from Southern California. L.A., she was pretty sure, since she had several clients in the area.

"Siren Sys-Secure. Lauren Miller speaking."

The caller's silence sliced through her like a blade of ice. Her body clenched, with the exception of the jackhammer of her heartbeat. *What if I was wrong last night? What if the boy was just some troubled teen, spooked by the sight of Brent's gun, and had nothing to do with the Troll King whatsoever?*

"Hello?" she ventured, scarcely able to breathe for the dread that crowded into her throat.

But instead of the monstrous digitized voice and hateful words she half expected, she heard only the soothing tones of a sonorous male voice that would sound at home on late-night radio. "Hello, Miss Miller? This is Reynolds Hadley, a producer for Monarch Entertainment. I'm terribly sorry to be calling at this difficult time, but—"

"Monarch Entertainment?" she echoed, snapping to attention. Because Lauren was a woman who liked to know her enemies—and Rachel's enemies were hers. "Tell me, Mr. Hadley, you wouldn't be the same bottom feeder who repeatedly called my sister asking her to speak to Jaycee Joiner on *The Vigil*, would you? How on earth did you get my number?"

She could have sworn she heard him swallow. Hard, as if her tone made him nervous. Which told her this producer had brains, because her anger damned well ought to.

"We . . . we do like to offer persons spotlighted in Ms. Joiner's—"

"Verbal crucifixions?" Lauren suggested, certain that Jaycee's spittle-flecked rabble-rousing amounted to nothing less. She pictured the woman, her flame-red hair flapping and her eyes lit by what looked like a demonic possession as she railed against the grand jury that had no-billed the "Blonde on Blonde Killer."

"In her *segments*, I was about to say," Hadley corrected, as if the gentler word might buff away the damage. "Anyway, we try to offer people in your sister's position the opportunity to explain their actions, to defend themselves."

It occurred to her that she should hang up, that this slimemonger might even stoop to record this conversation, but angry as she was, her mouth was running ahead of her better judgment.

"As I'm sure you know, even if her attorney would've allowed such insanity, my sister was nowhere near dumb enough to go head-to-head against a former judge in front of an audience of 'Vigil Aunties.'" Lauren remembered the day they'd talked about it, when Rachel had sounded so desperate to get out her side of the story that Lauren had gone into full-blown big sister mode and threatened to drive down and lock her in a closet if she mentioned it again. "Not that that stopped that mad cow from publically eviscerating Rachel anyway."

"Listen, Miss Miller," he went on, speaking so calmly that one might imagine he'd heard his boss called worse than a mad cow every time he had to make one of these calls, "I understand you must be upset. I understand and I respect that, and personally, I want to offer my sincerest condolences for the loss of your sister."

"Does Jaycee? Because she's the one who lit the fuse, the one out there on that vacuous cable cesspit you dare call entertainment using all that trumped-up pathos to incite her mob of morons. Not giving a single damn that those people *stalked* my sister, that one of them bullied and tormented her until she killed herself."

"You know, you're quite an articulate young woman. And I think you make an excellent point, about the bullying angle and all that. Hot topic for a segment these days."

"It's not any kind of *angle*." Her voice flattened, the heat in it cooling like magma as it slowly turns to stone. And Lauren began to wonder how much grief she could cause Jaycee Joiner and *The Vigil*, and Mr. Monarch Exploi-tainment, if she set her mind—and maybe a few of her online hacker friends—to the task. "It was my sister's life. The sister I raised after our mom died when she was little. The sister who was all that I had left."

"Perhaps you'd like the opportunity to speak to Ms. Joiner personally," he rushed to suggest, as if he had just thought of it, "to lead a conversation on-air to explore the topic of media responsibility?"

She rolled her eyes at the suggestion. "Go to hell, Hadley. Or better yet, get yourself another job, because as far as I can figure, you're already working for the devil."

Before she could disconnect, she heard him shouting into the phone, sounding small and eager. "Please, Miss Miller, I know you have a lot to think of, with the funeral today. But if you change your mind, we'd absolutely love to have you. You're a very intelligent, extremely photogenic woman, as pretty as your sister . . . I'm sure the audience would carefully consider whatever it is you want to say."

Photogenic? As pretty as her sister? How the hell would he know what she looked like, unless he'd visited the memorial website defaced last night by the troll? To Lauren's knowledge, there wasn't another photo of her anywhere online.

She thought of threatening him, warning him not to call again or he'd be sorry. But with revulsion making her skin crawl, she finally did what she should have in the first place, and hung up without another word.

***

Hollowed out by grief, Lauren struggled to get through Rachel's graveside service later that afternoon. As Mr. Brashear, the funeral director, a beaky man with the starched gravity of an old-school British butler, made a few sadly generic remarks, she shivered in the cold breeze, her gaze cemented to the pearl-white casket she'd had blanketed in delicate pink flowers.

Better that than looking at the dozens of other mourners in attendance, all of whom she imagined were glaring at the back of her head and the simple chignon she wore to downplay her newly dyed blond hair.

Nerves buzzing like a super-caffeinated wasps' nest, Lauren told herself she was being ridiculous, thinking that anyone gave a damn about her hairstyle. The mourners weren't thinking about anything except the loss of the sweet, vibrant young neighbor, friend, or coworker they had come to bid goodbye.

As strung out as Lauren was, her defenses were far weaker than usual against the phobia that plagued her. So by the time Mr. Brashear nodded to indicate it was time for her to step forward and deliver the brief eulogy she'd prepared, she was trembling and perspiring while every word fled her brain. She wanted desperately to run, to flee these people and their expectations. But a quiet voice in her mind whispered that Rachel deserved better.

With her heart thumping and her eyes downcast, Lauren managed to mount the small podium, where she took a shaky breath and wet her lips before beginning. "I-I'm no good at this sort of thing, nowhere near as good as Rachel would be. Sh-she should be the one here, helping us all through this. M-making us laugh at one of those dumb puns of hers, reminding us that death sucks, but it's still worth the pain—worth whatever price you pay to get to love someone so special."

Lauren fell silent, the pain that filled her lungs making it impossible to breathe. Did she really believe what she was saying? Could anything be worth what she was feeling now? *How could you do this to me, Rachel? How could you let some sick bastard convince you you had no choice?*

After that, she stammered through something—heaven only knew what—looking forward to that moment when she could flee this nightmare. Could sleep her way back to a day before she'd ever heard of Cruz Jimenez or received his devastating news. Back to a day when she had never met or spoken with or made love to or spent half of the night worrying herself sick over a man named Brent Durant.

Abruptly aware she was no longer speaking, she blinked down into a sea of sympathetic eyes. With a nod of thanks, or perhaps of apology for subjecting them to her nonexistent speaking skills, she stepped down and forced herself not to flinch away when Mr. Brashear touched her arm and assured her she'd done "well," a polite lie if she'd ever heard one.

Though a number of people pressed forward to offer their condolences, Lauren's gaze went to the huddle formed by Rachel's inner circle. Their faces pale and eyes red, they hung back, skittish and standoffish, as if they feared that tragedy was catching.

Lauren could hardly blame them, with the shocking news of Nikki's murder so fresh. With her name released, but no details, they could be forgiven for taking their leave without speaking.

Even without them, Lauren was having enough trouble fending off the hugs and tears of Rachel's coworkers, ex-boyfriends, and fellow students from her college years. Though Lauren remembered, for her sister's sake, to thank people for coming, she couldn't control her tendency to stiffen with each stranger's touch, no more than she could stop herself from either clamming up or blurting something awkward—or awful, as she did when a well-meaning older woman, a former neighbor of her sister's, assured her, "Rachel's in a better place now, honey."

"You mean here, in this casket? In this hole in the cold ground, where no one who loves her will ever see her again?" Heedless of the way the woman shrank back, Lauren glared at her, resenting the graying hair, the wrinkles, seeing them as achievements that her sister would never know. "Do you honestly think *that's* a better place for a twenty-five-year-old?"

"I-I'm so sorry, dear. I never meant t-to upset . . ." began the woman before tears sprang to her eyes. Turning with a sob, she fled, her departure making Lauren feel worse than ever—so much smaller and crueler than the generous, caring person her sister would have wanted.

After her outburst, the remaining mourners gave Lauren a wide berth. As they ebbed away, she heard their whispers, faint as the cold breeze rattling through the grove of gnarled trees that edged the old cemetery.

But the trees, she realized, were not the only things that stood there. Among them, she first made out a glint at approximately eye level, a reflection of the weak winter sun off a piece of glass. Was that a camera lens?

Her pulse accelerating, Lauren took a few steps in that direction. Mr. Brashear stepped up to ask her a question, but she didn't hear a word of it. Instead, she took two more tentative steps, her attention riveted to a silhouette shifting among the branches.

A burst of heat suffused her as it came to her what she was seeing—and who must have sent the man holding the camera. Temper boiling over at the intrusion of one of Jaycee Joiner's minions on this private moment, Lauren started toward the movement, her long strides straining the fabric of the black skirt she was wearing.

"Wait, Miss Miller! Don't go in there!" the funeral director called after her.

Looking back, she shook her head. "I can't believe it. They're filming—filming her funeral after I expressly told them I wanted nothing to do with them."

Clearly alarmed, he didn't give up, saying something about homeless encampments. But Lauren ignored him, kicked off her heels, and broke into a run, far more furious than she was afraid.

"Hold it right there," she shouted at the male figure scrambling to get away.

She stopped short, sucking in a breath as something in his silhouette—maybe the breadth of the shoulders—reminded her of Brent. At the same instant came the pounding of footsteps behind her, the heavy breathing that had her whirling around to face the funeral director.

Except it wasn't Mr. Brashear. She shrieked, her heart jerking at the sight of a stranger in a gray suit and tie running at her—a fit, dark-skinned man with close-cropped black hair, a thin mustache, and the intensity of a wide receiver positioning himself to catch a pass. As she lurched to her left, attempting to avoid him, she saw his hand rising, clutching something that glinted in the winter sunlight.

Gun! He's going to shoot me. But a splintered second later, recognition kicked it—*Not a gun, a badge*—along with his shouted warning.

"Austin Police, Miss Miller. Stop where you are, for your own safety."

But she was already falling, tripped up by her own bare feet. She came down in an explosion of bristly grass and dry leaves, the wind knocked out of her.

"Are you all right?" he asked, hesitating while another man—Detective Jimenez—raced past them, his gun drawn as he ran among the trees.

Her mind full of Brent and the possibility he would be captured and arrested, she tried to call Jimenez back. But she couldn't speak, couldn't even draw breath for what seemed like forever but probably only lasted no more than seconds.

At last, the air came back to her lungs in a noisy rush, and the man beside her reassured her, "You're okay. Everything's okay. Can you tell me who you were chasing?"

Once she could breathe again, she ignored his question to press her own. "Wh-why? Why were y-you staking out the funeral?" It was obvious to her that was what they'd been doing, without her knowledge or permission. Probably afraid she'd somehow warn off Brent. Maybe they knew that only an hour before the service, she had broken down and tried to call his cell phone.

Not that it had done her any good, with her call going straight to voice mail. She'd ached to leave a message for him, to ask him how, and where, he was, but she wasn't sure whether the police had already gained access to his phone records, now that he'd been implicated in a homicide.

"Just making sure you stay safe, Miss Miller."

His steady gaze and tone, she knew, was meant to reassure her and to keep her busy while Jimenez hunted down the man who'd been her—what exactly *had* Brent been to her? Abductor, partner, friend, or lover, or some deadly combination that kept her from wanting him caught and locked away.

"I'm Detective Wallace, from the Homicide Unit." He offered her his hand. "I understand you've met my colleague, Detective Jimenez."

She nodded and let him help her to her feet before explaining, "I thought I saw a cameraman, filming the funeral after I made it clear I wanted nothing to do with those vultures."

Wallace glanced anxiously in the direction his partner had taken. "He was filming? From the trees here? You're sure about this?"

She shook her head. "I might've been mistaken."

"If you're all right, I want you to wait right here. Or better yet, go back to the fellow in the black suit while I check on my partner."

Seeing the detective's concern, she didn't argue, so she walked back to find the foolish, impractical heels she'd bought for this occasion and stuffed her feet back into them before hobbling back to the funeral director, whose reproachful sniff let her know that her behavior had left his dignity affronted.

"Don't worry," she said as she approached him, "my sister would've expected nothing less of me."

Despite, or maybe because of, her worry over Brent, the thought made her grin, and she mentally added *Inappropriate behavior at solemn occasions* to Phillip's list of grievances against her.

Mr. Brashear struggled to compose himself, sputtering a few comments about how "irregular" this all was before the manners borne of his experience seemed to fail him. Giving up at last, he busied himself speaking with the cemetery workers while Lauren said a silent prayer that Detective Jimenez would come up with some charges to discourage the photographer she'd spotted.

But when the two detectives came walking through the trees, a handcuffed man between them, her stomach dropped as she saw her hopes had been dashed. For this red-faced, sandy-haired man was no photographer who had been caught spying on her . . .

Nor was it Brent whom they escorted toward her, his eyes downcast, his face averted.

But Lauren knew him nonetheless—Megan Rutherford's now-beardless widower, who had gone out of his way to track Lauren to the hotel bar, where he had hit on her while calling himself Jack Steelman.

***

According to the last rap sheet Brent had read on his one-time informant, the man's real name was Leonard Arnott, and he was thirty-three years old, five years younger than Brent himself.

Except Lenny, as everybody called him, hadn't aged well, with his fish-belly white skin pocked with scabs and poorly healed scars, his tufts of straw-dry brown hair, and his teeth rotting in his sunken mouth. The "sampling" that had wrecked his health—and sent him tumbling from drug network mid-level manager to pitiful junkie in a span of just a few years—had taken a toll, too, on the man's brain, leading him to repeat himself to an extent that made Brent want to choke the snot out of him.

"'Magine me, doin' *you* a good turn this time 'round," Lenny said for the fourth or fifth time since he'd awakened on the bare and filthy mattress where he'd crashed, going from deeply unconscious to wired for sound in an impossibly short span. Tweaking—which he preferred to do by smoking crystal from a heated glass tube—had only made things worse.

"You thought I'd never do it, didn'tcha? Thought I didn't mean it when I said I'd pay you back for keepin' me outta the pen."

As badly as Brent's head was aching as he lay on the gritty, sway-backed sofa, he almost regretted the act of mercy from his old life. In reality, he remembered, it hadn't been so much about compassion as it had been about convincing Lenny to give him the leads he had needed to dismantle the Texas arm of a meth distribution network that was cutting a violent swath across the Southern US.

From the looks of Lenny, he would have been a hell of a lot better off in federal prison, with at least a chance of getting clean through one of the rehab programs the system offered inmates, than in the cramped, trashed condo with someone else's eviction notice tacked to the front door. Lenny didn't have the key to it, so he'd left it unlocked, allowing people to wander in and out throughout a night Brent only half remembered.

After realizing the situation was far more dangerous than he could have predicted, he had struggled to stay awake and on guard. Yet in spite of his efforts, pain, fatigue, and blood loss had taken their inexorable toll.

Rocketing to his feet, Lenny strutted around the apartment, his bare feet kicking aside old soda cans and crunching fast-food wrappers. "But who answered your call?" he crowed as he thumped scabby knuckles against his thin chest. "Who came'n gotcha straightaway without no questions? And today I'm gonna find that guy—that guy I know who used t'be a doctor—or maybe a nurse's assistant or something—before he got himself fucked up. Imagine me, Lenny Arnott, doin' a freakin' Fed a good turn instead of laughin' in his face when he called in his favor." He ended the pronouncement with a hooting cackle.

Yeah . . . it's now official. I've died and gone to hell. But as Brent attempted to sit up, pain ripped through his bandaged arm and his plastered neck, assuring him he was still alive enough to hurt. A groan slipped through his clenched teeth, unstoppable as the progress of the sun across the sky.

"Hey, pal. You look pretty rough. And you're bleedin' through—gettin' blood all over."

Brent swore, but there wasn't anything he could do about it, since he'd left the extra first aid supplies in his car. And there weren't enough antibiotics in the world to convince him to use anything he found in this apartment to bind an open wound.

"You sure you don't want a couple oxys?" Lenny licked his cracked lips and scratched his cheek, a crafty look darting through his bloodshot eyes. "You, um, you gimme the money and I'll score you some, maybe hook up with another tweak, too, while I'm at it."

"I—uh—no thanks, man." Nauseated with the pain that hit him every time he shifted his position, Brent desperately wanted the opiate, wanted anything it took to knock back the agony so he could get on his feet again. But even in the unlikely event that Lenny would come back with the oxy, Brent knew, as he had known last night, that he couldn't afford the luxury of a pill to give him comfort. Unconsciousness would end up costing him dearly, most likely at the hands of one of Lenny's fellow squatters.

Already, Brent realized as he looked over at the duffel of belongings he'd grabbed from his motel room before he'd left, the zipped top was wide open, the contents spilling from it as if someone had pawed through them. His laptop sleeve lay on top, conspicuously empty.

Brent thanked God that his encrypted data was automatically stored online. Still, he swung an accusing look toward Lenny as he readied himself to stagger off this crap sofa and hammer the little junkie flat.

Apparently sensing danger, Lenny skittered backward on cockroach-nimble feet. "It wasn't me, man. Wasn't me. I told Shorty last night not to fool with your stuff while you were sleeping. But at least I kept him out of your pockets—"

"The hell you did," Brent said as a half-forgotten nightmare twisted back into the light, a "nightmare" of someone skulking nearby until Brent had wildly slashed with the knife he'd fallen asleep holding. One glance at the blade, at the dried red-brown substance on its honed edge, told the remainder of the story. "Looks like I found my own methods of persuasion."

"I'm sorry, pal. That damned Shorty—seems like you can't trust anybody these days not to take your shit and hock it for a half ounce. But let me go'n score your pills. 'Cause you look bad, man, really awful."

The thought was sobering, Brent decided, especially considering it was coming from a guy who looked like his next stop was the county morgue. If he'd had any idea Lenny was so far gone these days, Brent would have never risked calling him for help.

The problem was, there were precious few people—let alone decent people—a man could call when he was covered with blood and fleeing a motel room with two bodies in it. And even fewer places he could think to run to now.

Eventually, Brent did come up with one place—a place he knew would be one hell of a gamble, once he got rid of Lenny by giving him the money to go buy the oxy as he'd offered.

But the level of risk no longer mattered because, whether death or the cops were the first to catch up with him, he'd be damned if he would go down in this wretched squatter's hell.

CHAPTER NINETEEN

Lauren felt the blood drain from her face as it sank in that Jon Rutherford had been skulking near her sister's final resting place. Why on earth would he have come here, much less taken pictures of the funeral of a woman he had blamed for his wife's drowning? Could this mean that Rutherford and not the boy from the café had been the one who'd stalked and hounded Rachel to the grave?

Heart pounding out her fury, Lauren hurried to meet the approaching detectives and the handcuffed man between them. As she drew nearer, she saw that the item hanging on a strap around Rutherford's neck wasn't a camera after all, but a pair of binoculars instead.

"What are you doing here, spying on my sister's funeral?"

He looked away, flush deepening, so she caught Jimenez's eye. "Did Rutherford tell you he's been stalking me? Using a fake name to try to hook up at the hotel bar?"

Jimenez jostled his prisoner. "Is that right, Mr. Ruther—?"

Rutherford looked up at her, his hostility like a hard slap. "When it comes to fake names, you should talk, *Celia Blanchard*."

"Can't imagine any woman in her right mind would hand over her real name to some Saturday night stranger. I only wish

I'd recognized you that night, before—Why, Rutherford? Why would you go after Nikki? Why would you want to hurt—"

"You bitch. Don't try to pin that—"

"That's enough," Detective Wallace interjected, his voice firm as he and his partner exchanged a brief but pointed look. "Why don't I take this gentleman to headquarters for a chat while you two talk a little further?"

As Wallace hustled Rutherford toward the cemetery entrance, she looked at Jimenez. "Why would he shut me down like that? That lunatic showed up at my sister's funeral and I can't even ask him a few questions?"

Jimenez waited, watching his partner and Rutherford until they were out of earshot. "We can't have him confessing here. On the off chance it does turn out he's somehow involved in a homicide, we don't want to blow the prosecution in the first few minutes."

"What do you mean, blow the prosecution?"

"We'll want to record it all—both the reading of his rights and, if we get lucky—a confession. *If* this guy's really good for anything you're suggesting."

A dozen questions clamored in her brain, but they were choked off by the painful awareness of where she was and what she should be doing.

"It's too much, Cruz. All this." She made a sweeping gesture that ranged from the pair's receding forms to her sister's casket and Mr. Brashear and the cemetery workers waiting with strained patience for her to clear the area so they could go about their business . . .

A business so grim and so final that the thought of it drove the breath from her lungs.

"Of course," he said, laying a hand on her shoulder. "But might I drive you to the hotel afterward?"

Still without a car, she had previously arranged for one of Mr. Brashear's assistants to drive her, but she saw in Jimenez's dark eyes that there were things he needed to tell her. She only hoped that she could find the strength to bear them. She nodded. "I actually moved my luggage and my dog back to Rachel's apartment earlier today—"

"After our conversation last night?"

"I'm not afraid of Brent Durant." She said it boldly, realizing that she meant it, despite her earlier doubts. The man who had touched her so tenderly, who had put her pleasure before his own, would die before he hurt her. "You didn't—you aren't here to tell me you've found him, are you?"

A grimace marred Cruz's handsome features. "I wish to hell I had. Considering the amount of blood in his car, he could be in serious trouble. And of course, we have a lot of questions. But we did find one thing of interest."

"What's that?"

"A GPS tracking device, affixed with a magnet to the bottom of his car."

"A tracking device? But who would—" She stopped herself as the pieces snapped together. "That has to be how the troll knew where he was staying. And how he realized we were heading for the café in time to run out of there. Don't you see? It's proof. Proof positive Brent's not to blame for Nikki's—"

"Don't get too far ahead of yourself. There could be some other explanation."

She waved off his cautious attitude, impatient as ever with others' slowness to latch onto intuition, to trust it and run with it to obvious conclusions. The tendency had gotten her kicked out of advanced math classes in high school because of her refusal to complete the useless proofs the teacher had demanded. With the answer as clear as window glass before her, should she waste time proving that the sky was blue and water wet while she was at it?

"So are you taking me to the apartment or not? I have things to do there."

Though he didn't look happy about it, he gave way. "All right, Lauren."

"Okay, then. Just give me a moment, will you?"

"Take all the time you need," he said, the warmth of compassion flowing through his words. "I'll wait."

She left him for a few minutes, first to speak to Mr. Brashear and then to linger one last time before her sister's casket. She had thought, when the time came, she might find the right words to say a better goodbye, certainly something better than the awkward eulogy she had delivered. Something to let Rachel know how much she'd meant to her.

But as Lauren laid her hand on the casket's cool side, it came to her then that she'd been wrong before, telling that poor older woman that her sister was in this cold box, that she would be in the ground. For whatever became of the body her sister had taken leave of, the presence that had animated her, the essence so precious to Lauren, had gone elsewhere.

She could only pray that Rachel had taken with her the memory of how deeply she'd been loved. No, not *had been*. *Was* loved, for as upset, even angry, as Lauren sometimes felt with Rachel for her last, desperate act, she would always love her sister until that day when she would be laid to rest in the empty plot beside her—the plot whose purchase guaranteed a future where the sisters would never again have to worry about being parted.

Eyes sliding closed, Lauren whispered, "Leave a light on for me, sweet girl. I'll be—I'll be along before you know it."

As she rode beside Jimenez in an unmarked gray sedan, he respected her silence for about ten minutes before clearing his throat and speaking gently. "If you're ready to talk, Lauren, could you tell me more about what went on between you and Jon Rutherford at the hotel bar—you said Saturday?"

She blew a breath through her nose. "All right. It was like I said. I'd gone downstairs to the bar, and he came over and started to chat me up, playing like he was some horndog business traveler. We talked for a few minutes, and then I blew him off and left. Only later, I happened across a picture of the Rutherfords and realized it was him, the husband. The same guy who threatened Rachel after her accident."

Jimenez frowned at her. "You mind telling me what you were doing down there drinking in the first place, Lauren? Hadn't you had calls by this time? Threatening, disturbing phone calls?"

She stared out the side window, watching the small, closely spaced houses slide by. With the hour growing later, a few of them had lights on, cars crowding the driveways. Families coming home to talk, to eat, to argue, never thinking for a moment that their time, as a single unit, had an expiration date.

"The noise inside my head that night was more disturbing. And silly me, I thought I might be able to drown it in a drink and the sounds of other people." She shook her head, amazed at her own flawed logic. "I don't even *like* alcohol. And I can't stand other people. Mostly."

Jimenez clicked on his turn signal. "At the cemetery, you accused Jon Rutherford of going after Nikki. What would make you think that, especially considering how last night, you suggested the boy you saw struck by the pickup had been the one to kill her?" He slowed to make a right. "*And* leave her inside Brent Durant's motel room afterward."

"The truth is, I don't know which of them it was," she confessed. "I mean, Rutherford or the kid from the café. But I have reason to suspect them both, as I explained to the officers last night, and I'm absolutely sure it wasn't Brent."

She half expected Jimenez to challenge the last part of her statement, to try again to talk her out of continuing to stubbornly stick up for a man she would still swear she was half-afraid of. Or maybe afraid *for* him was the right term, for the thought of him, hurt and on the run, on foot, made her stomach feel as if the world had been ripped out from underneath her.

It was not until that moment that it occurred to her that, somehow, against both her will and her better judgment, Brent Durant had become a rare exception. One of those few humans on the planet whose company she craved.

Brilliant choice, some obsessive-compulsive fugitive who's bound to either get you killed or arrested.

But it didn't matter how she mocked herself; she knew it for a blue-sky, wet-water kind of truth. The kind so clear and obvious, no proof was necessary.

The thought made her swallow hard, her throat tight and painful.

Stopping at a red light about six blocks from Rachel's apartment, Jimenez shook his head. "I have no idea what Rutherford's doing back in town or why he'd want to seek you out, but that boy from the café—you could've been right last night when you claimed he's somehow involved."

She straightened. "So you got into his laptop?"

"Not yet, as far as I know. But fortunately, someone at the medical examiner's office remembered seeing a missing persons flyer out of Houston and thought it might be our hit-and-run vic. Houston PD had the fingerprints, and we were able to get a match confirmed—and a little background from the investigator on the case."

"So who was he? What's his story?"

The light changed, and Jimenez accelerated smoothly. "His name was Chad Henderson. Rachel ever mention this guy?"

"No, but Rachel wasn't talking about anything that was going on with her. And what troll has the guts to use his real name anyway? They're cowards, every last one."

"It's still not established he was out there trolling, but his personal history was definitely troubled."

"In what way?"

The detective braked as a ragged-looking, older woman with a lumpy bundle strapped to her back stepped into the street. "Hold on a minute, will you?" he asked as he turned on the car's hazard lights and got out.

Lauren couldn't hear the conversation that followed, but she saw the detective take the homeless woman by the arm and gently steer her back to safety. After a brief conversation, he passed her something that made her smile and give him a hug. Money from his own pocket, Lauren was guessing, though the suspicious part of her wondered if he was putting on a show of kindness for her benefit.

The truth was, he might be drop-dead gorgeous, but she still didn't trust him. Didn't quite buy that his solicitous act was genuine. Or maybe she simply didn't want to like Jimenez because she wanted so badly for Brent's theory to be right, for *him* to be all right, in terms of both his health and sanity.

Jimenez climbed back into the car and continued his earlier conversation without missing a beat. "This teenager—Chad Henderson was his name—had everything a kid could want.

Doting parents, good schools, nice neighborhood, and all that, but it seems he was the original bad seed. Frequent disappearances. Lots and lots of problems."

"What kind of problems?"

"A history of restraining orders and charges dating back to his eleventh birthday. And not just minor-league busts for truancy or vandalism, either, but serious offenses from extortion and sexual harassment to the torture of stray animals he'd decided it would be *fun* to douse with gasoline and light up—"

"That sick little bastard." She shuddered, remembering the day she'd found poor Dumpling huddling helpless on the roadside, and thought about what might have happened had some sadistic monster spotted her first.

"Apparently, the parents had the money to spend on fancy lawyers, counseling, and a series of private schools when he kept getting kicked out of one after another. This past October was the last straw. He was expelled from a place for troubled teens after he confessed to planting kiddie porn on a male teacher's laptop following a disciplinary referral."

Suspecting that such an accusation, however unfounded, would have permanently destroyed the man's career, she felt a stab of sympathy. "Suddenly," she said, "I'm feeling a little less traumatized about that whole brains-on-the-windshield moment I witnessed."

As soon as the words were out of Lauren's mouth, it came to her that Rachel would have called the thought one of those "inside-your-head moments" not meant to be shared with others. To his credit, however, Jimenez only nodded.

"I know we should all be mourning the loss of such a young life," he confessed, "but if you ask me, whoever ran him over spared the world a future killer."

"Not future. That kid was definitely trolling Rachel, at least online," Lauren insisted. "And Brent might be right about him doing the same to all those others, including his wife, Carrie. Maybe the kid didn't physically lay hands on them, but isn't it possible he tormented these vulnerable women, who were already under fire and feeling guilty for their part in accidental tragedies, to the point they took their own lives?"

Rather than arguing, Jimenez considered it for a minute, no doubt weighing Rutherford as a suspect against one very screwed-up teenager. And weighing both of them, she suspected, against Brent's recent behavior, along with the discovery of two bodies in a room filled with his prints. "The kid was sixteen when he died. So you're suggesting, at only fourteen, he could've manipulated an adult woman into taking her own life?"

"I think you might be surprised, Detective, at just how many kids are out there hacking, trolling, using social networks to viciously destroy their classmates. It's like the worst bullying we ever saw back in school, except on steroids."

"And you know all this, because . . . ?" he prompted.

She mentally kicked herself but recovered quickly, answering with a shrug. "You're aware I'm in computer security, so I read everything I can find on related subjects and attend all the latest conferences to keep up."

The last part wasn't true, exactly, since she'd rather be dragged facedown over a sandy beach with her eyelids sewn open than show up in person to a seminar. She did, however, watch live-streamed and recorded sessions online. And there was no way she was admitting how much of her knowledge was derived from her extracurricular activities.

"One of the things I learned was, some of the most destructive hackers out there aren't old enough to drive," she added.

"We didn't deal much with cyber-crime there, but I used to work in Gang Suppression. So I do get what you're saying. Some of these kids are really too adult for their own good—and everybody else's."

Jimenez signaled and then turned into the lot at Rachel's old apartment complex. Lauren caught herself scanning the area, looking for any sign of Brent's car. The realization that, of course, he wouldn't be here caught up with her an instant later, riding a wave of fatigue that had her vision swimming.

"So what else have you found out? What else is going on with Nikki's case?" she asked.

He shut off the car's engine. "I've told you all I can for now, probably more than I should have."

Indignation pierced her exhaustion. "Considering that I'm, what? A *suspect*?"

"A material witness is more like it, which means a wiser man wouldn't want to contaminate your testimony. So in other words, you're going to have to wait for official news to break from this point forward."

"In that case, thanks for the lift." She reached for the door handle. "But I'm pretty tired after everything, so if you don't mind. . ."

"Let me walk you upstairs, at least. Make sure everything's okay up there."

"If that makes you feel better." Her voice flattened. "But if you're coming up hoping to pick my brain some more, I've already told you everything I know."

His look sliced through the layers, sliced through flesh and struck bone. "I sincerely doubt that, Lauren."

So it was as she suspected. He might have been pretending to be her friend, but Detective Jimenez considered her either in league with Brent or under his power. As if she were incapable of thinking for herself.

She took a deep breath, struggling for calm. "Well, I've told you everything I can remember, considering I'm running on about three hours' sleep."

Without waiting for an answer, she bailed out of the car and started for the staircase. Behind her, she soon heard the heavy thunk of Jimenez's door and the sounds of his approach. Instead of slowing her pace, she moved faster, forcing him to hurry to catch up.

As she started up the stairs, she pulled the keys from her bag. Whether it was the jingling or her footsteps that did it, Dumpling started barking desperately, her toenails scrabbling at the inside of the front door. Tired as Lauren was, she only thought of getting into the apartment and grabbing the dachshund's leash before she had an accident.

Then she recalled how she'd left the dog shut up with her treats and water inside the apartment's bedroom. There was no way she could have possibly gotten out on her own.

At the same instant that realization struck, Lauren saw it on the doorjamb—a smear of blood just below the level of the knob. Fresh blood, not yet dried. Her breath hitched and her hand clenched, the keys digging into her palm.

The blood, she realized, her pulse thrumming at her eardrums, was at the level of a grown man's forearm—*Brent's* injured forearm? When her gaze flashed downward, she saw a drip by her foot and heard the change in Jimenez's footsteps as he moved from the metallic top step to the solid concrete of the landing.

Whipping around to face him, she leaned up against the door, the dachshund barking up a lung behind her. *Stuff a sock in it, Mutt.*

"Everything's fine here," Lauren said brightly as her foot slid to cover the stain. "I'll just need to take Dumpling out before the neighbors start complaining. Then I'm going to crash on the couch for about twenty hours."

"You're dead white. Are you all right?" The detective studied her, his body tensing as if he were preparing himself to catch her—or shove her aside and rush past her.

Lauren tasted fear, a metallic current in the back of her mouth. Nervously, she scuffed her foot, the frenzied barking at her back seeming to vibrate through her bones.

"I'll be fine. Like I said, I'm just tired, and maybe a little dehydrated, too." She scuffed the bloody drip again and raised her voice, praying it would be loud enough for anyone inside to hear. If that anyone was still both conscious and alive—and not deafened by the dachshund's racket. "Quiet, Dumpling! We'll be in in just a second."

Jimenez stretched his hand out, his gaze narrowed and his expression serious as only a cop's could be. "The keys, Lauren, right now. And then you'll need to step aside."

She stared, heart pounding, trapped between the detective's demand and her own wild impulse to duck beneath his arm and run or hurl the keys into the empty space beyond the railing.

He stepped back, pulling the gun from a hidden shoulder holster in one swift and seamless motion. And the look etched into his handsome face offered her no choice at all.

CHAPTER TWENTY

Jimenez's gun wasn't exactly trained on Lauren, but her pounding heart didn't make much of a distinction.

She opened her mouth to argue with his order for her to back away from the apartment's front door. He shut her down with a look, his eyes warning she had damned well better remain silent if she wanted to avoid a night in jail—or worse.

Praying that Brent had left the apartment after discovering her absence, Lauren resentfully thrust the key at the detective and moved to a spot near the metal railing. He motioned for her to wait there.

Too afraid to shout a warning, she froze in horror while he unlocked the door. He stepped to one side and slowly, cautiously, pushed it open, as if he half expected bullets to come flying out. Instead, Dumpling ran past him, barking, and made a beeline toward Lauren, who bent to lift her wriggling, wagging companion.

"Take her downstairs right now," Jimenez ordered quietly. "I want you to stay there until I come for you."

Sick of being treated like a suspect, she answered, giving him her most glacial stare. "Whatever you say, Detective. But you're going to be seriously embarrassed when it turns out you're acting like an ass for nothing."

Dumpling made quite an armful, but Lauren carried her downstairs as she'd been directed. She strained her ears for any sound from inside the apartment, her nerves winding tight as she braced herself for a shout, a cry, a gunshot—staccato bursts that might add up to death. Her eyes filmed with hot moisture. Would another life be lost in the apartment where her sister had died?

Unable to bear the tension, Lauren hauled the dog around the corner and set her down on the grass. Instead of making the slow, lumbering break she was often prone to attempt when unleashed, Dumpling wound nervously around Lauren's ankles in an effort to stay close.

Lauren hugged her waist and wandered a few steps, then glanced up at the rear balcony that jutted from the building behind the apartment's sliding glass door. Her eyes widening, she gasped at a horrifying sight.

It was Brent.

His gray face was frozen in a grimace as he stared straight ahead. His muscles strained as he braced himself in an impossibly precarious position. His right foot rested atop the railing of the balcony, his left was wedged against an old air-conditioning window unit.

He's going to fall, she realized, certain that disaster was inevitable. Even if the metal railing or the rusted AC unit didn't give way beneath his weight, the rivulets of sweat streaking his ashen complexion and the blood staining his bandaged wounds warned he might collapse at any moment or lose his balance and go crashing to the concrete sidewalk far below. If he lived—and she was well aware that people often died in falls from lesser heights—he would likely break a leg or worse. Even if he didn't fall from his exposed position, anyone passing by or looking out from one of the balconies or windows opposite could see him and then dial 9-1-1.

But there was nothing she could do. Nothing except brazen it out and pray that Jimenez would leave quickly.

A loud crack from the old AC had her pounding heart leaping to her throat. She clenched her eyes and jerked her head away, terrified to see his fall, to bear witness when flesh and bone struck concrete.

She heard nothing more than Dumpling's growl, so Lauren gathered her courage to look again. Brent remained on his ungodly perch, though he'd shifted his stance slightly. He was peering down now, too, staring straight at her.

He looked surprisingly calm. Resigned, as if he'd made peace with whatever else life threw his way, now that he'd survived the worst. Though she'd never been the best at reading faces, she would swear she saw something else buried in his expression. A longing for a second chance, a wish that things could be different.

Maybe she only wanted to believe it, to imagine that in spite of his obsession with the past, he might yet take the first steps toward a future filled with more than dreams of justice and revenge. She needed to believe it was possible, needed to know a person could survive having his heart smashed into a million jagged pieces, could somehow find a way to risk the pain of reaching out again.

Dumpling spotted Brent, and let out a single *woof* before Lauren snatched her up and told her to be quiet. Startled into silence, the old dog was distracted—at least until Jimenez, still inside the apartment, swept aside a curtain to look out through the patio door.

Lauren froze, unable to breathe as the detective's sharp eyes swept the balcony. If he opened the sliding door and took a single step outside, there was no way he would miss Brent. No way in the world.

As Dumpling struggled in her arms, Jimenez turned away, letting the curtain fall behind him. A few minutes later, Lauren heard his footsteps coming down the stairs. Not wanting him to find her in a spot where he might look up and see Brent, she hurried around the corner to meet the detective.

"Everything all right?" she asked, "or did you find Al Qaeda hiding up there under the dust ruffle on my sister's bed?"

"No terrorists, but that's not what I was afraid of and you know it."

Even though he'd been right to be suspicious, she wasn't in the mood to let him off the hook. "You mean to tell me that sticking your damned gun in my face wasn't simply your way of comforting me in my grief? Because if it is, you need to seriously work on whatever you cop types call a bedside manner."

He kept his dark gaze leveled at her eyes. "For the record, Lauren, the gun was never in your face, never pointed at you. *You* were acting suspicious, just off enough that I figured you had something to hide."

"Here's a news flash, Detective. Even on my very best day, I'm *just off enough*. And today's one of the worst days of my life. You understand that?"

"I understand you're upset, and you have every right to be, but—"

Desperate to get rid of him, she kept talking, burying his reason in a landslide of indignation. "So cut me some slack, will you? And leave me alone to get some rest like I asked in the first place."

"All right," he said, his voice tight. "And I'm sorry today's been so upsetting. If you'd like, I'll call you in the morning with any updates I can share."

"I'd appreciate that," she conceded, toning down the cranky act a notch, "and thanks for the ride over here. Obnoxious as you were, I'd still take you and your gun over those damned funeral people every day, always pushing tissues at me and suggesting one more expensive offering would be *a fitting testimony to my sisterly affection.*"

He tilted his head. "Are you serious? They really did that, even after the arrangements were made?"

"If I told you *yes,* would you go arrest them? Or shoot 'em a little, maybe, so they won't do it again?"

He pretended to consider for a moment before shaking his head. "Makes for too much paperwork, even when you shoot 'em just *un poco.*" He held his thumb and index finger a fraction of an inch apart.

She faked a smile and counted out the heartbeats until he returned her key and said goodbye. Only when he walked away did she dare draw breath again. Still, she forced herself not to rush upstairs, instinct warning her that Jimenez still didn't really trust her, if he ever had. The fine hairs behind her neck rose as she imagined him turning around and watching from behind some bush until she went inside.

Terrified Brent would fall before she reached him and paranoid about Jimenez, she was so nervous it took several attempts to jab the key into the lock. Once she and Dumpling were inside, she quickly locked the door behind them and then raced into her sister's bedroom.

An instant later, she pushed the curtain aside, and cried, "Oh, thank God!" when she saw Brent jump down from rail to balcony, his limbs shaking but his mouth set in a look of pure determination. After lifting the broomstick from the sliding door's track, she opened up and said, "Hurry! Get inside. Jimenez could walk around and spot you any second."

He came in, and she closed the door, praying she'd been fast enough—or wrong to suspect Jimenez was playing her somehow, wanting her to think he'd given up on the idea that everything, from her "misguided" belief that Rachel had been driven to her death to Nikki's recent murder, stemmed back to a special agent driven mad by grief.

But all she could think of at the moment was throwing her arms around Brent and leaning her head against his broad chest. Over and over, she murmured, "You're here. You're back. You're not dead," not caring about his filthy clothes or stubbled jaw, not caring about anything but his solid presence.

He wrapped his good arm around her back and kissed the top of her head. "Lauren, I need . . ." Pain and exhaustion creaked through his voice, and coldness radiated from his flesh.

As much as she feared Jimenez might return with a demand to take a second look through the apartment, there was no choice except to pull back the comforter and top sheet of the freshly made bed and help Brent sit on its edge before he passed out on his feet.

"I'll get it dirty," he protested. "I'm bloody and I stink from—"

"Shh. Just be still and let me help you. Take off your boots and—"

"But I—"

"Do you want me to call back Detective Jimenez? Because if you don't quit arguing, that's exactly what I'm going to do." Maybe calling would be best, since Brent would at least get medical attention that way. But he'd come here for her help, and she couldn't bring herself to betray him after he'd risked trusting her again.

"Just lie back," she said. "That's it. Lie back and rest a while. You're safe now."

His brown eyes searched hers, and Lauren saw the enormous strength it must have taken for him to fight his way back to her, let alone to manage a balancing act she couldn't have pulled off at her fittest. But even great strength could be worn down, the way that wind, water, and time would eventually grind the tallest mountains into dust.

And lead brought men down even faster, not only the initial shock and blood loss from the bullets but also the infection that could follow. If he kept fighting rather than dealing with the problem, he could spiral downhill and end up as dead as Rachel.

"Lean back," she repeated, gently pushing his chest. "You need to rest now."

He remained upright, expression tensing, telling her she'd been wrong to think that coming here had been anything but an act of desperation. He might want to believe in her, might desperately need to, but he still wasn't there yet.

"Don't worry," she coaxed, her gaze avoiding the bloody droplets leaking from beneath the bandage on his neck. "We'll get you fixed up. Promise."

He didn't budge until Dumpling jumped up against his leg, her big, brown eyes pleading for attention.

Leaning forward, he reached down and stroked the graying head, his hands jerking through the simple movements. "So you're on my side, are you, dog? I figured you'd've gone over to Jimenez's team by now."

"Dumpling doesn't really have a side. She's happy to shake down anybody she's pegged for a pushover. Which I'm pretty sure explains all that crust missing from my pizza the other night."

"I wasn't being a pushover. I was—I was grooming an asset. That's law enforcement-speak for—"

"Trying not to get bitten on future visits?"

He managed a weak smile. "Could be I was more worried about *your* bite than the toothless wonder's."

"Good call, but you'd really better lie down. You're white as a sheet behind all that grime and . . ." She shuddered and left the part about the blood unspoken before squatting down to help him remove his boots.

Still he resisted, pulling his foot away from her. "Don't do that. I've got it."

"C'mon, Brent. You can't possibly manage one-handed." She glanced down at his stained sleeve and quickly looked away as dizziness fizzed through her brain. Though the sight of her own blood had never bothered her, she hated seeing those close to her injured and in pain. And like it or not, Brent had gotten far too close for comfort.

"I can use my arm a little," he insisted. "Managed well enough to make it out onto that railing."

"Seriously, you're going to argue?" She stood again and backed off, shaking her head at his stubbornness. Or maybe it was just easier to pull back, to be mad at him instead of sick with fear. "You scared ten years off me, you know that? I honestly thought you'd end up splattered on the sidewalk."

"Me, too, for a minute there," he admitted, as he used his opposite foot and left hand to take off the first boot. "As escape plans go, it left a lot to be desired. But it all worked out."

"It didn't work out. You *lucked* out."

"Considering that that little son of a bitch hit me twice in a dark alley last night, I figured I was due a little luck today." The second boot came off, but when it tipped over, she spotted a black handle sliding out from one side. Though he grabbed the boots and jammed them underneath the bed, he wasn't fast enough to keep her from glimpsing a flash of what looked like honed steel, which had slipped an inch or two beyond its sheath.

"What the heck is that?" she asked, realizing that was why he hadn't wanted her messing with his boots.

"Insurance," he said, "and last night, I was damned glad I had it after I lost my gun in that alley."

"I've heard of cops carrying a backup weapon, but why a knife?"

"In a lot of circumstances, a blade's faster and more lethal than a handgun. And I'm comfortable with using one. Grew up with them on the ranch."

"You grew up on a ranch?"

He nodded. "My grandparents raised and trained cutting horses in West Texas."

She frowned, considering. "So, they teach you some kind of fancy rope trick for breaking into locked apartments, too?"

He shook his head. "Got lucky there, too. Cheap latch on that front window snapped right off when I tried to force it."

"Okay, but I still don't get it. How'd you manage to drop the broomstick back into the sliding door track after you went out on the balcony?"

"I didn't, of course. There's no way I could've done that."

"But when I came in here, it was back in." Which had to mean that Jimenez had spotted the stick and dropped it into place, she reasoned. Had he done it to secure the apartment for her safety, or . . .

She hurried back to the sliding door and pushed aside the curtain. There, she spotted a partly dry smear of blood just above the door handle, which Brent would have left unlatched. Whirling around to stare at him, she said, "Jimenez knows. He knows you're here. He was just pretending that he bought it. Which means he's coming back, probably with reinforcements."

"*Shit.*" Throwing aside the comforter, Brent came swiftly to his feet.

Too swiftly for a man at the end of his endurance. The remaining color draining from his face, he stumbled forward two steps before dropping to his knees.

"Brent!" cried Lauren, hurrying in an effort to break his fall. But even if she'd been quick enough, there would have been no way to stop it. No way to handle the weight of a grown man as he crashed down, falling forward on the carpeted floor.

"Wake up!" She dropped to her knees beside him . . .

And sucked in a sharp breath as three knocks—heavy and insistent—struck the apartment's locked front door.

CHAPTER TWENTY-ONE

Pain gnawed through the darkness, slowly dragging Brent back to awareness.

He tried ignoring it, shifting his arm to a more comfortable position. But the movement sent fresh agony streaking straight to his brain, and he clenched his teeth to keep from crying out.

Can't let them hear you, he told himself, not wanting to imagine what would become of him if Lenny's squatter buddies figured out how bad off he was.

Wait, that's not right. In the murmur of quiet conversation that came to his ears, he picked out a female voice that was definitely no crack whore's.

Lauren's here. She's come to find me. At the thought, he lurched toward wakefulness, wondering if, instead, he might have somehow reached her and forgotten. Or was her voice a mere hallucination, a dream of heaven from the depths of hell?

No, that was wrong, too, he thought, his pulse throbbing fast and hard at his throat. *He* was wrong to imagine he'd reached paradise. His instincts warned of danger, some threat close at hand.

His eyes cracked open, and he found himself on the floor of a dimly lit bedroom, a clean room, furnished with a modular bed, dresser, and nightstand of the kind twentysomethings seemed to favor. The place was perfectly neat, too, other than the black skirt and dark print blouse flung just inside the closed bedroom door. Hadn't Lauren been wearing those just a second ago?

Uncertain how long he'd been unconscious, he realized he could be wrong about the timing. His gaze snagged on the lace-edged, black bra and panties tangled with her other clothing, and his mind froze with the fear—a fear that he had no real right to— that she was out there, completely naked, with some other man.

Smooth-talking Jimenez and his pretty-boy face flashed through Brent's brain, and pure rage brought him to his feet. Once up, he swayed, the pain and dizziness that had downed him once nearly pulling him back under. But it was the thought of the way his former colleague had been sniffing around Lauren, attempting to use her to bring him down, that kept Brent up and moving to the door.

There, he paused to rest, weakness dragging at his limbs. His head pounded, too, his blood roaring like floodwaters in his ears. As he stood there, doubt seeped in, making him wonder if the detective's interest in Lauren might be more than subterfuge. She was more than just a resource to be exploited. She was a beautiful woman with a razor-sharp mind, and if Jimenez really was rebounding from a divorce, he might just be attracted enough to risk his career seducing the family member of a victim.

A voice at the back of Brent's brain whispered that his suspicion was delirium talking. Still, Brent drew a deep breath and carefully turned the knob. Cracking the door open a fraction of an inch, he peered out but didn't see anyone, only the dusky gloom of the short hallway and the unlit living room beyond it . . .

Remembering the sofa where he and Lauren had made love earlier, he gritted his teeth and opened the door a little wider. As he edged into the hallway, he struggled to hear the low voices.

He tried even harder to imagine they weren't out there plotting his betrayal.

Instead, he caught sight of Lauren, wrapped only in a towel as she spoke through the cracked front door.

"I'll eat something in a bit, I promise," she told someone. "It's really nice of you to worry, but there's some food in the freezer and the pantry, and I really need some time alone now."

The person she'd left standing outside the front door spoke. Though the words were indiscernible, his subtle accent bled through, along with the persuasive tone he'd heard Jimenez use to dismantle the resistance of suspect after suspect.

But Lauren held her ground. "Listen, Detective, I left the shower running." The hissing from the bathroom backed up her claim. "And I'd love for there to be some hot water left when I get in it. Call you tomorrow."

Though his head was spinning, Brent grinned to hear how firmly she rebuffed Jimenez and how coolly she pretended that she had no idea he was onto Brent's presence here—if indeed he really was. Better yet, she'd gone back to calling his rival *Detective* rather than *Cruz*.

Once Jimenez had left, Lauren locked the deadbolt, then hesitated for a moment before peeking out through two slats in the blinds. With a sigh of relief, she relaxed her grip on the towel and started back toward Brent, so temptingly naked that he wished like hell the light were better.

The light was apparently good enough for her to make out his silhouette, though, judging from her startled cry and the way she scrambled backward, covering herself again as best she could.

"Brent?" she asked, tucking one corner of the towel into the top of her makeshift wrap. "You're awake. Are you all right?"

Shaking his head, he explained, "I heard voices, and—not that I'm complaining, but what the heck happened to your clothes?"

"You passed out and there was knocking, pounding at the door. So I started shucking stuff like crazy and ran to turn on water and grab a towel, thinking that the fastest way to get rid of Jimenez was to act like I was getting in the shower."

Brent doubted he had ever met a woman who thought on her feet more quickly. She would have made a hell of a special agent—if she could follow orders. "How'd you know it would be him?"

She paused, considering. "For one thing, he has a cop knock."

"A cop knock?" Brent echoed, but come to think of it, he knew what she meant. Hard, authoritative, the kind of knock that didn't take no for an answer.

"Yeah, a cop knock. But at least he didn't try to force himself in to arrest you, not yet at any rate." She turned sideways to slip past him, where she flipped on the bedroom light and stared at his face. "Whoa, Brent. Get your rear in that bed. Right now."

A smile tugged at one corner of his mouth as his gaze roamed her mostly naked body. "So you're saying I've still got it."

"What I'm saying is I don't want to break my back trying to pick you up off the floor, you big lug. Now quit ogling and let me help you."

"I can make it on my own." Despite the show of bravado, when he turned around, the room kept spinning. His knees loosened as well, leaving him no choice except to lean on her while she guided him to the bed. *Rachel's* bed, which reminded him of the ordeal Lauren had just been through.

"How was—how did the service go?" he managed, sorry for putting her through this stress on such a day. If there'd been any other choice, any way he could have left her alone to mourn in peace . . .

Eyes glistening, she shook her head. "I don't want to—I can't talk about that right now. Come on, Brent. Please lie down. Let's get you taken care of." This time he didn't resist when she shoved him back into the pillows.

Looking up, he saw her struggling to push back her grief, to channel it into activity just as he had poured his own into the hunt for the man he held responsible. If he could find the strength, the courage, he would warn her that the dark tide could not be forever held back, that eventually, it would drown everything that made life worth living. All the amazing things that made her so special.

A tic played at one corner of her mouth, and she abruptly headed for the door. "Be right back, Brent. Don't move."

From the bathroom, he heard the shower shut off, followed by the sounds of drawers and cupboards opening and closing.

She soon returned with a pill bottle and a small white plastic box with a red cross on the front. "Something for the pain," she said, shaking out a couple of ibuprofen tablets. "Just over-the-counter stuff, but maybe it'll take the edge off. This first aid kit's pretty lame. Better than nothing, though, I guess."

Grimacing, she shook her head, grunting in frustration. "This is ridiculous. You've been shot. You need a hospital, not some half-assed attempt to paste you back together."

"I need rest, clean bandages, maybe some antibiotic ointment and the pain tabs, that's all," he reassured her. "The neck thing's just a graze wound, and the arm's—I'm not even sure there's a bullet in there."

"Anyone can see you're seriously hurt. And don't try to tell me you haven't lost a lot of blood. Because you're wearing it, leaking it. And probably half rotten with infection."

"I'm not half rotten," he said, her bluntness taking him aback. And reminding him that infection was a very real possibility. One that could cost him big time.

"You will be if we don't get you patched up and cleaned up. But first, let me get you some water so you can take those pills."

She stopped by the walk-in closet first, where she found a robe to cover herself. Clearly more to Rachel's taste, it was made of some satiny, emerald material that only made Brent want to run his hands over Lauren's curves. Not that he was in any condition to do them the justice they deserved.

After belting the robe securely, she disappeared again and returned with a stack of folded towels and a tall glass of cool water, which he drained after taking two of the tablets.

"There, now I want you to lie back. I'll need to take a look at those wounds. The neck first." She shuddered at the thought.

"Maybe you should let me do that. We don't need you passing out, too."

She sniffed, two patches of color coming to her cheeks. "I'm not fainting. I can do this. I'll just need—let me get a washcloth and a pan of water."

She came back, her mouth set in a look of determination, but the horror shining in her eyes said something else entirely.

While she dabbed gently at the wounds to clean them, he did his best to distract them both, asking her if she'd heard any more about the kid struck by the car last night.

"I did, and it's not pretty," she said, telling him what Jimenez had shared about Chad Henderson's troubled background. "He's younger than you thought, sure, but isn't it possible that this kid had a gift—an evil, horrible gift for ferreting out and exploiting others' vulnerabilities?"

Brent shook his head, or tried to, grunting with the pain. As best as he'd been able to tell, the bullet's passage had formed a shallow groove along the side of his neck. Had it sliced a little deeper, he would've bled to death in seconds.

"Hold still. You'll start it bleeding again," she warned as she blotted the wound.

He clamped his jaw, closing his eyes until the pain subsided. But the more he thought about Chad Henderson, the less sense the kid made to him as the Troll King. "You're right that this kid sounds like serious trouble in the making, possibly psychopathic. But even the sickest juvenile offenders generally prey on those within their circles—a classmate or a neighbor, a relative or friend. They don't randomly settle on blondes who've gained a little notoriety. Heck, how many teens now even watch the news? And no way would some kid have the level of sophistication to frame a pursuer the way the Troll King set me up by leaving those bodies in my motel room."

"I tried to convince Jimenez that had to've been what happened. But they think there was only one body left there. The guy from the hotel had a bad heart, and they figure the shock of discovering Nikki like that—"

Brent started to nod, but remembered his neck and stopped himself in time. "He was still warm when I walked in and found them, much warmer than she was."

After she finished washing and drying his neck, Lauren used white first aid tape to secure some folded gauze, one side of which she'd smeared with an ointment that felt cool and soothing against the raw nerve endings exposed by the graze wound.

Her blue-green eyes searched his. "What about Nikki? Could you tell how—Do you think she suffered?"

He thought back to the violent bruising he'd seen around her throat, the red spotting in the whites of her eyes from broken capillaries. Signs of strangulation accompanied by the stench of a traumatic death. A painful, terrifying death, but there was no need to bludgeon Lauren with such gruesome details. "I think it probably happened fast, too fast for her to feel much," he said. "She might not've even seen him coming."

She released a tremulous breath that made him feel slightly better about massaging the dark truth to spare her. Turning her attention to his injured forearm, she said, "Jimenez thought you might've done it to force the authorities to listen to you about the Troll King."

"Me? That's insane."

"Well, since your sanity's in question . . ."

The more he thought about Jimenez, the more it bothered him. For months, the two of them had worked long hours, shared a few beers during those rare evenings when they cut out early, and given each other the kind of grief that guys do when they're buddies. "Cruz really believes that bullshit theory? He thinks I'd do something that sick just to prove a point?"

"I'm not sure what he thinks now, not since they found the tracking device on your car."

"The *what?*" Even as Brent asked the question, he realized it explained how the Troll King had found Lauren at the Omni and how he'd figured out where Brent had been staying. How could he have been so careless?

She pulled out more first aid tape from the roll. "GPS device, attached underneath your car with magnets. Maybe that's the reason Jimenez hasn't come back to root you out. Or maybe he's a better friend than you thought."

"Or he's out there in the parking lot, waiting for that SWAT team van to show up." Brent grimaced, picturing the heavily armed and armored officers taking bets on who'd get to bag an ex-Fed.

"If he really is, I can't see that we can do anything about it."

She was right about that, Brent knew. In his current condition, he'd collapse before he made it three steps. And considering the adrenaline spike inherent in a stand-off situation, any move he made might end up getting someone hurt. An image of Lauren on the ground filled his mind, the emerald robe gaping as blood soaked it. A possibility he refused to chance, no matter what the cost.

"If they come, I'll turn myself in. I'll find some way to make Cruz listen."

She hesitated and then nodded, returning her attention to the more serious injury on his arm. Paling as she washed away the layers of caked blood and grime, she worked as gently as she could, but he couldn't help but groan as pain flared with her touch. At one point, his eyes rolled back in his head, but her words returned him to himself.

"You may be right that you weren't really shot. I'm seeing something in the wound. It's a chunk of wood in there, I think."

"I heard it, right next to me, a bullet slamming up against a wooden gatepost when he popped out from behind a shed and fired on me." A piece from it must have been driven into his flesh. "Whatever got in there, it hurts like hell. Don't touch it."

She shook her head. "The flesh is already really red and swollen. Warm to the touch, too. Whatever's in there has to come out, unless you want to lose that arm—or your life."

He winced, the thought of his arm being taken somehow bothering him more than the death he'd willingly courted for so long. "You'll have to pull it out then."

"Not me. I can't do that. There'll be blood, lots of it, and I don't do—"

"You're doing fine now."

She shook her head, her breathing hard, her eyes wide with alarm. "Listen, Durant, I'm not cut out for this. The only hacking I'm up for is the kind—"

She cut herself off, flushing furiously.

He fought an impulse to smile. "Don't hold back on my account. I know all about that. Or enough of it at any rate."

She glared at him. "How much? How much do the Feds know?"

"They figure the majority of what you do is related to your business. Whatever isn't amounts to harmless recreational stuff. Mostly, anyway. Isn't that right, Litef00t?"

Her eyes widened, and he could almost smell her synapses sparking in a rapid-fire sequence. He spotted panic, too, but she contained it so quickly that he sensed that his friend Cisco at the bureau didn't know the half of what she got up to online. And Brent wasn't about to ask her.

"There's more I have to tell you," she said, hurrying to change the subject. "Something else that happened earlier today."

"I'm listening," he said, though part of him wondered if she was stalling for time, not wanting to think of probing his wound.

She told him about Jon Rutherford, hiding near her sister's funeral, and how she'd at first mistaken him for a freelance photographer sent by the television producer who had called her that morning.

"From *The Vigil*?" he asked. "I shouldn't be surprised by any-thing those muckrakers will do for a story. But Rutherford . . . Did he give any indication why he's been following you?"

"No, he didn't, but I figure there's a chance he might've been obsessed with Rachel after his wife's death, a chance he could some-how be involved, too. Jimenez's partner's questioning him now."

"No way Rutherford's the Troll King, either. Whatever his agenda is, it's all about the wife he lost, not the earlier women."

Lauren looked up from squeezing more of the ointment on a square of cotton, as if that would make a difference with a foreign object embedded in his arm. "I agree his beef was with Rachel, not any of the others. But you still aren't buying that the Troll King was Chad Henderson, that this is finally over. Because it is, Brent. I know it is, and the police will prove it, as soon as they get a good look at the contents of that laptop."

As certain as she seemed, his instincts warned this wasn't over by a long shot. Maybe the real Troll King had enlisted the teenager, but the troll Brent had hunted for the past two years, the person smart enough to try to turn the tables on him, had a genius, a maturity far beyond some damned delinquent.

Changing the subject he asked, "That first aid kit have any forceps or tweezers? I'll need something to dig out that chunk of wood."

"Are you kidding? You can barely stand it when I blot it, you've already passed out once, and you think you're going to pull that out yourself?"

He sucked in a deep breath and studied the uncovered wound. Surrounded by a garish ring of bruising, it was a ragged hole a little larger than a dime. His forearm was more than twice its normal size, but he realized he was lucky. If he'd caught the bullet instead of an outsized splinter, there would've likely been an exit wound, too—and far more damage.

"I'll handle it," he told her, reminding himself he'd survived injuries before, from a compound fracture of one leg after a horse had fallen on him in his teens to a dislocated shoulder after grappling with a suspect. And his wounded arm would only fester if he didn't remove the foreign body.

"Jimenez is right. You're crazy—and way too macho for your own good."

"Jimenez thinks I'm macho?"

She rolled her eyes. "That part was all me, Goofball. But I'm telling you, you're going to black out."

As she found and unwrapped a pair of sterile plastic forceps, he reached out to take them.

She shook her head. "Aren't you right-handed?"

He winced, realizing that would complicate things but unwilling to give up. "I'll make this work. You watch me."

She grimaced, her face paling. "I was really hoping to avoid that."

In spite of her obvious misgivings, she helped him cushion his wounded arm with towels to help absorb any further bleeding. When he took the forceps from her, she blurted, "Let me take you to a clinic. We can say you were fixing a door or doing yard work and had an accident."

Convinced he'd be arrested the moment he set foot in any medical facility, he shook his head, his focus shifting to a cautious exploration of his arm. But his left hand shook so badly, he could barely control his movements, and pain exploded in his vision, pain that opened its black maw and swallowed him headfirst.

***

After she pushed Brent's slumped form back onto the pillows, Lauren shook her head and sighed. "What did I tell you was going to happen if you tried that?"

Out cold, he had no answer. But his unconsciousness did put him beyond pain, so she swallowed back her squeamishness and took the forceps from his hands. Closing her eyes, she took several calming breaths and told herself she'd try. That's all. If the wood was too deeply embedded, she'd quit and bandage the wound—or maybe call Jimenez and beg him for help. And if the bleeding was too bad, if Brent grew any paler, she would do what she had to and call for an ambulance.

She knew he wouldn't want that, knew he would be furious to be taken into custody. But he would be alive and safe then, both from his wounds and the obsession he clung to so tightly.

The idea slid uneasily through her mind, the thought of him safe behind bars, inside a locked ward, or in the numbing fog of psychiatric medications. Safe but miserable, beyond the reach of hope. Would she really give him up, consigning him to the same rule-bound idiots she'd fought all her life, to those more interested in classifying, moderating, and burning away her differences than understanding her as a person—or at least getting the hell out of her way?

"I'll do my best by you," she promised and leaned forward to press her lips to the warmth of Brent's forehead. "But if I scream like a girl and throw up, don't say I didn't warn you."

She probed the wound with the forceps, her nose wrinkling as she worked. Within seconds, it was over, as she pulled a bloody chunk of wood about the size of the top half of her pinkie finger from the hole.

"Gross, gross, gross," she said, wrapping the thing in plastic and laying it in the kit's lid. To her relief, she didn't get sick or even feel lightheaded; instead she did what was needed with calm efficiency.

In under ten minutes, she had Brent's arm cleaned up, wrapped tightly, and elevated on some extra pillows she'd found on a closet shelf. He was breathing easier, as if he were asleep rather than unconscious. His face looked more relaxed, too, and his color was so much better, she was dizzy with relief.

With a fresh cloth and a clean towel, she washed and patted dry his face, too, and as much of his body as she could manage without disturbing him too badly. As tired as she was, she was glad to have his needs to tend, glad to have him—and the distraction of his bare chest, with its enticing array of dark hairs—to take her mind off Rachel.

Still, the pain was with her, embedded in her heart like a chunk of wood that no forceps could reach. She knew she would carry it all her life, scar tissue eventually growing tough and hard around it, like the other losses that she carried. But underneath, the tender spot would never quite heal; she would only learn to live around it . . . if she found a way.

Leaning forward, she pulled the sheet and comforter over him and watched the gentle rise and fall of his chest for a long while. Dumpling waddled over and half jumped, half scrambled onto the bed, where she curled up and rested her chin atop his legs. Lauren moved to shoo her off but stopped herself, knowing how much comfort a little canine contact could bring.

Eventually, she joined them, curling on Brent's uninjured left side, opposite the little dachshund. She meant to lie there only a few minutes, but instead her breaths deepened and grew deeper until they matched his own, and the long, stressful day took its toll, pulling her down, down, beneath the roaring river of her grief.

***

A tap was all it took, a tap delivered to the bulb he'd wrapped in an old T-shirt to kill the noise, and the security light shattered, without a peep from anybody inside. A second pop took out the neighbor's light, too, throwing the two-apartment landing into darkness.

Darkness was the operator's good friend, a friend to all those in his line of business, especially those with the misfortune of having an impatient woman like the contact breathing down their necks. Once he was certain no one had heard him, he used a tiny penlight to pierce the pristine blackness, a thin beam he blocked from view using the bulk of his body. Using it, he checked the door. Though it was locked, he was happy to find the deadbolt was a cut-rate, five-pin deadbolt model he'd easily picked on any number of past occasions. Just for the hell of it, he shone the light on the nearby window's inner latch, too, since a man never knew when he might find some point of entry left carelessly unlocked.

A thrill of pure exhilaration sparked up his spine when he saw the window latch—a cheap, old piece of crap a toddler could snap off—simply lying there, broken behind the blinds, though someone had pushed it close so a casual glance would not reveal it. Half-expecting the painted casement would prove an obstacle, he carefully attempted to force the window open. It gave easily, noiselessly, as if someone had recently worked on it, and he grinned in triumph. *I should play the fucking lottery. Today's my lucky day.*

It was true, he'd had a run of good luck, spotting last night's drenched blond witness the following afternoon heading to the graveside service of a young woman by the name of Rachel Miller—a service that the contact had suggested he check out. Blending near the back of the mourners in his dark suit and darker glasses, he had discovered that his target was the dead chick's sister, Lauren Miller, and minutes later, he had overheard a couple of young women gossiping about how "weird and creepy" it was that she was staying alone in Rachel's apartment.

He wasn't sure about the "weird" or "creepy," but he was positive it was a stroke of fucking luck for him. After leaving the graveside service before it even really started, he'd hit the Internet next, where it didn't take him long to get an address on the dead chick.

There was more online about Rachel Miller's suicide this past Friday, along with some posts referring to an earlier accident she had supposedly been at fault in, but that had been where he'd quit reading.

Curiosity, like a conscience, was a liability he couldn't afford, one that could only serve to get him hurt or killed. Better he should keep his mind on the goal of silencing Lauren Miller before she managed to ID him—and searching for that laptop on the off chance she might have it. He hoped to hell she did, or knew where it might be, for its timely recovery might make the difference between spending six months or a year or more exploring tropical ports aboard his beloved sailboat. It was an expensive hobby made more expensive by the string of women he went through every season, but fortunately for him, there were always people who needed killing—and others willing to pay handsomely to see to it that it happened before nature took its slow course.

With the window standing open, he kissed each bicep in turn, something he did dutifully at the outside of each operation. Next, he paused to screw the suppressor onto the threaded barrel of his pistol and check the magazine. He hoped to avoid using the gun, since even a "silenced" weapon could be heard through thin apartment walls. Besides, his own huge hands—and the massive arms that powered them—were weapon enough for most occasions, but he liked to allow for every possible scenario . . .

Except, of course, the one where Lauren Miller walked out of here alive.

CHAPTER TWENTY-TWO

It was fully dark when Brent woke, hearing something—was that scraping sound coming from inside the apartment? Dumpling was only half a step behind him, jumping down from the bed and growling her way toward the front door.

Heart thumping, he extricated himself from the sweet prison of Lauren's embrace and sat up, his teeth clenched against the pain. He heard the scrape again, followed by a light thump, and realized the sounds had come from outside the apartment. Whoever was out there could easily get in—all he had to do was discover the broken latch and raise the front window, the damned window Brent had meant to find some way to secure before he had passed out.

Dumpling's growl deepened, and Brent called to her, "Hush," before she could start barking.

"Wha—What's going on?"

Now that his eyes had adjusted, he could make out Lauren sitting up beside him, her form striped by the illumination from an outdoor security light sifting through the blinds on the rear window.

"Shh," he warned. "There's someone out there, outside the front door."

"Police?"

"Possible." He was already bracing, breath held, for what Lauren had termed the *cop knock*, but when it didn't come, he swung his legs over the side of the bed. "I'll check on it."

She grasped his left arm, her nails digging into his flesh. "No, Brent. Let me. You're in no condition. And if it *is* the cops, maybe I can get rid of them."

The pounding in his chest picked up speed. "What if it's the Troll King instead, here to do to you what he did to Nikki?"

"He's dead. He has to be."

"Are you willing to bet your life you're right about that? Because I'm not."

"If I'm wrong and he's alive, he'll have a hell of a surprise." Springing from the bed, she hurried to the dresser, digging into what he realized was her purse. And coming out with her gun.

He rose with a grunt. "No, Lauren. Give me that. You go waving that thing around the police, you'll be dead before you know what hit you. I need you to wait here, in the closet. And don't even *think* of arguing."

"Fine." She handed the gun over. "But just so we're both clear on things, I've performed all the surgery today I plan on doing."

"Deal," he said. "Now, in the closet." He headed out to the living room, where the dog had ceased her growling.

Was Dumpling really that obedient to his command, or had their late-night visitor left the front porch? Imagining the intruder taking off, Brent wondered if he had spoken too loudly when he'd called to quiet the dog. Or had the person at the door heard the growling and realized she was about to raise the alarm?

Neither possibility pointed to police, since they'd likely use a metal ram to break in the door and toss in a stun grenade— what law enforcement called a flashbang—to temporarily disable anyone inside. Instead, he figured the intruder for a lone assailant—the Troll King, who clearly wasn't dead at all.

The bastard could be fleeing now, getting away while Brent stood here debating. With the thought, his pain and weakness fell away, replaced by the roar of adrenaline in his ears. Risk or not, he couldn't let it happen. Couldn't allow the man who wanted to hurt Lauren—to rip her from him as he'd ripped away Carrie—to escape. He refused to leave the troll alive to strike again, hurting him or anyone else.

Flinging the door open, Brent burst outside, gun at the ready, not caring if it killed him, as long as he struck first.

***

No way was Lauren cowering in the closet, not when her own quick explanation might keep the police from shooting Brent down. Instead, she stood near the bedroom doorway—until he threw open the door and launched himself like a missile toward the darkness.

Dumpling barked at the commotion, and Lauren sprang after Brent, her fear that he'd get himself shot overcoming her instinct for self-preservation. It was pitch black beyond the front door—as if someone had knocked out the landing's lone security light, but she charged forward.

"Lauren, look out!" Brent shouted over the dog's riot. Shouted from a point directly in front of and beneath her.

The warning came too late, her shins striking some obstacle as she ran straight into it. Though it slid forward as she kicked it, she tripped, her momentum sending her tumbling headlong toward the landing. Already down, Brent grabbed her as she fell, breaking her fall but grunting with the fresh insult to his bandaged forearm.

"Shit. What *is* that?" she asked, kicking at whatever obstacle had tripped them.

Moments later, the next-door neighbor's door opened, the light spilling out from his apartment. "What's up with that racket? Anybody hurt?"

"Dumpling, hush," Brent said, and the dog fell silent. "Front light's out, and someone left this damned box right on the front doorstep."

"Are you okay?" Lauren asked him.

"I will be. You?"

"I'll live." As Brent helped her to her feet, she noticed he had tucked the gun behind a lidded white box, the kind used to store files or reams of paper.

"Hang on. I've got a flashlight," the neighbor told them. When he returned a moment later, the blinding brightness made Lauren raise an arm to shield her eyes.

The beam dropped to the box, and Brent nudged it with his socked foot. When it slid a few inches, he said, "Not very heavy, whatever it is, but I don't see any labels."

The neighbor approached, and Lauren saw he was a bearded, middle-aged guy wearing a plaid bathrobe. His sparse hair was standing straight up, as if the noise had dragged him from his bed. Approaching, he offered up the flashlight. "Here, you can return it in the morning. I'm Cooper by the way. Brian Cooper."

"Thanks, Mr. Cooper," said Lauren. "And sorry we disturbed you."

"I've been meaning to tell you how sorry I am about your sister."

"Yeah, I know. Everybody's sorry. But nobody can ever, ever make it right again."

Cooper shifted, glancing toward his door as if checking his escape route.

"But thanks," Brent put in, having mercy on the guy.

He hesitated, peering at Brent another moment before his shoulders stiffened and he stepped back, his demeanor flipping like a switch. "Wait—I know you. You were here before, banging on her front door. I told you to get lost before I called the cops."

Lauren's heart raced with the accusation. Then she recalled how Brent had told her he'd been here before.

"That was me." Regret hung heavy in Brent's words. "I was worried about Rachel, damned worried she might—"

"He's a friend." Lauren edged in front of Brent in the hope of blocking his bloodstained clothing. With the neighbor already suspicious, he might head in to call the police. "I live out of town, so I asked him to stop by here and check on her for me."

The neighbor stood a moment longer, as if weighing her explanations, before his shoulders slumped. "Bless you both, then," he said, his words sounding genuine. "And keep the flashlight as long as you need it."

Once he'd locked his own apartment door behind him, Brent ordered Lauren, "Go on inside. I'm going to check this out before I bring it in."

"It's a casserole, I'll bet," she told him. "After my dad died, people came and left food, hams and pies and more cakes than I could eat in a decade." Then she'd made them feel uncomfortable, even when she tried to say the right things, and they left, too. Very quickly.

"In the dead of night, after shattering the only lights? Shine that flashlight over next to the door, will you?"

Underneath the empty fixture, an array of thin shards caught the light. She swung the beam toward the neighbor's door and saw the bulb to his light had suffered the same fate.

Casting a worried look at the box, she asked, "You don't think it's dangerous?"

"Guess I'm about to find out. Now listen to me for once and go inside. Get in there."

Her face grew hot. "You don't have to get so damned huffy about it."

But the look he turned on her was so fierce, she hurried inside the door and waited with the dog, where she braced herself and screwed her eyes shut, then counted down the seconds, her palms sweating and her body shaking.

A half minute later, Brent came in, dragging the box with his good hand. "The next time I run into Cruz Freaking Jimenez, remind me to kick his ass."

"Jimenez?" she asked as Brent kicked the door closed.

"Yeah, Jimenez. Look at this." He flipped the top of the box to the floor. "That son of a bitch nearly broke our necks and gave me a damned heart attack for *this*?"

Dumpling ran to the open carton, her tail wagging with excitement. If Brent hadn't grabbed her collar, she would have clambered over the side and dove into the newspaper wrapping paper.

As a spicy, cheesy aroma hit Lauren, she understood completely. Her stomach was practically climbing from her throat in an effort to get to the foil-covered tray that had to be . . .

"His mama's famous chicken enchiladas." Brent groaned and shook his head. "I can't believe he'd do this. Bastard *knows* I can't resist those. They're my damned kryptonite."

"Oh, the horror," Lauren said, coming forward to pick up the tray and take it in the kitchen, where she set it on the stovetop.

"And it's still warm, too. Maybe we should file a complaint for police brutality. Oh, my gosh, are those Hatch green chiles I smell in there? She didn't!"

As Lauren struggled to control her drooling, Brent brought in a bag that had also been in the box. Picking it up by one corner, he dumped it on the counter. The clothing was most obvious, an inexpensive sweatshirt, a pair of jeans, and fresh socks with the discount outlet tags still on them. Two pill bottles tumbled out, as well, prescription bottles with their labels torn off. Someone had marked each with a piece of masking tape, the words *Antibiotics, 2x daily* on one and *Pain, every 4 hours,* on the other.

"Wow, I guess Cruz is a better friend than you figured after all," Lauren said. "A much better friend. I still can't get over— why did I never think of putting green chiles in my enchiladas?"

But Brent brought the box over and started taking out the newspaper, his movements incredibly precise for someone whose stomach she heard growling from across the room.

So paranoid, he can't even accept an act of kindness, she thought as she pulled two plates from the cupboard. *Do you really think there's any chance he'll ever let go of his suspicion?* As painful as it was, as deeply as it hurt her, to imagine Jimenez had been right from the beginning, the sight of Brent gritting his teeth against his agony as he smoothed out page after page, shattered the hope that kept falling on some fertile patch of her heart, no matter how she tried to weed it out.

Then she heard a click, quiet and high-pitched enough that Brent missed the sound. But Dumpling's sharp ears perked up, and Lauren hurried to intercept the greedy dachshund before she reached—and gulped down—whatever had fallen to the floor.

She recognized it as a tiny microphone taped to a small battery that had been disguised by wrapping it in the newspaper. Except for Brent's "paranoia," they never would have seen it. Never would have known that Brent's "good friend" had offered up this kindness as a way to spy on them.

Brent cut her a look that informed her he had seen the device—and recognized it for the betrayal he'd expected. "Let's get this trash out of here." His calm tone belying the intensity of his expression, he crumbled up the newspaper—loudly and close to the receiver—and gave Lauren a nod.

Rather than crushing the thing, she deftly plucked out the wire that connected the mic to the battery. As far as she was concerned, it was bad business to wreck a perfectly good bug when she didn't have to. A person never knew when one might come in handy.

"So you still think that son of a bitch is a *good friend*?" Brent's voice dripped with sarcasm.

"That all depends," she said as she opened a drawer and pulled out a pair of forks and knives, "on whether or not he comes crashing through the front door before we finish off those enchiladas."

***

The operator had never been religious, but he was superstitious as all get-out. It had been in this vein that he'd taken to those two ladies his south-of-the-border brethren sometimes called on, tattooing the skeletonized personification of death, Santa Muerte—a Mexican folk saint often depicted with flowing blond hair—on one bulging bicep and Santa Maria Auxilatrix—whom some consider the patron saint of assassins—on the other. It had been a damned fool thing to do, since any sort of body art made it easier for the authorities to ID him, but tonight he was thanking both from his spot behind the bushes below the Miller chick's apartment. Thanking his lucky ladies for the miracle that had gotten him downstairs off the landing when his burner phone vibrated insistently in his back pocket.

It had been his very own patron saint calling, though there were plenty who would dispute the contact's holiness, if only they were alive to squawk about it. Inconvenient as her timing had been, he'd been forced to lower the window and then leave the landing, because a guy who wanted to stay on the right side of the grass did not ignore her calls.

"Is he gone now?" she asked in his ear, waiting until he judged it safe to hold a two-way conversation.

"Yeah, he's gone," he whispered as his balls descended from the place they'd fled in panic. Because the man delivering the white box had been packing, no freaking doubt about it. As he'd walked past along the sidewalk, carrying his burden, the operator had seen the way his jacket had snagged on his shoulder holster. And shoulder holsters often meant cops, though why this one was making a delivery after midnight was just as big a mystery as why he'd slipped away in such a hurry. "And everybody else went back inside."

The operator had already explained that Lauren Miller wasn't alone—which was too bad for her boyfriend or whatever, since he, too, was going to end up the victim of a "botched robbery" attempt later tonight. As soon as everyone had settled down and had a chance to get back to sleep.

"There's just this one thing," the contact told him, once he'd briefed her on his strategy. "You see, the client's called me, and there's a little change of plans."

He clapped a hand over the mouthpiece so she wouldn't hear him swear. A change of plans, *now*, with the target all but dead?

"Which at this point in the game," she continued, "required a substantial renegotiation of the finances of this deal. Putting it in terms you might appreciate . . ."

She named a figure that made him smile, imagining at least a year and a half—maybe two if he was careful—living aboard the boat. He was already tasting the daiquiris and picturing a leggy brunette with a Brazilian—and he wasn't thinking *blow-out*—when the contact went on to say, "This woman's death can't be murder, or look like it. And an accident, the client insists, would be way too suspicious."

"Which leaves us with exactly *what*, then?"

"A woman so saddened by her sister's death, she decides to join her . . ." A pause stretched long and fragile as a strand of spider's silk on the breeze. " . . . in an act of suicide."

CHAPTER TWENTY-THREE

It was a testimony to Brent's hunger—and to the almost magical properties of Señora Jimenez's enchiladas—that he was able to choke down half a plateful of them. Between his throbbing wounds and his worry about Jimenez's next move, it was all he could do to sit there instead of lurching toward the bathroom to be sick.

"No," he said in answer to Lauren's eager question, "I am definitely *not* calling Cruz to ask him if his mama will share her recipe. Since you're so damned friendly with him, why don't *you* call?"

She rolled her eyes at him. "I was only thinking it might be a good way to open a dialogue between the two of you."

"Open a dialogue, my ass. I don't have anything to say to him."

After warning him not to even think about getting up to help, she stacked the plates and silverware. "Even I know you should probably start with *thank you*. And people say *I'm* dense about the social stuff."

"Thank him for what? For trying to talk you into thinking I'm a killer, or putting a bug inside that Trojan-horse care package of his?"

"He brought food—the best food ever"—she eyed the leftovers longingly, as if she were considering whether she could cram in another bite, and he decided he liked it that she wasn't one of those women who pretended to live off the fumes of self-denial—"and clothes and medicine. And I'm betting none of these things were authorized by his department. In fact, I'd go so far as to say he hasn't even mentioned his visit here to his partner."

"And how would you know that?"

"Seriously? The prescription bottles with the labels torn off? That spliced-together bug of his? Cops can't really do that, can they?"

"For all I know, he's working with my former colleagues from the FBI on this. Could be part of their plan to make us believe he's off the reservation," Brent said. "You ever think of that?"

She pressed her lips together thoughtfully and carried the plates to the sink, but at least she didn't call him paranoid this time.

She scraped Brent's uneaten portion into the sink, ran the disposal, and loaded the dishwasher. Once she had put the wrapped leftovers in the fridge, she turned toward him, studying his face. "You're looking pretty rough. You'd better take that medicine."

"How the hell do we know they aren't some kind of tranquilizers to knock me out cold so the cops can waltz in and take me into custody?"

She made a rude noise. "And I thought *I* was neurotic. Come on, Brent. If they'd wanted to dope us up, why not just lace the enchiladas with sedatives? Though that would be a crime against all that is holy."

"The food . . ." he said, realizing his condition was dangerously undercutting his thought processes. It would be the perfect bait and switch, focusing his suspicions on the pills while drugging food he knew and trusted.

"Considering that I'm not unconscious after the plateful I ate, I'm sure the food was fine," she insisted. "More than fine, and I'm betting the medicine will be, too."

"Betting with my freedom. Or are you telling me you'd take some random pills delivered by a guy who's trying to arrest you?"

She put a hand on her hip. "If the alternative was debilitating pain and infection, I'd consider it. But you're right. I'd check 'em out first—the medications, that is."

"How do you propose to do that?"

"How do I do anything?" She picked up her laptop from the counter and brought it to the table. "Pass me those bottles, will you?" she asked once she was seated next to him.

He shoved them toward her and she popped the tops off and shook out one tablet from each. Then she typed the words *prescription pill identifier* into her search engine.

He pulled his chair closer to hers and watched the fluid dance of her fingers on the keyboard. There was an untamed grace in the way she moved, the way she zeroed in on her query with the tenacity of a tigress stalking prey. It made him want her again, made him need to recover the strength to make love to her for as long as it would take to discover every facet of her, to kiss away her grief and the million tiny scars that a bad marriage had left on her heart.

But he didn't have that kind of time, no more than he had the right to saddle the woman who'd reawakened him against his will, who'd entered into a relationship with a man on the wrong side of the law. So instead, he kept his focus on her search for the medications Jimenez had provided. "So you've done this before?"

"No, but I have faith that the net can give you almost everything you need, if only you can figure out the way to ask it."

Her first guess proved a winner, leading her to a site that allowed her to type in each pill's color and shape, and any markings imprinted on the side.

The first he recognized as a generic painkiller commonly traded on the street. "See this?" he asked, pointing at the warnings that listed it as potentially addictive and sedating. "This stuff'll put you under if you're not used to taking it."

"Oh, come on," she said. "Doctors prescribe it all the time. I took it myself after I strained my back a couple years ago. I didn't turn into a junkie, and nobody came and threw a net over my head."

"I could point out that you probably hadn't kidnapped anybody, either, or been mentioned as a potential suspect in a murder."

"So you're finally admitting it was a kidnapping." Triumph glinted in her gaze.

"I'm admitting that there are those who might interpret it as such."

"Including any rational person, but you do have a point about the cops' motivation." She nodded toward the second tablet. "Here, let's try this other one. Can you read those little numbers on the side for me?"

He did so, and they soon found the pill was exactly what the bottle had claimed, a frequently prescribed antibiotic used to treat "moderate infections." Only this one had less worrisome side effects.

"So, I'll take the antibiotic," he said.

"You'll take them both. Come on, Brent, please. You're white as a sheet and you're exhausted. Trust in this and sleep. Or, better yet, trust in me. I've got your back. I promise. Dumpling and I will guard you tooth and nail."

He smiled at her, but when her gaze softened, he saw how serious she was. In spite of the emotional fallout of her sister's funeral, she would stay up to watch over him, making certain he was not caught unawares. Looking into her eyes, he realized that of all the people on this crowded planet, Lauren Miller was the only one he had left to trust. And it didn't matter what deception and distrust had followed their first meeting, no more than it mattered that she was some kind of vigilante hacker as well as an unaccomplished liar.

All that mattered in this place, in this moment, was that she was willing to take a chance on him. And that he loved her for it with a fierceness that took his breath away. Or maybe he was grateful, that's all, grateful he had a woman as capable and as cunning as Lauren at his side, an ally he could count on after so long on his own.

"I trust you," he said, reaching for the pills still lying on the table and downing them with the remainder of his water. His glance banked off the dachshund. "But I'm not so sure about your sidekick. Pretty sure she'd sell me out for a forkful of those enchiladas."

"You're probably right, but honestly, for the recipe to *that* stuff, I might just sell you out myself."

He snorted. "Now you tell me, *after* I take the damned pills."

She stood and moved behind him and leaned over, her hair falling loose over his left shoulder, her warm breath tickling his ear. The teasing note in her whisper was seductive enough to get a rise out of a dead man. "You have nothing to worry about, at least not as long as those leftovers hold out."

When he reached for her, she pulled away. But his fingers found one silken lock, which tangled in his fingers. "You better be careful, coming this close." His gaze snagged hers and held it fast. "Otherwise, you might be the one with something to worry about."

289

She grasped his wrist and disentangled her hair, then straightened. "Don't you think we both have enough worries for the time being?" A wry smile tilted her mouth, belying the concern in her eyes. "Come on, let me help you back to bed before you get any loopier."

"Medicine couldn't have possibly hit me that fast," he protested, stung a little that she imagined he must be drugged to come on so strong.

"Considering it's well after midnight, you're exhausted, and you're hurting, I wouldn't be surprised at all." Despite her clear attempt to keep her tone light, anxiety bled through her words. "Can you get up on your own, or do you need some help?"

"I'm getting up." Hating the strain he was putting on her, he used his good arm to push himself to his feet. "Last thing you need is to hurt yourself trying to lift me, on top of everything else."

The room began to spin around him, forcing him to close his eyes.

Her voice reached out to him, sifting softly as moonlight through dark shadows. "It's all right. Wait it out. I'm right here if you need me."

When his head had cleared a little, she guided him back to bed and covered him as he lay down. Sitting at his side, she leaned over and kissed him on the temple, her lips so sweet and full of promise, his defenses melted away.

He looked into her eyes. "Someday you're going to make a hell of a mother, you know that?"

Sadness veiled her beauty, and she shook her head. "It was a stupid dream to start with, Brent, especially for someone like me. I'd probably let a kid starve while I was on one of my marathon coding sessions. Or turn the poor thing into another hermit cyber-freak like me."

"That dachshund of yours clearly isn't starving, and your sister was a social butterfly. And you practically raised her, didn't you?"

"Yeah, and look how well that all worked out." Lauren shook her head, her voice clotted with emotion. "I'll never forgive myself for not being there for Rachel when she needed me, much less risk my heart to another."

He grasped her hand and brought it to his mouth to kiss it. "You can't see it right now, but your heart has a hell of a lot more room inside it than you might imagine. Don't let this destroy you. Don't let it change you into someone your sister wouldn't recognize."

She sat in silence a few moments before shaking her head. "In two years, have you forgiven yourself for losing Carrie? Will you ever find a way to move on?"

He heaved a tired sigh, blackness clouding the edges of his field of vision. "In my case, there's a hell of a lot more to forgive."

"Maybe. Or it could be that it feels safer to blame yourself than deal with your anger with a dead woman."

"Believe me, I tried blaming her, tried being angry for the longest time. But it was all a waste of energy when I was just as much to blame. More, really."

Lauren squeezed his hand, her eyes encouraging him to explain. And it came to her that she deserved to know just how big a screwup he was before she got in any deeper.

"Carrie and I had been trying for years to have a kid of our own. She wanted it so desperately, I would've done anything to make it happen—would've gone to the ends of the earth just to make her smile again. Unhappy as she was, I should never have agreed to let her watch our neighbors' little boy. I should have seen how it was eating at her, watching over the one treasure she could never have— since she refused to look into an egg donor or adoption."

"That must have been tough for you, too."

"Eight years of that was no picnic, I can tell you, but having that little guy around in the evenings did bring some kind of spark back. I think we were both pretending, just a little, that he was ours. Our son . . . And maybe I was hoping having him there would convince Carrie a kid didn't have to be biologically related . . . for us to love him like our own." Brent's eyelids drooped, but the stream of truth flowed freely, the poison he had kept walled up inside him cascading through his system.

"Sometimes I'd buy him things," he continued, "just little things, for the pure joy of seeing him light up. Like the kiddie pool for our backyard. We filled it every night that summer so he could splash around and burn off a little steam while Carrie put together dinner. And because there was a pool, of course, there had to be a tugboat."

"A tugboat?"

"Sure, a little toy tugboat. Just a cheap piece of plastic—blue and white with bright-red trim around the edges, but I'd had one just like it, back before my mom and dad's wreck." He paused, getting the connection for the first time, how that stupid toy— that freaking boat that still haunted his nightmares—had forged a link to a past he'd thought long forgotten. "He loved the thing, just loved it when I surprised him with it that last night. So much that he had a meltdown when it was time to come inside and eat. I said we'd get it later."

He went quiet for a long time, drifting back to that night, to how he'd bargained with the squirming toddler, to the fragile bubble of his wife's voice as she'd called, *Come on guys! It's getting cold.*

Just as crystalline, another memory cut deeper: how he hadn't taken that extra minute to empty out the kiddie pool and flip it up against the back fence to drain, as he normally did each night. By the end of dinner, thunder boomed, one of those huge, crashing storms that so often built up on hot June afternoons around Oklahoma City.

Adam, it had turned out, was scared to death by the noise, and the three of them had cuddled up like a real family, along with their cat—called Wonton, since he'd been rescued from the dumpster behind the local Chinese takeout—until Adam's mother had shown up to shatter the illusion. Afterward, he'd caught Carrie crying, saying she couldn't do this, didn't know how much longer she could survive having her heart ripped out and torn to pieces night after night.

As usual, he'd done what he could to appease her, to distract her from what he'd told himself was only one of her passing spasms of emotion, intensified by yet another round of hormone shots. They'd ended up making love that night, the last time she had ever welcomed his touch, and later, while he'd held her, he'd given the little pool a fleeting thought just as he'd drifted off to sleep.

"I told myself I'd catch it in the morning," he told Lauren, a stab of regret rousing him enough to realize he'd been speaking all along. "But I had an early meeting, and it—it slipped my—it slipped my mind."

"We all forget things," Lauren supplied when his voice choked down to nothing.

"Not things like this. And not that goddamned tugboat floating in the middle. The one I'd bet my last cent Adam was reaching for when he fell face first that afternoon. Fell in and drowned in just a foot of water."

"Oh, God, Brent. I'm so sorry. I can't imagine how horrible you must've felt, how hard it must've been for everyone." A tear dripped off her cheek to splatter against his skin. "But it was an accident. A horrible, tragic accident, but it wasn't your fault."

"It damned well wasn't Carrie's, either. But she never forgave herself for forgetting to lock the back door after she let Wonton out right around the time Annabel dropped off Adam again that next day." He shook his head. "She was distracted, sure, worried how Annabel was going to take the news that she was quitting, but Carrie never for the world would have intentionally done anything to hurt that little boy."

Tragic as Adam's drowning had been, no one would have ever believed it to be anything but a horrific accident had it not been for Carrie's stiffness, her abruptness that morning when she'd announced she wouldn't be babysitting any longer after that day. Coupled with the emotional shock that initially made her appear indifferent to the news that Adam couldn't be revived, it had been enough to prompt the police to take a closer look at her role.

Yet even after the death had been officially ruled accidental, rumors spread like wildfire, sparked by the media's eagerness to air Annabel's grief-fueled accusations. And six months later, Brent returned home to pull his wife's pale corpse from the cool bathwater . . .

The bathwater on which a tiny tugboat bobbed.

***

As Brent slept, Lauren brushed away tears for a little boy lost too soon, for a woman who had been destroyed by grief and guilt and what might very well have been the malice of a psychopathic teenager. But most of all, she wept for the man who had carried such a burden for so long all on his own.

The question was, could he ever again set it down? Would he

face the fact that the Troll King had been killed and find a way back to his real life?

Not his former life, she realized. That much was for certain. In his quest, he'd gone too far, smashed past too many orders, directives, and even laws, for the bureau to ever accept him back into its hidebound ranks. And heaven knew, the tragedies that had destroyed Brent's former life had changed him forever, changed him into someone who would never allow his need for justice to be shackled by the rules.

But was he sane enough to make himself a different kind of life? And was she even crazier for allowing his tragic past, his stubbornness and honor, to seep past her own defenses?

Restless as a caged cat, she wandered the apartment, peering out one window after the next. Part of her wanted nothing more than to escape what she was feeling, to catch a bus or bum a ride back to her lonely farmhouse on the wind-scoured prairie. There, she could barricade herself in perfect isolation, pretending that the next weekend phone call from her sister—a touchstone Lauren had once lived for—was only a few days away. Pretending that loving someone, anyone, could ever be worth the pain that pierced her like a white-hot needle.

She thought about it for a long while, her tired mind working through the logistics involved in abandoning her sister's apartment, with making a break for it at 2:53 a.m. Through fantasies of running to escape the panic coiling inside her, the grief and the anxiety that made her want to shriek.

But she couldn't do it, couldn't leave Rachel's things to be pawed through by uncaring strangers. And she could no more abandon Brent to his fate than she could leave her little dachshund, who lay curled up at his side snoring softly.

Eyelids heavier by the moment, she turned away from the sight, from this pair who had somehow, against her will, staked a claim on her heart. Then she went to the kitchen and logged on to her laptop and into the virtual escape that was all that she had left.

CHAPTER TWENTY-FOUR

Brent jerked awake, his heart thumping at the muffled sound of a small and eager voice. Adam's voice, he'd swear on his life. He scrambled from beneath the covers, determined that this time, he would reach the boy before it was too late.

As his brain caught up with his panic, he stood breathing hard and shaking. Then he heard again the sound that had penetrated his dreams: peals of childlike laughter from somewhere outdoors.

Still breathing hard, he peeked out through the sliding glass door, where he blinked at the bright sunlight. As his eyes adjusted, he made out the receding forms of a woman with two small children on the sidewalk, and he realized one of them had been the cause of his adrenaline-soaked wakeup. An echo of old grief swelled to fill his chest.

But he was awake and steady on his feet, feeling stronger and in far less pain than he had been in the night before. Better yet, he was still free, which either meant that Jimenez was playing the long game or really out to help him.

When he left the bedroom, Brent discovered Lauren at the table beside her open laptop. Slumped forward with her cheek leaning against her crossed arms, she was fast asleep, dressed in jeans and a loose-fitting University of Texas T-shirt, her blond hair splayed across her shoulders.

She looked so pretty in the morning light, so carefree and unguarded that he ached for a day when she could know such ease while awake . . . a day when she could navigate her own grief without risking wreckage on his shoals.

The longer you stay, the more you're dragging her down with you. In choosing to help him, she was not only likely to draw Jimenez's suspicions, but she also risked being sucked into the same emotional quicksand that had cost him everything. Did he really want to strand her in the same grief-soaked half life he'd inhabited so long?

But instead of gathering his things, Brent grabbed a woven throw from the sofa and gently settled it over her shoulders. She slept so soundly that she barely stirred, even when he softly kissed her temple and clumsily slipped a sofa pillow underneath her head.

Convinced last night's medications had done him a world of good, he again risked taking both pills before heading to the bathroom to wash up and change into the clothing Jimenez had dropped off. When Brent came out, Dumpling whimpered at him and pranced near the front door, her brown eyes pleading for relief.

"All right, all right, dog. Keep your fur on, will you?" he murmured, hooking up the leash before she woke her mistress. At the door, he hesitated, tempted to tuck Lauren's gun beneath his shirt in case the cops were waiting for him, but he decided he'd caused grief enough already without risking getting into a shootout with a former colleague.

Still, his stomach knotted as he walked the dog around the grassy edges of the sidewalk. His anxious gaze darted to a thick-waisted woman in a skirted suit, who clutched her keys and scurried toward the parking lot. He spotted a long-limbed younger guy as well—a student, maybe, judging from the shaggy hair and backpack slung over one shoulder. A hulking mountain of a coverall-clad maintenance worker sauntered by next, in no particular hurry to make it to his next appointed chore. Any one of them could be surveillance, but Brent forced himself to keep moving, though Dumpling's deliberate approach to finding the ideal spot to relieve herself left his raw nerves buzzing with impatience.

Back inside the apartment, as he made coffee, his gaze settled on Lauren's open laptop. He ground his teeth at the reminder that his own computer was probably on its way to some low-rent pawnshop, but what about his backup files, the work that might just lead him to whoever had been pulling Chad Henderson's strings?

Unable to resist the temptation to reassure himself he could still access his work, he reached for Lauren's machine and scowled in frustration when a security login popped up with the message, *FINGERPRINT ID NOT FOUND.*

He glanced at Lauren, hesitating for a guilt-slick second before he took her limp hand. He lifted it carefully, holding his breath, certain that at any moment she'd spring awake and chew his head off for this breach of trust.

Moving her hand to the biometric scanner, he positioned an index finger over the reader. He sucked in a sharp breath when the damned thing gave a noisy chirp of recognition and she pulled her hand back, mumbling before she repositioned herself and dropped straight back to sleep.

Breathing at last, he moved the laptop to the pass-through counter and noticed the open browser window on the screen.

In the search box, Lauren had typed *Jon Rutherford Houston*, reminding him that days ago, she'd mentioned that the widower had moved back to a suburb of that city, where his parents could help care for the children. Curious about what she might have found, Brent clicked the search history and saw she'd also checked for links containing *Chad Henderson* and *Houston*.

Of course, he thought, irritated that he'd missed the geographic connection last night when she'd told him what she knew about the dead teen. Though it was a long shot, considering that the Houston area encompassed thousands of square miles and millions of people, Henderson and Rutherford might have connected somewhere in the city.

Lauren murmured in her sleep again, and he fought off a twinge of guilt, convincing himself she would have told him about her search anyway. He dug deeper and was just about to give up when he came across a two-year-old puff piece about some high school junior inventors team in Austin, which listed Jon Rutherford, of RBW Group Engineering, as a volunteer advisor.

There it is, the link . . .

Or it could be, if Rutherford had volunteered in a similar capacity after his return to Houston, possibly to help him get past his simmering anger over Rachel Miller's role in his wife's death. By that time, the grand jury would have declined to indict her and the insurance company would have settled his suit; but while he worked with the teens, had Rutherford seen, in Chad Henderson, another avenue for revenge, then twisted the budding psychopath toward his own dark purpose?

If it had really happened as Brent suspected, Rachel's death might well be unrelated to the other supposed suicides. Which could mean, he realized with an icy jolt, that the Troll King he'd been pursuing had never been a single person after all but some fucking bogeyman he'd conjured to make sense of the senseless string of deaths that had begun at his own doorstep.

With no answers to be found, Brent returned to checking on his online vault. He typed in his password, and his heart staggered at the red-lettered message *LOGIN NOT VALID*.

Shit. Had Jimenez or an FBI team somehow found a way into his files and changed the settings to lock him out? Were they downloading copies now, using them as evidence of Chad Henderson's crimes—or of Brent's own spiraling mental state?

He was breathing hard, sweat streaming from his hairline as he tried the login once more, his fingers fumbling through the keystrokes. With another blood-red blink, the message returned to taunt him *LOGIN NOT VALID*. Only this time, a warning followed: *1 ATTEMPT REMAINING*, a reminder that after three failed logins, the system was set to block him from trying again for the next twenty-four hours. Twenty-four hours he might not have, not as a free man, anyway.

He swore quietly and forced himself to slow down, to take a deep and calming breath. Feeling steadier, he tried again, praying that the only problem had been his own poor typing and his rush to get inside.

A few more clicks, and he grinned in triumph as the welcome message appeared: *ACCESSING FOLDERS*. Half-afraid that it would disappear, he quickly double-clicked the icon for the project that had consumed his every spare minute for the last few months, the website that would do him no good if he ended up arrested—or worse yet, committed somewhere—before he launched the pages. Up until this point, he'd put it off, telling himself it would do more harm than good to let the Troll King know how close he was to putting everything together. But with Henderson dead and his own freedom in question, Brent figured he had nothing to lose by stirring the pot at this point. And he knew of no better way than posting his work.

The home page opened, a stark testament to a chain of wasted lives. As had happened so many times before, the heart-rending photos sucked him down into a dark vortex, leaching away his awareness of the coffee in his hand, the dog curled near his feet, and the woman sleeping nearby, her blond hair alight with strands of sunshine that sifted through slim gaps in the blinds. Sunlight, he failed to notice, that was slowly working its way toward her lidded eyes.

Taking a deep breath, Brent clicked a button to take the site live. As the pages uploaded to the Internet, his gaze focused on an image of his Carrie, the woman he had loved and failed . . . and sometimes, God forgive him, even hated. The warped memory of a woman who had been his chief companion on this journey.

Was it really time to put her to rest, to admit that her death and all she'd suffered, all his attempts to atone for failing to protect her, amounted to nothing more than a disturbed teenager's entertainment? His gaze wandered over the other victims, through the "suicides" whose life stories, summarized beneath the photos, had grown as familiar to him as his own history.

In the images, each woman smiled, her beauty framed by pale or gold or sandy-colored hair, her blue or brown or green eyes alive with amusement, happiness, or hope in the weeks or months before tragedy smashed her joy to pieces. And before the cruel, judgmental world had come to feast on the remains.

As much as he wanted to believe it had begun with Carrie and that the Troll King's death would make Rachel's murdered friend Nikki Watson the final victim, Brent knew to his core that the problem went far deeper. With the world still sucking the dried marrow from the bones of long-dead beauties like Marilyn Monroe, Princess Diana, and so many others through its blood-stained teeth, there would always be a market for those out to exploit a fresh sadness. A market that would fuel the fantasies of sick bastards like the Troll King.

A market . . . marketplace. Brent blinked hard, his thoughts spinning like a thousand tumblers, whirling and very nearly locking into place.

***

The coveralls were freaking tight, constraining the operator's massive shoulders and cutting into his crotch. But XXL had been the largest he could get his hands on, and uninspired as the maintenance worker disguise was, it had rendered him all but invisible as he walked around the complex and pretended to check off items from a list on his clipboard.

Better yet, the ruse also afforded him an excuse to carry the tool kit he would need to gain access to the apartment. But going inside, taking control of the witness, and staging a sup-posed suicide in broad daylight still posed a host of challenges, not the least of which was the tall, capable-looking man he'd spotted with a waddling old dog—one of those obnoxious lit-tle bark boxes the operator would rather stomp to death than scratch behind the ears.

He had prayed the two would keep going, heading out for a newspaper or some donuts, maybe, or walking to the nearest park. But the man he'd spotted last night with Lauren Miller had a sharp gaze and a purposeful stride, or as purposeful as he could manage, with the canine anchor at his heels. Losing patience after only a few minutes, he gathered the dachshund under one arm and hustled back inside.

"Interfering pain in the ass," the operator muttered, his gut churning with the pressure the contact had put on him to get this job done quickly.

But as eager as he, too, was to finish so he could retire to his sailboat, the operator had been in business long enough to understand the crucial role of patience. If he didn't find his quickly, along with a secure spot from which to watch for his chance, he might as well pull out the gun he'd brought for Lauren and eat a bullet now instead of saving it for her.

Sooner or later, he assured himself, his chance would arrive. And when it did, he would seize it by the throat and claim the spoils, just as he had so many times before.

***

When the light first reached her eyes, Lauren unconsciously swatted at it as if it were a pesky gnat. When that didn't work, she shifted and felt the soft warmth of a blanket slip from her shoulders and fall to the floor.

She opened her eyes to see Brent seated, his back to her, at the pass-through countertop. Staring at the screen of her computer.

Alarm crackled through her, bringing her to her feet in one swift motion. Startled, Dumpling danced back, but Brent was too intent on the screen to notice.

Struck speechless by her panic, she could only gasp. How the hell had he gotten into her computer, and what had she carelessly left for him to find? But moments later, she breathed again, recalling that she'd been noodling through some searches rather than working on any extracurricular—and seriously illegal—mayhem.

Relief cascaded through her system, not so much because she imagined Brent would report her for messing with the scammers, malicious hackers, and purveyors of kiddie porn who were frequently her targets, but because she didn't want to implicate him or leave a trail that might possibly entangle any of the other hackers of conscience with whom she'd formed a loose confederation. But as Lauren took in the web page he was uploading, judging from the progress bar, her relief collapsed into a cloud of bitter ash.

The rows of beautiful blond faces made it impossible to breathe. And seeing her sister's smile among them, just another trophy in the conspiracy Brent believed in, hit her like a body blow, all the more painful when she read the garish banner: DRIVEN TO DESPAIR—SUICIDE BLONDES OR MURDER VICTIMS?

"What the hell have you done?" Her voice shook with outrage, a thin veneer that barely hid her pain.

Brent whipped around, his handsome face flushed with what looked for all the world like shame. Recovering an instant later, he pushed aside the laptop, turning it to hide his handiwork as if the damage had not been done already.

"Tell me you didn't do this," Lauren pleaded, her eyes blurred with hot tears, with the realization that if she didn't end this now, didn't find some way to pull back from her involvement, Brent would smash her heart to splinters. "Tell me this obsession of yours isn't just the flip side of that troll's insanity."

"Please, Lauren, calm down. Calm down and listen to me."

As she lunged for the computer, he jerked it out of reach—or at least she assumed that was what he meant to do when it went sliding off the countertop and crashing to the floor.

"No!" she shrieked as the lid snapped shut on impact. Startled by the near miss, Dumpling yelped in fear and cowered.

"Oh, hell. I'm sorry, Lauren." Brent bent to reach for the computer. "I didn't mean to—"

She leaned in, reaching past him and snatching away the machine she'd spent endless hours and thousands of dollars customizing for her needs. As she turned her back to him to set it on the table, she said, "You had better damned well hope it isn't broken."

Dumpling whimpered, her tail tucked to her belly and her small body shaking. Too upset to calm her, Lauren gingerly raised the computer's screen and groaned at the sight of the wrecked display, where a mishmash of gibberish appeared with a patchwork of vertical and horizontal lines. None of it was readable, yet inside the laptop, she heard a whirring sound, what she guessed might be Brent's upload still in progress. An upload she no longer had any way to stop.

"I'm sorry about the computer. I'll find a way to fix it. I'll—"

"You put up my sister's picture," she accused, "made her part of some sick menagerie that you've collected."

"I only thought if I could get the media's attention—if I could make them see the similarities among the victims, we might—"

"No. It's done. I'm done with this. Done with you. For a crazy minute or two, I thought we might—but I was so wrong. Your wife and all those dead blondes—they're the only women you have room for in that head of yours."

"Lauren, I will solve this," he swore, his gaze searching hers for understanding. "I'll lay them all to rest, and then maybe . . . maybe you and I can find some way to—"

"You really think Rachel's hanging out here with Carrie and the others waiting for you to make it right. They're gone, Brent. Their problems are all over. Only the survivors are left to go on with their—with *our*—lives or not." A tear gave way to gravity, breaking free to streak down her face. Because impossible as it seemed that she could have fallen so swiftly and completely, she loved this man. Maybe it was because, for the first time in her life, she recognized a passion and intensity that exceeded even her own, a drive to do the right thing, no matter the cost.

"All I need to do is prove it," Brent insisted. "Prove Chad Henderson wasn't acting alone. Then, we'll flush out the real Troll King. We'll lure him out into the open and we'll—"

"No, Brent. There's no *we'll* in this, because I just can't do it. Don't you understand? With Rachel gone, it's all I can do to keep on breathing right now. I don't have any more than that to give, to you or anyone."

He opened his mouth as if to argue. But with a spasm of emotion, his expression shifted, and at last, he shook his head. "The truth is you have more to give, and more to offer, than I could ever deserve."

He took a step nearer to look down at her, temptation and obsession warring in his brown eyes. She ached for him to give in, to lie to her if he had to, to pull her into those strong arms and kiss her until she lost sight of all the reasons why this relationship could never work.

Need thickened in the air between them, desire that hung heavy as a humid summer sky. She saw in his face that he wanted nothing more than to drag her into the bedroom and pretend for both their sakes that a pair of grief-ravaged near strangers could somehow save each other.

Instead, he shook his head and straightened his spine, determination hardening his gaze. "You know what, Lauren? You're right about me, about everything. I'm not letting go of this damned thing until I'm absolutely sure. I can't, which is exactly why I'm leaving before I ruin your life, too."

Lauren felt the breath leaking out of her lungs. Her throat too tight for speech, she stalked away and locked herself in the bathroom so he wouldn't see her cry.

Not wanting him to hear her either, she turned on the ventilation fan and climbed up on the counter, where she sat with her arms wrapped around her knees. Sat alone staring at her mirror image and thinking for a long time in that same room where her sister had lost her battle with despair.

Fresh grief knotted painfully in her throat as she made out the muted thump of the apartment's front door closing. Of Brent walking out of her life without saying goodbye.

She trembled as she asked herself, by letting him go without a fight, was she doing the same thing as Rachel, crumbling to the fear of more pain than she could bear? In turning her back on the only man she'd ever truly felt at home with, was she blinding herself to other possibilities, including the chance that Brent might actually be right about Chad Henderson's not having acted on his own?

Outside of the bathroom, she heard the scratching of Dumpling's toenails on the closed door, followed by an insistent whine. A lonely whine, now that Brent had gone, leaving both of them forever.

Panic thumping in her chest, Lauren lunged for the door she'd locked behind her, thinking there might still be time to catch him. To help him. To be the partner that he needed to finally put this all to rest.

As she left the bathroom, Dumpling raced toward the front door and started barking. Barking as the lock clicked, then turned, and the door began to open.

Pure relief bubbled up through Lauren's chest. Brent had changed his mind! Except the tone of Dumpling's barking warned her, shifting from a welcome to a warning in an instant . . .

And the joyful greeting on Lauren's lips gave way to a scream.

CHAPTER TWENTY-FIVE

Brent cut through the parking lot, a desire to turn back dogging his every step. A desire for a woman he had no business wanting, a woman whose equal he would never find again.

He told himself he had been right to leave Lauren, right to free her from the ghosts that would haunt him to the grave. She'd been through enough without being shackled to the rotting albatross of his own guilt, or the growing suspicion that his sanity had passed the point of no return.

He had barely left the parking lot when a dark gray Explorer raced around a corner and whipped to the shoulder beside him. As the passenger side window rolled down, Jimenez appraised him over the top of a pair of dark sunglasses.

Pulse hammering, Brent stepped between two parallel-parked cars and craned his neck to scope out an escape route along the mostly residential street. If he could make it as far as the nearby alley, he might be able to backtrack and then hop a fence into the Texas State Cemetery, where Jimenez couldn't follow in his SUV.

Unless Brent had missed other cops lurking nearby, waiting to swoop in and cut him off if his old friend gave the word.

"There's not going to be a foot chase, is there, *compadre*?" Jimenez asked him as a rusting hatchback passed by. "Because I haven't broken in these shoes yet, and I'd really rather buy you breakfast. There's a pretty decent taquería just a couple blocks from here."

"I might take you up on the offer," Brent said, taking another step toward freedom, "if the last meal you brought didn't have bugs in it. And I'm not talking *cucarachas*, either."

Jimenez shook his head and snorted, possibly at the notion of cockroaches breaching the holy ground of his *madre's* cooking. "Should've known anybody as paranoid as you are would sniff the damn thing out. But you can't blame a *vato* for trying—"

"Don't play the homeboy with me, *ese*," Brent said, scoffing at Cruz's attempt to act as though he'd come from the streets rather than big money. Everybody knew the guy's Mexico City family had millions, even if he was marking time slumming as an Austin homicide detective for some reason.

"If I were half as loaded as all you cowboys think," Jimenez said, his voice rough with emotion, "I'd buy some peace for Nikki Watson's parents. And some answers to their questions about why that little bastard dumped her strangled body in your motel room."

Brent froze, the hair behind his neck rising. "So you know it was Chad Henderson that killed her and not me?"

Jimenez nodded. "Kid might've thought he was playin' in the big leagues, but we found that sick shit's fingerprints on the duct tape he used to bind that poor girl. On that GPS tracker we took off your car, too, which tells me you've been edging way too close for comfort—"

"Because I was right about the suicides—Rachel Miller's, at least."

Jimenez dark eyes burned a hole in him. "Which means you must have valuable information. Answers I'm gonna need to close my case."

"Only your case, Cruz? What about the others? What about my wife's?"

"If any hard evidence of his involvement turns up, you know I'll follow through. Just like I'll follow through on any leads you might have for me."

Brent's next step placed him between a parked car and the wrought-iron front gate of an older bungalow, on a narrow and uneven sidewalk. "Oh, so now you want to listen to me, want to pick my brain—before you lock me up, that is."

Jimenez opened his door and stepped out. "Come on, man. Think this through. If I'd wanted you locked up, I would've done it last night."

"Or maybe you mean to play the friend card until I cough up whatever you need. *Then* you'll turn me over to the Feds."

Jimenez heaved a sigh steeped in exasperation before raking his jet hair off his forehead. "Maybe someone ought to. You ever think of that? Because you're getting people killed now with all your unsanctioned bullshit. And it looks to me like you just about got yourself killed, too."

"I'm sorry about Nikki. Sorrier than you can even begin to imagine. But I can see your shoulder holster there under your jacket, the cuffs you're going to slap on me, as soon as you—"

"Isn't this what you've wanted, *compadre*, for someone to hear out your bullshit theories and look at all your evidence?" Jimenez stepped between the parked cars. "Or do I have to go talk to your girlfriend?"

Brent wandered a few yards farther. "Lauren's not my girlfriend . . ." Much as he wished the bond between them could be so easily summed up.

"Accomplice then, or I imagine that's the way the DA and the federal prosecutors are going to see it. Guess it depends on what we come up with once we start digging into her phone and computer."

Brent's stomach dropped at the thought of the activities they might come across if they somehow found their way past whatever safeguards she had in place. "Leave her out of this. She hasn't done a damned thing."

Jimenez narrowed the gap between them. "She's lied to my face more than once, abetted a felony—"

"Her own abduction? And since when is it a kidnapping when the so-called *victim* helps out?"

"Come on, man. I'm trying to help you. Both of you, but that doesn't mean I'm willing to let this rogue agent bullshit go on one day longer."

"Then you can expect some fucking blisters, *compadre*," Brent spat the word sarcastically and planted his good hand on the fencepost he was about to vault. "Because you're about to break in those shiny new shoes of yours after all."

***

Lauren might be terrible with names—with people in general—but she was an ace at recognizing faces. Especially a face seared into her brain the way the driver's in the previous night's hit-and-run had been.

He must have seen her standing in the shadows, witnessing what her instincts told her had been no accident but an act of murder. A murder he meant to reprise, if the expression on his ugly face was any indication.

Launched by her mistress's scream, Dumpling hurled herself at the huge man in a barking, snapping frenzy. The intruder charged straight past her, oblivious, reaching out for Lauren.

Undeterred, the dachshund leapt, clamping down with her few teeth and hanging off one meaty hand.

"Freaking rat!" he shouted, slamming the animal's spine into the doorframe, where she collapsed with a pained yelp and struggled to drag herself out of the way.

"You son of a bitch!" Lauren cried, white-hot rage ripping through her as she struck out with the heels of both hands.

She'd meant to shove him back, to slam and lock the door behind him to buy herself time to grab her gun. Time to shoot the bastard or dial 9-1-1 for help.

But at the impact against his chest, shockwaves pounded up her arms. She might as well have hit a concrete post, for all the effect her strength had on him.

Dumpling screeched in pain, still unable to get up, and Lauren heard her neighbor's front door open.

"Hey, you!" Cooper shouted. "What are you doing to that animal? I'm calling the police now—"

Moving faster than anyone his size had a right to, the huge intruder spun around, ripped a handgun from his coveralls, and fired twice. The gunshots sounded oddly muffled, but that didn't stop the bullets from dropping Lauren's last hope like a stone.

With no way past the threat and no way to get close enough to scoop up her injured dog, she spun away, charging for the bedroom—and praying she could reach her weapon before a hail of bullets dropped her, too.

***

If not for the freaking rat-dog, the deed would've been as good as done, his stunned target overpowered and on her way to join her sister. Instead, the operator had this unholy mess to deal with, including a freshly ventilated neighbor and an animal shrieking like someone was ripping its damned tail out by the roots.

Honed by years of experience, his mind dropped back to fallback mode. The suicide plan was history, no matter how pissed off about it the contact or the client was bound to be. At this point, his immediate survival was the only thing that mattered—and that meant killing Lauren Miller as expediently as possible and getting the hell out of Dodge before he had more witnesses to deal with or, worse yet, the cops.

He needed to shut the dog up fast, he knew, but he was already charging after the target, desperate to get her under control before she could cause more trouble. Only a step or two ahead of him, she slammed the bedroom door in his face. Unable to stop, he smashed into it at full speed, knocking it off its hinges and punching one fist through a center panel.

His target cried out as the door struck her, and he reached through the hole and grabbed her, his left hand clamping around the front of her neck. She jerked backward, pulling free, and though he ended up with a fistful of her shirt, he could hear the fabric tearing, could feel it giving way.

Stop this right now. Shoot her, even if it does get messy.

But as he lined up his shot, her struggling sent a fragment of the wrecked door swinging around to knock the weapon from his right hand. At the same moment, the bitch bit down on his left, sinking her teeth into the knuckles still clutching part of her shirt. Shocked that she would have the nerve—that she would fight him like a hellcat instead of bowing to the inevitable—he reflexively let go . . . and felt her pull away.

Jerking free of the broken door, he shoved past the remains and saw her lunging for the dresser, for the purse lying atop it. Certain she was after either a cell phone or a weapon, he leapt for the bag . . .

And snagged a strap at the same moment that she grabbed it.

CHAPTER TWENTY-SIX

Brent ducked around the corner of a backyard storage shed and leaned his hand against the wall, where he gasped for breath and waited for the world to stop its spinning. His injuries, along with the crap food and brief snatches of sleep he'd given his body lately, had taken more of a toll than he'd expected. Or maybe it was the sedating effect of the pain pill he had taken, which made each step feel like a slog through deep mud.

Still, he'd gotten lucky, losing lead-ass Jimenez somewhere among these houses. Maybe the detective's shoes were really pinching—or perhaps he'd jogged back to pull the keys from his still-running SUV before some enterprising opportunist helped himself. It was just as possible Jimenez didn't have the heart to chase a former colleague, not one he considered guilty of nothing worse than a grief-spawned breakdown.

For the first time, it hit Brent that he had put his old friend in a position that might come back to haunt him, one that might call Jimenez's involvement, even his ethics, into question. Regret needling his conscience, Brent continued moving toward the cemetery. Though he hadn't yet decided where he was heading, for now, he needed to put some time and distance between himself and the two people whose lives he'd complicated beyond bearing.

He didn't get far before he realized he was weaving like a drunkard. Determined to overcome his weakness, he fought for focus, but his mind kept drifting back to Lauren, to the hurt he'd seen in her eyes before she'd turned away. Had he taken the high road, leaving before he could cause any further damage? Or had his departure, without thanks or apology or any kind of good-bye, been the cruelest blow of all?

He thought of where he'd left her, in that bathroom that still smelled of the disinfectants used to scrub away her sister's blood and brains. He pictured moonlight blond waves, floating in a tub.

What the hell is wrong with you? You can't leave her there. What if Lauren—

An image of a plastic tugboat surfaced, bobbing overtop a nightmare memory. Nausea pushing at his throat, he spun around, knowing he had to go back, needed to face her, face his demons and his future before it was too late.

But as Brent's vision cleared, the only thing he faced was Cruz Jimenez's drawn gun.

***

"Give it here, you bastard!" Lauren shouted at her attacker as the two fought for the purse.

A lopsided battle from the outset, it ended with the bag jerking from her grip and slamming against the wall.

Thrown off balance for a moment, the intruder stumbled in the act of reaching for her. Out of options, Lauren swept aside the curtain just behind her, her heart hammering as she kicked aside the broomstick, unlocked the sliding door, and yanked it open.

Huge hands grabbed at her back, but the swinging curtain tangled his thick fingers, gifting her with one more second. One

last adrenaline-fueled second, she was certain, as she sprang forward, attempting the same mountain-goat escape route Brent
had taken . . .

Attempting to leap out of the monster's reach, onto the
rusted AC unit.

Except that Lauren, in her desperation, missed.

CHAPTER TWENTY-SEVEN

Lauren's cry echoed between the two rows of apartments, reverberating off the glass and brick and concrete below the second-floor balcony.

With nothing to grab on to, she dropped like a falling stone. And landed badly, an audible crack coming from her right ankle as she came down on it in the grassy margin of the sidewalk.

Pain struck an instant later, agony shooting from her ankle to her upper body, as her shoulder and elbow came down on the concrete. She lay there breathing hard, afraid to move for fear of another jolt—until the footsteps banging down the metal steps of the outdoor staircase brought her back to her senses.

He was going to kill her if she didn't run.

She pushed herself up using both hands, but when she came down on the injured ankle, a white-hot bolt made her scream. Worse yet, she collapsed to the ground, inky splotches bursting across her vision—splotches that warned she would lose consciousness if she again tested her right ankle.

Crawl for the bushes, her sister's voice urged. *Now, before he sees you.*

Lauren did her best, dragging the injured leg behind her. But a glance over her shoulder told her she was too late, as the giant reached the bottom of the stairs.

Their gazes clacked together like two magnets.

In his fury-reddened face, she saw her own death. An ugly death.

Panic roared up in response, an inferno that had her screaming, "Help! Please, somebody help me!" The killer charged in her direction. "Fire!" she tried again, desperation dredging up something she'd once read about bystanders being too afraid to intervene in violent confrontations. "This place is on fire! Everybody outside! Call 9-1-1 before we all burn!"

"Shut your damned mouth, right now!" The man jerked his weapon from his coveralls but abruptly hid the gun as two heads popped out of upper-level doorways and a mousy-looking woman in red-framed glasses stepped outside about a dozen yards away.

"Where? Where's the fire?" She glanced nervously toward the roofline. "I don't see any smoke."

The killer's demeanor transformed in an instant. "My wife's a schizophrenic, and she's off her meds again." His voice downshifted from rage to concern with shocking efficiency, his expression following suit. "Poor thing leapt right off our balcony like she figured she could fly, but we'll get her fixed up, good as always."

"No! He's lying!" Lauren argued, but he talked right over her.

"Now if you people'll quit gawking, I'll get her to the hospital where she belongs."

"Please, you have to help me," Lauren begged as the woman gave her a pitying look and hurried back toward her own door. "He's going to kill me, just like he shot Mr. Coo—!"

The woman's door slammed shut, and when Lauren looked back to the balconies, she saw those tenants had also retreated. Panic stabbing at her, she realized that whether they had bought the killer's story or were hurrying to call the police didn't matter.

Rachel's sweet voice reverberated through her mind again, sounding sad instead of frightened this time. *By the time help finally gets here, you'll be dead either way.*

***

To the operator, death was strictly business. Business it didn't pay to get too emotional about. He didn't kill for pleasure or out of anger, either. He left that to the amateurs—and left getting caught to them as well.

But as he bore down on Lauren Miller, his bloody knuckles stinging from her bite, his business needs and his personal feelings intersected. Because he was going to feel damned good about finishing off this troublemaking bitch—good enough that he swore he was going to freaking take pains to make her pay for exposing him to God only knew how many witnesses.

Still, she didn't give up. Though she had to know she was about to die, she struggled to crawl away from him—at least until he "accidentally" kicked the leg she was dragging with one of his steel-toed work boots. She screamed in agony and curled into a ball. But even that much was beyond her as her eyes rolled back and she suddenly went limp.

He fought back a feral smile, not wanting any potential witnesses peering out from behind their curtains to see his expression change. Bad enough that they'd seen his face, that they would remember what he'd said and how he'd spoken.

Hoping to confound them further, he stooped beside the unconscious woman and tenderly, reverently brushed her hair out of her pale face. Next, he lifted her like a small child, or as if she really were the mentally sick but much-loved young wife that he had named her. As if his brain weren't shouting at him to twist her freaking head until the neck snapped.

On the way to the parking lot where he'd left the older Buick he had stolen, he heard the dog's cries from above. He remembered he'd failed to close the front door behind him as he'd run out of the apartment. He cursed himself, wishing he'd taken an extra few seconds to kill the damned noisemaker and drag the neighbor's body back into his apartment. But he couldn't take the time now, not when he was certain that someone was bound to head up to investigate—or have the cops check out the disturbance—within a few short minutes.

Minutes he meant to use to put as much distance between himself and this clusterfuck as possible. Then he would have to jack another ride, because the way his luck was running, someone was bound to notice that rather than carefully strapping his "darling wife" inside the car, he was dumping—and locking—the bitch inside the trunk.

***

Jimenez clenched the wheel of his idling Explorer so hard his knuckles went white. Knuckles Brent was absolutely certain were itching for an excuse to punch him in the face.

Glowering at his request to return to Rachel's apartment, the detective shook his head. "Listen, Durant, I've stuck my neck way out for you already, so don't test my patience any further."

"Then how about your friendship, *compadre*?" In the seat beside him, Brent gestured for understanding, counting himself lucky that Jimenez had accepted his promise not to resist in lieu of the handcuffs the detective had been ready to slap on him. But that didn't mean he wasn't plenty pissed off.

"Who the hell says we're still friends?"

"Come on, Cruz. This is important. I'm only asking for a quick stop to check on Lauren. Then I swear on my life, I'll come willingly to the station."

"I'll tell you what. I'll call her." Jimenez produced a phone from an inside pocket of his jacket. "I've got her cell phone number right here."

Brent knew he shouldn't push his luck, but he couldn't resist a surly "I'll bet you do. I've heard the way you talk to her, all that bullshit about how you've been through a divorce, too, how you—"

"Maybe I exaggerated just a little. But Deborah did file on me in November. Probably won't be finalized for another—"

"Then the last damned thing you need or want is one more blonde on your scorecard. You should definitely—"

"What? Stick to my own kind?" He turned a warning look toward Brent.

Brent grunted in disgust at the assumption. "How 'bout just stick to somebody other than the sister of a woman whose death you're investigating, for starters? And everybody knows you hit on every good-looking woman you cross paths with during an investigation—especially the hot blondes. In fact, I'm betting that's why Deborah—"

"Watch your mouth, *pendejo*," Jimenez warned, "and who the hell are you, anyway, to lecture me about bending a few rules to get information? Now if you're finished marking your territory, let me make that call."

Jimenez pressed a button, then held the phone to his ear and waited.

"Come on, Lauren. Pick up," Brent murmured, willing her to shake off her funk to get the phone.

"No answer," Jimenez said before leaving a voice mail. "Lauren, if you get this, call me right away. I'm taking your pal, Durant, over to the station, and he's worried about you."

Worried was an understatement. Brent's stomach had shriveled to a writhing ball, and his skin prickled with what felt like a host of stinging fire ants.

The moment Jimenez ended the call, Brent argued, "She was upset when I left her. She'd locked herself in the bathroom. The same place where—"

"You left her crying in the same room where her sister took her life?" Jimenez made a three-point turn and hit the gas. As they lurched forward, he demanded, "What the hell is wrong with you?"

"I thought I was doing her a favor getting out of her life." Brent shook his head, his throat tightening as he realized what a fool he'd been. When it came to their partnership, Lauren had already long since passed the point of no return, just as he had. "But the more I think about it, the more I realize I could've left her vulnerable to something even more dangerous than grief."

Jimenez sent an annoyed look his way and turned in the direction of Rachel's apartment. "About damned time you engaged that brain of yours for something that makes sense."

"So you believe me now about the Troll King going after all these women?"

"Look, you were right about Rachel Miller. I'll give you that much. About her being targeted by Chad Henderson, at least."

"You've confirmed it," Brent guessed, judging by the certainty in his voice.

"As of about an hour ago. FBI flew in a team of their best tech guys, and they spent all night working on that hard drive.

They still haven't gotten very far teasing out the data, but they've found enough to—"

"So the FBI's in on this? *Now* they're interested?"

"After I spoke to your old boss, Fremont Daniels, about the Nikki Watson murder yesterday, they sure were," Jimenez said, referring to the special agent in charge of the Oklahoma City division. "Although I sense their involvement may be more about damage control than any real commitment to your idea about a serial stalker."

He was probably right, Brent realized, imagining the embarrassment it would cause if a disgraced former agent was proven to have been right all along in a case resulting in the deaths of so many young women. If that tidbit hit the news media, it wouldn't spin well for the bureau, which was already facing harsh criticism for failing to stop a recent bombing by domestic terrorists. Brent figured Daniels was getting pressure from above to head off another PR nightmare, either by bringing Brent back into the fold somehow or finding a way to keep him under wraps—in a federal prison or a facility for the criminally insane.

Or was he simply being paranoid, as so many had suggested?

As the apartment complex came back in sight, a spasm of anxiety squeezed his gut. And he realized that it didn't matter whether he was right or not about the Feds' involvement. He didn't care what happened to him, not as long as the dying was finally finished and Lauren had a happy, healthy future. Not the half life she'd imagined suited her, but the kind of life she truly deserved. A life filled with people who would love her—people who were worthy of the love she had to give.

"It wasn't just this dead kid hunting blondes in the news," Brent insisted, willing Jimenez to listen this time. "There had to be somebody else, some partner pointing him in their direction. That's what really scares me, that I might've left Lauren with this—"

"As soon as we've confirmed that she's all right, we're leaving," Jimenez told him as they pulled into the parking lot. "No argument, no tricks, and if you try to take off, I swear on my badge, I'm shooting you myself. In the damned back if necessary. Mostly because, thanks to you, my damned blisters have blisters—and these freaking expensive shoes are going in the trash."

In a desperate bid to hide his fear, Brent snorted, thinking that for the only grandson of the founder of one of Mexico's premier media empires, the cost of shoes didn't make a single peso's worth of difference. "Maybe you should go back to counting your family's millions in Mexico City, because this stint in homicide's turning you into a peevish old man. Or maybe it's this divorce. That Deborah was something special." He'd met the woman a few times, a former Dallas Cowboys cheerleader who was as outgoing and sociable as Lauren was reclusive.

"If you're trying to get yourself shot right now, *ese*, bring up my wife again," Jimenez warned a split second before he stomped the brake. "What the *hell*?"

He was springing from the vehicle before Brent caught sight of a pair of legs on the ground, legs jutting into the front of the parking space that they were pulling into. He scrambled from the Explorer, joining Jimenez beside the fallen male form.

The man held his hands over his belly as blood oozed up through his trembling fingers. His pale face gaped in wordless torment, his gaze fixed on the sky.

Brent blinked "Jon Rutherford? Is that you?" What the hell was the widower doing here, in the parking lot of Rachel's apartment complex?

When the victim didn't—or couldn't—answer, Brent swung his gaze to Jimenez, who was already dialing on his phone. "I thought you had this guy in custody."

"Didn't have enough to hold him . . . Mr. Rutherford, can you speak? Who did this to you? Who?"

Panic ripped through Brent as he thought of the gun Lauren kept in her purse. Had the two of them had a run-in that had ended up with Rutherford being shot? Or would Brent find her bleeding, too, or even dead, in the apartment?

Rutherford's gaze flicked to Jimenez's face, but he only groaned in answer. Then the call must have connected, and the detective started talking to what must have been the 9-1-1 dispatcher.

"Heading over to check on Lauren." Brent neither knew nor cared if Jimenez heard him as he took off running, the pain of his injuries flaring with each step.

He pushed past the discomfort, terror fueling his muscles as he reached the staircase and raced up the metal steps, already hearing what could only be Dumpling's pained yelps.

On the landing, a woman with drab hair and bright-red glasses stared up at him from where she knelt beside a still form. "I-I heard the crying dog and c-came up." Her wet face gleamed in the sunlight. "That's when I found him lying here, dead."

"Brian Cooper," Brent said, remembering the neighbor's name. But he was already loping for the open door of Rachel's apartment, shouting, "Lauren? Lauren, where are you?"

Hearing nothing but the crying dachshund, he steeled himself to go inside. "Shh, Dumpling," he said as he walked past the dog, who was struggling to stand, her pleading brown eyes full of pain. "Stay down. Don't try to move, girl. Be right back after I find Lauren."

Whether it was his words, his voice, or his presence, the dachshund wagged her tail and immediately fell silent, as if she trusted Brent could somehow make things better. But how could he manage that with fear knifing through his lungs as he caught sight of the broken bedroom door, lying in smashed pieces just inside the room?

Brent ran past it, shouting. "Lauren! Lauren, where are you?"

She was nowhere to be found, not in the room or under the bed, or in the walk-in closet. After a cursory check of the bathroom, living room, and kitchen, he returned to the bedroom, where he spotted her purse next to a wall, its contents spilled and one strap broken. Checking it, he found her phone and handgun, and his stomach spasmed at this evidence that she'd never had the chance to call for help or get off a single shot.

He picked up the gun, not caring that his fingerprints would probably come back to haunt him. Not caring about anything but finding Lauren before whatever violence had erupted here claimed her life, if it had not already.

A breeze stirred the sliding door's torn curtain, prompting him to check the balcony as well. Finding no sign of Lauren there, either, he tucked the gun into the waistband of his jeans and headed back out to the landing. "My friend's missing—Lauren Miller," he told the woman kneeling there. "Good-looking blonde wearing a UT shirt when I last saw her."

Behind the thick, red frames, the woman's green eyes filled with tears. "He's taken her—that awful man. A huge man in a maintenance uniform. He must've done this, too."

CHAPTER TWENTY-EIGHT

"I w-wouldn't have ever hurt her," Jon Rutherford stammered, his face translucent as skim milk. But his belly was a crimson lake, the hands he clasped there barely holding back the tide. "I j-just wanted to t-tell her I'm sorry. Sorry for what happened to Rachel. I never meant to push her so far. Never meant for—suicide."

"Wait," Brent interrupted, still breathing hard from his race back to question the injured man about what he'd seen. "You mean *you* were the one calling her? The one who posted on the Internet about how she should kill herself?"

As Jimenez called in the report of Cooper's body on the landing, sirens wailed in the distance.

If Rutherford heard them at all, he didn't react, focusing on Brent instead. "Hell, no. I—I wouldn't do that. I meant with the lawsuit, and the interviews I gave. I was pissed, yeah. I wanted her to pay for what she did to my family, my kids. B-but I never wanted her dead."

"Forget that and answer the question I've been asking. Where the hell did the guy who shot you take Lauren Miller? What was he driving? Tell me now, damn you, or I swear you'll never see those kids of yours again!"

"Back off, Durant." Jimenez returned to kneel beside Rutherford, glaring a warning that he was the one in charge of this scene. "I know you're worried, but you've got to give me some breathing space here. You're not a freaking federal agent anymore—"

"I'll give you some room the minute this son of a bitch tells me where that bastard took Lauren. And who the hell he was."

But Rutherford seemed stuck on own agenda. Either that or he was too far gone to understand Brent's questions. "Only— only wanted to tell Lauren I was sorry for—for her loss. B-but I didn't know how. Was afraid sh-she'd blame me, so I came up— with that lame story in—in the hotel bar."

His eyes slid closed, and his head drooped to one side.

Shit. Too desperate to give up, Brent reached to shake him, but Jimenez shoved him off balance and turned to try on his own.

"Rutherford?" he said sharply. "*Jon.* This is important, man. So don't you dare die on me."

"At least not yet," Brent murmured, but his eyes were drawn to the *plink* of Jimenez's keys as they fell out of the detective's pocket. Keys he pocketed while Jimenez was distracted.

As the sirens neared, Rutherford's mouth moved again. This time, both Brent and Cruz leaned closer, trying to catch what might be the man's dying words.

***

Agony arced through Lauren's ankle, eliciting a groan as she stirred. The throbbing consumed her, nauseating in its intensity. Moments later, adrenaline spiked as she recalled the attack, the fall, the shock of the kick that was the last thing she remembered before she'd blacked out.

Her eyes flashed open to darkness, and her breath came in a panicked rush. Beneath her, a rough vibration rumbled.

Familiar, but off somehow, so it took her a moment to realize she was feeling an engine's thrum and hearing tires on pavement. Tires taking her away from the dubious safety of the apartment complex, carrying her to some secluded place from which she'd never return.

At the thought of Nikki's strangled corpse left in Brent's room for him to find, Lauren gasped and reflexively tried to sit up. Her head cracked hard against a low ceiling. Starbursts exploded in her vision, and she fought back a cry, her instincts warning her not to let her abductor know she had awakened. Awakened inside what could only be a trunk.

Shuddering, she pushed at the unyielding lid and felt around for an internal release. Hot tears burned at the realization that this car didn't have that safety feature. Maybe it was older—or maybe her kidnapper had prepared the vehicle to double as a prison.

She balled her fists, fighting back the need to sob, along with the bone-deep certainty that death awaited at the end of this ride. A death she wasn't ready for, not by a long shot.

Then quit freaking and start thinking. Think this through before you're one more face on Brent's website.

The car slowed, and the driver honked, pushing her pulse into the red zone. Was it already too late? Had they reached their final destination? She groped desperately in the blackness, feeling for a tire jack, a spare umbrella, any weapon she might improvise to surprise the killer when he popped the trunk.

She felt nothing, nothing at all, and her attempts to shift position sent fresh pain shooting up from what had to be a shattered ankle. An ankle that would never bear her weight if she did manage to escape, nor allow her to lever herself to try to kick at him when he came for her. Panic igniting in her pounding chest, she thought of screaming, banging her fists on the trunk lid, or attempting to kick out a taillight. But she held off, paralyzed by the fear that her captor would hear her and rush to quickly shut her up.

Moments later, the vehicle inched forward, and when she strained her ears, she heard other engines nearby. She felt, too, the slow stop-and-go progress of what must be a traffic slowdown.

Traffic means witnesses; witnesses all around us. Maybe it would be safe to try to attract someone's attention.

Though she knew she'd only get one shot at it, the idea still calmed her somehow—or maybe it was the image of Brent's handsome, haunted face that did it, the knowledge of how devastated he would be, how he would blame himself if she failed to survive. Either way, she dug deep and found the strength to mentally snip the cord connecting her brain from her emotions.

The cord. Of course. That could work.

This car might be old enough to lack an internal release, but it might still have a lever allowing the vehicle's driver to pop the trunk from inside the cab. Which meant there would have to be a cable. Feeling around, she pulled back a thin, woolly layer of insulation from the floor beneath the lock mechanism. At first, she found nothing, but eventually her shaking fingers grasped a cable, close to the driver's side.

Praying she had really come across the trunk release rather than a wrapped mass of tail or brake light wires, she waited for the car to stop again before jerking the cord toward the front of the car. With an unmistakable *clunk*, the lock released, and Lauren shoved open the lid just as the vehicle began accelerating. As the car picked up speed, she used her arms to push herself up and over the trunk's lip, despite her fear that the fall would doom her to another brand of violent death.

***

Brent's gaze darted to the rearview mirror, scanning for the flashing lights of any cops who might attempt to pull him over in Jimenez's stolen Explorer. Brent could have asked permission but didn't interrupt as Jimenez gave CPR to Rutherford, who had stopped breathing after sputtering that he'd interrupted the "maintenance man" in the act of dumping Lauren into the trunk of a faded-green sedan. When Brent had asked if the shooter had taken off in the direction of the freeway, Rutherford had shaken his head no. Or at least that was what Brent thought—or hoped—he'd meant.

For the sake of Rutherford's two motherless children, Brent hoped, too, the man would make it. But with anxiety clamping down hard, Brent soon forgot about Jimenez, the police, and the wounded man he'd left behind, forgot everything but his search for the older green car that carried his beating heart locked inside it. The problem was he couldn't be certain the driver had actually come this way, and even if he had, with every intersection Brent sped past, the chances lessened that the car remained on this road.

Wave after wave of doubt broke over him, doubt and fury with himself for ever having called himself a special agent. It was bad enough he'd failed his own wife, even worse that he'd failed to track down the Troll King to stop the killing. But he'd damned well *known* there was another killer out there, yet he'd still left Lauren vulnerable to what he suspected had been the puppet master's attack.

Had her abduction been prompted by him posting his website, or had Chad Henderson shared the news that Brent was closing in before the teen had been run down? The latter made more sense, he thought, but either way, the certainty that his actions had drawn death to her doorstep made him want to drive off the nearest overpass.

He passed a few small businesses, along with dozens of well-tended older bungalows. His gaze darted from parked car to passing vehicle to each pedestrian he spotted, the knot in his stomach tightening as the minutes ticked away. As hope gave its last gasp, he caught sight of a bank of flashing brake lights down a narrow side street to his left. He jammed the brakes and wrenched the Explorer's wheel. Tires squealed and horns blared as the SUV's rear end slung around.

An approaching car slammed on its brakes, but Brent accelerated out of the driver's path. Moments later, he screeched around the corner he'd passed, praying he hadn't nearly caused a wreck for the sake of some run-of-the-mill traffic slowdown.

But whether instinct had made the connection or he had unconsciously glimpsed the green vehicle among those angled across the street, Brent's heart pounded with the growing certainty that this was what he'd come for. As he floored the accelerator, he spotted several visibly distraught drivers—two women and an older man in a sports jacket and tie—leaving their cars and running, all of them making for the same spot. He spotted, too, an older green Buick speeding away.

With the stopped vehicles blocking his way, Brent jerked to a standstill, leapt out, and raced in the same direction the other drivers were moving. Raced toward a sight that had his throat knotting and horror searing his eyes.

A body sprawled in the street. Though his view was partly blocked, both by the angled vehicles and the drivers running ahead of him, he glimpsed the burnt orange of a UT T-shirt and the blond of her hair.

"Lauren!" he shouted. "Lauren!" As if the grief tearing at his center would change the fact that he was too late.

Startled by his shouts, the two women moved aside, and the silver-haired man wheeled around to gape at Brent, but he was already pushing past them, only steps away now.

Steps away when he saw Lauren lift her head and look at him, her blue-green eyes leaking tears.

Falling to his knees, he threw his arms around her, so choked by his relief, he couldn't get a word out. Behind him, the older man bent to squeeze his shoulder. "I'm calling the police now. I got that son of a bitch's license plate, too."

"Thanks," Brent managed, relieved, since he had been so zeroed in on Lauren that he hadn't even tried to make it out.

Lauren sobbed. "When I heard the door, I thought—I hoped you were coming back. But he—he broke in. He hurt Dumpling—"

"Your neighbor's taking Dumpling to a vet clinic," he managed, needing to reassure her with the promise the woman with the red glasses had made. "What about you, Lauren? Do you need an ambulance?"

"She fell out of a moving car," the older man put in. "I'll have 9-1-1 send paramedics."

"My ankle's killing me," Lauren said as he moved away, already punching in the numbers. "I heard it snap when I fell off the balcony. And then that bastard k-kicked me."

He'd kicked her. Kicked her broken ankle and tossed her in a trunk. Rage spilled over, red and molten, but Brent forced himself to breathe past his fury, his need for revenge.

"Other injuries?" He scanned her face, her hands, the whole of a woman he could scarcely believe was still breathing. Her color was washed out and her skin smudged with dirt, but he saw no obvious wounds—except for the fear and trauma written in her face.

"Scrapes and bruises, maybe. I don't know. I only—" She stopped to wipe away tears, and Brent wished he had a handkerchief to offer. "When I woke up inside that trunk, I thought I'd never see you again."

He hugged her hard against him, kissing her forehead and swearing, "I'm never leaving again. Never. At least not until Jimenez throws me in jail for making off with his SUV."

She pulled back, her brows rising. "You really stole a cop's—"

From down the street, there was a squeal, the sound of tires sliding around a corner, and one of the female drivers shouted, "Look out! He's coming back!"

Brent surged to his feet, scarcely able to believe what he was seeing. The old Buick barreled toward them, picking up more speed by the second—and coming far too close.

"Get her back!" he yelled, moving between Lauren and the big sedan roaring toward them. Behind the wheel, the huge driver leaned forward, his jaw set in a fierce scowl and his gaze locked on Lauren.

Brent ripped Lauren's revolver from his jeans and took aim. Adrenaline flooding his system, he took a few steps toward the threat and moved off to one side, meaning to draw off the killer with the more immediate threat.

Yet the driver lowered his head, every atom of his focus intent on running down his target. On taking out Lauren before Brent's very eyes.

"The hell you will," Brent said, squeezing off a shot and then a second and a third before he lost count and finally clicked down on an empty chamber.

Despite the tight cluster of bullet holes piercing the windshield, the car appeared to pick up speed, so close now that Brent turned, frantic to make certain Lauren had gotten to safety. But she remained where she had fallen, no one risking death to help her.

In that last, desperate moment, their gazes flew together, and he saw the terror in Lauren's eyes replaced with sharp regret. Regret for what he sensed had been the same possibility he had tasted when they'd come together—a chance for something real between them, a chance that would never come again.

Unable to drag his gaze from her, he cried her name aloud. Which was why he never saw the driver of the speeding car slump—

And why Brent failed to react when it abruptly veered his way.

CHAPTER TWENTY-NINE

The sounds of the collision echoed through Lauren's dreams: Brent's truncated shout, the heavy thud of his body falling onto the hood, the crack of the Buick's windshield as his head smacked hard against it. There were screams, too, her own ragged shriek among them as the car plowed into one of the vehicles that had stopped to avoid her after she'd escaped the trunk.

Unable to stop herself, she had lurched to her feet to get to Brent, to see if he was dead or badly injured. But the resulting shock of pain had her plummeting into blackness.

Sharp as vipers' fangs, panicked moments pierced her darkness. She fought her way back to herself inside the ambulance, screaming, "Where is he? Is he alive?" but passed out again after glimpsing the troubled look that passed between two uniformed EMTs.

Sometime later, her eyes opened to people in blue scrubs and masks staring down at her. A woman with kind brown eyes patted her arm and implored her to calm down as Lauren cried out, "Where's Brent, the man I came in with? Is he being treated—Is he—"

"You're going to be all right," a male voice reassured her. "We're going to stabilize that ankle, put a pin in—"

"Don't—don't give a damn about that. Just tell me—is Brent Durant still alive? Is he going to be all right?"

As she struggled against the hands holding her down, she fought unconsciousness, but dropped off again just as she heard someone asking, "Was there someone else brought in with her?"

After that, she lost track of time's passage, lost track of everything until she finally opened her eyes to see a seated figure with her in the dimly lit room. As her eyes adjusted to the light from a muted television, she blinked hard in an attempt to bring her wavering vision into focus.

"Brent?" she rasped.

Detective Jimenez looked away from his soccer game and down at her. "Hey there, pretty lady. How are you feeling? Can I get you some water?"

She nodded and accepted the drink he held for her, swallowing just enough to make her sand-dry throat work. "Please, Cruz, where's Brent? Just come out and say it." Her voice fractured. "Tell me if he's dead."

Jimenez captured her hand, enfolding it in a firm grip. "I won't lie to you, Lauren. He took a pretty hard knock to the skull when that bastard plowed into him—but if anybody in the world has a hard enough head to make it through this, it's definitely Brent Durant."

"Where is he? I have to see him."

"You just had your ankle cobbled back together. You're not going anywhere."

"Find me a wheelchair. Please, Cruz, take me to him right now." When he didn't move fast enough to suit her, she found the call button and pushed it.

"You can't see him, not now. Neurosurgeon's evaluating him, trying to decide whether he'll need a medically induced coma or surgery to relieve intracranial pressure."

Her eyes flared with shock. "You're saying—saying he has some kind of brain injury? That he might die?"

Horrific as the thought was, Lauren's mind leapt to an equally overwhelming fear. What if he survived but with so much damage he was no longer the man she'd come to love?

"I don't know. No one knows yet. But the first neurologist who came in told me that depending on how he does tonight, things could go either way."

"So there's still hope?"

Jimenez nodded. "Hope and room for prayer."

Tears rolled down her face, and he handed her a wad of tissue from the rolling table. While she wiped her face, he laid a hand on her hair, smoothing it back.

She flinched away from his touch, a level of disquiet rippling through her that she didn't understand. "If—if Brent makes it, then what? What'll you do with him then?"

Jimenez was quiet for a time, his dark gaze burrowing into hers, but finally, he sighed. "I wish it were up to me, *mi cielo*, but the FBI has placed a guard on his room. They're not about to let him slip away again."

Mi cielo? Lauren thought back to her high school Spanish but had no idea why the detective would be calling her *my heaven*. Was he merely showing kindness, or was there something weird about the way he acted toward her?

Deciding that it didn't matter, she shook off her misgivings and returned her thoughts to Brent. "You can't let them lock him up. Because he was right about this all along, no matter how crazy his methods might seem at times."

"I promise I'll put in a good word for him." He pulled a notepad and pen from an inner pocket of his jacket. "Now, I'm going to need to get you to answer a few questions for me about what happened today at Rachel's apartment."

She swallowed, her throat aching. "That man who came—the one who tried to kill me—Is he—"

"Dead at the scene, of gunshot wounds, courtesy of Brent."

She shuddered at the memory of the monster knocking the bedroom door off its hinges. "Thank God."

"Do you have any idea who he was? We're running descriptions of his tattoos through the federal database, but—"

"He was the same man I saw run down Chad Henderson and then steal from his body." Two muffled bursts echoed through her memory. "The same man who shot Rachel's neighbor, too, when he heard the noise and came out of his apartment."

"Brian Cooper, yes. I'm afraid he passed away of his injuries. I'm afraid, too, that Jon Rutherford was shot in the complex parking lot. He's in pretty rough shape, but they're saying he'll pull through."

"Rutherford? Why on earth would he have been there?"

"He claimed he wanted to tell you he was sorry about what happened to Rachel. He said he felt responsible, what with the lawsuit and his comments to the media about her."

"But then, why—Do you think he was involved with the murderer somehow? Like maybe he hired that gorilla to take out Chad Henderson before he was caught and led police—or Brent and me—back to him. Because it's possible those two connected. They were both in Houston, after all."

"We're looking into it, but if Rutherford hired the big guy, then why would he have placed himself at the scene?"

"He could've changed his mind, had an attack of conscience. Maybe he decided to try to stop things before anyone else got hurt—" Lauren stiffened, remembering the day's smallest victim.

"Dumpling. That monster hurt Dumpling. Slammed her back into the doorframe when she tried to protect me."

"Your dog, of course. Yes, a neighbor of your sister's gave me the number of the vet clinic where she was taken. I called while you were in recovery and was told there was a ruptured disk, but considering the dog's age and the expense of surgery—"

"Oh, my—no." Her heart drummed and her eyes filled. "Tell me they didn't put her down. Please."

"I told them to do the surgery," he reassured her. "Told them I'd cover the cost myself if you couldn't—"

"Oh, thank you. Thank God. But that won't be necessary. I'll take care of Dumpling. And Brent, too, if there's any way."

"Maybe when it comes to Brent, we should wait and see if he—"

"I've already lost one person I love dearly. I'm not taking a chance on losing another."

"It might not be your choice," he said. "But I'll be sure to keep you posted . . . if he makes it through the night."

***

Two Days Later . . .

Grinding and insistent, the headache chewed its way through Brent's awareness. He did his best to ignore the pain of what the doctors had called a concussion, but a strained voice—a voice he had feared he might never again hear in person—had his heart stuttering in response and his eyes cracking open.

"Just a few minutes," Lauren was telling one of the two special agents who'd been taking turns guarding his room. "That's all I'm asking. You have to let me see him before you take him."

Before they took him? *Hell.* Did that mean the neurologist had seen through his attempts to feign unconsciousness

341

and signed off on his transfer? Brent's stomach spasmed at the thought of being taken to some sanitized, well-secured "hospital" where his former agency could interrogate him. Or maybe they cared less about getting answers about his recent conduct and more about keeping him quiet about the lives lost due to his superior's refusal to listen to him earlier. Either way, his best shot—his only real chance—at escaping was to keep up his act on the off chance that one of the two special agents sent to watch him in shifts would let down his guard.

If he missed his chance, Lauren would remain at risk. Brent had overheard the special agents saying that the man who'd died behind the Buick's wheel was a professional, one known to be part of a small network of contract killers run by an elusive female mastermind. Which meant that someone had paid to have him sent here—someone who might try again.

Panic spiraled in on him, driven by the knowledge that he had to find some way to warn Lauren she was still in danger. But how the hell could he pull that off while playing the part of a vegetable?

"What?" she popped off in response to the special agent's murmured answer. "You really think I'm going to smuggle him out in my damned wheelchair? Please, before it's too late. At least, let me say goodbye."

He made out the low rumble of some bullshit about how the special agent had his orders before a phone began to ring.

"Sorry. Just let me shut this off." Lauren quickly silenced her cell phone. "It's only that idiot Reynolds Hadley again. If he's not pestering me about appearing on his damned show, he's bugging me to ask Brent—"

"The press is after Durant for an interview?" the special agent asked, his voice flat with disapproval.

"Look, you can hold on to my phone while I go in. Or keep it if you want. Those vultures from *The Vigil* and all those other shows can go to hell. I only want a chance see Brent, to thank him for saving my life and tell him that I—"

The special agent started to argue before Jimenez interrupted from the open doorway. "Come on, man. She's with me. I'll make sure there's not an issue."

She's with me. What the hell did that mean, Brent asked himself, anxiety tightening his hands into fists. Had Cruz really moved in on her so quickly, or was he only watching out for her for Brent's own sake?

Or is that just what the bastard's wanted me to think all along? The thought set disparate pieces tumbling through his battered skull, pieces whose gleaming edges mocked him as they spun just out of reach.

Except this time, at long last, the fragments returned to come together, clicking and locking into place. He remembered Lauren asking, *How did he even get my number?* Though at the time, she'd been speaking of the Troll King, the real question was how had the media—*The Vigil* in particular—gotten her contact information to pester her for an interview. How had they approached all those Texas-area blondes who had come under scrutiny during the investigations into accidental or suspicious deaths?

Investigations a police detective with interdepartmental task force contacts would be able to find a way to access . . . a police officer with family ties to a far-reaching media empire, not to mention a known preference for attractive blondes.

Cold sweat soaking the tangle of sheets around him, Brent kicked himself for the loyalty, the false fucking friendship that had prevented him from putting it all together earlier. But what the hell could he do to warn Lauren without coming off as some psychotic—or getting himself sedated or maybe even shot?

Moments later, Lauren rolled into the room, her wheelchair pushed by the very man Brent felt certain had almost had her killed. But as clear as the *how* of it seemed, the *why* continued to elude him. Why on earth would Jimenez want to drive any of the women to suicide? Was it some sort of long-standing hatred of a particular blond woman or a twisted desire for justice, borne of his frustration with the limitations of the system? Had Nikki and Lauren been later targeted to warn Brent himself off—or had Jimenez meant to punish him from the very start?

Brent racked his brain, wondering if the reason could be more personal than he'd imagined. Could Carrie have been the first victim chosen because of some perceived slight or betrayal that had turned his own casual friendship with the detective into smoldering hatred?

Nothing came to mind, and Brent couldn't focus anyway, with Lauren's beautiful, bruised face lighting up as she rolled up to his bedside. Rather than a robe or hospital gown, she wore a long-sleeved T-shirt and a pair of sweats with the right leg cut off at the knee to accommodate a bulky, neon-green cast on her lower leg and ankle. A plastic bag with the hospital's name was tucked by her side, clothes maybe, and she held a folded sheaf of what he realized were her discharge papers. His gut twisted with the realization that she was leaving . . . in Jimenez's tender care.

"You're awake! Oh, thank God, Brent! I thought—I was so worried that the accident had—"

"Left me with an IQ somewhere between a turnip and a cauliflower?" Terrified as he was for her, he instinctively forced a smile to ease the worry in her eyes.

"Something like that," she admitted, struggling to lower the leg rest that held her wrapped leg on a nest of pillows.

"Don't do that," Jimenez scolded, as if he gave a damn about her well-being. "Here, let me turn the chair."

"I'll be fine," Brent told Lauren, his voice rough from disuse. "What about you? How's the ankle?"

"Oh, I'm all right. Or I will be." She leaned in to hug his arm as he reached for her. "Cruz is mother-henning me like you wouldn't believe."

"I do believe it," Brent said, looking up over her head to study Jimenez's face. "I believe it absolutely. My buddy, Cruz, here, he's one of a kind. Though I didn't always realize *what* kind of friend he is."

Jimenez shifted his weight, discomfort arcing across all-too-perfect features. "You'd have done the same for me, *compadre*."

"No," Brent said, tension coiling in his muscles. "I don't believe I would have, no matter the circumstances."

He had more to say—much more—but Jimenez was watching him warily, and Lauren was pushing herself out of the chair. Balancing on one leg, she threw her arms around him and leaned forward to plant a searing kiss on his mouth, a lingering kiss that almost made Brent forget where he was and what was at stake.

When Jimenez turned his head, giving them a moment's privacy, she moved her mouth to Brent's ear and said, "I think I have it figured out, Brent. I know, and as soon as I get to Jimenez's place and get access to a computer—"

"Not there. Not with him, Lauren," Brent warned. "You're not safe—"

"Where would she possibly be safer"—a spark of anger lit Jimenez's dark eyes—"than in a one-story, wheelchair-accessible lake house with a police officer watching over her?"

"No. You can't," Brent told Lauren.

"Relax, Durant," Jimenez said. "It's actually my family's place on Lake Travis. You've visited. Remember? Only now, my mother's living there full time. And believe me, nobody plays the chaperone quite like Maria Elena Jimenez de Soto."

"Besides," Lauren said brightly, "once I'm getting around better, Cruz promised me he'd talk her into teaching me to make those enchiladas of hers."

If you live that long, Brent wanted to argue, but at that moment, the young bull of a special agent who'd been guarding his door stepped in and insisted, "Sorry, folks. I have to clear the room now."

"But we're not finished," Lauren argued. "Please, just another few—"

"You asked for a chance to say a quick goodbye, Ms. Miller, and you've had it. But transport's here, and it's essential that we get him prepped for—"

Pure panic jolted through Brent at the realization that the bureau planned to have him drugged and trussed up before they hauled him off to a secured facility God knew where. That whatever he had to say about Jimenez would be buried, just as Lauren would before it was all over.

"No, Lauren. You can't go with him. Goddamnit, Jimenez! I know what you're up to! I know what you're planning to—"

A nurse came running into the room, a needle in her hand. Before Brent could pull the IV out of his arm, Jimenez and the special agent both grabbed Brent, one on each side, holding him down while she injected the sedative into the line.

Maybe it was the concussion making him so vulnerable, or maybe it was the pounding of his heart that did it, carrying the drug throughout his system with such ruthless efficiency. He bucked against the firm grips, fought to get out one last warning, but his muscles slackened within seconds. His mouth moved but he couldn't force a single word out. The best that he could do was fasten his fading gaze on Lauren's tear-stained face . . .

The face of another woman he'd failed.

Another woman, doomed to die because he loved her.

CHAPTER THIRTY

Far from the homey lakeside cabin Jimenez's description had led Lauren to expect, the sprawling "retreat" he drove her to had to be worth millions, with its native stonework, exotic woods, and antiqued tile. Though Lauren had never been much interested in such things, her eyes were immediately drawn to the floor-to-ceiling windows that overlooked a picture-perfect deep-blue cove beneath the lowering sun. The view alone, along with the iron-fenced, landscaped bluff where the house sat in splendid isolation, made her add an extra million to her initial estimate.

In an elegantly appointed kitchen that smelled faintly of chiles and spices, Jimenez's mother had left a note of welcome, explaining that she'd gone out to play bridge but would return soon.

"*Soon* may be a relative term"—Jimenez grimaced as he passed her the bottled water she had asked for—"given how my *madre* and her friends enjoy their cocktail hours more than their card games." He glanced at the glowing numbers of the micro-wave clock, his frown deepening when he saw it was already nearly six p.m. "I only hope that this time, she doesn't . . ."

The words trailed off, but his exasperation lingered, hinting that his mother's socializing—or more likely her drinking—had caused issues in the past. But what made a cold pit open in the bottom of Lauren's stomach was the dawning realization that she and Cruz were all alone. She tried to shake off the anxiety thrumming through her, assuring herself it was only an offshoot of her worry about Brent's situation.

All the way out here, her mind had replayed his disturbing outburst, the way he'd lashed out at what might be his last friend in the world. Was he really so worried Jimenez was attempting to seduce her—or had the blow to Brent's head caused his suspicions about whoever had sent the assassin to veer sharply off course?

A third possibility worried her even more: that Brent was as dangerously unstable as both Jimenez and the special agents who'd come to talk to her in her room implied. But she reminded herself that Brent had been right about the existence of the Troll King, whose laptop, according to Jimenez, had yielded thousands of saved images related to female bondage and medieval torture, along with a history of searches on each of the "suicide blondes" Brent's web page had named. Coupled with the Troll King's disturbing history, the evidence all pointed to the rapid development of a young serial killer, who had "graduated" from psychological torment to hands-on murder when he'd killed Nikki in an attempt to either frame or scare off Brent.

Still, Lauren reasoned that Brent must have been right, too, to insist there had been something—or someone—linking Chad Henderson to the women he'd targeted. Someone so desperate to keep the connection from being discovered, he or she had apparently sent a contract killer to eliminate the teen, along with her, the one witness who could testify Chad's death had been no accident. But who would have both the resources and the motive to hire an assassin? As her mind worked furiously, doubts burrowed into her heart, undermining her confidence in the theory that was beginning to come together.

Turning away to hide her troubled expression, she wheeled herself into the living area to take in a sprawling view, burnished by the sun's last rays. "Wow, Cruz. You've got an amazing place here."

"It's a little far from town, but it's been good staying with my mother—at least 'til my divorce is final."

Lauren turned in her chair to spear him with a look. "Didn't you tell me you went through a divorce last year?"

"I should have said a separation."

"Should have, but didn't," she said, thinking aloud, "because you wanted me to open up more about Brent."

He shrugged. "Guilty as charged, I'm afraid. I might not be quite as obsessive as Durant's always been about things, but in the heat of an investigation, I've been known to make use of whatever tools I have at hand."

She bit her lip, suspecting those tools included the handsome face and taut body that so many women would find irresistible. Was his apparent kindness just another façade, a way of taking down the man he'd seemed so determined to get off the streets for good? Was he really as troubled as he pretended to be when he saw Brent in federal custody?

He was the first to break the unwieldy silence that took shape between them. "Let me show you to the guest suite."

"And my laptop?" She couldn't wait to get her hands on it, to find out if it could be repaired.

He nodded. "I left it in there with your suitcase."

"Thanks so much for picking up my stuff from Rachel's. And for what you did for Dumpling, too." Earlier that day, she'd spoken to the vet herself, and learned the dog was recovering well and should be ready to come home in a day or two . . . once Lauren figured out where "home" would be, at least for the short term.

He took her to a tastefully decorated room, with its own bathroom, sitting area, and French doors leading out to the deck—and that spectacular sunset view. But Lauren wheeled herself straight to her computer, which rested on top of an antique writing desk.

"I hope it was okay to plug it in to charge the battery," Jimenez said. "I know you said it had been damaged, but—"

"That's perfect. Thanks. I just need to check the motherboard, see if it's toast or just knocked—"

When his cell phone rang, he gave her an apologetic look. "If you'll excuse me for a minute . . ."

By the time he returned, Lauren had already dismantled the back of the computer with a small screwdriver she'd found inside the desk drawer and was absorbed with tightening connections.

"I'm afraid I have to leave you."

"Is something wrong, Cruz?" Her mind flew to Brent, her stomach plunging.

"There's been an accident—my mother's car."

"Oh, no. Was anyone hurt?"

"I'm not sure. There were sirens, and she was so upset, I could barely understand her. Upset and maybe . . ." His face darkening, he shook his head. "Damn that woman's stubbornness! I've warned and warned her not to even think of getting in the car after she's been drinking—especially after what happened the last . . ."

A spasm of what looked and sounded like raw fear choked down his voice. "I have to go now, Lauren. Will you be all right?"

"Of course, Cruz. I'll be fine," she said, suspecting that he wasn't only worried about his mother being injured but also intoxicated—or arrested for drunk driving.

351

"There's food in the fridge, fresh towels on the bathroom counter."

"Just go. Don't worry about me here. Call me when you can and let me know how your mom's doing." He nodded tightly and promised that he would before he left her to a sprawling, empty house.

As soon as he was gone, Lauren heaved a sigh. As much as she hated the idea of something terrible befalling Cruz's mother, she felt nothing but relief to have him out of the house instead of here with her.

It was enough to make her rethink her own suspicions, along with the last-ditch plan she was still mulling over—a risk she knew would either end this or result in another hired killer being sent to take her life . . . assuming one was not already looking for her.

With the laptop's motherboard firmly back in place, she powered on the laptop and sighed in relief when it booted normally. Afterward, she lost track of time, forgetting about food, about her isolation, about everything as she immersed herself in digging deeper into Chad Henderson's background. She tried a number of social networking sites, from the mainstays to the upstarts favored by the younger crowds. But teenager or not, he'd been careful to remain invisible. She'd give him that, and her searches gave her no clue as to possible usernames or passwords that would help her hack any online storage or e-mail accounts.

The same, however, could not be said for the man she suspected of having a connection with him. Her search started slowly, but gradually, his paltry safeguards crumbled, giving way to the battering ram of her relentlessness.

It was not until hours later, when she looked up to see light from countless stars reflected off an ink-black lake, that it occurred to her that Jimenez had neither called nor texted. Had he gone to the hospital with his mother? Or was he at the police station, trying to keep her from being booked? Misgivings swam around Lauren's stomach at the idea he might be stalling his return for some other reason, but she told herself she was just nervous. Nervous about the phone call she was finally prepared to make.

But first, she spoofed a number, just as had the Troll King.

As she waited to connect, she murmured, "Let's see how you enjoy a taste of what you put my sister through."

From somewhere in the house, she heard a soft beeping, quickly silenced. Her pulse fluttered in response, her grip tightening on the phone. But before she could hang up, she was distracted by a man's anxious voice in her ear.

"Who the hell is this? Why are you calling me?"

***

The man who entered the lakeside retreat punched in the alarm code and sighed softly when its beeping fell silent in an instant. Next, he stopped to listen, worried that he might have been heard. At first he heard only the light hum of the refrigerator, the warm breath of the heating system, and the tick of an antique clock hanging just outside the kitchen.

Comfortable, familiar sounds, yet he didn't relax. He couldn't until he knew for certain exactly where she was.

Stepping out of his shoes so he wouldn't be heard moving across the fine Italian tile, he slipped the gun out of his holster, tested its weight and heft, and smiled at the way it fit in his hand. He hoped like hell he didn't have to use it, prayed he wouldn't need to call in more backup, either, but his instructions were specific: get Lauren Miller and get out fast, while she was here alone.

He stopped, pulse jumping, the moment he heard a voice from down the hallway. An unexpected voice, far too deep to be hers. So who the hell was in there with her, sounding so harsh and angry?

This could all go to hell in a heartbeat. But there could be no backing out now. He might never get another chance to end this all for good.

Adrenaline coursing through his system, he crept cautiously in that direction, the grip of his pistol growing slick with sweat.

***

"Answer me, will you? What the hell is it you want?"

The man on the phone sounded angry but not frightened, Lauren noted. Or not yet, anyway, but she would damned well fix that.

"Is this some kind of joke?" he demanded over the speaker-phone, a hint of uncertainty slicing through his bluster. "Hello?"

She laid the phone beside the laptop speaker, then typed in a response. The computer read the text aloud, the words slow and cruel, words she'd digitally distorted to resemble the monstrous male voice Chad Henderson had used to torment her . . .

And to drive Rachel and so many others to their deaths.

"You imagined I would die so easily? That I'd just go away, after everything we've been through? You ought to know I'll never leave you—not when you still owe me for those numbers I got for you."

"You—Ch-Chad? Is this really—Hell, kid, I'd heard you'd got yourself killed in some kind of accident. It made the papers, even."

As quickly as she typed, the distorted response lagged only a little. *"You, of all people, should know not to buy into everything the media reports."*

"Well anyway, what the fuck are you doing calling me on this number? You're supposed to use the burner, and you damned well know it."

White-hot rage burst into flame at Lauren's center, fury mingled with relief at this verbal confirmation that this man was really the root of so much misery. But she felt something else as well, a pulse of pure, sadistic pleasure at the rising panic in his voice. Was this how Chad, the Troll King, had felt, when he'd pushed his first victim, Carrie Durant, to take her razor to her bath?

At the thought, the smile died on Lauren's lips, and nausea coiled low in her gut. But when she thought of that animal hammering at her sweet sister's psyche until she'd shattered like fine crystal, of him destroying everything Brent cared for, Lauren typed her next response.

"The rules are different now. I make them, ever since you paid that animal to kill me."

"I don't know what you're talking about. I swear it."

"Did you really think you could hide your online financial transactions from me? I have the proof you paid that driver," she wrote. *"Proof you hired him so no one would ever realize that all those women died because of your greed and ambition."*

"All those women died 'cause you're a straight-up nut job, that's why! You're the one who went off-script, stalking them, driving them to suicide, when you were only supposed to get their contact information. What kind of sick fuck even does that? What the hell is wrong with you?"

"I got their numbers like I said I would. The rest was none of your damned business."

"What the hell do you mean, it was none of my business? If anyone ever finds out that I'm connected, that *The Vigil* had anything to do with some psycho kid who gets off on torturing blondes to death, we'll be ruined, all of us."

"So you decided that you had to stop it."

"Hell, yes, I had to stop the killing, to stop you from destroying everything I've worked for. As soon as I figured out what you were really doing—"

"You paid for me to be run down like a damned dog in the street," Lauren finished, chill bumps erupting as she realized that regardless of what he said about putting an end to the so-called suicides, Reynolds Hadley's true interest in eliminating Chad had been all about self-preservation. Had he sent the same man after her as well out of fear she knew too much? Or had that been the killer's idea, to eliminate her as a witness?

Lauren decided that it didn't matter. She had reason enough to take down Hadley either way. Just as he'd had reason to shut down the kid he'd hired to do a little light hacking when it became apparent that, for reasons no one would ever fully understand, Chad's torture fetish and antisocial tendencies had taken a lethal turn.

"I only wish he'd flattened you the way I paid that woman to arrange," Hadley fired back. "Now I'm hanging up, you little bastard. And if you know what's good for you, you won't call back again."

"Hang up, and my next call goes to your wife, I swear it." Lauren's fingers raced to vent the heat of hatred. *"Or how about Judge Jaycee? Maybe she'll be next to end it all when she finds out what she's done with her show."*

"What *you've* done, you twisted little shit. I never wanted anyone hurt. You were just supposed to get their phone numbers so we could book them for the show. And Jaycee knows nothing about it. She can never know a thing about our arrangement. She can't—"

"She needs to know what was done in her name. Needs to understand The Vigil's *burning down around her, and you're the one holding the gasoline and matches, Reynolds Hadley."*

Over the speakerphone, she heard the television producer panting in his desperation. In his soft moan, she heard, too, the dawning realization that what must have once seemed a simple plan to hire an online hacker to get the jump on his show's competitors was about to consume his life. That like the job he'd risked so much for, his marriage and his freedom, would soon, too, be forfeit.

"Just like Brent Durant's," Lauren whispered to herself, feeling whatever pity she might possess dry up like a streamlet in the hot Saharan sun. *"On second thought, maybe I'll come by and explain it all in person. How your ambition, your need to feed fresh meat into the machine, left those women vulnerable to . . . my suggestions."*

"I've got a gun, right here in my desk. You come anywhere near my wife, within a mile of either her or Jaycee," Reynolds swore, "and I swear to God I'll use it on you."

Lauren could have stopped there, should have been satisfied with the admissions she'd recorded, with the price he would pay once she leaked them to the Internet and brought them to the attention of investigators. She couldn't stop thinking, though, of what this man had cost her, of how he'd stolen not only her sister but also whatever chance she and Brent might have cobbled out of tragedy for themselves. And deep inside her, something twisted, snapping off like a blade's tip, lodged in the fault lines of her heart.

So instead of showing mercy, she slipped deeper into the dead teen's poisonous persona . . .

And Lauren Miller, lifelong champion of lost dogs and lost causes, crowned herself the Queen of Trolls.

***

"Why not turn the gun on yourself instead?" came the cruel words, words spoken in a warped, computer-generated voice.

But Lauren was behind them, Brent understood as he watched her type. As he watched her doing to Reynolds Hadley—the man he clearly should have focused on, rather than his innocent friend, Cruz Jimenez—what he'd so long dreamed of doing to the man responsible for so much misery.

So why were his lungs freezing solid, making it impossible to breathe as Lauren chose the same dark path he'd once embraced? *Did you really imagine that revenge would be easy to look at? That it wouldn't demand a higher price than you ever thought?*

The question was, was he prepared to watch her destroy herself to satisfy his obsession?

"Isn't life as you knew it over anyway?" the distorted voice demanded. *"Because it's coming out, all of it. Everything you're responsible for, all the things some sick teen—I—did to all those poor women."*

"Stop this, Lauren." Slipping the gun back inside his holster, Brent stepped inside the room behind her. A surge of pure adrenaline smashed past the remaining dizziness and weakness from his injuries. "Stop it right now."

At the sound of his voice, she gasped and turned her head, her eyes wide with shock and fear and what looked to him like shame. Shame he understood, for the monster he'd glimpsed bore no relation to the shy and gentle woman who, despite her fierce intelligence, loved with an even fiercer passion.

Snatching up the phone, she held her hand over the microphone. "B-Brent, how did you—Are you all right? Are you on the run?"

"Listen, Chad," said Hadley, apparently too upset to notice Lauren's slip. Over the phone's speaker, his tone turned wheedling. "Please, just listen to me. I can—I can get you money. Just leave Jaycee out of this. And my family, too. Please."

"Stop this," Brent repeated, never taking his eyes off Lauren. "It won't bring Rachel back. Won't bring back any of them. It'll only take what's left."

"Chad?" Hadley asked. "Are you still there, kid? Talk to me. Let's work this all out, before it's too late."

Lauren's face went pale as moonlight, lit by her computer screen. "*What's* left, Brent? Because I can't see it. Please . . . tell me that there's something. Some future for either of us, some way past this pain."

He strode to her and took her hand, gently pried her cell phone from it. Without a moment's hesitation, he disconnected the call, because no revenge could be worth the soul he'd come to treasure.

"More of a future than I ever could have imagined," he answered, "thanks to my old boss, Fremont Daniels, and the agreement that I just signed."

"Agreement? You mean they aren't shipping you off to some . . . facility?"

He shook his head. "Not since I'm taking part in an active, ongoing investigation, same one I've been working on every day since Carrie's death."

"But you were fired."

"I've been *un*-fired, retroactively. Which means the results of my investigation won't blow up in the bureau's faces. Well, except for having to smooth over some ruffled feathers about grabbing Jimenez for questioning tonight."

"Then his mother's all right?"

"She will be, if she gets help for her drinking problem like she and Cruz both promised. She's just lucky no one was hurt in that fender bender today. I gather it's not her first incident, not by a long shot."

Lauren took a deep breath, clearly struggling to take in what he was saying. "So you're really a special agent again?"

"Not exactly. I'll be working in the capacity of paid consultant on a brand new task force. A task force focusing on hunting down and stopping cyber-stalkers."

"Sick sadists like the Troll King."

"Yeah, but even after more than two years, I told Daniels I'm still no expert on the tech side. I need someone with the network security skills, someone by my side to honestly let me know when I'm in danger of slipping over the edge. Losing my perspective."

"If you're thinking of me, Brent," she started, shaking her head slowly. "I've lost my own way, too, since Rachel." She gestured toward the open laptop. "I had all the proof I needed to take down Reynolds Hadley, everything the authorities will need to—"

"We'll take him down, I promise. Only we'll do it legally. And civilly, I imagine, once the families file lawsuits. He'll be judged and punished for hiring a hit man to hide his connection to Chad—for all the crimes he's committed."

"I get that, but *look* at me. Listen to me, acting as insane as—"

"You slipped for just a minute, exactly the way I had before you dragged me back from the edge. But I swear to you on my life, we can keep each other in check. Help each other through our grief."

"Is that even possible?"

"I can tell you this much for sure. I'm done with obsession, done with revenge. I've glimpsed my future, and it's about saving other lives, not slogging endlessly through my own loss and anger. It's about moving forward, with you, Lauren, if you'll have me. Because I've discovered that I love you far more than I hate anyone."

When he reached for her, she drew back, shaking her head. "But I screwed up my marriage. I'm not the right woman—not normal, when it comes to—"

He took her hand and pulled her from her wheelchair, his strong arms supporting her as she stood on one leg, instinctively leaning into his embrace. As he squeezed her close against him, he whispered into her ear, "Who the hell is normal, Lauren? Who the hell would even want it? Because once you've tasted the extraordinary, everything else is boring as hell."

He freed one hand to stroke her gently, his caresses feathering along her side and up to her jaw. As her breathing lengthened, deepened, he gently tipped her head back to claim a lingering kiss.

Her hand came up between them, her fingers splaying against his chest and stiffening as if she meant to push him away, to reject the chance he offered. Brent's heartbeat drummed with the fear he'd come on too strong, too fast, scaring her back to her windswept prairie stronghold and away from him forever.

Instead, beyond the windows of that sprawling lake house, a billion stars bore witness as the Queen of Trolls retired her crown, her fears, and the last of her doubts . . .

COLLEEN THOMPSON

Her resistance melted into mist like dry ice, leaving them both free to embrace the promise of a future they never would have imagined possible. The kisses that followed began as sweet and full of yearning, then gave way to a passion that made him forget his aching head, the agents waiting outside—everything but her.

When finally, she pulled away, she gazed up at him and whispered, "Anybody ever tell you, you're pretty damned extraordinary yourself?"

With a soft snort, he shrugged a shoulder. "Maybe not in so many words."

"Then it's about time I amend that," she vowed, "every single day from here on out."

"So you're really going to tell me I'm extraordinary? Every single day?" he teased.

"Absolutely . . ." A wicked smile twitched at the corner of her mouth. "As long as you keep proving it every single night."

ACKNOWLEDGMENTS

The popular image of the lonely writer in her cramped garret is romantic, but it's also (in most cases) an enormous lie. I rely on some fabulous folks to help me bring each novel to fruition, and I want to take a few moments to express my appreciation.

First off, on the home front, a special thanks to husband Michael and son Andrew for the encouragement, plotting/research assistance, and most especially for knowing to refrain from interrupting when I look up from my laptop with the Atomic Death Glare. I should thank my rescue dogs, too, for occasionally forcing me to get out of my chair, thereby saving me from the resulting blood clots, but they prefer their payment in biscuits and chew toys to a bunch of inedible, unsniffable (and therefore useless, as far as they're concerned) words.

Thanks, too, to agents Karen Solem and Nalini Akolekar and everyone at Spencerhill Associates for believing in *The Best Victim* from its earliest stages and for all they do to help make my work life easier. Additionally, I want to express my sincerest appreciation to editors Kelli Martin, Helen Cattaneo, and the entire team at Montlake Romance for their work with and enthusiasm for this story.

I rely on a number of beta readers and critique partners, each of them a talented author in her own right, to help me make the story as focused and error-free as I can get it. Thank you so much for sharing your wonderful friendship, your perceptive insights, and your virtual red pens, Jessica Trapp, Patricia Kay, and all the members of The Midwives: T.J. Bennett, Wanda Dionne, Joni Rodgers, and Barbara Sissel.

Finally, I would like to express my sincere appreciation to computer forensic investigator William Simon for his assistance with research on some technical aspects of the story. Any errors, omissions, or exaggerations in the service of the story are my own responsibility. Or go ahead and blame the dogs. They aren't overly concerned about that either.

ABOUT THE AUTHOR

RITA-nominated author Colleen Thompson first cut her teeth writing historical romances under the pseudonym Gwyneth Atlee. But she couldn't resist the draw of intrigue and neither could her readers. Together they've traveled the twists and turns through her more than fifteen tales of romantic suspense. A native of New Jersey, Thompson now calls Texas home. When she's not out and about exploring the Lone Star State with her husband, she's at home writing or playing with her two rescue dogs.